THE ORACLE AT
STONELEIGH COURT

THE ORACLE AT STONELEIGH COURT

STORIES

PETER TAYLOR

Alfred A. Knopf

New York

1993

THIS IS A BORZOI BOOK
PUBLISHED BY ALFRED A. KNOPF, INC.

Most of the stories in this collection were originally published in *Encounter,*
Kenyon Review, New Virginia Review, The New Yorker, Sewanee Review,
Shenandoah, Southern Review, and *Virginia Quarterly Review.* "Familiar Haunts"
was published in an earlier version as "Two Images" in *Presences: Seven Dramatic
Pieces,* Houghton Mifflin, 1973.

Library of Congress Cataloging-in-Publication Data
Taylor, Peter Hillsman, [date]
The oracle at Stoneleigh Court : stories / Peter Taylor. — 1st ed.
p. cm.
ISBN 0-679-41990-X
I. Title.
PS3539.A9633073 1993
813'.54—dc20 92-54283
CIP

Manufactured in the United States of America
First Edition

For Eleanor, again

Contents

CONTENTS

THE ORACLE AT
STONELEIGH COURT

The Oracle at Stoneleigh Court

MRS. AUGUSTA ST. JOHN-JONES was now seventy-five years old and had lived in Washington for nearly half a century. She was the longtime widow of a Tennessee congressman who had in fact died of a heart attack while midway through his maiden speech on the floor of the House. This widow of the late lamented Congressman Jones (she hyphenated her maiden name and her married name only after her husband's death) was actually a lady from Middle Tennessee and was generally known to us—her various nephews and nieces, that is—as our Aunt Gussie Jones. But from the time of her husband's early death our Aunt Gussie had stayed put in Washington (her own phrase) until the present day of this story I am about to relate.

As for myself, I was already a grown young man at the time I speak of—in the year 1943—and was now serving as an enlisted man in the United States Army. I had, moreover, been placed for several weeks on special assignment for temporary duty in the District of Columbia. And this was when, out of obscure needs quite beyond my own comprehension, I made a point of seeking out this great-aunt where she was currently living, in the stylish Stoneleigh Court Apartments on lower Connecticut Avenue. I did so ostensibly in order that I should make the old lady's real acquaintance for the first time since I was a small child. Yet there were other and more profound reasons for my looking up my aunt, which were at the time by no means self-evident or in the least bit comprehensible to me.

THE "PRESENT DAY" that I made reference to above, regarding my aunt, and the "now" and the "nowadays" that may creep into my narrative during these first pages must not ever be construed as having reference to the trite "present day" or the banal "nowadays" that such a one as I have lived on into. Rather, the time I shall have in mind will be the vibrant "now" of fifty years ago when the Second World War lay before us and I was that staff sergeant on temporary duty in the District of Columbia. I do believe in my heart that this is the period when the young people of my generation imagined ourselves most fully alive—whether we were some avowed conscientious objector, such as I had actually listed myself with the Memphis Draft Board, or whether we were one of the more warlike spirits amongst whom we were inevitably cast in the ranks of the army.

Whatever we were, all of us imagined ourselves most fully alive then. And yet somehow, at the same time, how often it was we felt bored to distraction with our lives! There in Washington we rode the streetcars and stood in line at the cafeterias, to which we were allotted tickets, and at the movie theaters, which seemingly were on every corner of the downtown. Yes, to all of us it was the most exciting and the very dullest of times. We had before us—the would-be conscientious objectors or the ordinary draftees—either imminent death in the global war of our day or, if spared, then we had the prospect of a stagnant life in a world we all dreaded and that we sensed we should certainly come to know when the war was over.

I HAD BEEN DRAFTED before our country was actually in the war. As a result of this I had picked up many a trick from the old-time regular army soldiers in our organization. I had been drafted so early as I had for fairly obvious reasons. It was because of my having tried originally to register as a conscientious objector! On my draft registration form I had made a somewhat naïve-seeming statement, objecting to any sort of peacetime draft and "defying any contractual coercion to do murder at any future time." My impression is—as I shall illustrate later on—that there were a number of like-minded young men right there in Memphis at the time, young men who were willing in a halfhearted way, like myself, to resist any sort of peacetime draft.

On the draftee special train transporting our group to the Reception Center at Fort Oglethorpe, Georgia, I sat next to a slight acquaintance of mine, a young man by the name of Alex Mercer, and Alex was certain he was being drafted early only because of some almost inadvertent remark he had put on his own registration form about the peacetime draft. When he and I were back home again after the war, he was still as certain as ever about why he was "called" so early. And so I am sure that what happened to me was not merely a figment of my imagination. In fact, it was to the young woman secretary at the Draft Board office that I—and possibly others like me— could trace my own special brand of discrimination. When I questioned her about why my registration form had been sent on to Washington, instead of being reviewed first by the local board, she replied with indifference that she supposed my phrase "the act of murder" referred to "some act of Congress," and said she with a patriotic grin, "I left it for Congress to interpret, instead of the local board." I had no recourse, after that. I could only wonder even then that the fates of how many draftees would at last lie in the hands of that young woman clerk. In any case, the result for me was my being forthwith catapulted into the first peacetime U.S. Army draft.

Yet once any of our sort was drafted and sworn in by some anonymous adjutant-general army officer, then we were from that moment forward not noticeably different in our general behavior and performance of duty from the other soldiers we found ourselves in the midst of. From then on, indeed, our only and foremost concern, so it seems in retrospect, would be to prevent our companions in arms from learning how it was that we had originally enlisted ourselves with our Draft Board at home.

In my own case, extraordinary feelings of guilt would sometimes sweep over me when I was deceiving all those around me about my real nature and my halfhearted conviction—and these feelings were followed by a period of profound depression. And oftentimes there would be only the unaccountable depression without any consciousness of guilt.

At any rate, it was with the typical connivance of any old peacetime dog-faced soldier that I managed to obtain an extended temporary duty away from Camp Forrest, where I was then stationed. And I had done so in order to be near a fantastically good-looking girl named Lila Montgomery, a young lady who had just recently left Tullahoma, Tennessee, and had accepted an office job in Washington, D.C.

It is important to say that that temporary assignment of mine in the District was not something that just happened by chance. It was something that I finagled rather deviously in order to be near that fantastically good-looking girl. To my commanding officer back at the Post I had explicitly stated that before our outfit shipped out for overseas, which was bound to occur a few months hence (for our country was by now in the war), there was an aging relative in Washington that I wished to see before departing these shores. It had been precisely the right approach to make to the young C.O., and I congratulated myself, as I often had occasion to do in those days, on my very thorough understanding of commanding-officer mentality.

IN RETROSPECT, I am not sure it was my Aunt Augusta St. John-Jones I was pretending to have in mind when I spoke my piece to the officer. The fact was, in our family there were always various great-aunts, and their like, who lingered and lurked about Washington—even in so late an epoch as that of the Second World War. Generally speaking, these were the widowed spouses of politicos, of one kind and another, who tarried on the scene for years and years after they had any official position in the place. They were mostly the remnants of past political administrations, ladies who had caught the Washington bug and would not willingly give it up. To other Washington residents, even in that day, these kinswomen of ours were bound to have seemed an anachronism. Like most others of their sort they existed as the widows, the sisters, the daughters of what were now forgotten men—that is, those men amongst us who from time to time had represented our family (as well, incidentally, as the state of Tennessee) in the seat of government of what they termed the "Federal Union."

But all that aside, the girl I have spoken of, the fantastically good-looking girl named Lila Montgomery, was then residing in Washington in a women's hotel on upper Connecticut Avenue. She was one of those thousands of girls who hurried off to Washington during the war to work in the bureaus for the duration; in Lila's case it was only now—only just very recently—that she had taken up her job there. (When I am tempted sometimes to slip into the present tense, as I sometimes shall do, I think it is largely because all stories about young people—especially young people who have participated in war—seem to cry out to be told in the present tense. For them there seems to be no past, so to speak, no future, only the present.)

Lila Montgomery was actually someone I had met scarcely three months prior to our fateful Washington reunion, had met at a U.S.O. dance while she, a genteel country girl from what is known in Tennessee as the Highland Rim, was then staying with relatives in Tullahoma, and when I was still in basic training in nearby Camp Forrest. I say I "met" her just as though she and I were properly introduced at that dance in the Camp Forrest canteen, which was hardly the case, and which mattered considerably in that day and age but which would hardly matter at all in years ahead after the war. The truth is I had watched this girl on the crowded dance floor that night without having any idea who she was. I had no idea whether she was one of the regular hostesses or merely someone brought there by one of the headquarters company enlisted men. The important point for me is that I would almost have been content to stand there on the sidelines of the dance floor all night, merely watching that girl. And a sad sight I must have made, in my polished high shoes, my spotlessly clean uniform, my overseas cap tucked neatly in my belt, perfectly got up for a U.S.O. dance, but drawing a long face that bespoke a draftee contemplating an imminent overseas shipment. But even in my forlorn state of mind there was something about watching Lila that was a satisfaction in itself. That is to say, even later after I got to know her and wished to be constantly in her company I believe it was, first and last, the very expressive mobility in the girl's gestures, every slight movement of her whole person, the quick, responsive and ever-changing expressions of her face—like lights and shadows that came from within her—that utterly delighted me, and delighted me to the exclusion of everything else involved in our acquaintance. She seemed such a natural part of the scene that she somehow became the scene itself. And perhaps it was the scene itself I was enamored of—or thought I ought to be enamored of, as a normal young male animal. It may be that so long as I was acquainted with Lila Montgomery this perception on my part would alienate and in some degree estrange her from me and prevent her from ever allowing me to become acquainted with what was probably her essential nature. But I could not be sure of this. And in the end it would be left for my old Aunt Gussie to perceive and act upon.

After we began going about together, Lila often complained that I never made sufficient effort to develop any conversation with her and that I often failed to listen to her when she spoke to me. She said I had a way of seeming always to be listening to other voices across the room or across the street. But merely looking at Lila Montgomery would be for me the greatest pleasure to be derived from being in her company. The animated features of her face, the long, quite golden hair pushed behind the pretty little ears just showing under the brim of the G.I. hat she sometimes affected, as well as the single strand of pearls about her neck, the pale blue sweater she had herself knitted, the wide pleats of her dark skirt constituted altogether my greatest pleasure. I didn't allow my observations or my thoughts to carry me any further than that. The total, ultimate beauty of this girl I did not let myself think about. I suspect that during wartime soldiers will demand either total satisfaction of their aspiration with regard to persons of the opposite gender or almost total sublimation.

From the stag line that first night at the canteen dance I saw her personality and to some extent her very physiognomy change utterly with every new partner that broke in on her. Her face changed, her step was altered of course, the very angle of her arm on her partner's shoulder was altered, as well as her posture and the very animation of her entire person. In her wonderful kind of innocence or sophistication—it was hard to say which it was—she seemed responsive with every fiber of her being to every man that came near her. Anyhow, with no pretense at having an introduction that night I at last stepped out and touched the elbow of her current partner. And Lila, instantly responding to the agitated expression I must have been wearing, tried desperately hard to hold on to that corporal's sleeve. It was as though she suspected at once I might be bad medicine for her. It was as though she were endowed with a wonderful intuition that I would complicate her life in some way that she did not want it complicated. But nevertheless as a sergeant I more or less pulled my rank on the unhappy corporal and with Lila in my arms I glided away in my old-fashioned Tennessee two-step.

By the time I was cut in on by another soldier (this one outranking myself and who was clearly a real acquaintance of Lila's) I had already learned her name as well as her street address and telephone number in the nearby city of Durham. By then the wonderfully pouty expression that had come on her face when first she saw me touching the corporal's elbow had vanished altogether. And now I felt a certain alarm at how quickly she had adjusted to me and to my dance step. It made me begin wondering even then whatever in the world this well-adjusted and infinitely adjustable girl could have in common with my ill-adjusted self. She had come here tonight out of a sense of duty or just for the fun and adventure of attending a dance on a military base while I was a lowly draftee who was and would ever remain ill adjusted to any aspect of wartime adventure.

Yet when I yielded to another soldier who was breaking in on me, I saw her looking that pouty way again. But I saw too that it was only a pretense this time. I turned away from her, saying nonchalantly, "See you later, dear girl," as though losing her as a dance partner was a very small matter to me. And as I ambled away to the cluster of stags standing nearby I heard her calling out to me in a hoarse whisper, "You've got your nerve, you know, Sergeant!" Then she gave me a big, forgiving smile that invited me to come back soon, I felt. The invitation was more in the tone of her voice than in her words or even the smile on her face. I stood at the edge of the dance floor watching her for an immeasurable time it seemed—watched the shifting overhead lights and the occasional shimmerings and shadows they threw on the planes of her expressive countenance, seeming to coincide sometimes (or so I imagined) with the inner lights and shadows of her wondrously articulate personality. I gazed at her with an objectivity previously unknown to such a raw and callous youth as I perceived myself to have grown into since the day I put on uniform. (It seemed to me that I had been older and more sophisticated before I went into uniform.) Lila appeared to me from my first sight of her indeed like one of some species I had never before set eyes upon. I watched her lovely neck as she bent forward and backward, all the while that she was making animated conversation with each successive partner, and watched too the slender body that seemed transfigured entirely somehow in response—and nothing more than that, perhaps—to the different and unpredictable dance steps that she was called upon to follow.

It was merely watching Lila Montgomery always that gave me the greatest kick—only a "kick" and possibly nothing more. It seemed to me that she possessed a natural genius for quick responses to other people. It never occurred to me what she might otherwise be like or be unlike. But of course it was her manner and grace that would make me characterize her—when at last I spoke to my Aunt Augusta St. John-Jones on the telephone—characterize her, that is, as "simply a fantastically good-looking girl" whom I wished to bring to see my aunt. And this was how I most often thought of Lila during the long, lonely hours while she was at her daytime job and my Aunt Augusta was not "receiving." (Aunt Augusta St. John-Jones never received any visitors before five in the afternoon.) During those empty hours I found myself pacing the streets of the capital city, trudging mostly from circle to circle and from avenue to avenue with no definite purpose or destination in mind, with no purpose perhaps but to follow the routes suggested in the guide books. Studying and following the routes recommended in the guide books was simply my way of not thinking about my present life and my future and my non-future.

One day in my wanderings I catch a glimpse of myself in a mirror on the wall of a drugstore on Dupont Circle. Undoubtedly the weary figure and the unthinking face I behold there is that of a common soldier who carries inside him a burden he doesn't understand or in any way comprehend. And from that moment I perceived myself during daylight hours of my Washington stay as a lonely wayfarer without any direct notion of why he should bear his burden or even of what his burden is. (It was as though I were keeping my secret from myself.) Is it only being young and in uniform? To have all thoughts of future time blocked out just when one feels the strongest urge to take one's own course? And I do understand somehow that all this has to do with my strong feelings about Lila Montgomery and why they seem to remain so persistently shallow. I am aware that to others I seem lively, adventure-some, even high-spirited. Other soldiers in my barracks at Camp Forrest know of and approve my going off in pursuit of a girl. But what they do not know of nor would approve of is my reserve with Lila, my failure to demonstrate any and all affection I might or might not feel for her. And others of my acquaintance—older and closer friends from my curtailed civilian boyhood and young manhood—would scarcely believe that during my Washington stay I have not frequented the art galleries and great museums nor even visited the Senate Chamber wherein my most illustrious grandfather long ago distinguished himself with his rhetoric and wit.

BY DAY ALWAYS awaiting the night—blessed nighttime—for Lila to emerge from her bureau I try to sleep till noon in the temporary barracks that are used to house soldiers on duty in the District. But the sergeant major in charge always rousts me out before noon. And so I get up and make myself scarce, as he wishes me to do, and begin my wanderings through Washington once again. It seems to me that at each circle where I stop and rest my feet, pausing there to admire the equestrian statue of whatever little roundabout park I happen to stop in, that particular parklet immediately empties of all other people when *I* arrive, and I am alone there with a grim General Sherman or an icy George Washington.

THE SEASON OF the year is not yet winter but it is no longer autumn either. Again and again I see streaks of light in the great lifeless sky that I cannot account for. It all seems significant or even ominous in some way that is quite beyond my understanding. What is the matter with me? I ask myself. More than once I see or imagine I see a man on the edge of a high, flat rooftop who is clearly contemplating a leap into the street below. But he always turns away. I find myself on the verge of calling out to him, "Go ahead! Leap!" At every street crossing I find myself not looking at the traffic light which is meant to protect my life but peering instead at the watch on my wrist. ... During every day of sightseeing I begin to imagine that my temporary duty in Washington will never end. It seems that

I am suspended in time and it is not an altogether unpleasant sensation. My observations are but another means I have devised for not thinking about what my present mode of life signifies.

THAT DAY AS Aunt Gussie and I talk over the house phone from the high-ceilinged lobby to her sixth-floor flat I detect a tremor in the old lady's voice that suggests to me her very great age or perhaps the excitement of having one more young person from Tennessee turn up in her life—at her door. I feel that even the tremor in her voice is intended to mean something to me. As Lila and I ride up the old bird cage of an elevator, with the old hunchback of a man operating it, I imagine that I have already become the victim of some spell cast by the tremor of that melancholy voice on the phone and that I am somehow restrained from making mention of it to the girl beside me, she who watches intensely and questioningly as the elevator ascends. I smile inwardly at myself as we pass each floor, imagining as I do new dangers at every level.

After we leave the elevator and its humpbacked old man, and as we traverse the brown-carpeted corridor to Aunt Gussie's little flat on the very top floor and at the very back side of the Stoneleigh Court, there, suddenly, the old creature stands before us in the doorway of her tiny cell-like apartment with her arms stretched out to receive us and wearing on her face what appears to be a circus clown's smile painted all around her thin old lips, and on her hollow cheeks orange rouge so besmirched that I think at first she is blushing. Black eyes shine forth at me from the deep recesses of their sockets with a brightness that cannot be artificial. And now she throws her skeletal old arms around me, being ever so careful not to stain my fresh uniform with either her orange rouge or lipstick. Now she peers up into my eyes with a stare that is at once analytical and affectionate, and now she explains, "How I do love a uniform, especially when topped off with so handsome a visage."

Now she is pulling me inside the tiny apartment and presently she is beckoning Lila to follow, without seeming to look directly at her. I don't know when the old creature first looks directly at the "fantastically good-looking girl" I have brought with me. I *think* it is only after Lila has softly closed the door to the entryway behind her and is stepping into the cluttered and untidy living room. Even now, without taking Lila's hand or making any gesture or effort to do so, Aunt Gussie merely stares severely in her direction. "So that is your fantastically good-looking girlfriend!" she says to my embarrassment of course, since she is obviously quoting from the note I sent her earlier in the week. But Lila only raises her hand to her mouth to conceal a smile.

As my aunt leads us farther into the crowded little apartment—crowded, I knew, from accounts of my sister and those of my older cousins who came to Washington long before my visit, crowded, that is, with furniture from larger apartments she formerly occupied in her more affluent days at the Stoneleigh Court—she at last gives Lila one appraising and condescending glance—or so I imagined it to be—that I shall observe a while afterward during that afternoon's visit.

What I am not at all prepared for, strangely enough—I say strangely because it *has* all been described for me by my older sister and to some extent by my parents—is first of all the mauve silk scarf tied about her old head, gypsy fashion, and the array of rings on the knobby old fingers, all set with stones seemingly with every hue and color of the spectrum. There is also the tiny, cluttered living room itself seeming to come forward at me all at once with its jumble of furniture and catching me unawares. Along one wall of this minuscule parlor of my aunt's there is hung a sort of arras, and there are inside window blinds with half-opened louvers casting stripes across the Turkish carpet. In the center of the crowded room and directly under the shaded chandelier is a table with a paisley cloth, and on that cloth is a set of unfamiliar playing cards laid out in vertical rows as if someone has been playing solitaire. With a second glance, though, it occurs to me that my aunt has been telling someone's fortune there. Then all at once as I press forward she sweeps up the cards into a disorderly pile, though not bothering to put the deck out of sight. It is as if she doesn't wish me to see what the fortune—her own or someone else's?—reveals. Then she looks at me with the coyness of a child—a child that has perhaps written some nasty, naughty word in her sand pile and then defies me, the adult, to fathom whatever word she has written there and which is now wiped out forever.

Presently she indicates with her right hand—and with precise specificity—the high-backed tapestried armchair that I am to occupy. And almost simultaneously with her left hand and in her most offhand manner she makes a wide, vague gesture that tells Lila she should avail herself of one of the little straight chairs—any one she likes, for it is no matter about her—just any one of the ordinary little straight chairs that are scattered here and there about the cluttered room. Even at the time her indifference seemed rather studied, though I could not be certain about it. It left me wondering for a few seconds. But presently I forgot this first impression. We three sit there together for the better part of an hour and as we drink our tea from the elaborate orange and black tea service that she produces from her little hole of a kitchen, my Aunt Gussie and I are not silent for a single moment. In this way, I suppose, the visit can be called a great success.

Lila, meanwhile, speaks not a word but only now and then gives me a knowing grin whenever I glance in her direction. It is as though she were seeing in this occasion something that I don't see. She is altogether left out, purposely excluded it would seem, as my aunt and I exchange family stories or at least make reference to stories and characters we are both of us familiar with. Our talk is not at all stiff or stilted as I previously thought it would surely be. I have even imagined the meeting might be disagreeable. But Aunt Gussie knows all the characters in our world so well! She can usually add something to any story or anecdote I make reference to. But she listens intently to all I say. Again and again, though, we interrupt each other.

More than anyone else in the family she refers to my maternal grandfather, who after serving several terms as governor was at last sent as senator to Washington. What a friend the Senator was to her late husband! How wise and witty he was and how sympathetic to the likes of her—even took her advice, too, in certain matters. "You can't know at your age," she says, "how humiliating it was to be simply a 'woman' in those days, to be a woman and be almost never listened to by men—with regard to serious, public matters, I mean. One *had* to do something to make oneself interesting. It didn't matter how silly it was, actually. But *he* listened, your grandfather the Senator did. He listened to everybody. That was really his genius! He would even take my astrology seriously at times and sometimes acted according to the indications I received—from up there." For a moment she casts her eyes upward toward the ceiling of her top-floor apartment. "He was an honest friend to me. And his wife, your grandmother, she was the best of all friends, and I would often cure her terrible headaches with certain powers of concentration that I possess. She even took my astrology and my palmistry seriously—even my devotion to the Church of Rome. But *he* always listened to all I said and it was more remarkable in a man to listen."

Lila is seated still in her straight chair—her sassy little hat at an angle on her head—a picture of patience. My own and Aunt Gussie's talk runs on and on. At last, there is an almost imperceptible twitch of Lila's left foot. I hope my aunt has not observed it, because I know it means that Lila's patience begins to be exhausted. Suddenly, as though she too had got the signal, my aunt goes to the table and takes a black notebook from the drawer there. I manage to get a quick glimpse of the entries on its lined pages but I cannot make out its real character. I think it is not a common address book, but she holds it so close to herself that I cannot at first be certain. Presently she asks for my temporary address and the telephone number at which I can be reached as well as my date of birth and even my army serial number. She gives me a quick glance and, blinking her little black eyes, she says, "You know, don't you,

that your parents' wedding date was five/one/ought seven?—
which all adds up to thirteen." I cannot resist now throwing
back my head and laughing aloud. Meanwhile, under her
breath almost and in the most casual way, as if it were an
unimportant afterthought, she solicits Lila's address and telephone number and the exact spelling of her name. Then the
old lady returns the notebook to the table drawer.

As Lila and I rise and are about to take our leave, Aunt
Gussie and I are still saying to each other how much each of
us has reminded the other of someone else in our various
Tennessee connections. Near the entry door she breaks off
suddenly and says with a searching look up into my eyes, "You
do look so like your late distinguished grandfather. And sometimes, you know, he comes here still."

Now I feel I have not been paying close enough attention.
I almost say aloud, "Who do you mean, Aunt Gussie?" Or
even: "What do you mean, Aunt Gussie?" Then I think surely
I must have misunderstood. And then I hear her saying,
"Wouldn't you like to see him sometime? He might come to
us if just the two of us were present. It would mean so much
to him, I think." I turn to look at Lila to see if she has heard
what I have been hearing. But Lila has already bolted. She has
opened the hall door and preceded Aunt Gussie and me into
the hallway. She seems oblivious to all that has passed between
us in the last minute or so. Presently I can recall my father's
once saying, "Aunt Gussie has moments of madness, but only
moments. Otherwise she is a thoroughly entertaining person."
And my mother's saying, "Madness maybe, but usually I can
find some method in her madness."

And after all, during this afternoon's visit, Aunt Gussie has
surely had only one lapse into madness. I *think* there has been
only one momentary lapse—that is, speaking of my late grandfather as she did and making reference to the signs of the
zodiac. I make no answer, of course, for I can't imagine what
on earth I might say. Presently when I'm just about to pass
through the entry doorway I see what I had not observed upon
entering. In a sort of alcove there, which I can only suppose

to have been originally a coat closet with its door removed to give the effect of an alcove, therein on the farthermost wall of the shallow closet and under a dim light from above is affixed an ivory-colored Saint Sebastian. On his ivory body are deep traces of blood, flowing from the arms and hands. At the very moment that I am struck by this gory sight and am inwardly debating whether or not the light from above the ivory figure had been shining there ever so dimly when we came in, just then Lila heaves an audible sigh which she follows with a sharp intake of breath. I cannot be sure whether she has glimpsed the dimly illuminated figure as I have done or perhaps has grasped the meaning of Aunt Gussie's reference to my grandfather's ghost. I instinctively raise my voice in order that Aunt Gussie not hear Lila's breathy exclamations out in the hall. And now having said several deafening goodbyes in the doorway I go racing after Lila who, without making any pretense of saying goodbye, has preceded me down the seemingly endless corridor. Before I arrive at her side she is already standing at the iron gates of the elevator shaft, jabbing in fierce desperation at the call button there.

As for Lila and my Aunt Gussie, I wrongly imagine of course that this will be the end of their acquaintance and this might have been the last of it for my aunt and me, so I told myself afterward, except that something has already been set going inside of me that will not let it come to just that. Something inside me has been stirred that will not let me be satisfied with only that one visit to Aunt Gussie's flat. By the time Lila and I have stepped out of the elevator and into the lobby downstairs we have kept silent except for mumbling our thanks to the decrepit operator of the bird cage which brought us down. As we pass out through the colonnades at the entrance Lila and I still have not exchanged a word. It is now that I again observe the familiar pouty expression on Lila's face. Her full, perfectly shaped lips, ordinarily among the chief features of her beauty, are now pressed ever so tightly and disagreeably together. I can tell she has resolved not to speak until she has regained command of her emotions. I can sense already that this will not be her last meeting with Aunt Gussie and that she can somehow perceive that there is some advantage to be had from their acquaintance.

From Aunt Gussie's stolen glances I now thought, too, that I detected some half hidden design on her part for Lila's attention. And I remembered my mother's once saying that with *women* Aunt Gussie always played a game of cat and mouse. It was now for the first time that I sensed it was not just Lila's responsiveness to people that is to be admired. After that day I can in retrospect see that Lila has the wish and power to detect when someone can be of use to her and her ambitions. And it is as though Aunt Gussie has managed to convey something to Lila that did not reach me. By now I know the girl well enough to understand that it will help her to discern her own feelings (which she does not at this moment fully comprehend) if I will only say something utterly uncharged with emotion, something indifferent to what is going on inside her. "Isn't she a queer old thing?" I venture tentatively. As we walk along the avenue Lila looks up at me with the same knowing smile that she gave me once a while earlier at my aunt's apartment. It is a smile that assures me now that there is a side of Lila's personality or character that I have scarcely taken into consideration before.

And Lila, the pouty expression suddenly all gone, looks up at me wearing that big familiar smile. "She certainly is a queer old soul," she says, obviously trying to catch my tone, "and she certainly doesn't fancy the likes of me."

Thinking to placate her, I say, "I guess she never liked women very much, not even my mother. Especially not when she is competing in the world of Washington—unless of course the woman is somehow famous or powerful to some degree—most especially in politics. Did you happen to observe on the little shelf above our heads the signed 'studio portraits' of Grace Coolidge and Alice Roosevelt Longworth?" As Lila and I walk together up the avenue to the apartment she shares with other girls like herself, I undertake to tell her whatever I can about Aunt Gussie. And as I hear myself repeating certain familiar anecdotes, I suddenly realize how little I really know about my aunt. The stories that have been passed on to me about her are concerned mostly with her striking good looks and eccentricities. I have of course this afternoon acknowledged the eccentricities and discerned traces and suggestions of her faded beauty. But the two elements do not somehow make a whole picture—not by any stretch of the imagination. As Lila and I make our way up Connecticut Avenue, my talk is all about Aunt Gussie and my thoughts are all about Aunt Gussie, but the two somehow don't coincide exactly—my talk and my thoughts. I am repeating accounts of the peculiar and outrageous things she has said or done at one time or another, repeating them in the very pejorative terms that my parents and older sister, as well as other relatives, have used when passing the stories on to me. But in my concurrent thoughts I am revising everything. Now I am seeing it all anew in my mind's eye, anew and in a more sympathetic light. As a girl she had had a great many admirers, as such a beauty as she had been will inevitably have. It was said that at twilight she had been fond of being accompanied by a beau on certain long walks, often following various circuitous routes to the town cemetery. On some occasions in the approaching darkness and at a moment when the beau had turned his eyes away from her she would go quickly and hide behind one or another of the larger gravestones, managing to conceal herself altogether from his view. She remained in hiding there while her young man went bellowing after her in the near darkness among the stone angels and the little marble lambs and an occasional granite cross. At last, utterly mystified and seized by panic the young man would run out of the pitch-dark burial ground and on throughout the streets of the old river town to pound at last upon the door of the girl's father's house, meaning to ask for help in his frantic search. The beautiful Gussie, meanwhile, dodging from gravestone to gravestone and taking a little-known exit from the cemetery and racing through the back alleys of the town had preceded her young man there by so narrow a margin that she was scarcely able to rest and catch her breath and appear in the doorway before her panting admirer's eyes, a vision of ghostly loveliness.

THE NEXT TIME I went to see my Aunt Gussie in her Stoneleigh Court apartment, I went there alone. It was on the Thursday following that Sunday's visit. She awaited me in her apartment doorway this time, not wearing the mauve scarf about her head, but instead a black broad-rimmed hat with a very low, flat crown perched rather nattily, I thought, on her head of white hair, almost as if she were a toreador. I assumed from her appearance that she was either about to go out or that she had only just come in. Neither was the case. She had been expecting me, and it was merely her old-fashioned Washington way of receiving people in a hat. And I was arriving at just the appointed hour of our visit.

"It is a pity you couldn't have come earlier," she called to me when I was as far as fifty feet down the corridor from her. "For *he* has just been here!" she continued as I grew nearer. And then when I was in reasonable speaking distance I raised my eyebrows as if to ask who on earth she meant. "The Senator!" she exclaimed. "Your own grandfather!" And now she seized my extended hand between her own two hands, which seemed almost transparent in their fragility. "He couldn't wait another minute," she contended with excitement in her black eyes, seeming to scan my face for any response. I'm afraid I seemed to deadpan it, although at first I simply could not take it in. Leading me into the open doorway and stopping to close the door tightly she further exclaimed, "He could not wait another minute though I made every effort to detain him—for you to see him and for him to see you."

I was still speechless and began wondering if I could ever speak again. My first thought was: "What an old fraud she is!" But I had scarcely placed one foot across the door sill before I found myself believing in her, accepting *her* view of reality, or wanting so to believe in her that I dismissed all honest thinking. The first thing I observed upon passing through the doorway this time was the dimly lit Saint Sebastian in the alcove. And I was aware, or thought I was aware, that on the first visit she had purposely arranged my seeing it only upon leaving, and now she manipulated my seeing it at once upon entering, and my seeing also above the lintel of the inner doorway to the apartment the design of the constellations of the zodiac represented in bright colors. Then after allowing me barely a glimpse of the Saint Sebastian and the signs of the zodiac she took me by the hand and led me across the room to "my chair." She said quite openly and casually, "I have to tell you that your signature, as well as your handwriting generally, disturbs me, and all your numbers disturb me, too."

"My numbers, Aunt?" I asked in genuine wonderment.

"Yes, all numbers pertaining to you. I have taken the liberty since you were here last of doing a tentative horoscope of you."

I could not help exclaiming with a smile, "Oh, you *are* into everything, aren't you, Aunt Gussie?"

"Such things I *am* 'into,' " she asserted with only a shade of sarcasm. "One sees the same thing everywhere. I principally see that at this time in life you are not a suitable partner for anyone." So saying, she drew back into her chair and spoke no more of this nonsense. But presently I perceived that she had drawn back only to regroup her forces—her ideas, that is. Closing her eyes momentarily, and keeping them closed even after she began to speak, she presently spoke very firmly. "I could see when you were here the other night that you are not attracted to the cards." She now made a wide gesture toward the nearby table.

I cut my eyes to where the deck of cards was now ever so neatly stacked. "I'm afraid," I said with another foolish smile, "that I was not able to see what kind of cards they were after you squinched them up so quickly. And I still don't know."

"They are tarot cards, my child," she asserted with a certain condescension. With her black eyes now wide open, as if she would penetrate through my own eyes to my innermost ignorance and stupidity, she said, "They are cards which possess great authority and which have done so since very ancient times." She had now gone to stand by the table, and she fanned out the cards on the paisley cloth.

"Oh, fortune-tellers' cards," said I, "like those gypsies use."

"Tarot cards," she corrected me.

"Why, they are all face cards," I said genially. "Is that quite fair?"

"You are not a serious person, I fear," said my aunt, with a wan, unhappy look on her face.

"Tell my fortune," I urged, hoping to divert her.

"You are too skeptical. It would be no use. Besides, I 'told your fortune' for my own satisfaction after you left the other day. I already know about you. I have read you in the twelve houses of Heaven." She was laying out the cards now on the paisley cloth. "I use only the Minor Arcana," she said, seemingly to herself since she knew I lacked understanding. The pictures on the cards seemed wonderfully significant and suggestive and decorative to me. On the face of each there was a great deal of nudity, like so many drawings of Adam and Eve. It occurred to me that such examples of nudity would not have been allowed in the household that I grew up in. Aunt Gussie gathered in the deck again, asked me to place my two hands on top of the deck, one on top of the other, and after first riffling the cards she shuffled them three times. Then she proceeded to lay out the cards on the table once again. "We use only the cups, the wands, and the swords," she explained. "*You* are the Verent, and *I* am the Reader. *You* are the Knight of Swords. And today I am using the Celtic Method."

At least it was something like that that she began with. What I actually remember most clearly in all this nonsense was what she would allegedly reveal about me. "Ah, yes, I am the Reader," she repeated, "and you are the Verent, and it all comes out just as it came out when I was doing my Meditation, when I was alone in the room and you and your gorgeous Lila had just departed." Suddenly she sat very straight at the table and with closed eyes she began to speak in a somewhat more convincing voice. I didn't then and don't now know whether she purported to be reading the cards or following mystical insights of her own. At any rate, with her eyes now open, she was mostly staring straight into mine as she spoke. "You are a domineering and willful person at this time of your life. But you will be better later on when you have found your true calling. You would be a poor partner for anyone now, but it will not be so later on. Now you are angry and uncertain about your future. It is because you do not use your imagination. You are moody and have moments of fear about your future. You must come to terms with these negative moods. You must learn to use your imagination."

I could not resist interrupting at this point to express further skepticism. "I am afraid the government and the army are using *their* collective imagination for and about me."

Presently she opened her eyes very wide. "So there's the rub!" she fairly gasped. I made no acknowledgment of her gasp but hurried on to say in a casual tone, "Do you know that I have one early memory of you at our Cousin Annie's house in West Tennessee? I was there with my mother and Cousin Annie and yourself. Suddenly an empty rocking chair made a slight movement, and you said to Mother that *her* mother— long since dead of course—had just got up from that chair and set it rocking."

"I suspect your mother said," Aunt Gussie interrupted, "that the chair's movement was caused by Cousin Annie's old brick house's settling on its foundations."

"I believe that's how she explained it," said I defensively.

"Well, my dear boy, your mother, too, was a skeptic. And I must tell you that if *you* don't learn to use your imagination you very well may lose what you most desire in life!"

"Do you mean lose that girl Lila, by any chance?"

"I mean that and ever so much more."

Presently she left the table where the cards were spread out and excused herself from the room for a moment. And now she returned with a tray of tea things, and she served us tea from the same orange and black tea set she had used before. "Next time you must manage to come earlier," she said with a slight suggestion of rebuke in her voice. "And of course I realize now that you must bring your young lady Lila," she said. I did not know then what I learned later, that she had had a meeting with Lila since our last visit on Sunday. "I want to get to know her better," she said. "You *are* fond of her, aren't you?"

"I think she is a 'fantastically good-looking girl,'" I said, laughing at myself, intentionally putting a certain crudeness in my voice. But I was really more interested in concealing how I was responding to her probing.

"And I can see well enough how fond she is of you," she said, still giving me a very straight look. "It's a perfect scandal how girls can't or won't conceal their feelings."

"Yes, I suppose she likes me well enough," said I, dissembling, unwilling to reveal whatever opinions I might have had on that score.

"Good. That's what I want to hear you say, my boy." But I reflected that she had other things on her mind, too. I felt that she had some evil intention toward Lila. I was altogether mystified. And it seemed to me at this point that after all I did know ever so much about this great-aunt of mine. Suddenly I could hear my mother's older brother (he, long since dead and in his grave) saying, "She can't keep her hands out of other people's business—particularly men's business. She's always stirring her witch's pot in search of trouble." And presently now I heard Aunt Gussie actually saying, "I wonder how much you know about Lila's people?"

I dared not tell her how little I cared just then about what the girl's people might be like or tell her that marriage was not particularly what I had in mind at this point in my life. I even laughed to myself inwardly that anyone should presume to make any reference to any future of mine. And presently I was struck with consternation by what I then heard this Great-Aunt Gussie of mine saying: "*My* husband never cared a hoot for what my people were like, either, until *he* married *me!* . . . Ah, not that he really came to care even afterwards, either."

It was as if my aunt had purposely made this opening for herself—to talk to me or to anyone present—about her own marriage to that Tennessee congressman who died on the floor

of the House. "My husband knew only that my people had all
got into politics somehow and that was what he longed to get
into himself above all else in the world." This she asserted,
leaning forward toward me and resting her elbow on her knee.
"He cared only about that. And that's all he could care about
at the time. It was more important to him than anything else
in the world. And after we were married there was precious
little in my family he could approve of then." For a moment
Aunt Gussie seemed to be waiting to see if I showed any
interest in what she was saying. Finally I obliged by asking
what it was about herself and her family that her husband so
disapproved of. She clearly wanted me to ask this very question. "Mainly," she began, drawing a long breath, "mainly I
guess it was that my people were people that no longer had any
money to speak of." Now she had got round to telling me the
things that she had set out to tell and that she had prepared the
way for telling. And yet she rambled on as though this were
not really what was on her mind. "My people—your father's
people—were cotton people in the old days. That is, before the
Civil War they were. And they owned land in the clay hills all
over West Tennessee." This was like all the old rumors I had
heard at home. There was nothing new about it, but it seemed
more significant somehow coming from her. Now she got up
and drifted about the room between the table and two small
cabinets and the variety of chairs, still wearing her black hat
set squarely on top of her head. It was as if she had really gone
into some kind of trance and as if my grandfather's spirit or
that of the dead congressman, her husband that was, and perhaps spirits of other relatives whose names I wouldn't even
recall might easily appear right there beside her. "It was said,"
she continued, still roaming about the room, "that our people
had a talent—or once had had a talent—for making cotton
grow even on the poorest land. But there came a time after our
disastrous Civil War when no matter how much talent you had
for it and no matter how high the cotton plants grew it wasn't
worth anybody's while to grow the stuff—at least not out there
in the clay hills of West Tennessee and not anyway if you had

other talents you could make use of! And we *did* have other talents we could use—the men in the family, at any rate, did have."

Now she was seated again and in her agitation was leaning forward toward me and waving one bejeweled but knotty old forefinger at me like an inverted pendulum. It was as if she were literally trying to hypnotize me, which in fact she may have been attempting and now perhaps without herself being totally aware of what she was up to. "Our men had another talent," she presently went on, "—a talent for language, a talent for logic—or so they elected to call it. It was a wonderful gift in its way. The gift of gab, their wives more often than not called it. And so our men when they had worn out the land went down to Memphis and they went over to Nashville as though the land didn't exist any longer and as though land were something mere women could manage, and in those cities our men took to the pulpit or took to the bar and bench. And they became the great preachers and lawyers thereabout. That was what they did after the war. And of course finally there they took up politics, which suited them best of all. And as for the women they could stay at home and be damned, or we could go along with them to Nashville or at last to Washington City and play the fine hostess if we liked. That's what women were good for. Which is to say, the politician's female side-kick."

Meanwhile, in her bursts of nervous energy, Aunt Gussie was first getting up out of her chair and then sitting down again. "That role of female sidekick I knew from an early time. It was one we all knew and had known since time immemorial. I knew it from a time when, as you have no doubt heard, I used to play a game of hide-and-seek with my beaux in the village graveyard." Here she laughed to herself rather breathlessly. "Oh, I taught them some lessons! But that's not when it began for me. It began even as far back as when I learned to show off as a little bitty girl. My papa would call me in to perform for his friends, and I would go on dancing and singing with such enthusiasm that he would at last have to stop me, saying,

'Let up, Gussie! Let up, for God's sake!' For I was too much for Papa and *all* the men in the family even then! But Papa's friends would tell me to go ahead, as if it were some joke on Papa for me to behave so. 'Keep it up, Augusta!' they shouted out. In effect they said, 'Show off! Show off! Show off!' as though through me they could discover what Papa was really like."

EVEN BEFORE my aunt had pointed out so obviously what the connection was between her showing off as a little bitty girl and as a girl in the cemetery, as well as the role she was destined to play as a mature woman—even before any of that I had begun to see the connection for myself or *thought* I had begun to see. I had begun to understand or to *think* I understood this old woman and what she was all about, with her magic and her spiritualism and even her own brand of Romanism. Her reputation for being a good little girl, and then for being a proper young lady, and afterward a virtuous matron and widow-lady had been impeccable and beyond suspicion. Her spiritualism and all that was something outside and quite apart from her ordinary life. Ordinary standards did not apply in that area. It was simply like having a good singing voice or being an accomplished musician on some instrument or other. It made one a welcome addition to any gathering. I understood for a certainty that she, Aunt Gussie, saw to it that her reputation as a female was above reproach. Among her great detractors in the family—including my parents—she was known of course as a busybody, a social climber, even a sometime liar, but her virtue as a girl and later as a woman was never questioned. As the years went by, her means—her funds—were gradually diminished and then she took herself back to Tennessee more and more often.

I had been told once by one of my older cousins that when she was in a nearby finishing school she used sometimes to go into Washington and spend a weekend with Aunt Gussie. Aunt Gussie would get her a date with some senator's son or

the like. But when hard times came Aunt Gussie had to re-
trench and move into her tiny, smaller apartment on the back
side of the Stoneleigh Court. After that she wasn't able to keep
nieces and nephews over a weekend. She couldn't afford even
to occupy the smaller quarters on the back side, herself, except
during the high season in the late fall and early winter. During
the rest of the year they allowed her to sublet the small apartment to some politician who liked to have a good address. The
Stoneleigh was, however, still a good address—the kind Aunt
Gussie thought she *had* to have in Washington during the
season. The rest of the year she would go back home to Tennessee and put up on poor and obscure kinfolks. And that was
when, as a boy, I had had my first glimpses of her. She would
be staying in the house of first one relative and then another.
She would be sitting about the house in all her Washington
finery, probably huddled over a wood-burning stove, or loung-
ing on a front porch swing, not helping with the housework,
not even making her own bed—according to the colored people about the place—but most often with her pince-nez
perched on her nose while she perused the pages of the *Washington Star*, which she had delivered to her wherever she was
currently domiciled. And if you asked her where she might be
found during the rest of the summer or early fall or late spring,
her reply was inevitably the same: "No definite place of abode.
Just visiting around."

In retrospect I cannot be sure how much the substance and
the impressions that came through to me during those afternoons in my Aunt Augusta St. John-Jones's flat emerged actually through words spoken or through ideographs artfully
presented or some manner of altogether comprehensible pan-
tomime—comprehensible to me, that is. After a while it would
seem to me at the end of a session as though I was distinctly
waking from a dream in which everything about Aunt Gussie's
life was revealed to me. I had witnessed her ambitious husband
experiencing his fatal heart attack on the floor of the House.
I had seen her alone in Washington for a time with no one to
turn to. It seemed I had seen my senator grandfather take pity

on her here in this very room, speaking words of consolation to the young widow, accompanied of course by his wife, my sainted grandmother (for she was always referred to thus), who would herself die soon afterward. And I saw my bereaved grandfather in the room being advised by Aunt Gussie about political matters according to her readings of the cards and later being advised about marital matters according to the signs of the zodiac, with the Senator laughing heartily at all her advice, yet clearly destined—as I somehow understood—to follow her advice even as to how he voted in the Senate chamber, as well as in making a choice of his second and even, later on, his third wife (neither of whom was represented to me very vividly there in my aunt's little parlor). And both the second and the third were women of great wealth and of the highest social standing in Washington, D.C., which Aunt Gussie duly pointed out. It was not till I had set out for my barracks after a session that I would fully realize to what degree I was falling under her spell. I began to suspect sometimes that *she* suspected precisely what *kind* of moments of depression I suffered from and indeed that she knew the nature of my great secret regarding my army registration. When I was leaving her place one afternoon she held my hand between the two of hers and looked at me in silence for a long time. While her black eyes bore into my own I imagined I could hear her saying to me quite distinctly, "I will be able to find a way to help you, no matter what you think." And when at night I slipped between the sheets of my metal cot it was always somehow a pleasurable sensation to understand that whenever I was under my aunt's spell I was relieved as by no other means of those periodic periods of depression and dread that possessed me during that visit of mine to wartime Washington.

IT WAS AN overcast weekend with intermittent rain when I returned with Lila on another visit to the Stoneleigh Court, and on this occasion Aunt Gussie seemed to pay Lila as little attention as on the first visit. The cards were not in evidence this time as they had always been before. And the arras along one wall of the little parlor was drawn back to reveal a grouping of family pictures. Most of the conversation over teacups today was about relatives and forebears represented there. Aunt Gussie was more voluble than on previous occasions and before long she sent us on our way. During the last minutes before we left I made a point of watching to see if there were furtive looks exchanged between the two women. I expected there to be some reference made to the occasions there had been when I was not present. But no such reference was made. During the next few weeks of my stay in Washington this would happen again and again. Lila would give me sketchy accounts of their meetings and made a point, I thought, of never mentioning anything more precise than the name of the restaurant where they had lunched. And Aunt Gussie made no reference at all to the outing. She never even suggested by word or look that the meetings were taking place. I can say truthfully that their secret rendezvous (so Lila, in her light-hearted way, referred to them) did not disturb me enough for me to make an issue of—not at first, anyway. If the girl and the old lady chose to have luncheons together, which I assumed was the character of their outings, it was of no concern to me. For, as I have indicated, Lila Montgomery was from the outset someone for whom I acknowledged that my feelings did not run very deep. She was a beautiful object which had come into my view on the dance floor at Camp Forrest's canteen and the innocent view of which continued to offer me great pleasure. Like Aunt Gussie's pretensions to magic, Lila was a charming distraction from my own morose spirits. From Lila's very popularity on the dance floor I knew instinctively and in all good reason what sort of girl she in all probability was. She was a "nice girl," and her vivacity and her charm and beauty and her very niceness itself drew attention from the horde of "nice soldiers" who lined up to take their turns at dancing with her at Camp Forrest and elsewhere. In her "niceness" perhaps she seemed a goddess—more powerful than I dreamed. She was a girl who as yet felt no urgent reason to make a choice amongst her multitude of admirers. And perhaps Lila's greatest single insight into human psychology was that any soldier who was consistently attentive to her, as I came to be, probably knew just how "nice" she was and probably valued her "niceness" and therefore was to be encouraged beyond the others. Beyond that I did not attempt to plumb the depths of Lila's psyche. I did not know and perhaps did not care what her deepest, innermost feelings were. Perhaps I had sufficient absorption in exploring my own. At the moment I did not care what it was in her nature that allowed her to permit herself to be drawn into Aunt Gussie's web of tea parties and luncheons. (Of course I did not reflect then how willingly I allowed myself to be drawn into the old lady's power.) I did not do so until, one fateful late afternoon at Lila's usual quitting time, I gave up my usual, aimless wanderings through the circles and along the avenues (with a copy of *Carp's Washington* under my arm) and stopped by the bureau where Lila worked and was told that she had been granted permission to leave her desk early that afternoon in order to have tea with her old aunt from Tennessee who, as I was informed, had come for her in a taxi. Somehow it dawned on me only in that moment that I wished to ask Lila Montgomery to marry me. It seemed that I had always intended to make her my wife, but the wish or idea had never surfaced from my subconscious till I looked at the empty swivel chair where I knew she usually sat. And I did not, at the time, myself know whether this represented a sudden surge of jealousy and a resentment of Lila's responding so readily to my aunt's intentional and possibly malicious distraction from her interest in me or whether it was merely the result of the long, lonely, miserable afternoon I had just spent in meanderings about the senseless circles and on the mindless and seemingly endless avenues which radiated so arbitrarily from those circles and led eventually to nowhere. But it did occur to me in a flash that love and marriage to this vibrant and sympathetic girl from whose company and very appearance I derived such satisfaction would do more to dispel the unbearable moments of gloom and depression which beset me during the idle hours

of the day than could all of Aunt Gussie's magic. In my mind
I set the two against one another in direct opposition. I did so
in the precise moment when I must have appeared (to the
onlookers in that government office) merely to stand, irreso-
lutely, in the doorway to the little cubicle where I was told Lila
was ordinarily employed. But I turned away and out the door
from the temporary one-story building wherein Lila's bureau
was housed, there in the greensward of the Capitol Mall. And
I then rushed off in search of a taxi, which I certainly was not
accustomed to riding and most certainly not accustomed to
hailing in traffic.

And of course it was no easy accomplishment to grab a cab
in wartime Washington traffic and particularly in that rush
hour I now found myself in. But with my book under my arm
I did manage to commandeer one that was caught in a stoplight
traffic jam, claiming to the sympathetic driver that it was urgent government business that this particular sergeant was on.
He asked me if I wished to be taken by a short route, by which
of course he meant a circuitous route that would avoid some
of the rush hour traffic. Cutting out of the through traffic and
finally on through certain narrow streets in Foggy Bottom he
did manage to deliver me at the arched entrance of the Stoneleigh Court in a very short time. It was to no avail, however.
Lila and Aunt Gussie of course had not gone there in their taxi.
As I would later learn, they were keeping a teatime or a cock-
tail hour engagement with high-placed acquaintances of my
Aunt Augusta St. John-Jones who inevitably of course would
reside somewhere much farther up on Connecticut Avenue.

It was not until the following night and after my own separate and subsequent teatime engagement with my aunt (on the
next day) that I would see Lila again. During my afternoon
meeting with Aunt Gussie (that next day) at an hour appointed
by herself, her show of magic and her exercise of hypnotism
seemed somehow frenetic. The paraphernalia of her spiritualism and her apparent religiosity were everywhere to be seen.
(I say "apparent" because during the entire span of time I was
in and out of her apartment I saw nothing but a few outward

trappings of Christianity.) When I arrived this afternoon the arras which hung across the wall where the family pictures were sometimes displayed was drawn as it had been on the first visit. Little charts and various scribblings on note pads lay about the table. Her costume was more exotic than ever before, with a magenta kerchief tied about her head and a bejeweled neckband about her throat and matching bracelets on her wrists. A colorful apron with many pockets was tied around her waist. Actually she resembled a female Mason, if there be such a thing. I believe there was a faint aroma of incense in the fetid air. When I first entered there was certainly some kind of soft radio or phonograph music coming from the room beyond the arras-draped wall.

She seated me at once in my by now customary chair and said, "There are many souls wishing to crowd in to see you today." I now took such pleasure in her showmanship and derived from it such utter relief from all my neurotic and depressed states of mind that I made no protest and did not make any inquiry or reference concerning meetings between her and Lila that had been taking place regularly.

"It is not altogether a blessing to be born under Capricorn," she began, apropos of nothing except that I was indeed born under that solar house. Next, taking my hand, she asked very earnestly, "Do you mind if I have a quick look at your palm?"

"Most certainly not," I said in a mock serious tone. "The fact is, I have only been waiting for you to ask."

Before looking at my palm she gazed up into my eyes with an expression of profound pity for someone so frivolous. Then she of course bent her magenta head over my outstretched hand. "What I look for is the answer to how you will ever find your true calling. For I do believe you will have a true calling." Bending farther and ever closer to my open palm, she muttered, "Ah, you have a long lifeline. I am glad for that. Certainly you will need time." Suddenly I realized that the hand of mine which I had extended and which she was now examining was visibly trembling. I had no idea of the cause. It was almost as though in the tight grip on my wrist she had touched some nerve there. "You will need a long life to discover your greatest talents. Your palm possesses very deep flexion folds." Now she lightly rubbed her free hand over my upturned palm. "Your palm for all its flexion folds is very hard and dry. The line of the head is superb, and that of the heart also. The line of the fortune is not so well defined. The mountains of Venus and Mars I do like the looks of. I see wisdom, good fortune, and prudence in abundance. My only fear is for the near future. Venus and Mars may be in collision. There is confusion and uncertainty there. By every sign I see you will finally become some kind of artist. This will come later—much later—after you have known experience. After much experience, love and success and understanding will come—after much traveling and still more experience in the world."

Presently I withdrew my hand and let it fall, a clenched fist, at my side. I found myself for one insane moment believing every bit of her nonsense, all that I had submitted to for entertainment and a distraction. And then almost at once I regained my composure and my disbelief.

The apparitions that Aunt Gussie produced that afternoon in her narrative or by her stagecraft or by her mesmerism—I know not which it was—momentarily made me forgetful of the drabness of my camp life during the previous year and a half and oblivious to my overseas experience which I knew lay ahead of me. I gave myself up wholeheartedly to the phantasmagoria that my aunt served up for my beguilement. My grandfather appeared to me first in the guise of a young man lecturing in the Chautauqua series of the 1880s. Then he appeared as the somewhat older young man touring the back country as an actor in a stock company. Then clearly under the influence of Aunt Gussie he appeared as the occupant of the Tennessee gubernatorial chair. Someone or something had made him change his course and become more seriously ambitious in his career. And at last I saw him in full feather on the floor of the Senate chamber, and delighting that body with his fine flow of rhetoric. Next there appeared my own sainted grandmother, managing to be both elegant and saintly in her suede gloves and her feather-covered hat. There were other members of the family, too, who had been only names to me in anecdotes told by my mother and father. I do not know what my principal feeling was. But I had a strong feeling of the richness of life and the pleasure that was to be had in looking back into things that were unchanging and seemingly unchangeable in the world I came out of. Upon leaving Aunt Gussie's apartment that afternoon I knew I had experienced what I had now come to expect: delightful flashes that made me wish for the moment to pursue the same rich human endeavors that my forebears had pursued before me and not to die in some Asian or European battlefield and never to know the satisfaction of taking to wife some truly glorious girl that fate had sent my way.

Now more than ever I knew that I must go right to Lila's women's hotel and make my proposal of marriage to her. She met me downstairs in the lobby when I arrived. She appeared to be in especially high spirits. She was in a smartly tailored suit which I knew that I had not seen before and was something that she had only recently purchased. Somehow it was like no other garment I had ever seen her in. Before we sat down in the lobby even, I made her my proposal. She looked at me in utter astonishment for a moment. And she led me to a nook in the corner of the lobby where we could talk without being overheard. But already I had assumed that there was something different about her other than the businesslike blue suit she was wearing—different from the Lila Montgomery I had known in Tullahoma or Camp Forrest. It seems to me now that things moved very fast from that moment. Before we scarcely were seated in our little corner I told her that I wished to marry her before I shipped out for overseas with my unit and that I wished her to at once meet my parents in Tennessee. Closing her eyes, she rested her head on the back of her chair. She commenced shaking her head in a most unhappy fashion. "If only you had asked me a week ago," she said. "It would have been possible. It would not be possible now."

I drew nearer to say, "I can wait. I can wait. I can wait." I supposed it was my imminent embarkation for the European theater of war that made her think it impossible at that moment. But it wasn't that. It was not because of something that was about to happen in *my* life. It was about something that was about to happen in *her* life. She bent forward resting her little elbows (she had never before seemed so diminutive to me) on the knees beneath her pleated navy blue skirt. She looked directly into my eyes. "It has to do with your aunt," she said. I felt my face flush. I thought of course of all the queer things I had heard my parents say about Aunt Gussie's interference in the affairs of young people. Momentarily I supposed Aunt Gussie had introduced her to a more eligible suitor than I. It occurred to me that Lila had been taken to tea and to lunch with the scion of some family like the Posts or the Guggenheims. (That's how out of date my notions of who the rich people in Washington were—notions handed down no doubt from my grandfather.) But it was not that at all. And it was only now when Lila began telling me what the luncheons and tea parties with Aunt Gussie had been like that I began to have some conception of what Lila herself was like and what there was in the world that would be more attractive in her eyes than would be her intimate friendship with me. I recalled that she had actually left the Tullahoma and Camp Forrest scene rather abruptly. I had gone to fetch her one night at the house of some relatives with whom she was living in Tullahoma and was told that she was setting out the next day for Washington to take a government job which a cousin of hers had found for her. I already knew that she had come originally from a smaller Tennessee town than Tullahoma and she was actually only renting a room from her relatives there in order to be able to take advantage of one of many civilian job openings in Tullahoma and out at Camp Forrest. It had been one night not long before that that I had undertaken to talk to Lila about how boring I found the army routine and about how grim was the prospect of going overseas and how awful it was not to be able to make plans for your life. "Yes," she said after only a few seconds' hesitation and smiling rather dreamily to herself, "but

I am afraid the war is my oyster. It may be my only chance
for something other than this life—something else, though I
don't yet know what."

I was too obtuse to see (though surely I ought to have seen
at once) or was too much preoccupied with the wonderful
good looks of this girl and her charming way with everyone
she met. Seeing that we did not agree on this subject I simply
hurried to other subjects on which we might find areas of
agreement. I know that I ought to have seen significance in her
high spirits when I first looked her up in Washington. She was
excited by everything she saw in that city and was exhilarated
even by the dull clerical work she was saddled with. She certainly said to me more than once that she tried to be always
aware of who the higher-ups were—those who came into her
office asking for information that only she and the girls working with her could provide. "Who knows," she had asked
herself, "when my efficiency might be observed and I might
be shifted to a more important bureau or might even be
shipped overseas to the headquarters over there?"

When Aunt Gussie had seemed not to like her at first, Lila
was really not particularly depressed by it. Then when the old
lady did after all take her up Lila was perfectly willing to be
taken up. On their first outing together Aunt Gussie had remarked that she had observed that Lila was not interested in
the sort of family matters that she and *I* had talked about. She
had observed that Lila was not even entertained by the magic
tricks she performed there in the little apartment. Lila told me
that Aunt Gussie had said to her, "I can see that you have other
matters on your mind—more serious matters. And I have to
tell you I too had more serious matters on *my* mind. Perhaps
you will say to yourself that it didn't get me very far. Only as
far as Stoneleigh Court—but for a young lady in my day that
was farther than you might suppose. But somehow, my dear,
one has to bring other people's attention to focus on what
talents one has. And since time began there have been many
ways for a woman to do that. I suppose it doesn't matter which
way you choose to do it so long as you keep your self-respect.

If you lose that, you may find that you have lost everything. I was, myself, never a really beautiful girl and never a particularly intellectual one. A flirt—no, *never* that. I was sometimes called the one or the other, but it wasn't so." It was as if Lila had memorized all that Aunt Gussie had said to her, knowing at the time even that she would have reason to repeat it all to me.

"I married early," my aunt had continued to Lila, "and my husband and I had very soon to face the certainty that he would not live long. I would have done anything, I suppose, to give him an early success or to make his life interesting for him while it lasted. It happened that in Nashville, after we first were married, there was a man named Mr. Ben Allen who entertained the set we travelled in with séances he held in his house on Eighth Avenue. He could hypnotize people very easily and was master of all things occult. He managed to make the dinner parties given at his house more fun than those we attended anywhere else. As we sat about the dining room table he could make everyone—one after the other—imagine that a cat was rubbing about their ankles. Almost by chance I learned that I, using an intense form of concentration, could make the imaginary cat cease to rub about their ankles. Mr. Allen was delighted by this discovery. That is, he was delighted when I revealed that it was I who was providing the interference. He told me that I had real psychic powers. And he offered to instruct me in the uses of hypnotism. It got so in Nashville and later in Washington that I entertained at parties we went to by demonstrating my hypnotic powers, sometimes hypnotizing one of the other guests. It made me very popular in whatever set we moved. And sometimes I would cure the headaches of friends with those newly discovered powers of mine. Even before we left Nashville some friends became dependent upon me for help. But it was not always a happy thing. For a time I cured the headaches of your young man's grandmother, the wife of the then governor of Tennessee. She and I and our husbands were then living in the old Maxwell House Hotel, since there was no governor's mansion at that time. I somehow developed such a power over her mind that I could cure her headaches without her being aware of the source. One day I sat on the mezzanine on the opposite side of the hotel lobby from where she was seated. She was sitting with her head resting in her gloved hands, and so I knew she was suffering. Within a few minutes she looked up cheerfully and gazed across at me. It was a very happy moment, but later the Governor learned of it, and he made strong objections to my having such power over his wife. I am not sure that his objections weren't largely due to powers existing in the person of a woman. Later, one awful time in Washington, I would undertake to cure the headache of my own husband. He told me at the time that I had succeeded, but afterward I was never quite sure it was a simple headache he was suffering from. I was present in the balcony of the House that very morning when he collapsed. He was making his maiden speech, and I was there to hear him. He lived barely long enough for me to make my way down the stairs and push through the crowd of congressmen to his side. He died there in my arms even before a doctor could be summoned. No one ever knew such loneliness as I did in the years afterward. But I was determined to stay here. And I held my ground!"

Lila Montgomery told me all this as we sat together in the corner of the residential hotel where she lived. But that was not the whole of it. That was hardly the beginning. She did not tell me then what the nature of her other meetings with Aunt Gussie had been. She was presently overcome with emotion and said she must go to her room now. She would tell the rest tomorrow.

Back in my barracks that night I slept only fitfully. Those moments when I did sleep my head was filled with uneasy dreams and when I lay awake my mind was filled with speculations about the more eligible bachelors Aunt Gussie would have introduced her to. Over the telephone the next morning she told me that on the day before she had actually quit her job in the bureau. She asked me if I would come to her place and go for a walk with her that morning. I went and found her got up in another brand-new tailored suit and in a narrow-brimmed hat of matching material. She looked an absolute knock-out and wonderfully happy. When I came in, she stepped forward and kissed me. It was the first time she and I had ever kissed. She took my arm, leaning on me, and we passed out through the entry and into the dull light of the October morning. I was prepared for her to tell me of the charm and the intellectual brilliance and the aristocratic background of some man that she was now engaged to marry. It seemed that her happy and affectionate manner could suggest only that. "Let's walk all morning," she began, "and do nothing but look in the shop windows at women's clothes—all the way to Georgetown and even beyond."

Our walk entailed going a short way up Embassy Row and around General Sheridan's equestrian statue, past the buffaloes and over the park bridge to Georgetown. I suppose we found some shop windows to peer into, though I don't remember anything I saw there. After we entered Georgetown we passed several high-ranking military officers, and more than once it was necessary for me to salute them. (Lila could not resist commenting on the smartness of the salutes we exchanged and she giggled to herself, saying she could hardly resist joining in the process and giving a salute herself.) This was the total business of the first part of our walk except for what Lila had to tell me about her lunches and tea parties with Aunt Gussie. It was always some senator or the right-hand man of some senator that Lila found herself in the company of when she went out with my aunt. It seemed that on every occasion the elegant gentleman ended by offering her a job or at least suggesting that he had a job to offer. But Aunt Gussie, without ever being observed by the gentleman, would shake her head significantly at Lila, indicating that what was offered or hinted at was not good enough. But once in spite of my aunt's head-shaking, Lila burst out with: "Oh, I'd be happy to be the girl in the outer, outer office. And you would be surprised at how little pay I'd need."

But Aunt Gussie had quickly come forward with: "Don't let

her deceive you, Senator. You can't imagine how little interest she has in such a job."

While we were in Georgetown, ambling up Wisconsin, suddenly the sun came out from behind the clouds and shone brightly for a very few minutes. But how wretched it seemed to me, how deceptive. It was not the real Washington at all. Yet instantly Lila was saying, "Isn't Washington beautiful! Whether cloudy or bright! Even the ratty little shops here on Wisconsin!" Then the sun did go under a cloud again. To Lila *it* seemed the real and wonderful Washington still. "Isn't it glorious even when it's overcast!" she persisted.

"But you were to tell me something," I reminded her, with a persistence of my own. "I suppose it's about why you have quit your job?"

"It is about that and about something more," she said with enthusiasm. "You see, I want so to be somebody who matters. Your aunt has introduced me to any number of people—people of considerable influence and importance, and quite a few of them have suggested that I might do for a job in their office. And finally there has come one that I cannot resist, one that is sure to open up bigger and bigger things for me, into worlds that I want to be in. I am afraid that you have never understood what an ambitious creature I am. It's my future I am wrapped up in, and I am afraid I can't give myself to anybody else while that is the case."

I looked down at her in utter astonishment, which must have been written on my face. Lila reached out her hand and rested it on the sleeve of my army jacket. "I *am* sorry, dear, if I have misled you about what I am really like," she said softly. I suppose it could not have occurred to her that I was most astonished at myself for having perceived so little of what Lila Montgomery really was like at all. But I quickly got hold of myself and said a number of silly, consoling things—consoling to her, though not to me. And I even thought that I saw a mist of tears in her eyes when I looked at her. I think neither of us was sure at the moment just how deep or how shallow his or her feelings were. I cannot be sure even now. We walked on up Wisconsin, as far as the cathedral. Lila asked me if I would like to go inside the great edifice and see the work that was still in progress there. I said that I could see it another time. I could not concentrate on the small talk that she and I were reduced to making and could certainly not have given my attention to the details of the cathedral under construction.

Finally we turned down Massachusetts Avenue and would eventually find our way to Lila's hotel. Before we reached there we found little left to say to each other. What a waste the furlough in Washington seemed. It accomplished nothing really but to reveal the difference in our two natures and how unsuited we were to each other. Only in retrospect would I realize what we each had been thinking about during the hour that we walked together. In retrospect I would feel sure we each had been thinking of my aged aunt, Mrs. Augusta St. John-Jones.

Only moments before we parted in the entrance to her hotel she quite suddenly spoke to me, speaking as though in our silence we had been having exchanges on this subject as we walked: "Your aunt, you must understand, never once spoke of or made reference to any of her magic business when she and I were alone. It was for *you* alone that she reserved all that."

"Me alone she condescended to dazzle," I said, "because I was a mere man—only an overgrown child as all men are to her."

"No, not at all," she corrected me. "Or at least your language is much too strong. It would be fairer to put it another way. She can see you are a person of imagination. And she sees I am an ambitious, literal-minded little chit, not worthy of her fireworks." And with that Lila Montgomery blew me a kiss and disappeared through the revolving door at the entrance to her women's hotel.

Perhaps such thoughts occupied me for the whole of my last two days in Washington. During those days I moved about not in my usual drifting fashion but seemingly with a purpose. On those two days I viewed the real monuments of the national capital, those one is supposed to see. I saw the interior of the Washington Monument, I saw the Spirit of St. Louis in the Smithsonian, went through the principal art museums, saw the work in progress at the unfinished cathedral, viewed the Lincoln Memorial from a great distance and then from within, saw a portion of the White House, and paid a hurried visit to the Capitol. When at the end of the second day I went by appointment to my aunt's apartment I of course reported what I had seen but made no mention of Lila. Nor did my aunt mention Lila's name. We spent an hour together, talking family. Just as I was leaving, she asked me if I had seen the Hall of Heroes that used to be in the basement of the Capitol. When I said that I had overlooked that, she insisted that we meet there next morning at ten o'clock before I took my train back to Tullahoma. We agreed to meet on the steps at the east entrance to the Capitol.

And there she was just on time, at the foot of the vast flight of steps, climbing out of a taxi. She was dressed very becomingly in a light polo coat and a jaunty hat. I had never seen her in such high spirits. She waved her little gloved hand to me as she turned away from the taxi and then ran up the broad steps like a young girl. It occurred to me immediately that it was being here at the Capitol that excited her so. We passed inside and went directly down to the rooms that housed the statues of heroes selected from the histories of all the states. Reaching down into the collar of her dress she produced her lorgnette and stooping a little now and then she would read the name and dates of each hero. Finally she insisted that I go a few steps ahead of her because she wished to read the inscription beneath each bust or statue. I wandered on, rather absent-mindedly, studying the stone faces and the stone garments of these heroes. Then, feeling I might seem rude and not properly appreciative, I turned back to join her. But she was not in sight. I began searching behind each piece of sculpture. I hurried up and down the long hallway, but she was not to be seen. Presently I was running up and down, calling out to her, "Aunt Gussie! Aunt Gussie!" There was no answer. I searched out a guard and asked him if he had seen an old lady such as my aunt. He neither nodded nor shook his head, only looked at me with pity. I went back to the wide portal which we had entered at the foot of the stairs. Then I ran up the stairs and on through the halls and passages to the east entrance. She was nowhere to be found. She had disappeared. She had purposely gone off without me. Then at last it came over me that that was what she had planned. This was how she wanted us to part. There was nothing I could do to change it. There was not time now for me to call her at her apartment and make my noon train. And so, not returning to the Hall of Heroes, I shouldered my duffel bag and made my way over to the Union Station. I kept telling myself as I hurried along that I would call her or write to her when I got back to Camp Forrest, but already I knew I wouldn't do that and imagined that Aunt Augusta St. John-Jones and I had said our last goodbyes. And once aboard the train to Tullahoma I found myself looking forward to seeing my soldier friends back in camp. It was they I yearned to be reunited with, rather than my own family. I longed to feel myself one among *them*. I wanted—I was determined—to forget the Washington furlough. As I sat with my duffel bag by the day-coach window I kept asking myself why this "temporary assignment" had been such a failure and such a fiasco. Was it my awareness of the war and a prescience of the role I was to play in it? Was it a vestige of a childish yearning for a magic that would constitute a cure-all for whatever troubled me? Was it merely the atmosphere of wartime Washington? Was it perhaps a simple case of disappointment in love? In any case, whatever the grimness of army life, I was going to that hiatus of real life, to a life where personal problems did not absolutely have to be solved, to where problems were solved by commands or unanswerable authority. I imagined that military authority and the war itself would last forever.

II

It was now three years after the war ended, and I was an acknowledged veteran and casualty of said war, still trying to sort out my own dismaying—and very nearly fatal—experience which had followed our unit's D-Day landing in Normandy. During the intervening time few thoughts had crossed my mind concerning that episode in Washington. For the most part, it all seemed literally quite unreal. And only now, when I had begun to recover from what the doctors euphemistically termed my "long invalidism," did I again hear someone speak the name of Lila Montgomery. Even now I did not take the trouble to make inquiries into what had actually become of Lila. For the time being, I was living at home with my mother and father down in Memphis, and I made a practice of not going anyplace at all where I might conceivably be recognized—recognized, that is to say, as the kind of war hero which during the intervening time and to my great discomfort I found myself to have become.

For the most part I saw only two friends during this period. And these were not among my oldest, closest friends. They were, rather, two young men who had had experiences similar to my own—not in the war itself but still earlier and with regard to their registration with the Draft Board at the beginning of the war. I cannot now say for sure that this significantly or intentionally was the case or whether perhaps it all occurred just by chance. At any rate, one of these friends, it may possibly be remembered by an attentive reader, was a man named Alex Mercer. The other was Alex's longtime friend Phillip Carver, and so it may well have been that they both were attracted to making my closer acquaintance by their special sensitivity to the predicament I found myself in at this point. On the other hand these two contemporaries of mine may unconsciously have lent themselves to my support without themselves fully understanding their own motivation. Anyhow, the case was that during the first months after I was released from my two-year stay in the army hospital and when I had first returned to Memphis the acclaim and the adulation that then became mine constituted a painful experience for me. And this was due to certain well-publicized exploits attributed to me by army communiqués on the first day after the Normandy beachhead—exploits for which my memory still even till this day presents a perfect blank.

Everyone in Memphis now knew, of course, that at the beginning of the war I had first listed myself as a conscientious objector. And this would only add luster to my image as the war hero I had now been acclaimed. I had no difficulty in recognizing the pleasure people took from the irony of my situation. For I all too well remembered the excitement generated (ten years after the First World War) by any public appearance of Sergeant Alvin York or by that of Colonel Luke Lea. The identity of the former is well known, of course. The latter was a Tennessee man who had led a party trying to capture Kaiser Wilhelm after that famous ogre fled to Holland at the end of the war. As a boy the exploits of both these men had seemed to me well worth celebrating. They remained Tennessee's two principal war heroes from 1917 until the Second World War, and now my own story whetted the public's appetite for another such hero. As a child I could accurately recall both those men and had myself participated in the adulation they received. I even once shook hands with the famous Colonel Lea when riding on an elevator with him in downtown Memphis. My father had recognized him and took that opportunity to introduce the two of us. On another occasion I was taken on a twenty-mile ride over rough country road— by an uncle of mine who lived on the Cumberland Plateau—to hear Sergeant York address the congregation of a country church.

For a time my only experiences with the present-day Tennessee populace were barely less remarkable for me than those men's experiences had been a generation earlier. Once while riding an escalator—I believe it was in Goldsmith's Department Store—I was spotted by a group of school-age boys riding upward on a parallel escalator. I of course heard their exclamations to each other about who I was and what I had allegedly done in the war. And I saw them presently begin running up the upward moving flight and saw them squeezing by people on the downward flight I was riding. Suddenly I took fright and myself commenced squeezing past my own fellow passengers until I had in short order reached the first floor of the department store. Then I ran out through the crowd and pushed through the revolving door and on out onto the sidewalk. When presently I went scurrying up an alleyway toward Front Street I saw two wooden sawhorses blocking my route and workmen digging up patches of the pavement. I also observed at once that a line of pedestrians were carefully making their way around either end of the sawhorses and through the narrow passageway between that impediment and an adjacent building. With no hesitation I took on greater speed now in the direction of the street blockade ahead. And when I had made my way past the workmen and the sawhorses in my path I was astonished to hear a generous round of applause from the onlookers. It was applause for me! I might have assumed their applause to represent only the great good nature of Memphis citizenry in general except that simultaneously I heard my own name being called out above the applause. They had recognized their hero!

During that first year or so after the war I was often so recognized and applauded wherever I went. The schoolboys on the escalator failed to overtake me that day, and the pedestrians did not pursue me. But as I came out on Front Street I spied a bench in front of one of the cotton offices and found it necessary to drop down there to rest. I found it necessary because even in the last moments after I turned into Front Street and with a glimpse of the waters of the Mississippi River not far ahead, myself panting and sweating as I certainly was (though it was not by any means a hot day), I experienced a flashing image of a certain steep path beside a green hedgerow in Normandy and with a similar glimpse of the English Channel just over a slight rise in the land. It was an image or scene which periodically presented itself to me after any moments of emotional excitement or after any strenuous physical exertion of almost any kind. But after that flash of memory there was nothing more. And there never could be more—not ever. Beyond this there was nothing in my memory till I woke many days later in an English hospital tent. What my acts of heroism had been, remained for me to discover from chance remarks I heard dropped from other soldiers who came upon the scene and from accounts I uncovered in old newspapers.

WHEN I WAS a boy no older then those boys who had sighted me on the escalator I had already by then commenced my own brand of hero worship. My choice of those heroes or non-heroes was, I am sure, a response in some degree to the conventional and decidedly bland mentality of my parents—and indeed of all members of our family except of course my Great-Aunt Gussie, whom I then knew of course almost entirely by representation alone. Both my parents always spoke with a certain condescension of Sergeant York and his "untutored, hill-country, plain-people" background. And despite the fact of his having so famously brought in a horde of German prisoners, my father was apt on all occasions to remind one that Sergeant York had begun his career as a conscientious objector, which was intended on Father's part to show how little understanding that country boy had had of what the world we live in is like. On the other hand, though he had been a political enemy of my grandfather, Colonel Luke Lea was generally spoken of at home with all due or undue respect. Despite the total failure of the escapade in which he and three fellow officers took over a command car and raced off across the Dutch border to try to capture the Kaiser, and despite the later scandal regarding his later business practices, and despite even his spending a period of time in a North Carolina jail as a result of those practices, I was required as a child to speak of him with the same respect I would have spoken of any other adult and

certainly any other "gentleman." And that day when my father introduced him in the elevator I observed that my mother,
whose father it was he had "betrayed" in politics, turned her
back on the Colonel and on the rest of the ride upward behaved
not only as though he did not exist but as though Father and
I were complete strangers to her. It was all a curious business
to me, and I often thought of it when I had first come home
a hero of a kind from my own war. During this period I took
an interest in discovering just what kind of endings these men's
lives had come to. I learned that Sergeant York lived out his
life in the region of Tennessee known as the Highland Rim
and died in the very cabin where he had been born. And
Colonel Lea of course had gone on to distinguish himself as a
showoff of a predictable kind in the world of business and high
finance and had died of old age in the comfortable house of his
estate near Nashville, only two or three miles from where he
had himself first seen the light of day.

BY THE TIME I came home from overseas my two parents were
now in their midsixties and like so many people who have
reached that age, they were especially sympathetic to anyone
of their acquaintance who was a decade or so older than themselves. Soon after I got home they began receiving word from
their relatives that Aunt Gussie Jones, still living in the Stoneleigh Court up in Washington, was in a bad state of health and
could not be expected to live for many months. After a while
my father began urging me to write a line to the old lady. But
he asked in such a casual way that I didn't imagine for a
moment that he really wished me to do so. It was only his way
of saying that he no longer had any interest in communicating
with the likes of Aunt Gussie. I had no thought of writing her
myself, of course, and without explaining why, I laughed
rather nervously at the very idea. I had been in such low spirits
after that visit to Washington and before my subsequent embarkation for overseas and the combat ahead for me that I had
not given my parents an account of my adventures with Aunt

Gussie and had scarcely ever mentioned the name of Lila Montgomery. It was only after I had been home for nearly two years that I heard her name mentioned by my mother.

I had not known for certain whether Mother knew the name of the girl I had gone to see in Washington. She gave me no indication. I can only suppose Aunt Gussie had mentioned it to her in a letter. It was a good many months later that I heard her, in passing, mention Lila's name to Father. Again I made no acknowledgment of my acquaintance with her—and certainly not that of any romantic interest on my part. I had by this time been having dates with Ruthie Ann Sedwick, who was a cousin of my friend Alex Mercer's. I had met Ruthie Ann while she was baby-sitting Alex's two children when his wife was in the hospital giving birth to a third child. I suppose it was the power of suggestion that made me begin to imagine that Alex Mercer's way of life, with his steady job and his growing family and his clear intention of putting down roots in Memphis, might be the way for me to go. The truth is, though, I made no mention of Ruthie Ann's name to my family either. I do believe that I loved my parents very dearly, but I had long since ceased to confide anything of a very private or delicate nature to either of them. Ever since the days of my stand on the matter of conscientious objection I had been convinced that there were many matters on which we could never understand each other and that should never be brought up for discussion. The fact is that from early childhood I observed that there were areas in which there could be no understanding or agreement between them and me. And until the war came along I had always assumed that in every instance they had been right and that I, through perversity and ignorance, had been wrong. For instance, at the age of four or five I had gone to Father at Easter and said that I had seen Mother hiding eggs in the grass and shrubbery and that I therefore no longer believed in the Easter Bunny. Father had quickly assured me that I was mistaken and that my mistake must remain a secret between him and me. And in fact I never again raised any questions on that score. It may seem incredible, but once at

Christmas when I was seven or eight (after I was of school age at any rate) I saw Father filling the stocking I had hung on my bedpost at bedtime. When I reported this to my mother she took a similar line to my Father with regard to the Easter Bunny. She said she was sure I must have dreamed it and that events in dreams sometimes seemed more real to us than real events. Once when I came home from Sunday school, during those years, I announced to my older sister that I didn't believe the story of Christ's resurrection was a true story. I said I could tell from the Sunday school teacher's tone of voice and from the look on her face that she did not believe it for a minute! My sister flew into a fury of rage against me. She said that I ought to be ashamed of myself and that if I knew what was good for me I would never say such things in the presence of our parents. I followed her advice and in the future kept any such thoughts to myself. . . . At the age of eleven I was sent to a summer day camp for boys. In the shower room at camp I had felt humiliated by the discovery of a difference between me and all the other campers. I was the only one of that group of boys who had not been circumcised. At the end of the summer I went to Father with considerable embarrassment but with firm resolution, and requested that the same operation be performed on me. At first I thought his sudden blushes meant that he was angry, but after a moment he spoke to me very gently. "I believe most of the boys at that camp of yours," he said, "must be of the Jewish faith. It is a matter of faith to them, and you must not wish to be like them in that respect."

AFTER I HAD been home from the war for somewhat more than a year Father received a long-distance telephone call from Washington—I can only suppose from subsequent events that the call was from Lila Montgomery herself—informing him that Aunt Gussie was to be removed from her hospital in Washington to St. Joseph's Catholic Hospital in Memphis. He was told the date and hour of the train's arrival and that she would be accompanied by both a "trained nurse" and by none other than Lila Montgomery herself. The call had come to Father's office on a weekday, and that night he told us no more about it than that. I received this news—along with Mother and my sister Agnes—and I had far less to say about the prospect before us than did anyone else present. I was unwilling to commit myself to showing interest either in my aunt or in Lila. That night I was to take Ruthie Ann Sedwick to a neighborhood movie, and I resolved not even to mention the matter to her. My sister Agnes was going to a country club dance with her fiancé, Hubert Madison, and I knew that she—and my parents when they went up to bed—would repeat a good many times the kind of remarks they had made at the dinner table before going upstairs. Their remarks there had consisted mostly of speculation about who had made the decision to send Aunt Gussie home to Tennessee to die. As for me, I had had a flash of insight at the very first moment of Father's revelation of his news. And, strangely enough, the flash came not from any previous understanding of Lila's character when I had known her in Washington but quite extraordinarily from a sudden foresight, a stunning unexplainable prescience of what Lila had become since I last saw her. I was not aware of having given much reflection to changes that might have taken place in her character since we parted in Washington. I know only that something deeper than thought or reflection had transpired somewhere within my being that informed me that if she would turn up in Memphis I must not expect to see the girl in the single strand of pearls and the hand-knit blue sweater and the pleated skirt and the neat low-heeled shoes. Nor was I to expect her to appear in such new clothes as she had put on just before she sent me away to the war. The sudden flash told me only as much as that about what *not* to expect in the Lila Montgomery who would come escorting the sick person which I knew Aunt Gussie now to be. This insight of course seemed to reach me through processes and channels that would not ordinarily be open or available to a young man of my sometimes unobservant and for the most part unintellectual temperament. In this instance my head—or I might even venture to say my heart—made associations and induced deductions and drew upon farfetched comparisons that it would never perhaps be able to do again. In a word, I knew that Lila Montgomery would be something different and mean something different from what she had been and meant before. And now for the first time I understood or perceived that nothing in this world would ever again be or mean what it had been or meant before the day I crept on my hands and knees along that path beside the hedgerow at the beachhead in Normandy.

WHEN LILA DESCENDED the steep little flight of steps from the Pullman car to the platform in the old Union Station at Memphis there was a party of seven of us to greet her—or rather present to meet Aunt Augusta St. John-Jones. Word had gone through the whole family connection that Aunt Gussie was on her way. Besides my parents and my sister Agnes and myself there were three cousins of ours whom Father had corralled into meeting the train. Two of the cousins were young men of my generation, to whom I bore some slight resemblance. These were nephews of my father's. The third cousin was a youngish spinster of an age somewhere midway between my own and my parents'. Her name was Andrea Lomax, and she lived alone in an old-fashioned apartment house on Cleveland Avenue where she had grown up with her family. As Lila Montgomery stepped down onto the footstool that the porter had provided I presently realized that only I of the family members gathered there would be able to recognize her. As a matter of fact I was not at first sure it was she I beheld on the metal steps coming down from the Pullman car. Even when she had stepped down onto the wooden railway platform I was not certain it was she. There was a crazy moment when I thought perhaps it was the rather plump nurse following behind her on the steps who might be she. Lila was so greatly changed that in that moment prior to my certain recognition of her she might have been any one of the half-dozen women following close behind her on the steps. And when I did recognize her for a certainty by the familiar grin that now played on her lips I became equally certain that during another moment Lila Montgomery was not at all sure which of the three young men in civilian clothes and endowed with a decided family resemblance was he whom she had known at Camp Forrest and in Washington. At some moment, however, she did become sure—perhaps only at the moment when I stepped forward to take the piece of hand luggage she carried and to place a kiss on her forehead. Or perhaps it should be put the other way around, for it was the kiss on the forehead that I had first in mind, and I am afraid it was a sort of Judas kiss—intended to let the rest of the family know who she was. The fact was, moreover, that once I had planted that brotherly kiss on Lila's forehead—or rather once, as it seemed to me, she herself was certain that I was who I was—she suddenly came up on her tiptoes and placed a kiss on my lips of a kind I most assuredly had never before received from her either at Camp Forrest or in Washington. In retrospect it seemed to me that our affair in those earlier days had been almost entirely platonic. Under present circumstances this kiss of Lila's was no less than alarming. For my most pressing concern at that moment was not for Lila but for Ruthie Ann and the serious turn her and my conversations had recently taken. I felt myself instantly withdrawing from this kiss of Lila's as though I recognized what it might suggest about her behavior and perhaps the general style of her life nowadays. And then during the moment of the kiss I heard the jolly little trained nurse behind her saying, "So this is why it was necessary for us to bring Mrs. St. John-Jones out here to a Memphis hospital." Then she gave way to what we all very soon came to recognize as her own characteristic burst of staccato laughter. And when presently she was introduced to me by Lila and I asked her how my aunt had borne the journey she suddenly looked very solemn and replied that she was afraid that Aunt Gussie had not borne it well at all. And carefully looking directly at me and possibly avoiding Lila's eye she asserted somewhat gravely, "I fear undertaking such a journey has been too much for your aunt."

Then she added solicitously to me, "Would you care to come aboard the train and see her? She's still in her berth in the drawing room."

Lila Montgomery had now descried at some distance up the platform a stretcher cart being rapidly wheeled along in our direction. She commenced waving with both hands at the stretcher bearers. The stretcher was clearly something she had ordered when setting out from Washington and hence was now on the lookout for. As she hailed the stretcher bearers with a certain authority, I glanced back at the assembled family members and was somewhat taken aback to see that none of them had yet come forward. Rather, they struck me as standing there still in open-mouthed amazement, so to speak, at the remarkable warmth with which I had been greeted by the good-looking young woman who had just stepped off the train. Perhaps this was only something I imagined, but it made me gesture with some impatience for all the group to come forward.

When I had introduced them all around, my spinster cousin Andrea Lomax touched my arm and said, "Don't you think you and I might go aboard and greet the old lady? I remember her very well from the old days when I used to go in from Miss Madeira's and stay with her at the Stoneleigh Court." And then Andrea turned to Nurse O'Neill (for so the attending nurse would presently refer to herself) and asked her permission to let the two of us board the train and enter Aunt Gussie's drawing room accommodation. In response to this Nurse O'Neill shrugged her shoulders in a most offhand fashion, saying in an exaggeratedly indifferent manner (so it seemed to me), "You may all of you go ahead if you like, though I am afraid she won't know any of you from Adam's house cat! For she is not at all herself." Notwithstanding this chilling response, Andrea presently climbed aboard. And I soon followed after her. I suppose I did so partly because I wanted time to adjust my thoughts to the ardor of Lila's kiss. As we went along the little passage that ran alongside Aunt Gussie's drawing room I heard Andrea Lomax ask querulously from over her shoulder, "Is that young woman someone you met in Washington during the war?"

To this I heard myself reply noncommittally, "More or less I did, Andrea," making it plain to this elder cousin of mine that it was distinctly none of her business where I had known "that young woman." For I was perfectly aware that this spinster cousin had observed the amorous nature of the kiss that Lila Montgomery had bestowed upon me when she stepped off the train. At the door to the drawing room Andrea hesitated and gave me a quick look that said we must be prepared to expect almost anything once we got inside and which suggested somehow that she herself had some old scores to be settled with this mutual aunt of ours.

The face of the old creature that presently peered out at us from under the sheet in the made-up drawing room berth bespoke nothing less than absolute terror. Presently now Andrea, to my delight, was addressing the old lady in the gentlest and most reassuring voice imaginable. But in response the dark, hollow eyes and near toothless mouth gave no distinct sign of recognition. The eyes seemed to stare right through the both of us, as though we were perfect strangers, or as though she hadn't the power to summon up whatever memory of us she might once have had. But after a time Aunt Gussie very distinctly spoke the name "Lila" as though that were now the only name that could mean anything to her. Simultaneously we heard the stretcher bearers first stumbling along the passage and then bumping against the open door to Aunt Gussie's compartment. To make way for them Andrea and I at once backed out into the first Pullman section. Through the window out there I had a glimpse of Lila Montgomery speaking very effusively to my mother and father and to other members of the family. Seeing her so engaged with my parents and my brother and sister suddenly all seemed like a confused dream to me: this admixture of people thus appearing from different moments and in different contexts of my life! And certainly no less confusing was the subsequent emergence from the drawing room of my little aunt, now supine on the stretcher and being wielded into the passage by two white-clad and rather pudgy young men and attended by the resplendent Nurse O'Neill, who had now joined forces with them. Andrea and I remained by the Pullman section window long enough to see the stretcher appear on the platform and be carted away by the vehicle waiting there. The cluster of family members could hardly have got more than a glimpse of Aunt Gussie as she was wheeled by. She must have appeared to them, as she had to Andrea and me, as little more than a corpse. Nurse O'Neill and Lila Montgomery, hurriedly calling out instructions to the family group gathered there about the disposition of their luggage, went running unceremoniously after their departing charge.

AND YET NEXT DAY when I was taken to see Aunt Gussie at St. Joseph's Hospital, allegedly at her request, she seemed— upon my entering the hospital room—almost her very same wizened, black-eyed self, even with the gypsy scarf tied about her old head. She greeted me quite familiarly, like someone who might have been near and dear to her for many years. "Come in, you young rascal of a war hero!" she exclaimed in that memorable, husky voice of hers. It said worlds to me! Somehow at the moment it seemed to tell me all I needed to know about Lila and Aunt Gussie and how close they had become and how much they might have talked about me— especially in recent months. Yet even before this first exclamation of hers was quite uttered, her voice began to trail off into what was at last little more than a whisper. It became immediately apparent to me that the hardy tone she had at first affected was done only with the greatest effort and could not be sustained for more than a few moments at a time. She seized my hand between her own two hands, which for all their old appearance of transparency were like steel in their grasp. Then she began again in a voice that would once again trail off into a whisper: "You young scamp you, you see I have hunted you out in the wilds of West Tennessee in order to return your 'fantastically good-looking girl' to your safekeeping! I think you will find her worthy of the war hero that you have become." So saying, like some child in a school play who has spoken its only allotted lines and then out of utter exhaustion has gone into a near faint, my Aunt Gussie slumped into silence and simultaneously released my hand from her steel-like grasp. Lila Montgomery was at that moment standing near me beside the high hospital bed. It was she who had this morning summoned me to my aunt's bedside in the hospital, and the thought occurred to me even then that Aunt Gussie had conceivably memorized those spoken lines in order to oblige Lila Montgomery, though it seemed equally possible that my aunt had done so in order to satisfy some deathbed scheme of her very own.

FROM THE MOMENT on the previous day when, out on the railway platform, I first heard Nurse O'Neill's burst of staccato laughter an uneasy feeling began developing inside me. I had felt some force at work within me that I knew I had best take note of. Perhaps it was Nurse O'Neill's unbecoming girlish irony, more than her laughter, that had alerted me to imminent danger of some sort. At any rate during waking moments of that night's sleep her words more than once rang in my ears: "So this was why it was deemed necessary for us to bring Mrs. St. John-Jones out here to a Memphis hospital to die?" And now at Aunt Gussie's bedside, with Lila beside me and Nurse O'Neill just opposite, it was easy to imagine myself trapped in a nest of armed combat troops—all of them appropriately outfitted with spiked helmets and war gear of the most threatening kind. Though I did not in any literal sense do so, it might have been tempting to try to equate this moment with that other moment when I alone had allegedly held off a horde of Huns similar to and equal to Sergeant York's own. But despite any battle shock or other permanent disability I had suffered I yet had more fundamental wisdom in my nature than to give way to such images. In the first place I knew with all certainty that

that memory was forever blotted from my mind. And I had too much respect—of almost the religious variety—for all under Heaven that is blessedly blocked from human memory and particularly for those horrors blocked from my own consciousness and the memory of events never to be recalled on that hillside above the Normandy beachhead—such non-memories being truly like the battle dead who had been left behind in that place—too much respect, I should emphasize, to allow me to think even momentarily of equating it with such a prosaic and pathetic scene as this at St. Joseph's Hospital. And true though it is that certain war correspondents and certain official military observers have since given relatively accurate accounts of what occurred that June day in 1944 and of the role I myself played among the hedgerows on that hillside, still in each case the journalist and the military narrator needed for his own purposes that which only *I* could supply. Of course I have not necessarily had to believe in the truth of their accounts. As I have read them I have gone along with said accounts (it has been a "learning experience" for me) because since I do not remember anything, I cannot therefore deny anything. For my own peace of mind and sometimes out of vanity I have accepted as truth all that I have seen put in writing. There have been moments when to deny anything at all would seem to deny *everything* and to have begun a great unraveling that might have ended I know not where. I therefore can deny nothing except in ridiculous instances like the present when I am tempted to make some petty and ignoble comparison between the present unworthy events and events of those heroic moments which all the world will continue to believe in and consider so until the day when I can truthfully make a denial.

THAT FIRST DAY on the railway platform it must have at some point been decided where Lila would reside during her stay in Memphis. The only detail I can recall is that when leaving the Union Station it happened to come to my attention that Lila's two rather large pieces of luggage were placed in the trunk of

Andrea Lomax's navy blue sedan. At noon on the second day of her stay in Memphis I received a telephone call from Lila requesting that I might be so kind as to fetch her in one of my parents' cars and take her out to dinner that night. Andrea was being very hospitable, Lila's old familiar voice assured me, but it would surely seem an imposition for her to turn up there for dinner every night. Besides, said that charming voice whose every engaging quality now rang familiarly in my ear, there were certain matters that she and I had to discuss.

At this very period in my recuperation from my bad war experiences my relations with Ruthie Ann Sedwick were becoming more and more intense. My immediate reaction to Lila's call was that either I had to break my engagement with Ruthie Ann that evening or somehow arrange to include her in any plans I might make with Lila. I decided that any version of the latter would be too awkward. And as I might well have predicted, that dear girl Ruthie Ann Sedwick was ever so understanding about the problem I was faced with. I scarcely needed speak of it. She seemed immediately to comprehend the whole situation. It was as though she said to herself, "Of course there must have been a girl in Washington, and what could be more likely than that she should accompany his Aunt Gussie on the train? Probably they became acquainted through his aunt." And how different this was from Lila Montgomery! During the first days after her arrival I would several times make a point of mentioning Ruthie Ann's name to her. She seemed deaf to the very sound of it. Until nearly the very end she would seem willfully unaware of Ruthie Ann's existence.

As a matter of fact it was Andrea Lomax who proved *not* so understanding. For the evening ahead she had prepared a rather elaborate dinner for herself and her house guest, during which I must suppose that she, as a curious-minded old maid, intended to extract whatever information Lila and I were concealing about our acquaintance. But Lila had overlooked telling her about our other plans for the evening! Andrea, though obviously disappointed, commenced insisting that we both of us stay on at her place for dinner. But Lila was adamant, insisting herself that it was too much of an imposition on Andrea. Afterward, I fear, they were unable to make it up between them. As a result, on the following day, Lila rented a small car for her own use, though actually she would make little enough use of it. She did, however, continue to occupy her room at Andrea's place for the duration of her protracted visit to Memphis, but she took her meals elsewhere.

As I followed Lila out through the entry doorway that night at Andrea's I saw Lila give a quick glance backward into the front room of the place, and her expression seemed strangely familiar to me. I could tell that she would prefer not to be coming here again. But I perceived too that it was somehow important to her to be staying with a member of my family. But clearly what was equally or even more important to her was that she and I should have this first evening together and entirely alone. The expression on her face was familiar to me but was assuredly not one that I could thoroughly have comprehended at an earlier time in our acquaintance. I read in it now a purposefulness about her that would have entirely eluded me at any previous time.

Yet when Lila and I dined together later that evening I recognized in her demeanor a cheerfulness and charm that would have seemed actually foreign to her nature in my former acquaintance with her. No semblance of the old pouty expression showed itself at any time during that evening—or at any time later, for that matter. That whole pouty business was obviously something left over from the personality of the child Lila Montgomery had once been. Neither was there now any evidence of the mixture of the once companionable and always impersonal feeling that had formerly marked her personality. Most striking, though, was the absence of the old mobility of facial expression which I had noted the very first time I saw Lila on the Camp Forrest dance floor nearly five years before. I became aware of this absence tonight first while introducing her to two casual acquaintances in the restaurant and again when merely hearing her place an order with our waitress after we had been seated at our table. The change in her manner—

the rigidity of it—had been noticeable even in such passing and casual exchanges. And it now seemed, in retrospect, that a change had been apparent to me two days before on the railway platform in the Union Station. It seemed to me that she had greeted my mother and my father and the other members of my family with approximately the same at once rigid and effusive manner that she had used just now while addressing our waitress in the restaurant. Above all, it was the peculiar mixture of rigidity and effusiveness of manner that most distinctly set the new Lila apart from the old. There was a oneness in her way of addressing people now where once there had been great shades and distinctions at hand for everyone.

But equally distinct was her way of dressing nowadays. There was something I kept referring to (only to myself) as her high style. There was the different era we had all moved into— men and women alike—and there was of course the difference in Lila Montgomery's present age. She had seen a good deal more of the world now—even there in wartime Washington she had, even in Washington which somehow always manages to give one the feeling of being in a bit of a backwater. One felt that she would not willingly have been seen nowadays in one of those outfits she had purchased when she went to take up the new job that Aunt Gussie had found her—much less in one of the little blouse-and-pleated-skirt "sets" she had arrived in Washington wearing. Without having a lot more interest than I could reasonably have been expected to possess in such matters it wasn't easy for me to put my finger on what the principal difference in her "look" was. What I finally settled on by way of close observation was that she no longer on any occasion wore a hat. I had noticed her hatlessness almost the first moment she stepped off the train. There was something I didn't like about it from the outset. It made her seem quite undressed in a way that I could never like. I believe I noticed too from that first moment when she stepped off the train that there was something different about her very carriage. Rather, I should say, there was something so altered about how that young woman stepping off the train at the Union Station "carried" herself that at first I drew a perfect blank. She manifested such "manner," such "presence," such consciousness of her own consummate good grooming that I quite frankly could not identify her as any person whom I would have been likely to make friends with in the past. Even the bestowal of her ostensibly passionate kiss seemed somehow so studied a performance that I doubted anyone else—not even Aunt Gussie if she had been able to witness it—could have believed it one more whit than I had. And someone with Andrea Lomax's suspicious nature would inevitably have suspected that things were not quite what they seemed.

Perhaps the most astonishing thing of all was the wardrobe that even I wouldn't be long in discovering Lila had brought along for her Memphis sojourn. The two large pieces of luggage that I had seen thrust into the trunk of Andrea Lomax's car must have been jam-packed with countless frocks for Lila to deck herself out in. (And perhaps there were other frocks to be shipped separately.) Already on only the second night she had appeared in three different garments, and during the remaining ten days of the visit she was destined to appear in as many ensembles as there were days. Ill equipped as I may be to judge such matters, moreover, I could not but compare habiliments of this present wardrobe of Lila Montgomery's and those I recalled from former days. Gone were the frilled frocks and shirtwaists that once had seemed so becoming to the young girl from Tullahoma, Tennessee, or even to the office worker in wartime Washington, D.C. Now she was all bright silk prints with low necklines and rather heavily ornamented bracelets and necklaces. There was nothing, to be sure, suggesting extreme bad taste, but there was everything that such a one as I could recognize, without knowing quite how I recognized it, that was part and parcel of the post–Second World War world that Lila Montgomery and I and everybody like us had lived on into. That was what she was or what she seemed like to me.

AFTER DINNER we sat and talked for a while about Aunt Gussie. It seems her illness had come on quite suddenly. For a year or longer she had existed almost entirely on a diet of raw eggs, which had seemed adequate and even thoroughly satisfactory until six weeks or so ago. Then she had begun to weaken. Lila Montgomery was sent for by Nurse O'Neill. Lila had not seen the old lady for two or three weeks before that. But she had always kept in fairly regular touch with her, visiting her almost on a fortnightly basis. This, in fact, was what struck me as most surprising. In whatever few thoughts I had about the matter it had never seemed likely to me that their friendship had been a continuing or in any sense an intimate one. Above all, it had never crossed my mind that Lila and Aunt Gussie together would have read accounts of my own Normandy exploits in the newspaper or that I could have risen to the rank of hero in their minds. And regardless of that it would never have occurred to me that Aunt Gussie might have kept a firm grip on her relations with Lila. But apparently this was the case. It came out presently, though with Lila's making only passing reference to it, that once Lila Montgomery had accepted her first job through my aunt's auspices, she reported to her on the progress in her career with what I would consider an unnatural regularity. When Lila told me about this I immediately and to my own dismay somehow visualized her seated at the card table opposite my aunt there in Aunt Gussie's tiny Stoneleigh Court apartment. I saw her leaning over a deck of tarot cards laid out on the table there. More clearly even I saw her participating in some sort of séance under Aunt Gussie's direction, caught up in a trance, as it were, and revealing to the old lady every detail of her work where she was currently employed. . . . But this was only the stuff of my imagination, of course. I cannot be sure of what the scene was like. But I did learn how frequently Lila had made a habit of reporting to the old lady's apartment and sometimes, incidentally, reading to her from the daily newspaper. And I do know that when

Aunt Gussie was taken ill and she was sent for by the frightened nurse, Lila had just then taken a new job at some different senator's office. And I do know that on the following day Lila resigned from that new and rather important job she had taken and had at once begun making plans to bring Aunt Gussie down to Tennessee.

When the telephone message reached her Lila had been greatly alarmed simply by the fact of a professional nurse's having been called in. She hurried to the taxi and rushed over to the Stoneleigh Court. She found it reassuring when Nurse O'Neill revealed herself to be not only a Roman Catholic but even someone who took a considerable interest in Aunt Gussie's spiritualist concerns. Nurse O'Neill had acted as companion and nurse for another old Catholic lady during her final days, one who had resided in the apartment adjacent to Aunt Gussie's. Upon the death of that neighbor lady my aunt more or less inherited the services of this good Catholic nurse, who also brought along with her a devout Catholic doctor. Lila saw at once that Aunt Gussie was in good hands and according to her she might not have renewed her old interest in *me* except that from the outset Aunt Gussie had talked incessantly about me and the great fame I had acquired as a war hero.

All of this came through to me while Lila sat talking after dinner that first night. What did not come through to me so clearly was whether it had been more Aunt Gussie's or perhaps Lila's wish that the old lady be brought back to Tennessee. Lila at no time made this quite clear to me. I had either to try to imagine my aunt whispering to Lila from her sickbed that she wished to be removed to St. Joseph's Hospital, in Memphis, or imagine Lila urging such a removal when she and Aunt Gussie conferred during the wee hours of the night. In any case I got the distinct impression that during a number of sessions held between them just prior to this one the two women had been almost exclusively concerned with the news of my having been awarded the Medal of Honor for my great exploits on the beachhead at Normandy. And it was this subject that occupied the two of us during the last hour of our talk that night in the restaurant. We talked until most lights had been put out in the little restaurant and until in fact we were told by the proprietor, in the politest Memphis way, that it was his closing time.

Lila really began this last part of our talk by inquiring of me if it were actually true that I had begun my army career as a conscientious objector. At first I thought she was going to take me to task for never having told her about that. To my surprise, she expressed her great delight and approval when I confessed to her, which struck me as quite ironic in view of the pains I had once taken to conceal the very fact from her. In my mind I could not resist comparing Ruthie Ann's indifference to what my status had been upon first entering the army with Lila's curiosity and her belated delight in it. And without my making any reference to it Ruthie Ann had seemed to sense from the first afternoon we met at Alex Mercer's house that I could actually remember nothing about the much heralded events at Normandy. It was something that between the two of us we were destined never to mention. When the subject arose in the company of others, Ruthie Ann would quietly turn away and busy herself with other matters. Presently it became clear to me that Lila's delight and approval were predicated upon my having become a war hero. Twice before I finished I had to describe to her my alleged exploits in greatest detail—all of which I had learned by rote, of course—our landing at Normandy and my reputed capture of two dozen German soldiers. I have to say that at first my manufacture of this memory was a considerably easier fabrication than when I had once found the necessity to conceal from her my role as a conscientious objector. I had by this time read so many accounts of how I had held off a whole company of Nazis and made prisoners of the two dozen of them that I now had no difficulty in picturing the adventure in my mind—how I had been crawling in the slimy earth behind the dense hedges there and taken the men one by one as they came out from a low brick archway—an archway so low they had to stoop to pass under it and so were caught off guard by the steel ring of my carbine, which kept firing away just inches above their heads—how the stupid krauts kept coming, as though they themselves were being fired from some automatic weapon, kept coming through that low archway in a peasant's barn till some one of them could see they were being made the captives of some low-ranking Yank, at which point they all more or less stampeded backward into the maze of cow stalls in the already roofless dairy barn, how I held them together there till I got some kind of relief from my cronies and then must have fainted away and struck my head on one of the barnyard stones. . . . But even before I got to that last part Lila had leaned across the table, seized my face in her beautiful hands and planted a kiss on my lips, and insisted that I repeat the whole fabricated account once again. It was as though she were looking or listening for some flaw that would give the whole thing away. But I did not betray myself. By now I had repeated the story so often to my family and friends that the hardest part had come to be making myself remember *not* to believe in my own pretended memory. At first I had had to labor at remembering that I actually remembered nothing. This was necessary to get myself released from the hospital and from the doctors that surrounded me—overseas at first and later back in this country. Pretending that the memory had come back to me was the way I could regain my freedom! And once I had returned to my family, the myth of my heroism became an even more profound necessity. Most wonderful of all, my unremembered heroism freed me from the old shame of having been a conscientious objector. I spent so many hours thinking about my old secret and my new secret that at last I could not fail to speculate about what secrets other people kept. Perhaps it was only a way I had of consoling myself. What secrets did my mother and father share? And what secrets did they keep for a lifetime from each other? What awful secrets had they kept about Aunt Gussie and about their own parents and about my own brother and sister and my spinster cousin Andrea Lomax? I realized perfectly how childish all this seemed, how like delayed doubts of childhood and puberty it was. Yet from the day I returned home from the war, nursing my secret—my "blankness," as I came to call my state of

mind—it was always with me. And it seemed the worse somehow because it was a secret nobody else could possibly know—
not for certain, they couldn't.

It was past midnight when Lila and I left the restaurant on
Front Street. We walked down the cobblestone embankment
and up Riverside Drive toward Mud Island and the New
Bridge. Lila had begun to talk about the time we spent together
at Camp Forrest and after that about those weeks in Washington. As we walked she hung on to my arm and pressed herself
very close against me. And she talked about those earlier days
in most romantic and sentimental terms. She had a very clear
head and remembered everything we had ever said to each
other. But somehow it always came out different from the way
I had remembered it. She spoke as if we had been *real* lovers
from the beginning and had parted only after a little spat and
a lovers' quarrel. She even spoke of that last long walk we took
through Georgetown as though it represented a lovers' parting. At last she looked up at me and said, "Let's go back to
Andrea's! She'll be wondering if we're going to be staying out
all night." And so we got in the car and headed back to Andrea's apartment at Crosstown. When I had parked at the curb
in front of Andrea's complex and after Lila already had her
right hand on the door handle beside her she leaned way across
the seat to kiss me on the cheek. It crossed my mind that that
meant "good night" and that she did not even want me to see
her to the apartment door. It struck me for a moment that she
was, after all, the same old Lila Montgomery I had known at
Tullahoma and in Washington. Then as if she had changed her
mind—had had it changed for her by some power outside
herself—she relaxed her grasp on the door handle and asked,
"Won't you come in for a while?" I was out of the car almost
at once and stood on the other side holding her door open for
her. Her change of heart—or mind—seemed irresistible to me.
She seemed so like the old Lila on the dance floor at Camp
Forrest. And we approached the front entrance on tiptoe, pretending we were afraid of being overheard and giggling at
ourselves like two schoolchildren.

There was only one table lamp left burning in Andrea's living room, as an indication no doubt that she had retired. We lingered in that room for a very few minutes—not speaking, while sitting very close beside each other. Then it was as though she had another sudden change of intention. Taking me by the hand, she led me back to the bedroom she was occupying at the end of a narrow corridor. She closed the door behind us, and now of course it became evident what her intention was. It became clear, moreover, that she was making no effort to conceal what we were about from my cousin Andrea Lomax in the adjacent room. There was no softness about the way Lila closed the bedroom door, and to speak plainly there was no effort to stifle the sounds of brutish love-making to which we would presently yield ourselves. What would afterward strike me as most extraordinary about this scene of fornication was not the evidence of my own gross wartime experience in the realm of casual sex (shocking as the present instance of it might be to me) and not even the convincing, the indubitable evidence as there clearly was of the similar experience by Lila Montgomery during the three or so brief years she spent working in the bureaus of wartime Washington, D.C., but rather other matters that pressed themselves more deeply on my consciousness when the episode had passed. When finally she had left the bed and had gone in unabashed nakedness to contemplate the streetlight just below and outside the window, I felt myself compelled to think of how driven she, throughout our lovemaking, had seemed by some other desire or some other power than her own.

For both of us it had seemed a mechanical and most unnatural performance. It had nothing to do with the two people who had once been intimately or affectionately acquainted. It seemed to me that we were now much more by way of being strangers to each other than we had been an hour before. More than anything else I felt the great intervention of some other power. Stupid as the idea struck me, it seemed momentarily that the war itself had intervened. And I was further distracted by another thought or impression. Could it be that Lila had consciously or even subconsciously wished to have Andrea Lomax overhear the noises we made tonight and identify the sounds? Was Andrea the other power or presence that I felt? While whispering good-night to Lila at her bedroom door and simultaneously thinking perhaps I had detected a light under Andrea's own door I even found myself wondering if there could have been some collusion between the two. But at once I thought better of this. And in the days that followed I came to think it almost a certainty that Lila had wished above all—or someone else had wished it—to place herself in the domicile of one of my relatives. It would have been a matter of strategy with her. Or had it perhaps been a strategy worked out between herself and Nurse O'Neill? It had even occurred to me that Nurse O'Neill had been the other power I had to deal with.

IN THE UPSTAIRS hall of my mother's house there was a curio case displaying all the various medals that had come my way in the war—down to the good-marksmanship and even the good-conduct medals. Mother was fond of saying of course that she valued the good-conduct above all others, adding piously that without that it was likely none of the others would have followed. She was speaking half in jest when she made this remark, as she was about half the remarks she ever made. When she made an opportunity to take Lila upstairs to see the curio case with my medals, Lila's wry comment had been that *she* herself valued the good-marksmanship medal above all others and it was likely that without *that* medal none of the others would have followed. This was a comment that Mother was not afterward able to forgive Lila, maintaining that it was too much like something our Aunt Gussie might have said. Perhaps Mother's half-pious, half-ironic note seemed to her within the bounds of old-fashioned convention and good taste, whereas with Aunt Gussie the measure of what was beyond those bounds was ever in doubt. Perhaps it was a fine line which my own masculine sensibilities could not grasp.

On the day after Lila and I had gone to Andrea's place, Lila arrived in the morning, self-invited, for breakfast at our house. And she would do so in fact every morning during the rest of her visit. She would arrive each day wearing a different dress, as I have already indicated. My mother and my younger sister, Agnes, were genuinely admiring of the rather brilliant ensembles she appeared in, and I am afraid they never failed to comment on this. I do not think that either of them meant to imply that Lila was dressing so for my benefit, or at least that either of them would for a moment have acknowledged as much to herself, nor do I think they were being critical of such bright, dressy colors being selected for a trip such as this one to Memphis. I think it was more likely an acknowledgment that these hues represented a particular kind of bright print now available and fashionable in Washington which, alas, was not available and fashionable down here in Memphis. Be that as it may, Mother on one particular occasion spoke to Agnes of how much these prints were like those once long ago affected by Aunt Gussie Jones. She said this in Lila Montgomery's presence, and I immediately saw Lila's face become diffused with blushes! It was as if for Lila there had been one too many references and comparisons made to Aunt Gussie. Though nothing was said about it by any person present, and though the blushes vanished almost immediately, I believe notice was taken by everyone—even by my father, who was also present though not previously taking a part in the conversation. Anyhow, it then struck me for the first time that in the eyes of all my family Lila was a veritable reincarnation of Aunt Augusta St. John-Jones and that Lila herself was somehow aware of this. I don't know at what moment or moments members of my family first received such an impression. Perhaps it was just after Lila stepped off the train from Washington. There was no physical resemblance between the two, of course, but there was, as my mother might have said, some sine qua non about her that bespoke Aunt Gussie herself. (My mother's speech, like that of other genteel ladies of her generation, was full of such Latin phrases and expressions, which she still retained from boarding school days.) It occurred to me at this moment that the great change I thought I had noted in Lila constituted nothing more or less than this influence on her of my aunt's personality. In any case, I had confessed to myself that my relatives observed this and articulated it among themselves well before I did.

One of my first observations about my parents after my return from overseas was that they showed far less interest in relatives, whether near or distant, than they had done before the war. Until news came of Aunt Gussie's illness her very name had scarcely been mentioned since I reappeared in Memphis. The old days that my parents had talked so much about in my boyhood were not often mentioned. Even old-maid cousins like Andrea Lomax were not often seen in our house, and the young men cousins who turned up at the train station—those two who looked so like me that Lila could not be sure which of us three might be the real me—even they had to be "contacted" by my father and forced to make an appearance at the station.

And in retrospect one felt that my father and mother and my sister had wanted the cousins present so that they themselves would not feel solely responsible for Aunt Gussie's care and well-being once she reached Memphis. And after the first day or so I was the one member of the family who turned up regularly at St. Joseph's Hospital. It might also be remarked that from this time none of my old boyhood friends was very much in evidence—none of those who as boys had hung about our house so regularly as to be considered almost members of the family; instead, only old would-be fellow conscientious objector friends Alex Mercer and Phillip Carver, and intentionally or not, my two parents always had difficulty in distinguishing who of these was who. Very soon Phillip left Memphis (without telling his family he was going) and went to live out the rest of his life in New York City. But even then Father was ever apt to address Alex as "Alex-or-Phil, whichever you are." It was as if ever after he and Mother lived in a kind of limbo and declined to try to connect either past or present with each other. Somehow I could not tell whether they were still more in a state of shock from my having signed up as a C.O. or from my having returned as a war hero. Perhaps it was neither. Perhaps they were simply two people who had reached a time in life when the past and the future seem equally unreal and undistinguishable from each other. Such a time comes eventually for every man and woman. But in this case it may have been only the war because for some sweet-natured people the mere existence of the war itself was sufficient to disorient them forever.

The fact was, my parents' life together seemed to me every day that passed more and more a secretive affair—altogether unfathomable to me. It seemed the two of them agreed on nothing under the sun, and yet I cannot recall their ever having spoken a disagreeable word to each other. Their peaceful coexistence was one of the great mysteries of life for me. But I have to insist that it was but *one* of the great mysteries. I seemed ever less able to comprehend the lives lived by those around me. I found myself constantly trying to remind myself why my two good friends, Alex and Phillip, had taken on the rôle of conscientious objectors. I always remembered why *I* had done so. It had simply seemed absurd to align oneself with men bent on killing other men who similarly had no reason for killing me. But I actually saw no reason why my two good friends—or anyone else—should necessarily feel the same as *I* did. But feeling as I did about this, it did not seem strange to me that I should let myself forever forget the men I had killed or captured at Normandy. And it was no easier for me to explain the one than the other. Yet there was one matter that disturbed my peace of mind as nothing else had ever done. I was not so much disturbed by my having thus casually taken Lila to bed— or permitted myself to be taken to bed—as by our having revealed to each other how accustomed our wartime lives had made us to such affairs. And I was considerably more disturbed by the great desire I felt, despite the awful mechanical quality of it, to repeat the performance we had allowed ourselves there in Andrea's spare bedroom. It was the continuing desire that made it torture for me for several days afterward and that made me wonder again and again about the callous feeling that now possessed me.

On the day after the evening I spent with Lila I went, before doing anything else, to see Ruthie Ann Sedwick. It was not in order to tell her what had happened the night before that I went to her. I wanted simply to stand in her presence and try to discern what my own feelings would be when she and I stood face to face. I found her in the basement of her mother's house, where she was experimenting with some tomato plants that she had pulled out of the ground by their roots the night before, this being in the fall of the year and at the time of the first frost. Ruthie Ann was a serious amateur horticulturist—not a mere genteel lady gardener—and she had read somewhere recently that if she hung her tomato plants upside down from her basement ceiling the fruit would continue to ripen without rotting. She had told me about this a few days before, and so when her mother had directed me to the basement this morning I was not surprised to find her so employed. She began at once to expound theories on why her plants were not doing so well as she had expected. I didn't listen of course. I could attend only to what my own feelings were upon seeing her this morning. My feelings about Lila did not seem to exist. That is, what had occurred to me the night before seemed to have no bearing on the present moment or on the undeniable love I had come to feel for this girl I had met by chance.

I had been seeing Ruthie Ann so regularly these past weeks that my dropping by like this was hardly anything out of the ordinary. I had even worked with her some in the big vegetable and flower garden, which was in a fenced-in vacant lot adjoining her mother's bungalow-style house there in Crosstown Memphis. Admittedly, what had appealed to me about her was her motherly posture and her beautiful patience with Alex Mercer's young children. There was an almost perpetual smile on her generous mouth, as though she were mildly amused not only by the Mercer children but by almost everything else that came her way. She had an adequate sense of her own dignity, yet when I had brought forth from my father's garage the motorcycle I had had since early boyhood she had not scrupled for one second about hopping on behind me or being seen riding all about that genteel old neighborhood, which was still there in Crosstown in those days. I believe she was always without personal ambition or vanity—more than anyone else I have ever known. Her father had died when she was still a small child, and Ruthie Ann seemed content enough to continue always living there alone with her mother, running errands for the old lady as though she herself were happy to be perpetually occupied by that and by reading aloud to her mother, who rather surprisingly had a decidedly highbrow taste in modern fiction. Neither she nor her mother ever expressed an interest in my having once registered as a conscientious objector or having afterward been hailed as a war hero. The only emotion Ruthie Ann would ever show in the latter was a kind of mild amusement. And even from our first meeting I felt that she suspected that I could not remember anything about my exploits at the Normandy beachhead. Best of all, perhaps, I sensed from the beginning that Ruthie Ann had not the normal quantity of secrets in her own life. As well as not caring to ferret out whatever secrets I might have.

When we were talking a while that day among the upside-down tomato plants, suddenly I found myself stepping forward and then leaning among those upside-down plants to embrace for the first time this girl I knew I had fallen in love with. Just as I was kissing the smiling mouth she turned up to me I heard the footsteps of her mother on the basement stair just behind me. She approached not seeming to take notice of how we were occupied and assuming certainly that it was not the first time we had so occupied ourselves. She fairly stumbled upon us as she made her way over the heap of tomatoes lying on the cement floor and commented ever so casually that we certainly had picked an awkward place to so engage ourselves. I was so amused and charmed by this that I could barely resist turning and embracing Ruthie Ann's mother herself. But, having received a telephone call from Lila just before setting out on my motorcycle, I had now to return to my house and exchange that vehicle for my mother's more suitable sedan in order to fetch Lila Montgomery from Andrea's place to take her to the hospital. As I hurried out of the basement I had heard the two of them, mother and daughter, laughing together at what they must have supposed to be my sudden embarrassment. As I rode my motorcycle home I could only think with pleasure of how wisely these wonderful women had waited the war out, making their garden, reading their "highbrow fiction," closing their ears to the noise of the war, insisting in their ways, as only women could really do, on a conscientious objection to the war.

LILA WAS WAITING on the front stoop of the apartment house when I pulled up at the curb. She was got up in yet another bright print dress—worn underneath a short navy jacket, it being a morning in late autumn. She wore no hat and had on a pair of shiny navy blue gloves that matched her low-heeled shoes as well as a flat purse under her arm. I believe I had noted every article of clothing before I had pulled up to the curb, even the smooth perfection of her silk stockings over her knees and her slender crossed ankles. I said to myself frankly that she would appeal to any man who ever lived and I was lucky she had not been snatched away before I got there. She remained seated on the stoop until I stopped the car, and then pushing back the fold of her glove she flirtatiously cast her eyes down at the tiny watch on her wrist. I was thirty minutes late! But in the blink of an eye she had sprung up from the stoop and rushed forward to the car, and sticking her head through the driver's window she gave me one of those impassioned kisses that she seemed to have discovered since the days that I first knew her. Still standing with her head pushed inside the window she said, "You know, don't you, that I've really come out here to Memphis to fetch you back to Washington with me!"

And I thought, "My God, I believe she really has!"

I drove us on to the hospital, again thinking mostly of what a power she was and wondering how conceivably I could ever do other than what she would tell me to do. And simultaneously I had begun wondering once more what was the source of the power she possessed or which seemed to possess her these days.

AND THAT'S HOW mostly it was for me during the two weeks that lay ahead. Though Lila had leased a car for her own use in Memphis, she called our house each morning, requesting that whoever answered the phone give me the message that she was ready to go to the hospital. It seemed little enough that someone from our household should escort her to and from St. Joseph's since Andrea was putting her up at her apartment and since after the first few days no one from our family was taking the trouble to visit Aunt Gussie at the hospital. Sometimes I would go with Lila to the door of the old lady's room. But usually I would only peek through the open door and maybe whisper good morning to Nurse O'Neill. Several times I crooked my finger and beckoned the good nurse to come to the door and give me a report on the patient. Once I asked her where she herself was staying. She laughed her familiar staccato laugh and said, "Oh, the nuns are taking good care of me"—said it in a way that somehow made me doubt that was really the case. If I asked how her patient was doing she would always frown and say, "She can't last long." Aunt Gussie had never slept well the night before and that was why she was always sleeping soundly when I stopped by in the morning. "She never wants to see anybody except her niece there." (That's how she always referred to Lila.) She always seemed to want to put me off. "And all she asks of the young lady is what kind of 'time' she's making with you." Then of course Nurse O'Neill gave her staccato laugh, and I took this as my signal to leave. Before I went up to the room, though, I would already have asked Lila about my aunt's condition. She would only shake her head and quickly change the subject. We would be sitting together in the cafeteria before we went up to her room, with me smoking a cigarette and with her sometimes holding my hand between the two of hers and smiling at me fondly. It was so often that way. I never slept with her again, though. I was spared that. But I fetched her from the hospital every afternoon, and I had always to take her somewhere for a spot of supper. I asked her out of the clear one day how long she thought she would stay in Memphis. She answered casually enough but with some certainty, "Oh, I'll be here till she's gone." She was always cheerful when I picked her up at the hospital entrance and always leaned across the seat to give me a kiss but it got so we didn't try to talk much. If she pressed me to do so, I would tell her one more time what it was like in Normandy. But we never talked at all about her life in Washington. She seemed to remember nothing about it.

I never had a clue about what might be going on in Lila's mind or about how to account for her persistence until one day when I ran into Nurse O'Neill in the hospital corridor. And I cannot be sure that it was by chance we had that meeting. The first thing I knew was that she and I had literally bumped into each other and had turned in the corridor. Instead of laughing in her usual way the woman wore a deadly serious expression on her face, and she stood there as if intentionally meaning to block my further progress along the passage. I smiled at first and then I frowned, trying to read the significance of her standing there so. At last she said, "I don't know how long she's going to last." Of course I took her to mean how long Aunt Gussie was going to last. "She's having a hard time of it," she went on, "and I don't think you quite understand." It began to dawn on me that it might not be Aunt Gussie Nurse O'Neill had in mind. But I didn't want to give my idle thoughts away.

"You think my aunt might be very near the end, then?" I asked obliquely.

"I don't know about your aunt." It was as if she had decided to bolt and have done with it. "It's Miss Lila Montgomery, I mean. I don't know how long she's going to last." She stood silent for a moment. It was almost as though she had changed her mind about bolting.

"You mean Lila's been under such a strain," I said, myself clearly implying more than I said. If she were going to bolt then I wanted her to go ahead with it.

"The old lady's got her under some kind of spell." She came very close to me and actually spoke in a whisper. "I think she's going to crack under it if you don't help her. Anyway, I can't help her. She's gone too far."

And before I could speak again she had swept off down the hall and through what I took to be the lab door. Only after she was out of sight did I realize she had been carrying some kind of plastic bottle or bedpan. And it occurred to me that that had only been her feeble excuse for hurrying along the corridor. And after she had passed through the swinging lab door she was immediately followed by two forbidding old nuns whose pace and deliberate hesitation so intimidated me that I did not follow her. Moreover, I stood there a moment in dazed reflection. I could not decide whether or not there might be collusion between Lila Montgomery and Nurse O'Neill. At last I decided I could not take the chance of being the dupe of such plotting. It was midmorning now, and I was due to pick up Ruthie Ann for lunch.

By the end of that week I was accustomed to having lunch every day with Ruthie Ann Sedwick and my two other meals—along with a couple of teatimes—with Lila Montgomery. As a matter of fact it was pretty nearly established that Ruthie Ann and I would regularly lunch together at home with her mother. Our lunch was not systematically nor on any principle planned as a vegetarian meal, but that's what it amounted to. It somehow was what their whole life was like. Nothing was generally based on any system of principle. Their bungalow was just a house they happened to be living in at the time of Mr. Sedwick's death. There just happened to be a vacant lot next door wherein they could plant a garden during the war years. When they could no longer afford to operate an automobile, they simply happened to be situated conveniently on a streetcar line and later a bus line. They merely happened to have inherited a cache of good clothing from a well-to-do late aunt. They planned nothing. They expected nothing. Everything simply came their way. "It's because we are so good," Mrs. Sedwick jested. "It's because we want so little," Ruthie Ann added a little more seriously. It was why they had been able to remain at peace with the world when everyone else had been going along with the babble—even taking advantage of it. And I had come upon them only just before it would have been too late, only just before the worldly Lila would have swept me up into her arms and made a national celebrity of me, the unknown war hero, made a national advantage of my nonheroic deeds in the great world of D.C., where it might matter most. What I recognized was that there just might be time for me to save myself.

But I had just enough feeling about Lila and the consolation she had once seemed to offer me that I knew I could not utterly reject the use she wanted to make of me now. The only defense I can make of my behavior after this point is that I did not speak of Lila and Ruthie Ann to each other—did not tell the one about the other. Every day there was the same leisurely lunch in the Sedwicks' bungalow, and each morning and night Lila and I ate together at a different little restaurant or joint. If Lila and I talked at all she wanted it to be almost exclusively about the "happy" times we had had in Washington or the "happy" times we would yet have there when "all this" was over. She refused to reveal whether or not Aunt Gussie was now in a coma. Lila's talk became ever more frenetic, ever persistent on the subject of our "happy" past times and future times together, interrupted by occasional references to my exploits in Normandy at the beachhead. On the two or three occasions when my parents dutifully dropped by the hospital, Lila received them in the waiting room and assured them that it would bring "no satisfaction" for them to see her now. From her conversation with me there was no positive indication of my aunt having her under "some kind of spell." And yet once it had been suggested by Nurse O'Neill I could not altogether put the idea out of my head.

A COMBINATION of events at this time suggested to me that nothing in the world could seem better to me than to get married to Ruthie Ann Sedwick—and to do so at once. She agreed to go across the river with me to Arkansas, on Saturday morning, and we were married by a justice of the peace over there. We both had grown up in Memphis, and since our early teens we had known a number of people who had made that decision and, in varying degrees, had been very happy about it afterward. It seemed the most natural thing in the world to do, and I suppose that was why we felt so good about it. We told neither her mother nor my parents but enlisted a young couple who "happened" to live next door to the Sedwicks—and who "happened" to need to go over to Arkansas to buy some whiskey—to accompany us as witnesses. Ruthie Ann's mother seemed awfully glad about it and at once began removing certain superfluous items from the guest room, which it was agreed we, the bride and groom, should occupy. At my parents' house, to which we took the news, the announcement was received without the raising of an eyebrow, and the same thing was true there of my younger brother and sister, who presently, barely stifling yawns, took themselves upstairs— presumably for afternoon naps. I think my father would not even have put down his afternoon paper if Mother had not specifically told him to. Mother herself smiled rather blandly and tried to say with some warmth that they had only just been waiting for us to "name the day." They made no reference to my having breakfasted and dined out with Lila Montgomery every day during the past two weeks. And it seemed to me in retrospect that when I had appeared at breakfast that morning and mentioned to them that I might have Ruthie Ann with me for dinner tonight they had scarcely acknowledged the infor- mation. It struck me now that likely they had not taken notice of my absence during the past three weeks or so.

It was while Ruthie Ann and I stood there burdening my parents with our non-news that I heard the slamming of metal against metal and heard the breaking of glass on the pavement of our driveway outside—the merest tinkling sound it must have been—seeming momentarily to reverberate throughout my brain and throughout the whole of the big house—upstairs and downstairs—in the most uncanny way. Simultaneously from the placid throats of my two parents came expressions of such shock and in such volume as could not ordinarily have seemed justified by the slight clatter we had heard from outside. And then also simultaneously and quite beyond any natural explanation I could think of there came from above stairs the resounding footsteps of my somewhat younger brother and sister as they leapt from their beds in the rooms where they had been napping and presently came bounding down the staircase and subsequently on through the open doorway to the front living room. By the time my two parents and those siblings of mine together reached the front windows of the house, the recent and upsetting noises in the driveway had become self-explanatory.

Without so much as a glance out any window I somehow—and without any natural explanation of the phenomenon—seemed to know precisely the source of the noise. I could not then and cannot now tell you how I had identified it, but I knew that it was the sound of the front bumper of Lila's little-used rental car colliding with the rear bumper and the left rear light signal of Mother's own sedan—the one which I had just used to transport Ruthie Ann and me to Arkansas and back. It will be said that I could not possibly have made such an identification without knowing more of events which had transpired earlier that afternoon, but I contend that there are events so inevitable in their sequence that persons in a certain state of mind cannot disengage either the sequence of cause and effect or any concatenation of the events. And from this point forward in this narrative I will not be held responsible for explanation or interpretation of events that follow with seeming mystery one upon the other.

But this I know for a fair certainty. Lila had left her vigil at my aunt's bedside earlier than was usual for her on this Saturday afternoon. Whatever had been her plans for the rest of the day, when she reached Andrea Lomax's apartment house on Cleveland Street she found her two pieces of matched luggage placed side by side on the front stoop with a note tucked under one of the leather straps. No doubt she had perceived this note there under the strap before she even got out of the car and no doubt the unattended luggage on the front stoop must have struck her as an ominous omen. Without any formal address or preface the scribbled note had read simply: "Away from town for ten days. Trust you can find quarters elsewhere. A.L."

Whatever frame of mind Lila had been in before that, she could not have been in the most placid spirit when, with no other place to go, she lugged her baggage into the rented car and headed for my parents' house. In view of the little use she had previously made of this car, having been transported mainly in my mother's sedan, she couldn't have been altogether familiar with the mechanical operation of the vehicle she was driving—could not have been aware of how soon or how powerfully to apply pressure on the foot brake. One could imagine, moreover, that the sight of the car parked in the driveway, in which she may well have supposed I had been chauffeuring Ruthie Ann about all this day, may have caused her temporarily to lose absolute control of the car she sat behind the wheel of. It will doubtless be noted that I have carefully refrained from making any suggestion that Lila Montgomery purposefully rammed the one car into the other. But at my first sight of Lila she was already, without stopping to assist in the damage that might have occurred to the car, striding across the paved driveway and up the steps to the wide, tiled front porch of the house. It was my luckless younger brother who stepped forward and opened the plate-glass front door. And as he did so he could not resist exclaiming in a joyful voice that reached Lila at the top of the front steps: "Brother and Ruthie Ann have got themselves married!"

Lila in utter astonishment halted outside the open front door. It was as if she waited there for him to speak again, and to make certain she was right about what she thought she had heard. And presently my brother did repeat precisely what he had said before. And now Lila without looking at my brother, without looking to the left or right at anyone, proceeded through the open doorway and back to that point where my mother and father stood side by side in the center of the hall. Looking directly at Mother, she asked, "Is there a room some-where that I could perhaps lie down in?" She hesitated that way in the middle of the question, as if she had at first not known what she was going to ask. Then as if trying to explain what would ordinarily have seemed obvious to everyone else present in the hall at that moment, she added, "I seem to be experiencing some kind of shock—some kind of electrical shock almost."

I had the ugly impulse suddenly to burst into laughter. That is, it seemed obvious that this was just what a person would feel after the series of upsetting things Lila had just been through. Then Lila said, "I think probably I'm going to faint. I don't know quite where I am. Oh, where am I? Where exactly are we?" And now with my arm about Ruthie Ann I felt a mixed compulsion again to laugh out loud and to go and try to say something consoling to the poor woman. But I said nothing and did nothing. And now Mother and Father together were leading Lila toward the broad, carpeted staircase that ascended the back wall of the hall. And Mother was speaking to Lila with a comforting warmth in her voice that I had not heard in years but that she had once used with all of us as little children. Before they reached the foot of the stairs, however, Lila had fainted away altogether, and with the help of my brother, Father had carried her to the first-floor bedroom that my parents used as their own.

When she fainted I looked immediately at my wristwatch. I think I did so because of the premonition I had. What had come to my mind of course was Nurse O'Neill's enigmatic reference to the "spell" Lila had been under. At the time this seemed too stupid to be mentioned to anyone. It still seemed so to me afterward. No matter if it later evolved, as it would indeed so do, that Aunt Gussie had died at the very instant of Lila's seizure, there were too many other immediate causes for Lila's hysteria and fit of fainting for this one to be singled out, or so it seemed to my mind. And so it would seem to Ruthie Ann when I pointed out the coincidence to her. It was not the sort of thing that Ruthie Ann and her mother were willing to discuss as a possibility. And yet when the call came from Nurse O'Neill an hour later, the time given for death coincided precisely with the other event. And when next day I insisted upon checking with the good nurse on the exact time of death she seized my arm, as we bent over the chart, and whispered fiercely, "Why do you ask? Why do you ask *that?* I have told you, haven't I, that Lila's name was on her lips as she drew her last breath?" But I made no answer to this. By now I was in complete agreement with Ruthie Ann and her mother. I did not want to be guilty of encouraging the superstition of this poor Irish woman, isolated as she was from all her own kind.

Events of the remainder of that evening are almost too painful to relate and yet in retrospect they may not seem at all eventful. Upon being given the news of Aunt Gussie's death, Lila showed no emotion whatsoever. Presently she said very firmly and quietly—almost under her breath, "If there's a train going back to Washington tonight, I mean to be aboard it."

There was such a train. And Lila with her luggage was put aboard it. It fell to my younger brother's lot to see her to the train. He drove her to the Union Station in her own rented car since her luggage was already loaded therein and since the rear light signal on Mother's sedan had been crushed—with its fragments of glass still lying on the pavement. Nobody made any mention of the broken glass during the rest of that evening and even when, after a while, Father and Mother went off out of decency to the hospital, they went in Father's coupe. I recall that Father had to hurry back into the house before setting off, to ask me for certain about which street the hospital was on—whether it was on Poplar or Jackson. They had been to St.

Joseph's so seldom as that! And I recall that it was my younger brother's lot next day to return Lila's rented car to the rental place. And it was his lot also to see after having the rear light signal on Mother's sedan repaired. It was too bad to leave it all for him to do, but I was a married man now, and, even so, since my injuries in the war I had been spared all such errands. I think, moreover, that my brother minded that sort of thing so much less than I did. I think he minded much more the note from Lila he had to bring home to me that night. Just before she got aboard the train, she rummaged in her purse for pencil and paper. On one side of the scrap handed me was the message left behind for her by Andrea Lomax. On the other side Lila had written simply the four words "I am so ashamed."

Just before Lila was preparing to leave the house, my mother, always with her sense of propriety, walked up to her and said, "Don't you want to stay long enough to attend Aunt Gussie's funeral service?"

Lila spoke her reply through her teeth: "That would be Nurse O'Neill's department. She's a Roman Catholic, and she will already have arranged about all that." Those were her last words. And she left the house as she had entered it, without looking to her left or her right—without making her goodbyes to anyone. It was hard to remember her as the same effusive young woman who had stepped off the train two weeks ago. At that moment it would have been easier for me to remember the independent and ambitious young girl who had walked out of my life three years ago—before she attached her fortunes to my aunt Mrs. Augusta St. John-Jones.

And just as Lila predicted, the good nurse had assuredly arranged the funeral service to be said two days later at the Catholic chapel across from St. Joseph's. My parents and the various other relatives, including Andrea Lomax and myself, put in a clumsy back-pew appearance at the mass, but we were not given much of a welcome by the young priest in charge. And we were none of us given the chance to say goodbye to Nurse O'Neill, who we had been told would go hurrying off to catch the late afternoon train to Washington. It had all been arranged, however, that my two parents would follow the hearse next morning up to the country town of Thornton. Aunt Gussie was to be buried there at the same town cemetery where she had once so long ago beguiled herself playing hide-and-seek with the suitors of her young ladyhood. My parents, in fact, lingered up there for a number of days, enjoying reunion with a number of old friends, some of whom they had not seen in many years.

Ruthie Ann and I took the opportunity to get ourselves settled in her mother's house in Crosstown. We three have lived there very happily together during all the years since, enjoying the uneventful seclusion we are all equally fond of, gardening, reading our favorite fiction, taking turns with the shopping. Even our old friend Alex Mercer has ceased to pay intrusive calls upon us. We have achieved such peace that thoughts about whatever may have become of Phillip Carver, that other friend who wanted to enlist as a conscientious objector—even such wandering thoughts as that never disturb us here.

Demons

HOW ARE THEY to be explained, the voices one heard as a child? I was seven. My father had left me waiting in the car for more than an hour while he walked over a tract of densely wooded bottom land he owned. I was not alone in the car. My older brother was there with me, but he soon fell asleep. I wasn't frightened; I was merely hot and bored. Since my brother had fallen asleep with his head against my shoulder, I dared not move a muscle. As a kind of consolation, I suppose, my father had left his pocket watch with me. It was a big gold watch, as thick as a biscuit, and it had once belonged to my grandfather. On the gold lid that snapped over the face were engraved the letters "L.P.," which were my own initials as well as my grandfather's and father's. On the face of the watch the hours were marked in black Roman numerals that I could not yet read with any certainty. I sat watching the second hand go round. The minutes passed very slowly. I heard the dry sounds of the insects in the tall grass nearby and listened to the thirsty cries of the birds flying over the low-lying woods toward the bayou. When at last my father returned, I told him about a voice that had spoken to me during his absence. At first, the voice had repeated my name very softly several times—"Louis Price . . . Louis Price . . . Louis Price." Then, later, in an even softer tone, it had said to me, "You are not Louis Price. You are the Lost Dauphin." My father laughed merrily when I told him all this, and afterward it became a family joke. One of my uncles said I was already manifesting a strong family trait—delusions of grandeur. The only thing about the incident that irritated my father was that I should maintain I did not know who the Lost Dauphin was, and had never heard of him before. But I maintain to this day that I did not and had not.

Now and then I find myself in conversation with someone who insists he never heard voices as a child—voices he could not explain. But I believe him no more than I believed the man I knew in the army who said he did not dream at night and was not able to imagine what a dream was like. Obviously, that man in the army was lying, and only for the sake of making himself interesting. But that's not the psychology of those who say they never heard voices when they were children. You will notice one thing about such people: it is not only the voices they don't remember, they remember almost nothing about their childhood. Whatever they do remember will be related, more often than not, to some experience connected with growing up, with putting childhood behind them, with mere recognition of the adult point of view. My brother, for instance, takes no stock nowadays in my talk about voices. He says I never heard anything he didn't hear, by which he means to say I heard nothing. But, mark you, though my brother is two years older than I, he has only the vaguest recollection of anything about that day our father took us with him to the low ground near the Forked Deer River, whereas I can recall almost every detail of the expedition—the deep-rutted red clay road we traveled from town, the elderberry bushes that scratched the sides of the car, a dead sycamore tree that stood alone on a little knoll ten yards from where we were left waiting, the sounds of the insects, the cries of the birds. But, on the other hand, why my brother and I happened to be taken along that day I have no idea. And when and why my father had acquired that tract of land and when and how he disposed of it are matters I know nothing about. These are questions that my brother might be able to answer.

When I was even younger—I will not say how much younger, for fear of not being believed—a voice once interrupted my play to speak prophetic words to me. On our front lawn, there in the little town in West Tennessee where I spent the first eight years of my life, were two giant chestnut trees. Since this was in the days before the blight, they were real chestnuts, not horse chestnuts. In September, the burs fell from the branches and covered the ground underneath. I learned early in life to open the burs with a minimum of finger pricking. And I devoured the meat of the nuts with such relish that the sound of my "mm-mmm"s sometimes reached my mother's ears through the open window of her sitting room. She used to declare that the first time she heard me out there she mistook the noises I made for the humming of bees under the apricot trees that grew nearer the house.

I not only ate the chestnuts; I used to play for hours with the burs, stacking them into neat pyramids or fashioning mountainous landscapes like none I'd ever seen, like none that ever existed, except perhaps on some other planet. It was while I squatted there at my play one afternoon that I heard the slow *clop-clop* of a horse's hoofs on the macadam street that went past our house. I may have experienced some premonition of who the rider would be before I looked around; I cannot be sure about that. I am sure only that before I looked I heard a voice that seemed to come right out of the tree trunk saying, "Ruin. Ruin." When I glanced over my shoulder, I saw that the horseman was our cousin Talbot Williamson. He was a big, barrel-chested man, and he sat very straight in the saddle. I got up off the ground and walked down to the iron fence that enclosed our place, and I stood there watching the erect figure on the horse until the horse and rider had passed all the way up the street and over the rise, beyond which, I knew, the town street turned into a country road. The sight of the straight figure sitting astride the horse stirred in me strange feelings of envy and admiration—and of dread. And when the figure had passed out of sight, the memory of it seemed no less mysterious to me than the voice I had heard coming out of the tree trunk.

Cousin Talbot Williamson was a man of about my father's age, and he lived five miles from town in an old clapboard house that my great-grandfather had built in the antebellum days. He farmed the old home place, and he and his wife lived out there without an automobile, without servants, even without electricity or plumbing in the house. All the relatives thought it their privilege or perhaps their duty to pay calls on Cousin Talbot and Cousin Carrie from time to time. A visit usually included a tour of the house lot, a look through the house, and then a half hour of talk about "old times." The women in the family disliked Cousin Talbot. They said he was a "vain egoist" and that he imagined himself a lady-killer. But they felt sorry for Cousin Carrie, who at thirty already seemed an old woman, and they thought her entitled to a little female company now and then.

I believe it was on a Thursday or a Friday afternoon that I watched Cousin Talbot ride past our house. At any rate, on the following Sunday my father decided it was time for us to pay a visit to the homeplace. I believe that there was nothing unusual about our visit that Sunday. Actually, it is the only such visit I can remember making, but in later years my mother assured me that we had spent many a Sunday afternoon out there. She said my father always imagined we were more welcome at Cousin Talbot's than we actually were. And I am absolutely certain that I had been there before, because in my memory of that day, nothing seems unfamiliar. After the preliminary walk about the place, the adults retired to the kitchen for their talk. My impression is that Cousin Talbot and Cousin Carrie occupied only two or three rooms toward the rear of the ground floor. The rest of the house was like a barn, and we children were turned loose to amuse ourselves wandering through the empty hallways and rooms.

We found little to interest us and we didn't have a very lively time. In what had been the front parlor, my two sisters, both older than I, discovered a ragged and faded old corset, and they quarreled over who had seen it first. But when the younger girl, who was my brother's twin, began to cry, my brother took her part, and the older girl had to give in. She had a moral victory, however, because as soon as she had relinquished the corset she pointed out that the stays had already been removed. There was nothing useful to be salvaged from it. Everywhere else, we found only stacks of old newspapers and empty cardboard boxes. In one of the upstairs rooms, Cousin Talbot kept rabbits, but since we had been warned not to go in there, we had only glimpses of the rabbits through the keyhole. None of us held back when Mother called from the foot of the staircase to say it was time to go home and fix Sunday night supper.

We must have left for home about four-thirty or five. Six hours later, the house my great-grandfather had built had burned to the ground. Talbot Williamson was not there when the fire broke out, and when the nearest neighbors arrived, Cousin Carrie was hysterical and could not make it clear whether or not she knew where her husband was. I suppose she might have been able to guess, but even afterward she never made it clear what or how much she knew. By the time Talbot arrived on the scene, his wife had been taken away by some of her own kinspeople. The two of them never saw each other again.

Those who were present at the fire reported that it was not long before midnight when Talbot Williamson came galloping up. His horse was in a terrible lather. Someone rushed up to assure him that his wife was safe, but the information seemed to make no impression on him. Without dismounting, he looked about him at the assemblage of neighbors and for several minutes gazed into the flames that were by then consuming the last of the oak timbers. Finally, he turned his horse away and rode off at a walk toward the watering trough and the barn. Everyone waited expectantly for him to reappear on foot. Instead, after ten minutes or so, he came galloping up from the barn on his horse, and, without looking to left or right and yet choosing a course between the onlooking neighbors and the fire, he galloped through the house lot, out the gateway in the picket fence, and down the lane to the main road. It was the last his neighbors would ever see of him; his relatives had already seen their last. Next morning, the body of his dead horse was found at the roadside ten miles away. Two days later, news came that a married woman in a neighboring town, whose name had long been connected with Talbot's, had vanished that same night.

I heard these details and others reported to my parents by eyewitnesses of the scene. I knew, without their saying, how erect he must have held himself as he rode back past the burning timbers of the house. And the image aroused in me the same feelings of envy, admiration, and dread that I had known standing by the iron fence a few days before.

PLEASE DO NOT attempt to find any consistency or try to uncover any *buried* significance in the kind of utterances I heard. Sometimes they were prophetic, at other times either genuinely profound or crudely sententious. Sometimes they were amusing, even joshing. They were exactly like the voices you remember hearing—unless, of course, you happen to be one of the number who have forgotten childhood and who think that a child is merely an immature man or woman. If that is the case, you will already have decided that I was an abnormal child and that I have never quite got over it. I can assure you that I have completely got over it—if abnormal I was. I move about the world like anyone else and enjoy a reasonable success in my chosen profession. And I abhor mystics. I shall not be making references to myself as an adult after this, but it may interest you to learn that I now have two adolescent children who already know next to nothing about what it was like to be a child. Further, like yourself, perhaps, I have been married not once but several times, and in each instance— But, no, I have said enough to convince you that my adult life has not been so very different from yours, or at any rate not so different from that of a certain number of your friends. No more about any of that.

Even when you are a child, it is difficult to get other children to admit to the voices they hear. And the mistake I made from a very early time was in speaking so frankly on the subject. I don't remember telling anyone specifically about the voice that came from the trunk of the chestnut tree. Possibly at that time my voices seemed such an ordinary part of my experience that I didn't always bother to mention them. But a few years later, I was forever making that mistake. I can still see the queer look—it was always the same—on the faces of children I made listen to me. It was not an expression of disbelief but one of disgust. They seemed to say, Don't you know, Louis Price, it is in bad taste to speak of such things? Still later, after I had given up hearing any voices but those of the people around me, I once saw precisely that same expression come over the face of an older boy to whom I confided that when I got out of school I wished to become either an actor or an artist. I knew before I said it that the boy had similar ambitions. But after that day he ignored my existence and never gave me a chance to speak to him again.

You can see that though I always did well enough in school, I was never quick to learn what people thought of me otherwise. I was born without the instinct to defend myself in a fight, or even the instinct to pursue an ordinary polite conversation with people I wished to make friends of. And yet these deficiencies of mine did not seem to matter so much in those days before I consciously began listening to the voices of other people and formally forswore hearing voices that came out of the air, from the trunks of trees, and even sometimes out of the mouths of small animals.

I WAS STANDING on the school steps one afternoon, waiting for my brother's class to be let out. Again I was feeling rather bored with life. We were no longer living in the old town in West Tennessee. My brother and I were in a city school, and my brother's class was kept an hour later than mine. Every day, I waited there on the steps until the hour when he was let out and our colored chauffeur came to pick us up. Sometimes there were other small children waiting, but on this particular day

I was alone. All at once, I saw a big dun-colored rabbit hopping across the green lawn. I hadn't then lived in a city long enough to know how thickly populated by rabbits and squirrels such "residential" neighborhoods often are. When presently the rabbit stopped and spoke to me, I was hardly more amazed than I had been by his very appearance there. He stopped in the center of the school lawn, lifted up one front foot rather daintily, and said to me, "Good morning to you, Bonaparte." That he should call me "Bonaparte" and that he say "good morning" when it was really afternoon seemed hilariously funny to me and sent me into gales of laughter. At the sound of my loud laughter, of course, the rabbit hopped briskly away into the hedge.

I was still laughing when my brother and his classmates burst through the doorway behind me. They wanted to know at once what I was laughing at, but as I began telling them, I saw the angry patches of red coming into my brother's face. I watched his lips as he drawled my name threateningly: "Lou-ou-is." Then I saw him draw back his arm, and before I could dodge the blow, he had struck me on the side of the head with the heel of his hand. I did not fight back and I did not cry. I simply sat down on the steps and remained there until all the others except my brother had gone. He leaned against the rail on the far side of the steps, looking at me with hatred. Finally, I got up and we walked together in silence to the car, where the chauffeur was waiting, as always, slouched behind the afternoon paper.

There is one incident from the earlier time—before we had moved, that is—which I very naturally find embarrassing but which must be recounted, because it is such a happy memory. I was seated on the toilet in the downstairs bathroom that opened off the back porch. It was summertime, and the door stood open. I had watched Alice, the cook, pass along the porch several times, performing little last-minute tasks. In those days, small-town cooks went home after midday dinner and returned at sundown to fix supper. Presently, I saw Alice start across the porch to the back steps, wearing her hat. She hesitated a moment and looked in through the bathroom doorway at me. She had been my nurse until a year or so before, when the old cook had quit. I was fond of her, and I knew that she was fond of me. She looked in at me with her lips pressed tightly together, but I heard a voice like hers asking, "Are you going to sit on that Christmas tree all day?" My voices rarely had such a definite character as that one had, and somehow that accounts for part of the pleasure I derived from the incident.

Alice disappeared for a moment but soon came into my line of vision again as she walked down the path through my father's vegetable garden. She carried a paper sack under one arm, and at the foot of the garden she slowed her pace and began rather boldly filling her sack with a half dozen or so of his ripe tomatoes and two or three cucumbers. When she had filled it, she lifted her free hand and waved to me. And when I waved back, it gave me a feeling of immense satisfaction.

As soon as she had passed on into the alley beyond, and out of my sight, I heard another voice—one of my usual voices, without any special quality or character—say, "Now what have you done?" The tone was both accusing and exultant. I thought about what had been said by both voices for a moment, and then I burst into laughter. I found the whole incident highly amusing.

IT IS A MUCH later time. It is a Saturday morning. I have somehow been roped into a game of baseball. Since I have no instinct for throwing or catching a ball—and as yet no learned ability—I am sent to the outfield, where I won't matter so much. The team at bat has one out and two men on base. Their best hitter steps up to the plate and hits a high, easy ball that begins an arc that I know is going to end right in my glove. I am hypnotized by the little planet moving so inevitably toward me, and I could not run away from it if I tried. And then there is the *plop* in my glove and I am holding on to the ball desperately. As if from far, far away, I hear the cheers of my teammates; immediately, and from the same far distance, they are calling out for me to throw the ball. Almost any throw will mean a double play and the retirement of the other team. I lift the ball in my right hand, draw back my arm. And over that shoulder comes the quiet voice: "Time passes. You haven't got forever." I freeze.

I remain frozen there, holding the ball high over my head. I know that I am not going to throw it. I understand that the words do not refer to my throwing the ball. Voices never instruct about practical things of the moment. It is only cruel irony when they seem to. Better for me to avoid even the appearance of not understanding them when I do. I could, in my clumsy fashion, get the ball at least as far as second base. It would be to my inestimable benefit and gain. But I continue to stand there holding on to the ball. I do not listen to the shouts of the other boys. I am tempted to listen, but the incentive is not great enough—is not clear enough yet. I must go on listening to the other voices for a few more years yet. I see my brother advancing toward me across the field, accompanied by a boy who is even younger than I am and who will be my replacement. My brother comes toward me with a look that warns I had just better not dare try one of my explanations on him. He is on to me now—for life.

I hand him the ball and give up my glove to the other boy. As I amble off in the direction of the new, big house our family has recently moved into, I feel no humiliation or regret at having been put out of the game. I only feel depressed by what the voice said. It makes no sense whatever to me; I understand it perfectly. I am filled with a deep, unhappy satisfaction. That's how it was.

I WAS EIGHT AND A HALF when we moved away from the country town. After the move, my mother and father were never happy together again. But they were not finally divorced until I was in high school, and their discontent with each other as man and woman did not seem to affect very much the happiness of our family life during those years. They never quarreled violently—or not in the presence of us children. Usually I was no more disturbed by the quarrels I did hear between them than by the bickering that increased among us children as we grew older. It seemed natural and inevitable. And when the divorce came at last, that seemed merely the same kind of event as the graduation of my older sister from college or the twins' graduation from high school. Perhaps it was because I didn't really listen to their quarrels that I was not usually disturbed. Sometimes, though, without even listening to what they were actually saying, I *would* experience a vague disquietude—really a dissatisfaction with my own state more than with theirs. I sensed that whereas our bickering always seemed pointless, their quarreling had a mysterious point to it that made it worthwhile.

After they had got their divorce, I was to hear each of my parents explain in almost identical terms what had happened to their marriage. They said that, following the move, the changed circumstances in their lives let them see how really unsuited to each other they had always been. This was the easiest thing for them to say and to try to believe, so long afterward. But I don't suppose they truly believed it. They were no more ill-matched than most couples are, and I doubt whether their first misconceptions about each other had been very extraordinary ones. I suspect the fact is that they had once been very much in love and that the babies born of that love gave them great satisfaction. Perhaps the satisfaction was so nearly complete that by the time their babies were no longer babies but little people racing in and out of the house, they knew the need again to feel and make felt their own separate individualities. It is not too shameful a possibility to consider, I think—not when you reflect that that is all that seems real to most of us beyond a certain point, and that beyond that point we are committed to nothing but pursuing that reality. I remember all too clearly the elation both of them expressed at the prospect of leaving the town where their children were born and had grown out of babyhood. I believe their elation was a joyful anticipation of something more than just my father's rise in the world. What I am most certain of is that the changes in their life—the move and their altered relationship—only just happened to coincide, and that it was for us children the happiest of coincidences. It was like meter and rhyme. The one thing made the other seem natural and inevitable. And if it had not happened so, we children might not have got the right impression about the naturalness and inevitability of either thing.

There is not much more I have to say about my parents. In his new life, my father took up tennis and handball, but I know that he never got to be any real good at playing tennis singles and that he disliked doubles. My mother teased him about persevering so in something that he could not excel in, and said she believed he fancied himself in his white tennis shorts and sport shirt. He was no more than forty at the time, and it was true that he did look rather like a college boy whenever he set out for the University Club in his tennis garb.

I remember his coming home late for dinner one night and explaining to us that he had been playing handball. My mother laughed skeptically and said, "Handball, indeed!" Father blushed and then he looked at her for some time without speaking. There was no quarrel, but on another occasion I remember his making a comparable remark to her. She was an excellent horsewoman. In the country town, and while her children were small, she had not ridden much. But in her new surroundings that was all changed. There was the fall horse show and the spring horse show, and it seems to me that she was always preparing for the one or the other. We usually went to see her ride and sat in a box applauding her every time she went by. Sometimes she rode her own horse, but more often it was the horse of one of her friends. Father had bought a small suburban estate, and some of our neighbors kept fine stables. Mother often rode before breakfast. Once, she returned just as Father was leaving for his office.

"We missed you at breakfast!" he called to her from his car.

"Sorry I didn't make it," she replied, peering down into the car from her horse.

"Out riding with the young squires again, eh?" he said. Then he drove off, without any further exchange between them. I am not sure whether he said "squires" or "squire," but I don't think it makes much difference which it was.

I became fast friends with both my parents after I was grown, and I make it a rule never to inquire into those parts of my friends' lives, past or present, that don't concern me. In the case of my parents as friends, I have possibly been spared gossip that mutual friends would ordinarily have supplied. And possibly, because they *were* my parents, my memory has spared me a good deal, too. But my memory has not spared me with regard to a dream I once had. It was a year or so after I had given up hearing my voices. In the dream I saw my mother and father seated side by side in a rope swing. They were terribly crowded, of course, and couldn't make themselves comfortable. Every time the swing went up in the air, one of them would almost fall out. And then I dreamed I heard one of my old voices saying, "Oh, ouch—oh, ouch, ouch, ouch!" I woke up laughing, and what seemed so funny to me was that that was not the kind of thing my real voices would ever have said.

BEFORE I CONCLUDE, before I tell you about how I finally hushed the voices I heard as a child, I must relate two incidents that involve my brother's twin sister. She was ten years old when we left the country town. From that time, she and our older sister were sent to a girls' day school. And from about that time the old closeness and loyalty between her and her twin brother ceased to exist. Suddenly it was as though she were two or three years older than he, and during the rest of their lives they have remained almost totally indifferent to each other. But she began to take an interest in me. She mothered me and played babyish games with me that she would not have played with anyone her own age—games of hide-and-seek, usually, in which even I didn't take much pleasure at my age.

Since our parents did a good deal of traveling in those

days—sometimes together, sometimes separately—we children were left alone in the house for relatively long periods
with only the servants to look after us. (These servants, I
should point out, were always imported from our country
town and were almost like relatives to us. One of them was a
woman of some education. She had gone up North to a Negro
college and had even taught school for a while when she first
came home. She used to help me with my lessons, and one
night, when we had put aside the books, I confided to her that
I wanted to be an artist when I grew up. "Do you love nature?"
she asked. I was stunned by the question, and after some delib-
eration I had to admit that I did not *love* nature. "Then you
can't ever be an artist," she said. She was a superior kind of
woman, but I am afraid I have never quite forgiven her for not
pursuing her education further before she came to work in our
kitchen. Another of these servants was a palmist, and she read
in my palm that I was going to be a fine musician. "You'll
probably play the fiddle, like your granddaddy," she said. But
I knew even at that age that I was tone-deaf, and I was a long
time in regaining my faith in palmistry.) When we children
played, the whole house was our province, and no games were
too rough. Things got broken now and then, but it didn't seem
to matter much. My brother and one of his friends, seizing two
curiously shaped sticks that I had brought home from a walk
in the woods, played at jousting one night in the front drawing
room. Suddenly the friend lifted his stick above his head and
struck directly into the crystal chandelier. It was an enormous
antique fixture that my mother had bought in New Orleans.
When the boy heard the crash above him, he threw down the
stick and covered his face with his hands, but he didn't move
from beneath the chandelier. For at least three or four minutes,
he stood there with his hands over his face while the prisms
dropped all about him like melting icicles. Another time, our
older sister and one of her beaux, in a fit of high spirits and for
no other good reason, rode their horses up on the front porch
and into the front hall. The scars that the horseshoes made in

the floor were too deep ever to be removed. But I don't believe there were complaints from my parents in either instance.

Whereas in the country we had been made to feel that nothing in our house was replaceable, now everything was apparently replaceable or expendable. I remember thinking that this was merely a sign of our increased prosperity, and in part it may have been that. At any rate, my sister and I seldom broke anything during our games. We played quietly, hiding from each other in such incredible places that it sometimes took three-quarters of an hour for one of us to find the other. One afternoon, I hid in a compartment of the sideboard in the dining room. I had been there for quite some time. I was in an especially cramped position, because this was the compartment in which my mother's cut-glass wedding presents were kept and I had managed to coil myself about cruets, pitchers, and decanters without actually touching a single piece. Before my sister finally found me, I had got in very depressed spirits and had heard a voice saying to me in the darkness, "There is no one god. And there was no beginning and there will be no end."

When my sister opened the compartment door, I told her immediately that I had heard a voice that said, "There is no god." I don't know why I censored it. Possibly I knew that "There is no god" would not sound so blasphemous to her as "There is no one god."

She looked in at me curiously, observing how I was coiled about the glassware. "Louis, you had better be careful," she began, and I thought she was going to say that I was apt to break a piece of the glass getting out. "You had better be careful," she said, "or you *will* turn out to be some kind of preacher, or something, the way everybody says."

This was the first inkling I had ever had that there was something "everybody" said about me, and it gave me a shock that I don't suppose I ever entirely recovered from. For the moment, however, I stuck it somewhere in the back of my mind. And its only immediate effect was to make me kick over one of the decanters as I was crawling out of my hiding place. The glass stopper rolled out onto the floor, and though the decanter didn't break, to my astonishment—and to my sister's—the thing turned out to be filled with a dark, sweet-smelling wine. Before I could right the bottle, some of the wine had gushed out onto the carpet and left a stain there that no amount of scrubbing and cleaning, on our part or the servants', could ever expunge.

Several days passed, or perhaps even more time, before I thought again of what the voice had said to me when I was hidden in the sideboard. Possibly this lapse of time and the revelation my sister had made to me combined to rob the message of any powerful impact. It was the only religious or irreligious—whichever—utterance I ever heard from my voices, and the impression it made was not very considerable. Any suggestion of infinity, however, could always depress me somewhat when I was a child. For instance, on the cover of my Baby Ray reader, in the first grade at school, was a picture of Baby Ray himself holding a copy of his Baby Ray reader with a picture of Baby Ray himself holding . . . , et cetera, et cetera. A glance at that cover could put me into a morbid frame of mind for the rest of the school day. I shall never forget the joy I knew when the teacher set aside the last hour of school one afternoon to instruct us in making brown-paper jackets for our readers; I believe the quickness and thoroughness with which I dispatched the job made a lasting impression on the teacher and may account for my getting off to a very good start in school. I used to be similarly affected by the seeming infinity of reflections in barbershop mirrors, and I would sometimes embarrass my brother by sitting through a whole haircut with my eyes closed. Anyway, the recollection of what I had heard in the sideboard affected me no more profoundly or lastingly than those experiences did.

Though my sister befriended and mothered me during this period, she was also my chief tormentor. She tormented me, that is, with her confidences. I don't precisely remember it, but I am sure that she must have begun pouring out her sorrows to me as soon as I had crawled out of the sideboard that day. I am sure of it because that is the way it always was. At least half the time we spent together was given over to my listening to her accounts of injuries other people had done her and to her grievances against her fate in general. I usually listened in silence, and at night I tossed in my bed thinking of how unjustly she was used and of how unhappy she was. She said she was the most unpopular girl in her class at school. The other girls ignored her and thought her clothes were tacky. And why shouldn't they think so, she would ask rhetorically. For although we had as much money as anybody else, didn't Mother make her wear some of the dresses her sister had worn to the same school two and three years before? And Mother and Father frequently included Sister in their social plans but said *she* was too young. They encouraged Sister to try out for the steeplechase but said *she* was too young. It was easy enough to see who *their* favorite was. None of her teachers valued her, either, and some of them went out of their way to find fault with her work and humiliate her before her classmates. She could not blame her own twin brother for being ashamed to walk down the street beside her. After all, she was already two inches taller than he, and there was no predicting how tall she might get to be before she was even given a chance to put on high heels. . . . She had inherited all the worst physical traits from both sides of the family. . . . She had never met a boy her own age who did not find her repulsive. . . .

One day, I made a drawing of her, working entirely, so I thought, from a small snapshot. I believe it was my very first attempt at human portraiture. Previously, I had spent many, many hours copying pictures of animals out of magazines and sometimes drawing our pets from life. My efforts had been very well received by all the family. My brother was especially admiring of my horses. I think it was the only accomplishment of mine he ever respected, though eventually he became disgusted with me even about that. At first, he took my horse pictures to school as gifts for friends. Later, he began selling them to the other boys. He grew impatient, however, when I could not fill his orders fast enough. When I was unable to teach *him* to draw the horses as I did, in order to supply the demand, he was irritated beyond measure. He would not believe that I knew no principles, no guiding rules, that I could pass on to him. He stormed at me, he broke his pencil across his knee and tore up his paper. I was dismayed and gave up drawing altogether for a while.

But after dinner one night, I brought out the drawing I had made of my sister. Both my parents were present, and both were delighted with the drawing. They exchanged the kind of warm glances that only something one of us children said or did could call forth in those days. They could hardly even believe it was my handiwork. Even my older sister and my brother were astonished by the "real likeness." But while these others admired the portrait, the subject herself remained in a far corner of the sunroom where we had gathered. As I have already stated, I was convinced that I had worked entirely from the snapshot, but there can be no doubt that I had also worked from memory—from the image of my sister's face as it appeared during those long confidences I had listened to. Presently, my mother said to my sister, "Come over here and see yourself. It's a fine likeness, and you're very beautiful." Then, laughing quietly, with her eyes on the drawing again, she added, "He makes you out rather a mournful beauty, I must admit, but—"

At that moment, my sister, whose eyes had been directed toward me all along, suddenly sprang from her chair, shouting at me, "How hateful of you, Louis Price! How dreadful you are! How cruel!" She had not even seen the picture, and I don't think it was Mother's description that inspired the outburst. She made a dash from the room, but she chose a route close enough to where the rest of us were gathered to get a glimpse of my drawing. "Hideous!" she said as she went by.

"I thought she might like it," I said after she was gone, though I am not sure I was telling the truth.

"You had better put it away for a while," Mother said. "It is just that she is at a very self-conscious age."

Regardless of whether I had thought she would like my doing the picture, I was genuinely sorry that I had so wounded her, and wished that I had not shown the drawing to anyone. I did not understand her self-consciousness. She was a great mystery to me, and though I wanted to explain to her what it was that had moved me to draw her picture, I did not even know where to begin. I was no more able to tell her *why* I drew it than I would have been able to tell my brother *how* I did it. All was over between my sister and me from then on. Like my brother she was now on to me—for life.

I WAS NOT YET on to myself, however. My voices continued to speak to me now and then for another three years, until I was a year older than my sister was that day. As an adult, I can see some kind of connection—I will not deny it—between that episode and what began soon afterward. But the connection is not relevant to my purpose. My purpose is to keep always in mind the value the events had for the child I still was, the child whose experience and logic I still do not contradict.

When I was about fourteen years old, I began imagining myself in love with nearly every little girl who came into my acquaintance. I say "imagining" because of course I know I could not have been in love as often as I seemed to be. I knew this even at the time. I knew that in some instances my love was self-deceptive and in others it was real. If I were to take the trouble, I could distinguish for you even now between the little girls I was truly in love with and those I deceived myself about. I recently came across an old schoolbook of mine in which the names of twenty-seven girls were listed in my handwriting on the flyleaf. Glancing down the list, I felt my pulse quicken as I caught sight of certain names. Others only brought a smile, or sometimes a frown, when I could not quite recall a face or even recollect if this was a girl I had known in our neighborhood or at the skating rink or at school or at dancing class. I find no difficulty in accounting for the large number. It was almost inevitable, since my attentions were invariably rejected. The little brunette or blonde or redhead was either frightened or sent into giggles by my sudden determination to walk beside her down the school corridor or to skate beside her, with hands crisscrossed, around the rink.

I am sure it was my complete silence that made me seem so sinister or so outrageously funny to all those little girls. But speak to them I could not. My attentions were always solemn and wordless. At dancing class, I once wrote the same girl's name after every number on my program and then walked over to where she was standing and held up the card for her to see, exactly as though she and I were two deaf-mutes. Unfortunately, from the girl's point of view, I had got to her before any other boy had had a chance to ask her for a dance, and she responded by bursting into tears. The dancing master reprimanded me, of course, but I can still remember how beautiful she looked with her face flushed and her eyes moist with tears, and I wasn't altogether sorry for what I had done. Before the next meeting of the dancing class, I had already given my heart to someone else—because it is quite as true for a child as it is for an adult that once he has been in love, being out of love is an unbearable state and one that he will not endure a moment longer than he must.

To some people, the child they once were is like a brother or a sister who died young. My father had a brother who lived to be only eleven; my mother had a sister who died at eight. How tenderly each of them has always remembered the child in the family who died—how tenderly and how dimly! That child who died is the child they remember the most about, and the least. What a wealth of details and anecdotes can be recalled! But what the true nature of the child's experiences was, what life really seemed like to him, is all beyond knowing and beyond mattering. The child is *dead*. The only difference is that the child who went on to death, instead of adulthood, will have many allowances and concessions made with respect to magical experiences he was said to have had. He wasn't like other children! He was in such harmony with the natural world about him! Or: It was almost as though she were never

fully committed to life in this world! Or: On his deathbed, only
a few minutes before he was taken, he rose up from his pillow
and said to his mother, "Don't you hear that lovely singing?
Is it the angels, Mother?"

My voices, whatever they were, were not the voices of angels. They never spoke except when they had something interesting or amusing to say to me. And I might never have given
up hearing them had they themselves not been finally so ame-
nable to the break and at the same time disposed to let the
decision be mine. Angels could not possibly have been so
self-effacing or so unwilling to stand in the way of all the future
happiness and unhappiness to which I was entitled.

Dancing class was held from eight until nine-thirty on Friday evenings. My brother and I were regularly delivered and
fetched home by the chauffeur. During the first half hour, the
boys and girls, in two separate rooms, were given instruction
in the dance steps of the day. At precisely eight-thirty, the little
girls were herded in through a door at one end of the main
ballroom, the boys through a door at the opposite end. For
several minutes, the girls remained huddled down at their end
and the boys milled about at the other—each trying to appear
unaware of the others' presence. But at last the dancing master
took his place in the center of the parquet, bowed formally to
the balcony, where there would be a scattering of parents and
a somewhat larger number of maids and chauffeurs, and then
raised one hand high above his head and clacked his black
castanets.

For the girls this was the signal to fan out across their end
of the room and take their "separate and individual" stances.
It was the signal for the boys to advance on the girls. And
advance we did, armed with our little purple pencils dangling
on gold cords from our program cards, and each of us—consciously or unconsciously—trying to imitate the gait of a father
or the strut of some older boy admired at school. As we approached the girls, a whispering went up from them like the
whispering of trees, and we marched fiercely and possessively
into their midst as into a lovely woods that we had been or-

dered to take at any cost—at any cost to ourselves, at any cost, presumably, to the lovely woods. Invariably, after such a beginning, everything about the hour of fox-trotting and two-stepping that followed seemed anticlimactic. The presence of the dancing master, his wife, and their two assistants, as well as that of the observers in the balcony, insured its being a dull, tedious, uneventful time.

But it was the custom that after the class small private parties were held at the houses of the members. And the time came when my brother got up one of these parties. Since it was to be held at our house, I was told that I might—that I must, in fact—invite one of the girls to come as my "date." The girl I chose was one whose name appears on that list in the old schoolbook I came across, and hers was one of the names that could, as recently as a few weeks ago, still cause my pulse to quicken. An unlikely kind of name it was, too, yet there it is in the old book, written down correctly, with all its many consonants accounted for and in their right order: "Yvonne Schmidt." (Alas, these few more weeks have not lessened its effect.) When I stood before her, holding on tightly to my little pencil and twirling the program card at the other end of the cord, and asked in a whisper if she would come with me to the party at our house, I could not really hear my own voice above the chatter there in the ballroom. Afterward, I was not certain that I had spoken the words. Perhaps Yvonne read my lips, or perhaps she read the invitation in my eyes, or perhaps she had wanted so for me to ask her that she imagined she actually heard the question. She accepted immediately.

There is no need holding back what happened at the party at our house. As soon as we had walked through the front door, Yvonne ditched me. She ditched me for the one she loved. I had not guessed it—there was no way I could have—but she was mad for my brother, and she wouldn't have scorned any means of obtaining an invitation to his party.

But from the moment she accepted until the moment when we walked together through the front door of my house was by no means a short period of time for one of my attachments to last. Even in retrospect, it seems like a rather long time. Remember that I was a child still, and that time passes differently in childhood. At any rate, the experience—if not quite the duration of the time itself—was comparable to an unfortunate first marriage that influential parents manage, by hook or crook, to end with an annulment. Yes, like that—followed by the same feelings of frustration, emptiness, betrayal. But in one sense it was also like that second marriage about which one has so many illusions and which one would do almost anything to save except that one has, quite by chance, overheard those amusing and unforgettable remarks about oneself exchanged between the wife of one's bosom and her lover. Yes, there was some of that same disenchantment with world and with self.

I rode home from dancing class with Yvonne at my side, the two of us sitting on the little jump seats in my mother's limousine. My brother and his girl were in the back seat. They kept up a steady flow of conversation. It never occurred to me to imitate their kind of drivel. Most of the way, I sat looking out the window, wishing I knew which kind of things Yvonne would most enjoy hearing me say. I finally decided that probably it would just come to me naturally once we were out of the car and inside the house. But, of course, I never had a chance to find out whether or not anything would have come to me.

Although dancing class was always so heavily chaperoned that we could hardly wait for the time to pass, the parties afterward were frequently without any real chaperonage at all. Apparently, it was only the public appearance and the good opinion of the dancing master that mattered to the parents of our generation. Sometimes a yawning father or a preoccupied mother would pass through the rooms of a house where a party was being given, but often as not they did not even bother to make an appearance. On the night of the party at our house, both our parents were away. The servants were on duty to see after our needs, however, and our older sister had been deputized to be on hand with her beau. My brother's twin, who considered herself too old for the dancing class set, was also at home that night. But she could hardly be thought of as a chaperon, and when urged to come down and join the party she declined, saying that she had letters to write.

The rugs in the front hall had already been taken up when we came in. That was where those who wished to would be encouraged to dance. Also, the piano had been rolled out from the drawing room to a place near the foot of the stairs. When we came into the vestibule, my older sister was seated at the piano in the hall, and her beau was standing beside her with one hand on her shoulder. They turned around immediately, and at the sight of me holding the door for Yvonne my sister's lovely face was suddenly made lovelier by a broad smile of approval. And then, as she stood up, she threw me a kiss. It was an exhilarating moment. I turned to Yvonne, but she had already passed ahead of me into the hall. My brother and his girl had come inside now, too, and almost at once other guests began streaming in. My sister introduced herself to the girls and led them back into the sunroom, where they would leave their wraps.

My sister's beau came up to me and asked, "What's your girl's name?"

"Her name's Yvonne."

"She's a very pretty girl," he said. "You've got taste, Louis."

And when my sister returned, I heard him say to her, "Her name's Yvonne."

I drifted into the drawing room with the other boys. When the girls joined us there, Yvonne would not even let me stand beside her. She kept slipping away from me, until at last I went out into the hall, where our chauffeur, having now changed from his driver's uniform into a white house coat and dark trousers, was seated at the piano and was beginning to sound a few chords. He often played for us children, and he had welcomed the opportunity to provide the music on this occasion. I knew that though he could not read music, he liked to have someone stand beside him and turn the pages of whatever sheet music happened to be on the rack. I stood there turning the pages for him almost as long as I remained at the party.

Once or twice, I saw my sister and her beau eyeing me.

Obviously they suspected something had gone wrong. Finally, the terrible moment came when my brother and Yvonne had been dancing together at the rear of the hall for some fifteen or twenty minutes. During most of this time, there were three or four other couples dancing, too, but the other couples were continually changing partners there on the floor, or going out for refreshments and returning with different partners. More than once I saw my brother's girl come to the drawing room door, glance out at him, and then look reproachfully at me. But it was my sister and her beau who finally spoke to me. They came from the dining room where the refreshments were set out, and as soon as they had crossed the threshold they began dancing. The young man guided my sister almost directly across the hall to me. When they got very close, they stopped dancing but remained in each other's arms while they spoke.

"Go and break on him, you little nut," my sister said.

"Yes," said her beau. "Show that little Yvonne what it's like to *really* dance."

I had no choice. I set off down the hall toward the pair. But when I was only a few feet away from them, I heard Yvonne say very distinctly, "Why is Louis the way he is? What's the matter with him?"

"Haven't you heard?" my brother said, smiling. "He hears voices."

"Not ours, I hope." She laughed.

"No, not ours. That's the trouble. *Other* voices."

"You're kidding."

Both of them saw me coming toward them, but I suppose they thought I really wouldn't hear *their* voices. And just as I was about to reach out my hand and touch my brother's shoulder, they turned and walked away in the direction of the dining room.

I shuffled back toward the piano. My sister and her beau were still dancing there, but they wouldn't look at me. I felt the chauffeur's resentful gaze when I didn't stop and begin turning the pages for him again. I put my hand on the bannister rail and started up the stairs. My other sister was seated at the top of the flight, peering down into the hall, but when she saw me she began writing on a pad of paper that she held on her knee. When I came up to where she was, she said, "Did you see Sister dancing with her eyes closed? Isn't she disgusting?" Without answering, I went up to my room.

I had switched on the light and was closing the door to my room when a voice said to me, "The number of steps in the stair remain always the a—"

"Hush!" I interrupted, closing my eyes and running my hand through my hair. "Won't you hush?"

"We can never hush," said the voice.

I opened my eyes and looked about at all my dear possessions that cluttered the room. It seemed to me that the voice had come from either the sea shells on the bottom shelf of my bookcase or from the leaf fossils there beside them. I took a step in that direction. It was the first time I had ever spoken back to my voices; it was the first chance they had had to answer me.

"Hush for a year," I said, "or five years, and then come back."

"We can never hush." This time it came from another part of the room—from the corner where my collection of knotty sticks and pieces of driftwood was kept. "But you may stop hearing us whenever you wish." I did not turn around. And after that the voice seemed to come from no particular object or direction. "You might as well stop hearing us," it said. "You have everything to gain and nothing to lose."

"But who are you?" I said. "I don't want to hear you, but I want to know who you are. I don't want to forget you." And suddenly, when I had said that, the room was filled with such loud laughter that I thought my eardrums might burst. I whirled about to make sure I was still alone there. I *was* alone. I clapped my hands over my ears, but the volume was not diminished. I ran to the corner, seized one of my sticks, and began knocking all my pretty objects off the shelves and off the bureau top, and smashing the glass that covered my moth collections. At last, I raised my voice and shouted, "I will stop

hearing you, you demons who persecute innocent children!"
The laughter ceased abruptly, or so it seemed to me.

The silence was awful for a moment. But presently I heard
my sister, who had looked at me so approvingly two hours
before, speaking to me through the door. "Your guests are
leaving, Louis," she said. "You'd better come down." She had
opened the door now. When I turned around and faced her I
could tell from her expression that she had heard the racket I
had been making. "This is not a very mature way for you to
react," she said, glancing all about. "I can see you've got a lot
to learn, Louis. Do you think you are so much better than
everybody else that you are never going to be jilted?"

"Has the little wench gone?" I said through my teeth. And
I threw aside my stick.

My sister laughed. "That's more the spirit," she said. Then
she took a step backward. "You had better not come down,
after all. Stay up here and pick up the pieces." At the door, just
before she went out, she elaborated. "Pick up the pieces, Little
Brother. Tomorrow is another day. And if it's not perfect, the
next one may be." It sounded trite to me even at the time, and
I am not sure she was not quoting some popular song of the
day. But she was trying to speak to me, and I loved her for it,
and I pitied her for having to say it that way. She was only
seventeen—not yet out of high school, even. Maybe for a girl
that is not so very young. But I know that when I got to be
her age I was still only beginning to grow up. Though I
stopped hearing the mysterious voices one hears as a child that
night in my room, at seventeen I was still learning to listen to
the voices of people—still discovering just how carefully, for
love's sake, one must always listen. And I was thirty before I
felt that love's recompense was adequate to let me say with
honesty the kind of thing that my sister had said at seventeen.

But still, how am I to explain the voices I heard as a child?
Why did I hate so to give them up? And why do I insist so
upon remembering them? . . . Well, I reject your explanation,
whatever it is. And, after all, they are *my* voices. The truth is,

I have come to like having them there at my beginning, unexplained, a mystery. My liking for the mystery of them has increased with every bit of learning I have had to do. Such a mystery becomes, finally, a kind of knowledge. It instructs and informs us about the arbitrary nature of most of the things we have to learn in order to walk the world as adults. Learn those things we *must*, but we know in our hearts that it might have been different. Our requirement might only have been to make sense out of what the voices were saying, and in that case those of us whose inclination was to go on listening always to our voices would have been the normal ones and not the rare birds we are. After seventeen, I became obsessed with learning from people—about people and the world. I listened to everybody. I became a wonderful listener, and still am. Everybody says so. The unfortunate thing, however, is that I have become eccentric in ways you might not expect. For instance, every time the season changes nowadays, I wonder what in the world has come over me and why I am so uncomfortable, until one day somebody happens to say in my presence, "Winter is really here now. This is the coldest day we have had," or, "Well, the hot weather is upon us, no mistaking it." After that, I change to clothing of appropriate weight, and I am all right again. One more thing, too. I *have* learned to love nature. And the memory of my unexplained voices has been instructive there. Whenever I return to the scenes of my childhood and admire the pale beauty of the sycamore trees and the glossy leaves of the oaks—almost like magnolias, some of them—I understand how far, in my mind, I have had to withdraw from trees in order to learn to love them. I go for walks in the woods with my family sometimes on my visits back home, and often I cannot help remarking on the absence of any chestnut trees in the woods. My family find it very curious that I remember the chestnuts at all, and tell each other it is evidence of how much I have always loved nature. But that isn't so. It is something I have learned. It is something strange and wonderful that I have learned to do.

The Witch of Owl Mountain Springs:
An Account of Her Remarkable Powers

DURING MY LONG LIFETIME, even since my early boyhood, there have been groups of girls of a certain lovely kind and character who have repeatedly turned up on my horizon. Again and again, in the variety of provincial places where I have lived, these clusters of charming girls have appeared with seemingly magical regularity. But whether they were little Sunday school girls living in a small Southern town or they themselves constituted a sophisticated postdeb set in one of our burgeoning cities or they came on my horizon as nubile young ladies staying at an old-fashioned family summer resort, which once abounded in our Southern highlands, still they have always and in every age had the same effect upon me.

I have found them nearly everywhere that I have turned—everywhere from Memphis to Nashville, from Chattanooga to Atlanta, and even on to Birmingham and New Orleans, as well as countless other more obscure points all over and about the countryside. But I may as well say here and now that no other group of girls ever had quite the same devastating effect upon me as did the girls at the summer resort at Owl Mountain Springs, a pretty little sylvan retreat perched high on the bluffs of the Cumberland Plateau in Middle Tennessee. It was this superb collection of girls that made their appearance before me—and seemingly for my own special delectation—during the hot Depression summers of 1933 and '34.

I was then indeed a very young man, little more than a boy really, and already there seemed to be girls everywhere. But to get right to the core of my story, and in order to make clear what those girls who summered at Owl Mountain Springs were like and how attractive they seemed to me, I must now make mention of a particular one among them. She was a girl named Lizzy Pettigru, and I suppose she must be called the heroine of this story. Lizzy was very much one of that group of girls at Owl Mountain Springs, yet she did not willingly acknowledge her own likeness to the others. That is the long and the short of it. That was really what troubled me from the beginning. She was a girl somewhat older than I, and in my innocence I imagined that the supreme compliment I could pay her was to say how perfectly integral she seemed to those older girls that I so greatly admired. But she would always reply, "Oh, no, I am not really like them at all!"

It will be easy for almost anyone to imagine what the girls at Owl Mountain were like. Groups of girls such as they, and those at other places before and afterward, seemed always to make their appearances on my horizon in intimate clusters of, say, twelve or fourteen. In my mind's eye their lovely arms were forever intertwined, as it were, and also—so I believed—their young lives. These intertwining postures, both figurative and literal, were ever to my mind the enchanting and captivating thing about them. It was the close and inviolate affiliation, the tender camaraderie itself that I always found most deeply affecting. It was this about them that I in every instance came so passionately to admire. From the outset I *had* to think of Lizzy Pettigru as a girl who was from that particular group. I have to say that altogether the bonding of such girls has constituted one of the chief delights of my entire life. My most vivid dreams have generally been not about some individual female like Lizzy; rather, my dreams have most often been how firmly and intimately such clusters of girls have seemed chemically bonded; I have dreamed about the sense of style they share, about their very evident awareness of their own closeness and congeniality and even their exclusiveness. I believe and hereby acknowledge that it is in this special preoccupation of mine that I am perceived to be in a certain degree different from other men of my acquaintance in our quaint corner of the world.

The girls that I would so much have wanted Lizzy Pettigru to be like came of the precise same stock that she did. The little resort had originally been founded as a gathering place for the principal Protestant sects in our region: Presbyterians, Episcopalians, Baptists, Methodists, and Lutherans. (In early days prayer meetings were held here daily—morning prayers and twilight prayers.) It was natural that no Jewish people would wish to go there. And in the very charter of Owl Mountain Springs Resort it was explicitly stated that the place was founded for the benefit of those of the Protestant faith and it was even stipulated for all the world to read that no Roman Catholic could ever own property inside the Grounds. And since there were of course but few blacks there in our Southern highlands, the summer people had to make do with what was known as mountain white help.

Perhaps a realistic presentation of the character of the place can best be stated negatively. No one imagined that Owl Mountain Springs itself was exactly a fashionable summer place, not even vaguely so—not in the eyes of the great world, at any rate. It was never thought of as any Blowing Rock or Asheville or White Sulphur Springs. It was never imagined to be a Rye or a Saratoga or a Cape Cod or a Nantucket. It would have seemed laughable to mention it in the same breath with Bar Harbor or Harbor Point. And yet it was quite as much respected for what it was *not* as for what it *was*. And Lizzy Pettigru did seem to represent—or I thought she represented—the very epitome of what outsiders and newcomers envied in the people who summered there always. I suppose those who vacationed there thought of themselves somehow or other as the special urban remnants of an old gentry out of another time, out of their remotely agrarian past. Surely it was the things they did not do that counted most with them. It was the things they did not have and did not want that mattered most. It was what they were *not* that made them *who* they were. Grandfathers of some had been generals in the old war, which they tried not to mention too often. They were proud mostly not of the great battles their generals had won in that war but of the great battles they had lost. One of theirs had been blamed or honored for the loss of Missionary Ridge. Another was held responsible for the debacle at Shiloh. In one family the Fourth of July was never celebrated because a grandsire had lost Vicksburg, and Vicksburg fell on the Fourth. At Owl Mountain we were all the grandsons of someone of a particular distinction of this kind. All, it should be said, but the Pettigrus! Perhaps *their* distinction was that they *needed* no single distinguished forebear. With their name, it seems, one need not ask for more. The Pettigrus' ancestry stretched back into eternity—through Virginia and South Carolina and Cavaliers and Charles the Martyr. But the families of all of us at Owl Mountain Springs could be traced pretty far back. And all of us still owned a good bit of land somewhere, and all had inherited or had managed to acquire—even the Pettigrus—a modest cottage on Owl Mountain.

Suffice it to say that when little Lizzy Pettigru was sixteen her manners were excellent, and withal so unassuming, and her face had such sweetness, and her charm was so beyond the banal of the merely beautiful or genteel young lady (of Memphis, of Nashville, and similar cities) that there was no goodness that could not be attributed to her. And I believe this was apparent to me without my having to be told of it by my elders. Her charm was so difficult to describe that, like everything else at Owl Mountain, it was usually said simply what Lizzy was *not*. Her nature was such that people expected more of her than others, and alas for Lizzy's sake, as it turned out, they forgave her more than they forgave others as well. That is to say, they forgave her kindness to anyone who did not quite fit in at Owl Mountain Springs. It was as though it were only *she* who could afford such kindness because of her goodness and her beauty and her being a Pettigru.

FROM THE BEGINNING it was an annoyance to me that Lizzy Pettigru did not willingly allow me to think of her as being like the other girls in that group at Owl Mountain. My perspective in those days is very clear to me now. I was fourteen in the summer of 1933 and of course fifteen the next summer. The girls I allude to, including Lizzy Pettigru herself, were two or three years older than I. But because boys at Owl Mountain were ever in short supply, these girls were glad enough to have such a youngster as I to "cut in on them" at dances in the Pavilion. I was a pumpkin-headed, freckle-faced boy, my full height barely reaching the shoulder of some of those girls. Still, I was well coordinated and a good dancer and fond of hearing myself talk to any girl. And though I had spent all my previous summers at a boys' camp, I was from one of the well-established families of the resort Grounds. "We" had been spending our summers there for three generations. Like everyone else we had our own Confederate hero as a forebear. Except for my age and my height I was an altogether eligible stag at the weekly Thursday and Saturday night dances. It was assumed by everyone that I had not yet obtained my full growth upward. (In this they were incorrect, for I would remain of very short stature all my life. As a college teacher I have sometimes sat on a large dictionary in my desk chair to give myself height with the students or even stood on the same behind my lectern.) It was also assumed that within a very few years the discrepancy in our ages would not matter to any girl in the Dance Pavilion. All in all, moreover, no one could have been more reassuring to me about my future prospects than was the beauteous Lizzy Pettigru herself. And as for me, I certainly could not then have predicted the calamity that would befall Lizzy in the relatively near future or the disastrous fate that would ultimately be her lot.

WHAT HAPPENED to Lizzy Pettigru the second summer was a calamity not only for herself but quite as much for her family and even, so it seems in retrospect, for the whole summer community at Owl Mountain. Perhaps with the end of the Great Depression already in sight such an old-fashioned resort was doomed to fall into decline. The same people who had once occupied the cottages there in past times began to have the means to go to more distant, cooler, and more prestigious summer places. But because of the sequence of actual events one cannot help associating Lizzy Pettigru's calamity with the decline of the resort, with the approaching end of the Depression, with the preparations for war which were then going on and with its attendant prosperity which itself made it inevitable that more and more cottages would stand empty at Owl Mountain.

During the war that was to come there would be great changes there. Army officers and their families from nearby military installations would leave and come to live in whatever cottages it seemed possible to heat in the winter. Also certain so-called bohemian artists and writers were ever on the lookout there for a cheap place to hole up in the war years. During this time the old clapboard Owl Mountain Hotel with its tier upon tier of gingerbread verandas was closed down forever, though it did not burn till several years later. It, along with a good number of abandoned cottages, became overgrown with kudzu vine and inhabited by squirrels and by various kinds of rodents. It was just before this significant decline in the place began and when the general exodus of old summer residents was beginning to take place that the Pettigru family felt themselves so demeaned and humiliated by an event in Lizzy's life that they could not return to their old, accustomed seat of residence in the lowlands. And so it was now that they established themselves at Owl Mountain Springs to live the year round. It may seem unlikely and almost inconceivable to young people of the present day what actually were those circumstances that seemed so demeaning and humiliating to the Pettigru family.

The event which in the Pettigrus' eyes had altered their position in the world they came out of—altered it beyond all possible repair—was nothing more or less than the public jilting of the incomparable Miss Lizzy Pettigru herself.

Of course from my very first acquaintance with Lizzy I realized that she had a degree of charm and beauty that the other girls in the little resort did not enjoy, that she had an intelligence and kindness in manner toward others that the other girls did not possess. Her beauty and her serenity seemed to me then, when we attended those dances at the Owl Mountain Pavilion, something that could never be changed. And to some extent even in very recent times—so many, many years later—when she had already got to be quite a pathetic old woman and we were still encountering each other now and again every season on the Middle Path at Owl Mountain, I could make out in her sharp old features and jutting chin some suggestion of the delicacy her features once had. By then Owl Mountain Springs had altered so that she and I would sometimes be the only summer residents actually occupying a cottage. But whenever we passed on the Middle Path, the grotesque old creature took no notice of me. In her near blindness it is likely she mistook me for one of the mountain people whom she had come to know so well and who came to sweep out the cottage every so often, or for some stranger who had wandered into the nearly deserted grounds. Or she may, on the other hand, have mistaken me for one of the other rare old-timers like herself, but not one she ever willingly spoke to. Regardless of that, she had long ago, before her cataracts came on, ceased speaking to anyone except those certain mountain people who seemed to be under her spell and were made to do her bidding. In most recent years I might look right into her face as I passed her there and receive not a glimmer of recognition. Old-timers and newcomers—the whole world—had now long since all become one to her. And with her sharp features and her head of wild white hair I could easily see why the mountain people had nowadays come to regard Miss Lizzy Pettigru as something more or perhaps something less than human and would sometimes speak of her as the witch of Owl Mountain Springs. The disappearance of any vestige of the old resemblance was what would at last seem to me our irreparable loss.

But surely, as I must here interject, surely boys of almost any generation—you, for instance, who are just becoming young men today—will understand the necessity that compelled me to try to identify the incomparable Lizzy as one of the wonderful Owl Mountain girls. For so perfectly did I invest that band of girls with my ideal of feminine beauty and my ideal of all the higher sensibilities that it was impossible for me to conceive of Lizzy's virtues in any other terms. And this is what is important for any present or future generation of readers to understand: a young man's preconceived ideals of feminine beauty and virtue, if he have such ideals at all, must be reflected in his own beloved—in his girlfriend, if you will. It is true in any generation, I believe, and will always be so. *She* must be the embodiment of all *his* preconceived notions of female excellence.

Why, as much as twenty years later when I would be back on the Mountain and would catch a glimpse of the youngish spinster Lizzy Pettigru across the Mall, I would find something about her to remind me of those other girls whose style or manner I had once so admired. Of course still another twenty years later, forty years after those summers in the 1930s, it was quite a different matter. By then her craggy old face and her unkempt hair could remind one of nothing that was human, much less of those long-ago charming girls. And I must say that to an extremely old man it was deeply disturbing and irritating that he could no longer find that resemblance.

But that was only toward the last. When ordinarily I continued to come back home to our family cottage, summer after summer—as indeed I seemed destined to do throughout the rest of my life—I could scarcely have avoided seeing Lizzy there on the Grounds even if I had wanted to. Through those years I would sometimes come great distances just to stay at Owl Mountain Springs for a week or two during July or August. She was always there. She would have been there even if I had come in midwinter, because as I have said, Lizzy and her always eccentric parents had very early come to the strange turn of remaining at Owl Mountain Springs the year round. After the *first* twenty years, of course, the father and mother were already dead and buried in the Owl Mountain village cemetery, and her having no brothers or sisters and never having married, she was already very much alone. I can see her when she was just past middle age, trudging alone from her cottage over to the village grocery store and back again. That was the only outing she permitted herself in that period. Or it was so at least whenever we summer people were in residence again—those of us who were still coming back then. Even when she moved along the Middle Path or across the Mall she took no notice of anybody—not of me or of whoever of her other old friends were present—took notice of nobody at all unless she happened to pass one of her special mountain people who sometimes worked about her cottage. At any rate, the point I make here is that whenever I saw her, either in early or in later middle age (sometimes with me staring at her from behind the lattice of the old Dance Pavilion before it collapsed or through the louvers of the closed window blind of my own fast-deteriorating family cottage), I then observed to what extent she still resembled those other lovely Owl Mountain girls, all of whom had now been scattered, and all of whom, like myself, now lived hundreds of miles away from Owl Mountain Springs, Tennessee. I must add that at this point in middle age Lizzy Pettigru wore her hair chopped off short like some plain mountain woman and had it pressed tight against her head underneath a wide looped net—a kind of hairnet I never saw otherwise except on mountain women and that I presume must have been sold over the notions counter in the Owl Mountain village grocery store. But even with her hair like that and her face already marked with deep creases and in her plain gingham dress that hung beltless on her macerated frame, still the sight of her at that age could somehow call up images of girls that my mind had likened to her in the summers of 1933 and '34. It would not be so at a later time. And it was this loss of resemblance that would be the most terrible thing to me about seeing her toward the end.

BUT WHEN I LONG AGO waltzed and two-stepped Lizzy Pettigru about the floor of the Pavilion, she spoke sympathetically to me about everything concerning myself and spoke generously about girls other than herself who appeared on the dance floor. I believe that from the earliest time she was never heard to say anything critical about those girls with whom she nevertheless did not care to be indiscriminately identified. While dancing with her perhaps I talked too much about myself (especially about my various intellectual aspirations and pretensions), but she managed to make me feel that she found the subject as engrossing as I did. Perhaps I also talked too much about the other girls all around us when we danced, but she showed no impatience with my enthusiasm for that subject either. Week after week I could not resist commenting on how very becomingly dressed were the girls who turned up at the dances at Owl Mountain, always including Lizzy herself in my generalizations on the subject.

It has been my observation before and after those two special summers when I was under the spell of the girls at Owl Mountain Springs that bands of such girls will always dress themselves in a fashion that is genuinely artistic in the total or group effect. That is to say, when they are gathered on public occasions there will always seem to be complicated color schemes running through their various forms of attire. To a careful observer like myself, certain shades of blue or green will appear in the hair ribbon of one and in the dainty collar of the blouse of another and on the hem of the skirt of still another, these colors complemented perhaps by reds or yellows in the costumes of yet others. And this is not something I merely imagined on one occasion. I have seen it everywhere, time and time again. There will be patterns of cloth or cuts of dresses in the most sophisticated or the most infantile of them that will seem designed to contrast with or draw attention to the felicitous designs or uses in other garments. And so one *has* to see them as a group if one is to get the beauty of them. One cannot but imagine that the effect has been achieved by one single hand, one eye, one exercise of taste, one sensibility. For instance, I remember observing some little girls who were in the third grade at Miss Fontaine's private school whom I would see skipping out to the little playground at recess with their pretty arms quite literally linked. They formed such a close, human chain across the graveled playground that it was impossible not to take notice of them. The starch in their little shirtwaists, the crinkled ribbons in their heads of carefully curled hair, the very flare of their short little skirts made it impossible not to think of them as all of a piece and to wish to seize them in one all-inclusive embrace or hug. I would be so moved by my own fond feelings for those little girls—and perhaps by the frustration that I felt but could not express—that I would immediately perform some act of badness there on the playground. Afterward when I was punished by Miss Fontaine, the head-mistress herself—my act having been so gross for a little boy in the third grade—I would not be able to remember what it was I had done and would hotly deny my act of badness. I was seized by one of those moments of amnesia which have re-curred throughout the rest of my life in moments of great stress, and I would deny that I had done the bad thing that I was being punished for.

I am reminded that at a much later time when I was ap-proaching middle age I had another, similar amnesiac attack in connection with another such moment of overwhelming emo-tion regarding a group of girls who were quite grown up. And I do believe there have been numerous other such attacks in my lifetime following moments of stress, though I suspect I have not always had reason to acknowledge them even to myself (since there was not usually a Miss Fontaine threatening me with corporal punishment). But in that much later instance I do recall that I was by no means any longer a very young man. Nevertheless, I was young enough to be attending the annual presentation ball given at the country club. Being a single man still, as I have remained all my life, I was invited to such events not as an escort for a debutante but as a sort of perennial bachelor or stag. During that period of the evening when the season's debutantes paraded about the parquet as they used always to do at such ritual occasions, I stood with the parents and the other relatives admiring with them the young ladies in the procession. I was acquainted with quite a few of the girls that were being "brought out" that year. A number of them were daughters of some of my slightly older friends. And I knew these girls well enough to recognize that they made up one of those unforgettable special groups with their own style. I watched them pass about the ballroom with considerable satisfaction and pleasure. The evening gowns that year were apt to have somewhat higher hemlines in the front than in the back, and these girls seemed to have adopted that feature as their very own. Their presentation gowns were not so alike, of course, that there was any monotony about them, yet there *was* that particular feature and there were *other* features of design and other complements of colors that suggested that somehow or other there had been some omniscient eye conscious of the total effect to be received. I am not suggesting that the whole affair had been choreographed by one hand or head but that the girls' own ideas of the proper dress and behavior that night was so well understood among them that there could have been no need for consultation beforehand. At any rate when the orchestra had concluded their rendition of "Pomp and Circumstance" and when the procession of new debutantes was ended, I believe that in my state of euphoria I must have broken into an inappropriately loud applause or perhaps even shouted "bravo" as if at the ballet, or possibly given vent to a prolonged and deafening whistle even with my fingers in the corners of my mouth. I do not remember anything like that, however. For any consciousness of what I did some Merciful Censor drew a curtain across events of the following two hours. The next thing I remember is that upon leaving the party, I know not how many hours later, I was shunned by some of my closest friends on the front steps of the country club. The only persons who treated me civilly as I was making my departure that night were certain slight acquaintances who possibly did not realize that it was I who had made the rumpus or scene somewhat earlier up in the ballroom.

THAT FIRST SUMMER at Owl Mountain Springs it was pleats of every description that were the great vogue among the girls I so greatly admired. Costume jewelry was also much in favor with them. I cannot say whether these fads of fashion were general all over the entire country that year. Perhaps they were. But I am afraid that I was never aware of any ladies' fashions but those which held sway in some special group which had captured my imagination. I remember that one girl that first year wore a little short evening cape consisting entirely of pleats. I found it stunning. There were a number of girls whose full-length pleated skirts swept about the dance floor. It seems to me that all the girls wore such skirts on one evening or another. And the elaborate costume jewelry contrasting with the simple and severe effects of the pleats could almost have been called the general motif of the summer. Strands of pearls and bright-colored beads along with pendant rubies and amethysts adorned the milk-white throats of those pure young ladies—gems and pearls that were surely imitative of ornaments intended for harem girls. And on their delicate wrists hung heavy bracelets suggestive also of the harem. The effect upon me of the contrast between those worldly seeming ornaments and the nun-like purity of their pleats was profound. And there was an especial excitement for me derived from the knowledge that so many of the girls' dresses were made by their own hands or by those of their mothers and that the costume jewelry was purchased at the ten-cent store in Nashville or Memphis or perhaps handed down to them from their mothers' collections of keepsakes and trinkets. For this was, it is to be remembered, the depths of the Great Depression, when wonderful economies were practiced even by these genteel folk who nevertheless continued to betake themselves to places like Owl Mountain Springs in the hot summer months of the year.

When I repeatedly "broke" on Lizzy Pettigru at the Pavilion dances it seemed to me not that I had selected someone different from those other girls but merely the foremost among them, the crowning beauty, the superior sensibility and intelligence of that remarkable assemblage of young women. But it seemed always to be Lizzy's principal aim to make me understand that underneath and essentially she was cut from a different cloth. "No, I am not like them at all," she repeated. Her general behavior like her dress and her social manner might be indistinguishable from those of the other girls but there was a mysterious essence in her being which she asserted was totally different. However, that mysterious essence was as far as I understood her assertion of difference. And the difference seemed to be one which she purposely withheld from any easy understanding. "You ought to *see* it for *yourself,*" she would tell me. And then she would laugh merrily. She declined always to be in any degree explicit about it. I knew only that her attraction for me was infinitely beyond that of any of the other girls, and I did realize that her receptiveness to any charm that might exist in the rather intense and overly serious adolescent that I was exceeded immeasurably any receptiveness from the other girls. They as a matter of fact—whose style and essence I held in such high esteem and regard—were given sometimes to actually patting me on the head as if intentionally to remind me of my shortness of stature and my relatively immature years. I suppose I condoned their behavior with one self-effacing thought: how could they, with all their grace and beauty and their wonderful aplomb in our little social world, their being themselves the elect and the elite of that world which appeared to me then as "our modern world" and appears to me now as an old-fashioned world almost beyond imagining, that is, how could they reveal the least uncertainty or even fallibility? It may seem incredible to someone of the present generation, but I was so enamored of the style and so respectful of the authority of those other girls that I could actually, without taking offense or for that matter without feeling mortally wounded, overhear one of them make reference to me behind my back as "that puny little intellectual." I can almost say I suffered such gratuitous insults gladly in order to be admitted to the weekly company of those girls at Owl Mountain.

But only Lizzy Pettigru treated me consistently with respect and—as I imagined it—with sisterly affection. She would do so even when she had been brought to the dance by someone else. Sometimes she and I would wander off as far from the Dance Pavilion as one of the high wooden footbridges which crossed over the ravine within the resort Grounds. We would stand there leaning on the rail of the bridge, with me talking about what one should do with one's life, but all the while stealing glances at the soft features of her oval face, at her lovely, long throat, at the rich brown hair that then fell about her shoulders and glinted in the romantic play of moonlight, yet neither at those moments nor during our daytime meanderings about the ravine and under the cliffside did I presume to speak directly to her of love. It never once occurred to me that she might have been receptive to my caresses—verbal or otherwise—much less that she might even have welcomed all such caresses. I never once asked her to one of the dances or to go out with me on a formal date—not so much as to attend one of the movies that was shown in the shackly old Youth Building, a structure which along with so many others has long since burned down. I was too conscious always of the two-year discrepancy in our ages and ever conscious also of the older boys—and one in particular—who sought her attention and her favors. But what I was not at all conscious of that first summer was how near Lizzy and the other girls were to being what used to be called a marriageable age. It would not have occurred to me that by the following summer a number of these girls would be officially betrothed to young business and professional men from their home towns or in some cases to the very boys who this previous summer had escorted them to the dances at Owl Mountain Springs. And of course Lizzy Pettigru would prove to be among that number. Before the season of the second summer opened her engagement had been announced in the papers. But by the first of August her betrothed had fled from Owl Mountain with a girl whom Lizzy had called her closest friend from back home, a girl incidentally of the Jewish faith who until that night had been present at Owl Mountain only as a houseguest in the Pettigrus' own cottage.

At an early age Lizzy Pettigru chose for her very best friend a girl from next door in her home town, named Sarah Goodrich. That the Goodriches were Jews Lizzy never bothered to learn or care about. Perhaps as a Pettigru she didn't need to care about that. The Goodriches were the Nashville and Memphis Jews who went "everywhere"—or nearly everywhere. (There were no doubt some in Birmingham, too, and in Atlanta and Louisville and New Orleans as well.) It was only to Owl Mountain Springs that the Goodriches generally didn't go. But when little Sarah Goodrich, at the tender age of nine, began to spend a large part of her summers as a guest at the Pettigru family's cottage no one took any notice of it—hardly anyone at all. By the time the two girls were young ladies Sarah was regarded by the Owl Mountain Springs young people as one of the "regular" crowd.

And when it turned out at last that Lizzy's choice for a husband was none other than one Tim Sullivan, everyone might have supposed that more notice would have been taken of that. The Sullivans were the Nashville Sullivans, and they were the richest Roman Catholics in Nashville. Roman Catholics at Owl Mountain were welcome only as visitors or tenants of Protestant cottage owners. In this latter day, under these conditions and for reasons of their own, the Sullivans were willing and content merely to lease someone else's cottage in the Grounds during July or August.

It was thought that the boy Tim Sullivan could be hardly aware of the special conditions of his family's tenure in the Grounds. Certainly he was regarded by the Owl Mountain young people as one of themselves. And when Lizzy's engagement to Tim was first announced it caused hardly a murmur on the Mountain. The idea of a marriage of the Sullivan money and the Pettigrus' gentility was widely approved and even applauded. The announcement of the engagement was featured along with large pictures of the bride-to-be in the Sunday society section in both Memphis and Nashville papers, and possibly also some mention was made of it in the papers of Birmingham and Atlanta and Louisville. For the Pettigrus had connections everywhere, and the name Sullivan was becoming increasingly well known. With a Pettigru connection the Sullivans would no doubt now be a force to be reckoned with.

It was well after the engagement had already been announced, of course, that the awful blow fell. No one had reckoned there could be any connection between the Catholic boy Tim Sullivan and the Jewish girl Sarah Goodrich. Least of all could it have occurred to the Pettigrus. Afterward it would be easy to say that it came about just because it happened right under the Pettigrus' noses, that it was too close for them to see. But this wasn't true necessarily. And in part it *was* true that all Pettigrus thought themselves above any such eventuality.

Lizzy Pettigru herself heard them talking one night—Sarah and Tim, that is. The two of them were together in what was known as the "little parlor" in the Pettigrus' cottage. Lizzy was off in her father's study looking up some disputed point in the fine print of the *Britannica* there. At first she thought she misunderstood what she had heard. She would tell me about it the very next day before her attitude toward me and toward the whole world seemed to freeze. Lizzy heard Sarah say the word "Jew" and heard Tim say the word "Catholic." She could not imagine the context in which these utterances were made. She believed she had never before heard either of them speak the words then spoken except in a most serious vein. But it seemed to her now as if they were joking. Perhaps they *were* only joking that first time. Perhaps it began with their merely teasing each other. When presently Lizzy returned to the little parlor, she found them standing halfway across the room from each other and they *did* seem to be regarding each other with what were clearly teasing expressions on their faces. And yet upon her entering the room, their expressions changed immediately. And what was most disturbing, there was now no continuation of whatever exchanges they had been making.

During this summer at Owl Mountain Springs, and possibly the one before, this same Sarah Goodrich and this same Tim Sullivan, this closest friend and this recently announced fiancé of Lizzy Pettigru, had manifested a common interest in one of the resort's young people's activities. That is, they had taken leading parts in the annual play that was produced in the old gymnasium, which was generally known as the Youth Building. The two of them were the acknowledged stars of the play being "done" there this season. Any number of nights this summer they had been closeted together in the Pettigrus' little front parlor or together out on the veranda practicing their lines. And so it had been on that night when Lizzy heard them speak their revealing words when she was bending over her father's *Britannica*. On previous occasions she had come and gone from the room or from the porch while the lines were being rehearsed. Probably she would never actually know on how early an occasion the personal teasing had begun—if teasing, indeed, was how it began. She knew only that it was Sarah Goodrich who spoke the word "Jew" and Tim Sullivan who spoke the word "Catholic." Lizzy could only imagine or surmise how exactly it had gone. But in the light of what her father would later overhear from his study on this very midnight of their elopement, Sarah would be saying in her youthful resentment and irony, "Oh, I'm only her token Jew" or "Oh, I'm only Owl Mountain's token Jew" and Tim would have been heard saying, "Oh, I'm only her token Catholic" or "Oh, I'm only Owl Mountain's token Catholic." Judge Pettigru (for he had once served briefly as judge in chancery court and was addressed ever afterward by that title), coming into his study much later, heard Sarah's and Tim's voices only indistinctly. He was in his study with the door slightly ajar. Probably the young couple didn't know he was there. And perhaps without even knowing it they somehow meant him to hear them. They were together in the little parlor just across the narrow passageway from the study. Judge Pettigru could only make out from their tone of voice that their conversation was of a personal nature, as he said. His own genteel nature and upbringing directed him presently to turn off his lamp and go quietly to the bedroom to which his wife had already retired. He did not mention to Mrs. Pettigru that night what he had heard in the front part of the cottage.

Lizzy waited until she knew her parents were asleep. Then she put out the light in her room and went into the passage that led to the front door. It was totally dark but she knew the position of every piece of furniture and the location of every throw rug, and in her bare feet she recognized the rough pine of the flooring in the passage. When she approached the front of the cottage she could make out that the door to the little parlor was closed. She could see the pale streak of light underneath the door and even the recognizable figure of light in the large old-fashioned keyhole to which there had never been a key. She knew without seeming to think about it and without any pang of conscience what she must do. Yet it took considerable physical effort for her to force herself to act out her part. In her nightgown and without slippers on her feet she forced herself down on her knees, and through the big keyhole she saw them. Afterward she would feel that in a sense peering through that keyhole was the most degrading part of the whole experience. They were on the Brussels carpet and what she first saw were the soles of their feet. She wanted not to see more but she knew that she must, and then suddenly she was distracted from the sight of their actual bodies by their faint animal-like sounds. Now she withdrew almost despite herself. And she retraced her steps down the long passage as silently as she had come. In her room she did not put on a light or think of going to bed and to sleep. She drew a straight chair up by the small bay window and there she sat the rest of the night.

THE NEXT MORNING the young couple was gone. There was no note left behind for Lizzy or for her parents. But sometime during the night Lizzy had discovered that Sarah's clothing and other possessions had been removed from the room they shared. When the girls finally did not appear for breakfast the next morning, Mrs. Pettigru went to their room and found that Lizzy, sitting straight in the chair by the window, was still in her nightgown and clearly had not been to bed that night. Lizzy heard her mother open the bedroom door and then go away without speaking to her.

The only note left behind by Sarah and Tim was one for the woman who was directing the annual Owl Mountain play that summer. It was a long, earnest and rather beautifully dramatic farewell note, full of regret that the two leading characters could not go on with the performance. It was thought beautiful, at any rate, by the woman director of the theater, who took their farewell and regret quite personally and declined to show the text of the note to anyone. To other members of the cast and to the managers of the resort's summer program she would allow only a glance—only a quick glance at the elaborate girlish script which would prove it was Sarah's handwriting and would identify the final signatures of both young people. When she announced to the assembled cast early that morning that the performance would be canceled, that the show could not go on without those two, she did so with tears streaming down her very full cheeks. And tears would also very soon be streaming down the young cheeks of all members of the cast. The drama of the moment was so satisfying to all present—that is, satisfying just because it was a young couple's having fallen in love that the show could not go on!—and seemed so satisfying above all to the middle-aged female director that suspicions were aroused among the resort managers. It seemed to the managers that the lady had herself been privy in advance to the plans for the elopement! What she revealed from the farewell note was that the two young people were not only in love with each other but had also fallen in love with the theater itself and that their intentions were to go away and together devote their lives and careers to the great American theater of the future! At the time no one seemed to think of Lizzy and the elder Pettigrus in their cottage, alone with their humiliation.

But late in the morning after the couple went away Lizzy came to our cottage, asking for me. I believe it was the first time she had ever been there, and not knowing her news I was mightily excited when Mother brought word up to me in my attic room. (Boys at Owl Mountain were always quartered in some sort of garçonnière up in the attic or in a lean-to in the yard. Boys were not thought highly of there until they were of marriageable age.) I didn't put on a tie but did comb my hair and then came stumbling down the outside stairs to greet her on the front veranda. I can never forget how she smiled at me on the stairs that morning, a pumpkin-headed, freckle-faced, teenage boy, as though I were some kind of knight errant or an angel descending from the sky. And she never looked more beautiful—or perhaps more vulnerable—to me. My mother was standing in the front doorway of the cottage, and before I was all the way down the steps, Lizzy was addressing me: "I thought you might like to go for a long walk this morning out to Forrest's Steep." I could not help observing the stunned expression on my mother's face. I suppose I glanced at Mother expecting just that. It was unheard-of that a young lady at Owl Mountain of Lizzy's age should call on a boy at this hour—or any hour—and herself invite *him* to go on such an expedition, unchaperoned and even unaccompanied in any manner. Forrest's Steep was situated in a cove way out at the edge of the mountain. It was the passage and steep by which General Forrest was said to have crossed over the Cumberland Plateau on his way from Stone's River to Missionary Ridge. It was not unthinkable, however, for us to take such a walk unaccompanied, and I replied, with another glance at Mother before we left, that I was in the very mood for such an outing.

I felt it was a decisive moment in my life or almost a decisive moment. At any rate I did accept Lizzy's invitation and did override Mother's silent protest, which consisted indeed of her remaining in the doorway until we were out of sight of the cottage. I think Lizzy and I said nothing to each other until we had reached the outer limits of the Grounds and had come into the larger undeveloped area known as the Domain. From there we followed the wagon road under the trees which would lead finally to Forrest's Steep. It was there that she would begin telling me all that she had heard and seen last night, sparing me nothing. We walked under the growth of sourwood and shad trees and I kept my eyes turned mostly upward into the leafy branches overhead. I suppose I was too shocked and too embarrassed by what she related to look directly at her. Then she told me all that her father had told her that he had heard and also whatever she had heard of the note written to the woman who had been directing the play. At the time I could tell she was stealing glances at my face to see how I would respond to all of this. Still I would not look at her until she had told me the whole story. When we reached the head of the cove we sat down automatically on the big flat rock that is there. Then I looked her full in the face, saying nothing still but waiting for her to state more than just the mere facts, which until now I was very much aware she had limited herself to. I had thought she would have burst into tears at some point. And if she had done so at this point I believe I would have put my arms about her and would have known how to comfort her. But even now she did not. When I looked into her hazel eyes now she said without emotion, "They have betrayed me and gone away without so much as telling me they were sorry they had to do it. And I do suppose they really had to do it. But I can see neither of them has ever appreciated the love I was able to give them and *did* give them."

Then I was able to speak. Whether or not it was from my heart was a question that did not occur to me. "They were neither of them worthy of you," I said. Maybe my logic was only the logic of someone who wishes to reform someone else. "Why did you have to waste yourself on them?" I blurted out. "They were not worthy of you—you of all people."

She looked at me as though she could not believe her ears. And still there were no tears which might yet have undone me. "Who *is* worthy of my love?" she asked.

I must have looked at her with the same logic in my eyes as before. "I can't imagine," I asserted. "I can't imagine." I really was trying desperately to imagine and I suppose I said the first thing that came into my head: "Why Lizzy, you have had the same wonderful chances that all the other girls have had." I became irritated with her. "You have refused to be what everyone knows you are, the very best of the whole lot. You ought to be glad you have been betrayed by what they are. It proves what *you* are."

Still she looked at me without tears and without belief. All at once she sprang up from the big flat rock and ran back along the wagon road and ran at such speed that it would not have been possible for me to overtake her before we were already inside the Grounds proper. And it would not have done on that day of all days to have Lizzy seen being hotly pursued down the Owl Mountain Middle Path by such as I. And Lizzy would never again through all the years acknowledge any acquaintance between the two of us.

As these years went by the Pettigrus would withdraw more and more to themselves, not only from the world they came out of back home but from the world of Owl Mountain. And as these years went by the old summer resort at Owl Mountain Springs became increasingly less popular with people from such places as Memphis and Nashville. After the Second World War such people as once frequented the place had largely ceased to identify themselves as a separate sort of people, as a separate sort of Southerner, as those whose forebears had not lost important battles or minor skirmishes in that old war that was coming to be mentioned less and less. They went "away" during the summer. They too went to Cape Cod and Bar Harbor and the like. For the most part Owl Mountain became a place you only went on a long summer weekend when you didn't want to stay home with the air conditioner and the television. And as those years passed there were fires at Owl Mountain Springs that changed the nature of the place entirely. First there was the old gymnasium. It was there that children and adolescents and even older young people gathered for games and for the rehearsals and actual productions of the annual play in August. It burned one summer night in July just a year or two after Lizzy's mother had died. (She died toward the end of one summer and was buried just outside the Grounds in the village cemetery.) Then there was the fire at the Women's Clubhouse, followed some years later by one at the Men's Clubhouse. And it was one night later that season that we had the fire at the Lecture Hall. That was the year that Lizzy's father died and was buried beside her mother in the village cemetery. At last would come the great blaze that was to destroy the old hotel with its shingled cupolas and its tiers of porches and the lobby with its wide oak staircase and the dining hall in which had centered most of the adult social life. The hotel, too, was burned on a hot night in mid-August, just as the chill of the night air came on. But this was of course twenty years and more after the fire that burned the old gymnasium. During the intervening years nearly all the other places of assemblage had gone up in flames. Only the chapel was spared, and it remains standing today. But many an empty cottage met the same fate as the other, public buildings. And meanwhile, year after year, I continued to return for a few weeks every summer when I was not teaching courses in summer school. And it happened that I was present on the night of the great hotel conflagration.

I saw the flames leap seventy-five and a hundred feet in the clear, cold air above Owl Mountain. I saw those flames light up the charred and scorched foundations of various burned-out cottages which had stood unoccupied both summer and winter for a good many years before the burning. During all these fires, and probably without exception, the now isolated and aging Miss Lizzy Pettigru had never joined the throng that invariably gathered. Rather, she would be seen by the rest of us wrapped in her plain cloth coat, sitting in a rocker on her front veranda, watching those others who came and went from the fire. If someone approached her cottage to ask if she might know how the fire got started, she rose from her rocker before even a foot was set upon her shallow porch steps and silently withdrew inside the front door of her cottage. It was always supposed that she might have seen someone passing in the direction where the fire blazed up. It was always suspected by the ever suspicious mountain people in the village that she had had a hand in each fire, if only through some magic or witchcraft that they, by this time, confidently believed she possessed. But if Miss Lizzy had made herself available she might have confirmed for them what some of them would already have suspected; that some one of those vagrants who were not from the village but who so often wandered about the Grounds had made a fire to cook his supper in one of the never-used fireplaces and out of carelessness or even malice had set the whole place on fire.

Between Miss Lizzy Pettigru and the mountain people there had developed a history in the years since she had come to live at her summer cottage the year round. This was particularly true after her parents were dead. Whereas the summer residents thought it unbecoming and not fitting for a genteel young lady to live there alone the year round, the mountain people thought it exceeding strange. And as time passed they came to think everything about her exceeding strange. The postmistress in the village, as well as others, became aware of the string of visitors that she turned away from her door. This "string" consisted of many of her old-time summer friends who came great distances to visit her. The postmistress could vouch that there had been letters, probably warning her of their coming. Another criticism they made of her was that she permitted no villager to come inside her front door and hired to do her work only vagrants and so-called covites, both of whom were looked down on by the mountain people of the village.

At any rate, I know that through the years Lizzy Pettigru did have visitors who came knocking at her door. I sometimes recognized them when I happened to be in residence, and I know that she insisted to them that she had had no forewarning and could not receive them. They were often friends from her childhood and came from far distant places where they had long settled—from Cincinnati, Miami, Chicago, New York. (The mountain people knew from their license plates what great distances they had come.) But Lizzy would not open her door to them. Or if it happened, as it often did, that they caught her rocking on the porch, she would get up and go inside as soon as she saw that they were turning up the footpath toward her place. The mountain people, with their usual imagination, wrongly supposed that she had purposely and magically some-how drawn these old acquaintances to Owl Mountain and then had turned her back on them. They would tell me so again and again when I came to stay for a while in my cottage. And they said, she always sent them away again without so much as asking them up on her porch. I knew that in all reason Lizzy Pettigru had never actually sent for those that came back like this. They came uninvited and unannounced. She had no more sent for them than she had sent for me. I knew that they must have come only out of curiosity, in order to discover what kind of being she, Lizzy Pettigru, who had once been so much like themselves, had now turned into. It could not be she who had brought them back; for what need had she now of *their* com-pany more than she had of *my* company? What need had she of their company more than of the company of the miserable mountain people whom she had clearly wounded by prefer-ring to them the covites and the stray vagrants who wandered into the Grounds? Had not the village mountain people found her a mere curiosity in her grief, a monstrosity in her lost life, a total anomaly in their world where one was expected to accept his lot in life and to die in just the same guise more or less that he had come into the world wearing? It was unlikely that she had a need of anyone now. But it was possible that those old friends that she had once seemed so like had a terrible need to see how one who had once been so like themselves could have been transformed into such an unlovely old being as I came to see each summer.

Yet gradually I began to accept that perhaps Lizzy Pettigru had, consciously or unconsciously, made a compact with some dark spirit which her imagination had conjured or perhaps with the very Evil One to whom the mountain people had come eventually to attribute the source of her "powers." But this alteration of my view of the possibilities came gradually over the long years when I saw her turning into the hag, the Witch of Owl Mountain Springs.

I SCOFFED AT them of course when any one of them said she had "powers." "She hasn't got 'powers,' " I told the postmistress more than once when she suggested as much to me. "She hasn't got 'powers'—or not of any sort you mean." Still, she was a solitary old soul, and one saw her sitting there on the veranda of her ramshackle, battenboard cottage, talking to herself, her thin old lips moving silently, somehow stealthily as if her fearful thoughts would be overheard by some ordinary mortal passing by. But now and then, as though it were irrepressible, she would give a cackle of laughter, a laugh at once mirthless and breathless yet withal audible in that twilight hour, audible across the wide, weedy lawns of the old resort Grounds and all the way out to the bluff's edge and past Forrest's Steep, perhaps halfway down the mountainside, too. And up there on the wisteria-draped veranda of her ramshackle, battenboard cottage she was like as not laughing at the very thought of whatever it was the mountain people had finally taught me to impute to her.

IT WAS THE mountain people, of course, who began all the talk about powers she possessed. But the mountain people would soon enough pass it on not only to me but to whoever of the summer people still came to the Grounds in July and August. We laughed at them at first of course. But they insisted. And they told us how during the dark winter months when there was nobody much to be seen in the overgrown Grounds or

strolling along the limb-littered paths and walkways of old
Owl Mountain Springs Resort, Miss Lizzy Pettigru would step
out on her porch and using a most obvious magic draw name-
less men of the vagrant covite sort up the path to her battenboard cottage. Hollow-eyed men they were likely to be, and
lean-jawed and chewing on a twig of sourwood. They would
have come wandering through the Grounds at that time of
year when the last straggling summer resident had gone for the
season and they—these hollow-eyed men—had strayed in to
pick up the junk—the near-worthless junk—that careless summer people would likely leave behind. It was just things on
their porches and in their yards—and none of it tied down as
it would have been if it were something they valued. It wasn't
exactly what you would call stealing that those vagrants did.
Such junk was all thought of as fair game for them. And as for
Miss Lizzy Pettigru, such fellows were no less than fair game
for her. Pretty soon she would be setting them to work in her
yard or even inside her old cottage, just as though it were all
by agreement. They were the only living souls she would
allow on her premises. Generally they were rough mountain
men from up the ridge or louts from down in the coves who
had probably never lifted a hand in all their lives to provide
either bread or keep—not until the unlucky day, so the village
people maintained, when they came up against the powerful
magic of old Miss Lizzy Pettigru. Of course, said the postmistress and the other ordinary mountain people, it was little that
Miss Lizzy cared for such talk about magic so long as she got
her leaves raked or her logs chopped for winter, chopped and
neatly stacked inside her shed. She laughed in the faces of those
solemn village folk who kept a careful eye on all she did. "You
had better watch out for such desperate fellows as them!"

Thus they would warn her about those men who came
wandering through the Grounds. All the while, I suppose,
they were really sounding her out about what powers she
exercised over those old vagrants of hers. "They'll cut your
throat some night," they warned her. But she would only grin
away at them, so the postmistress said. And sometimes the

postmistress would wink at me, as though she and I were the only two realistic persons in the world, and say that maybe it was not any "powers" she used to make the old vagrants work but certain cash money she slipped them from under a loose board in her floor or from behind some loose and unchinked rock in her chimney piece that drew them up to her door. It might be the crumpled two-dollar bills, so the postmistress said, that Miss Lizzy had been stashing away there since she was a girl that made the old men turn up her path. It might be the folding money she paid them, the folding money that the old-time summer people never used to pay mountain people. I would listen to the cynical postmistress, but all the while I was beginning to think to myself that there might be a power she had and had always had. There might be something that had kept *me* coming back. There was a power she had possessed always that was a curious strength of mind, a way of thinking, no less, that was different from how other people thought. It might be that she had a power of mind that could somehow prevent any harm that might come from those old men, that could prevent their returning to tear up the boards and dig out the rocks to obtain whatever money that might be hidden there.

There came a point when I began almost to be afraid of her. I listened too much to the mountain people and saw her too much as they saw her. I knew that for half a century now the bodies of the two parents had lain in the village cemetery just outside the gates of the Resort Grounds. I knew that a place was left in their burial plot for the interment of their unmarried daughter. And I had observed that a space was left on their double headstone where the daughter's name could be cut. I was told by the mountain people that all the year round Lizzy Pettigru would be seen visiting the little graveyard. And she would be seen just as regularly in all environs of the village. As the years had passed both the mountain people and the summer people came to feel that she had become more native to the place than any of the natives themselves. It was even said sometimes that when she came out of the woods, after a long walk therein, she would be followed by a deer or a fox or even a bobcat. But as soon as the wild creature became aware of the presence of any other ordinary human being nearby it would straightway turn back and vanish in the woods.

Old Miss Lizzy Pettigru knew where and when the blackberries ripened, and the huckleberries and the elderberries, and where here and there in a mountain recess an unblighted old chestnut tree survived and continued to bear. Most of the knowledge of where things grew she had acquired not from any mixing with the mountain people. (She was quoted by the postmistress as saying she despised folk wisdom. She was quoted as saying folk wisdom was the same as peasant ignorance.) Rather, her information came from certain musty old books on the dusty shelves of what had once been her father's study. And perhaps, it was suspected, her magic powers had a similar source in that darkened room, whose door was kept closed to any rare visitor that somehow gained entry into her cottage. She knew, of course, that that was the thing which made everybody call her a witch—both mountain people and summer people. I think it was that and the obvious fact that she didn't have "inside plumbing." Having no plumbing somehow put the fear of God in the summer people. Then there was also the fact that her battenboard cottage had long since had all its electric wiring removed. When children—mountain children or otherwise—would peer in her windows at dark or at twilight and see only her candles flickering, *that* above all else scared the daylights out of their little beings and made them scurry on home to their folks and report what it was that they imagined they had seen inside.

When the aged Miss Lizzy Pettigru crossed from the Corner in the village, carrying her little straw basket and stooping now and then to gather mushrooms (of a kind even mountain people would never eat), or if she passed through the village street clutching her fresh-garnered herbs (which they would not know where to find), she would laugh to herself, or she would laugh out loud if it suited her, at the suspicious chatter she heard (knowing that all around her thought her to be deaf) and at the ignorant talk she heard very clearly about herself as she kept her eyes straight ahead and went on her way.

When I went to Owl Mountain for the last time, only two summers ago, it was really quite painful to have to confront as an old ogress the girl who once had been the foremost beauty of the place. Yet despite myself I found myself spying her out through the louvers of my own window blind or from behind the still-standing stone chimney of some former neighbor's cottage that had been burned out. I was seized by a new kind of fear, a fear that I would once again have to face the old creature at close range. It was how totally unlike she now was to those other images of her I held in my mind that unnerved me. I told myself she was nothing at all to me anymore. Yet that summer I saw to it that we never again passed each other on the Middle Path. And unlikely as it may seem, for the first time in my long lifetime I found myself locking the outside doors to my old cottage at night. One night I even got up and locked my bedroom door.

It was now more than ever before that I made it my business to listen to the mountain people's superstitious gossip about the visitors who came back to call on Lizzy. And how should I have known whether or not I should have believed them? According to their reports the entirety of that group of wondrous girls had one by one come back to Owl Mountain and knocked on Miss Lizzy Pettigru's door. They came with their husbands and children from the far distant places where events in their lives had taken them. The postmistress told me that she saw letters from them that must have announced they were coming and saw letters go back to them from Lizzy Pettigru that must have told them they would be welcome when they came. (The postmistress was very open about all her observations and shameless in her speculations.) Sometimes it was postcards they would write her and it was welcoming postcards that she would send back. On those postcards certainly it was just as the postmistress suspected it was in the letters. But on the day of her visitors' arrival Lizzy would not of course let them inside her front door. If she were rocking on the front veranda when they arrived she would not let them come up the steps or she would get up and go inside the cottage and close the front door behind her. But there were worse things than that to be told.

For there were some persons, the postmistress insisted, who did actually come unannounced and uninvited. The postmistress was sure of it. And their coming or not coming was the queerest business of all. She and the grocer and the man who operated the little hardware store had all, at one time or another, seen at least one of those others moving about the village. There was a couple who, even after the death of the elder Pettigrus, had summered in the cottage next door to Lizzy. Sometimes during the season they would send over a casserole or a chicken potpie to Lizzy, though they seldom received thanks or acknowledgment for such kindness. And it was some years after this couple's empty cottage had burned that they were seen in the village one day. They made inquiries here and there about Miss Lizzy Pettigru and about whether or not she was still in residence there. It was while they were still in the village and had not yet entered the Grounds that long-distance telephone calls were put through to both the grocery store and the hardware shop (the operator having first tried to reach the nonexistent number of Miss Lizzy Pettigru) requesting that a message be delivered to that visiting couple. Their son was desperately ill, and it was urged that they return home at once. Without ever entering the Grounds, they hurried away. The poor son was not dead when they got back home and did not die at all. But that couple was never heard from at Owl Mountain again.

There was still another couple who had been close friends of the Pettigru parents and who at a very great age was making one last pilgrimage to the old resort. They had flown from somewhere in the Northeast down to Nashville, and a car and driver had been hired to pick them up at the Nashville airport. The plane had had a frightful collision on the airport runway. Many aboard the plane had been injured. And the old couple, though not injured at all, refused to continue the journey on to Owl Mountain. When the Nashville newspaper interviewed some relatives of that couple, it reported that the two old souls had hoped to visit the daughter of friends they had once had at Owl Mountain Springs. But they had decided that luck was against them and that they had best return home.

There was a ruthless wickedness implied in these two stories—if, that is, one did concede some remarkable powers to the now aged Miss Lizzy Pettigru. And events conspired that last summer to advance my disappointment and disenchantment with the old resemblance that I had used for so many years to see. My disenchantment was transformed into a kind of fear of Lizzy and perhaps then into something more positive than that. I recognized in myself even a kind of hatred for this creature I once idolized. I think it might have been otherwise than this if I had not happened to be in residence during the last of July and the first days of August.

During the morning of the last day of July Lizzy appeared over in the village blithely buying a box of salt, one small package of nails, even a page of stamps. I had glimpses of her through the windows of the three establishments she entered. I didn't in any instance want to see her, and I turned my face away each time I caught sight of her. But in my swiftest glance even I believe I saw a look of peace and satisfaction on her face that somehow frightened me. It somehow had the effect of repelling me far more than any vacancy of expression or any ignoring of my own presence had done in recent years.

But I didn't feel at all that the expressions I observed through the store windows were really directed toward those with whom she was doing business. In fact I think I observed that when I saw her again—somewhat later and at some distance away on the Middle Path and within the Grounds—she wore the same expression of peace and satisfaction. It was not something I merely imagined. And it seemed utterly bizarre to me that she at this point in her life would take up wearing such an expression. It inspired me momentarily with inexplicable feelings of bitterness. I went to my cottage and must have slept there for a while, which was an unusual thing for me to do in the middle of the morning. Just before noon I went back to the village to do the shopping I had meant to do earlier and had somehow forgotten. It was now, just after I had entered the post office, that the postmistress opened the little frosted glass door that is beside the letter counter across which she does her business. And she summoned me to her by crooking her finger.

"I suppose you have heard," she said in a lowered voice. "You must have heard," she said.

Having no idea of what she meant, I drew closer to her. "I haven't heard anything," I said almost resentfully. I confess I thought it was going to be something that Lizzy Pettigru had told her when I was looking through the post office window some while earlier. But, anyway, I had heard nothing of what she would tell me. It seems that two persons had been killed in a car that had been catapulted and subsequently capsized on the first of the sharp inclines and curves coming up the east side of the Mountain.

"I am told," the postmistress continued, now speaking almost in a whisper, "that the victims are nobody else but the old movie actress, Sarah Goodheart, so called, and who else but that man she ran away with forty years ago, the man who used his money to make her and himself into movie stars."

SOMEHOW THE FIRST, worst shock to me was the news of what had become of that infamous pair. As a former college professor—I had pursued that profession till I was past fifty—I did not of course keep up with what became of old movie stars. I knew—or had once known—that that outrageous couple had actually gone the way of Hollywood and had had some degree of success out there. Probably everyone in this mountain village knew more of their careers than I did. No doubt everyone else knew how long ago they had retired from the screen as well as just how much they were still in the public eye. Certainly I had never seen them once on the screen. I could not have said how great or how little their success had been. But with the shocking news of those old acquaintances' fatal accident I returned once again to my cottage and had once again failed to do the shopping I had intended doing. And once again I must have done the odd thing of falling asleep there—by what must then have been midday.

And queerer than that, I must have slept there on the couch in my sitting room for the whole of the afternoon. When I was awakened by footsteps on my porch, it was already growing dark outside. The Owl Mountain grocer and the hardware merchant, along with two men in dark business suits who were total strangers to me, stood outside my front door. The identity of the strangers was immediately explained to me. One was the coroner from the county seat, ten miles away at the foot of the Mountain, and the other was the county sheriff himself. The two merchants had shown the two other men the way to my cottage. They had come there in order to ask me to accompany them to the county seat and identify the bodies of the two victims of the early morning accident. It seems it was important they be identified before any disposition could be made of their bodies. And it seems that I was the only person still living in the community who would remember them and possibly recognize their faces. The only other possibility of course would have been to call Miss Lizzy Pettigru. Yet knowledge of the long-ago elopement was sufficiently widespread throughout the whole county to make this an impossibility for men with any delicacy of feeling. I had no choice but to comply with the request of the strangers who had come for me. I put on a tie and jacket and went with them.

BEFORE WE ARRIVED at the county seat and went straightaway into where the two bodies were stored, lying side by side on two mortuary tables, I had been informed of the circumstances leading up to the accident. It seems that the nattily dressed old couple had flown into Chattanooga by way of Atlanta. Ordinarily any Owl Mountain summer people from the old days would have flown in by way of Nashville. Chattanooga was physically as far as Nashville from Owl Mountain, but culturally and spiritually it was considered to be light-years farther away. I suppose this was because it was settled as a town only after the Civil War and had been settled by Union soldiers who had taken part in the long siege of Missionary Ridge. It was indicative of how estranged from the scene Sarah and Tim had become that they allowed themselves to be routed by way of Atlanta and Chattanooga. I would read in the newspapers soon afterward that only the man in the airport car rental service recognized them for the celebrities they were or had once been. And it is likely that that agent only recognized their names on the car rental forms which he had received in advance.

It was no ordinary car that the agency had managed to hire for the couple. I would also read in the Chattanooga newspaper afterward (for the two were still celebrities enough for the local press to make much of their dramatic end), I would read, that is to say, of a Chattanooga teenager's having observed them at an early morning hour in their dark glasses—their "shades"—and driving a cream-colored Cadillac convertible, moving at incredible speed on a stretch of highway that runs along the foot of Chattanooga's Lookout Mountain and which follows the curve of Moccasin Bend of the Tennessee River. The teenager said he had remarked to himself at the time that the driver and passenger in the car must be a gangster and his moll or perhaps country music singers of some sort. The reporter interviewing the teenager in the *Chattanooga Times* observed that it was wonderful that the car rental agency could come up with just such a car as the couple had specified in advance they would like to have. And the reporter philosophized further that it was wonderful how much being celebrities enhances people's lives—even such rather out-of-date celebrities as these.

I DIDN'T KNOW any of this, of course, when I went in to look at the two bodies, though in retrospect I have a feeling that I did know all of it. What I actually knew then was only what the sheriff and the coroner had been able to tell me at the time.

I knew that it had been a sunny midmorning, and that by the time the exotic pair, Tim and Sarah, reached the ascent up to Owl Mountain they had put down the top to the rented convertible. In that cream-colored automobile and in their dark glasses they must indeed have presented a spectacular sight as they came round the first bend of that winding mountain road. There were a good many people who had been coming down the mountain at that hour, people who nowadays commuted to work at the county seat. Afterward they would remember the begoggled couple and remember of course the great rate of speed at which they were taking other curves. The thing was, nobody actually saw the car leave the road. The car that was around the next curve above heard the great scream of the tires and heard the series of bumps and crashes as the behemoth went down the mountainside. And occupants of a car on a curve just behind heard it all, too. But no one actually saw the big Cadillac leave the road. As it made its flip upside down through the bright morning air the only witnesses to its fateful move through the air must have been whatever wildlife was present on the wooded mountainside. After other cars appeared, all to be seen were the marks in the tar and some gravel which had recently been put on that stretch of the road—that and some even deeper marks and ruts in the red clay shoulder on the left-hand side of the pavement. From the sound of screaming brakes it could only be surmised that some wild thing must have suddenly appeared from the wooded slopes above the road—some deer or bobcat or fox—and in braking the car at such speed on the newly spread gravel the driver must have lost all control of the vehicle. When the passengers in the next cars to come along stopped and went to the shoulder of the road and looked down, only the underside of the big convertible could be seen. Already a few long wisps of smoke were rising from the wreckage. From the very first there was no question of anyone surviving such a crash. When the police came and the wrecker crew soon after them and the ambulance people not long after, there was some effort made to find whatever wild creature might have distracted and confused the driver and sent the car out of control. Whatever it was must have stopped right in the car's path for a moment and then scampered to safety. But no identifying track could be found. No doubt the turf at the roadside was too ravaged and the loose gravel and the tar too scrambled for any footprints or hoof-prints to be distinguishable. Yet surely there could have been no other explanation for the frightful accident.

IN THE TEMPORARY morgue where I was taken it seemed now that one moment I was standing between the two covered bodies and the next moment, by the concerted turns of the wrists of both the sheriff and the coroner, the protective sheets had been drawn back simultaneously to reveal the faces of the two accident victims. And it was almost as though the sudden exposure of the two faces had been coordinated in order to increase the shock I was destined to experience.

I had been told already that in the morning's accident the faces of the victims had not been mutilated or even scarred. All that I had inwardly prepared myself for was how the ravages of time and a life spent in Hollywood might reasonably have altered the faces of my two old acquaintances. But the actual shock I received and which I believe made me literally take a step backward was the sight of the youthfully smooth and untroubled countenances of the two dead people—their dark heads of hair, the unblemished cheeks, the unwrinkled lids of the closed eyes, the serene expressions on their relaxed faces. Before me seemed to be the faces of Sarah and Tim as I had last seen them. Not until later did it occur to me that what I looked upon was the work of dye jobs and face-lifts and per-haps something of a local undertaker's work. But for the mo-ment it was the young Tim and Sarah lying before me. "Yes, yes!" I said, almost without thinking, and turning to the men who had escorted me there.

"You have no doubt, then," the sheriff said, he and the coroner coming forward at once.

"Oh, no. There can be no doubt," I said. And I could only

think to myself, "*She* did this to them!" It was as if she had done it long years ago on the night they had eloped. As they led me back to the waiting car the two men had almost to support me bodily. And on the road back to Owl Mountain Springs I had not a word to say to them. It was then that I began to realize what was the nature of the work that had been done on those faces. When the men returned me to my cottage they offered to stay with me for a while. But I waved them away. And when I closed the door behind me, I locked myself in my cottage. I had now but one line of thought. Why had I come back to Owl Mountain Springs all these years? Why had I been destined to live so long as to see all vestiges of what I could love in Lizzy's face and figure entirely vanish? And at the last I found myself asking myself: was I ever in her mind any different from the others? And did *she* still have some hideous fate in mind for *me?*

I WAS AWAKENED once again by the sound of hurried footsteps on my porch. I can only suppose—because I could not otherwise account for the time—that I had fallen into another long period of sleep. The lights were still lit all over my cottage, but certainly I was prone in a sleeping posture on the couch in my sitting room. At some point I had washed myself thoroughly and even got into pajamas. And at some point I had unlocked my front door. And now I was awakened as from a troubling nightmare of the kind you cannot afterward quite remember. Someone on the porch knocked once and then opened the unlocked door. He was a young mountain fellow, a total stranger to me like the two men who had come earlier. I sat up on my couch blinking my eyes at him. Panting for breath and with one hand on the porcelain doorknob, he told me he had been sent to wake me and tell me that Miss Lizzy Pettigru's cottage was on fire. He stared at me for a moment as if to see how I responded. Then he fled across the porch and I heard him calling out to other persons on the path.

I went to my bedroom and pulled on a clean pair of trousers

over my pajamas as well as a fresh shirt. Then I hurried out to join the village people who had assembled along the Middle Path and in the yard outside Miss Lizzy's cottage. There were mists of white smoke all about the cottage but there were no flames. Some semblance of an amateur brigade had pulled up a water tank with hoses and already had been at work spraying the shingled roof. In fact, those men were still attempting to spray water on the roof and on the battenboard siding when I arrived. If there had been any appreciable fire it had been extinguished without much effort on their part. At first I began to move directly toward the cottage, but I was restrained by the strong arms of the grocer's wife and the postmistress. "It's too late for you to be any help," one of them said. I could feel their powerful hands taking hold of me, and all at once I became aware of my age. I heard someone say, "They're bringing her out now!" The two women led me toward one of the stone benches beside the Middle Path and forced me to sit down. Other people gathered around where I was sitting and I felt they were all being protective of me and showing respect for my great age. I became aware that a crowd of mountain people were grouping themselves between me and the sight of the body that was being brought out. I knew it was out of consideration for my advanced age and for my well-known friendship with Lizzy Pettigru. No doubt I had grown pale and no doubt the trembling of my right hand had increased and was becoming noticeable, because the grocer's wife now began to urge me to return to my own cottage. When I firmly declined to leave the scene, the postmistress sat down on the stone bench beside me and said in a most reasonable voice, "I think you must be told the whole truth here and now."

And that lady proceeded then to tell me that it was not the fire that had taken Lizzy's life. She told me that the first men to arrive at the fire had entered the cottage, gone down the long central hallway, and found the old spinster lying already dead in her bed. And then for a moment the postmistress looked at the other woman as if to obtain her approval before continuing. "She was already dead when they got here, and there could not have been much of a fire. I tell you just what they told me. Miss Lizzy had had her throat cut." The grocer's wife began to cry in her handkerchief then, but the postmistress sat there looking me straight in the eye. She gave me the very worst of the details. They found blood all over the wall opposite the bed. And clearly the fire had been set as an obvious effort—a too obvious effort—to conceal the means of death. But the murderer had had no experience in such a business. The postmistress, and everyone else later on, pronounced it most clearly the work of one of the old vagrants from down in the cove. And this of course, as we all remembered, was something that had been predicted years before. Boards had been prized up from the floor and the chimney stones pried loose from the chimney. It was supposed to indicate someone had been in search of the poor old creature's money. But even the search for the money was somehow unconvincing. And there was evidence that the old soul had put up resistance. But there was something unreal about that, too. Chairs and tables were turned over and there were bloodstains on the floor and along the dado of the bedroom. And last of all the murderer's weapon was a knife from Lizzy's own kitchen. That itself would have been like one of those old fellows from the coves. But the handle of the knife had been wiped dry of all bloodstains and fingerprints, which would not have been like one of those old fellows at all.

I was protected from the sight of the body when they brought the old creature outside. And of course I never looked upon her face again. But the picture described to me of her lying there dead with her throat slit will never leave me. At last I was guided back to my own cottage. I was seen safely to bed by my two lady companions, who sat near me for the rest of the night. I slept not at all and sometimes I remembered that I had not eaten all day. Before dawn it had occurred to me more than once that in all likelihood the body of Lizzy by this time lay in the temporary morgue that had been set up at the county seat. And it was all too easy to imagine that she would be lying there now right alongside the bodies of those who had been victims of the highway accident. I had the impulse to remark on this to whomever I might make listen to me. But of course I found it too grim a thing to mention in the presence of the two ladies who were sitting the night through with me.

In recent days it has seemed almost incredibly ironic, too much of a coincidence to be believed, that Lizzy Pettigru should actually have met her violent end on the very same day as Tim Sullivan and Sarah Goodrich. But if there be skeptics about the truth of my account, they must go sometime and look up the dates beneath Lizzy's name on the tombstone she shares with her parents in the Owl Mountain Cemetery and then travel out to Hollywood and see that the same date is there on the magnificent marble monument that I believe Tim Sullivan and Sarah Goodrich share. And if this be after my death, it might seem worthwhile to go and seek out my own grave in whatever remote place I shall have taken myself off to, and learn just how long I was able to survive the end of such a story as I had to tell.

At the Art Theater

AS THEY PASSED slowly and patiently up the aisle of the dark movie house, accepting the pace set by the departing crowd, Ginnie Patterson reached out to take the arm of her fiancé, Alan Gunter. She slipped her hand under a stiffly held elbow and then hooked it over a firm forearm, leaning heavily on the arm, though not looking in the direction of the tall young man. . . . Ginnie and Alan had just attended the art theater's Sunday night showing of Ginnie's favorite Bergman film. But since Alan had not seen the film before, and had not been sure he wanted to see it, Ginnie may have been preparing herself for some unsympathetic comment on his part. Or perhaps she was still reflecting on the significance of that last powerful scene by the cold, northern sea. Afterward, she could not recollect just where her thoughts had been. Probably it did not matter. At any rate, she presently recognized the familiar deep tones of Alan Gunter's voice coming not from the man on whose arm she was leaning at all, but from directly behind her. "Ginnie?" came the voice over her shoulder. Not bothering to withdraw her hand at once, Ginnie glanced up at the stranger on whose arm it was she was leaning.

He wasn't anything at all like her fiancé. Instead of her young man in his vest and three-button jacket (this being several years ago, I should say), he was a young man with a beard. When Ginnie saw definitely that he was a stranger she did remove her hand, though somewhat reluctantly, as if she might fall without his support. And she said quietly, "I beg your pardon"—said it in a tone she might have used if she had merely bumped against him ever so slightly. After all, this theater was only the neighborhood art theater, a familiar haunt of Ginnie Patterson's; and the young man with the beard was obviously one of the students from the State University, just a few blocks away, where Ginnie's father taught political science. When she looked up at him through the near darkness he was smiling broadly down at her, his dazzling white teeth set off strikingly by the black beard and moustache. To Ginnie he seemed a not uncommon type for the art theater on a Sunday night. And what had happened was a fairly commonplace little mistake. Yet when she glanced backward at Alan she understood at once that he was equating the student's face with that of one of the characters in the Bergman film. She felt that with his own grimace Alan was making a mountain out of a molehill. *His* grimace actually reminded *her* of one of the characters in the film. . . . But that he should behave so was something to be expected, she supposed. She gave a little shrug and, continuing up the aisle, tried in vain to recapture her earlier vein of thought.

When they came out into the lighted lobby of the theater, Ginnie waited for Alan to come up beside her. When he came, she took his hand very gently in hers. She still could not recall where her thoughts had been when she took the strange young man's arm. But now, trying to concentrate on her real fiancé, she thought to herself that he looked tired. His spark, his alertness, his vitality, all of these qualities which she was accustomed to seeing expressed in his face and which made him such an attractive-looking person seemed momentarily in eclipse. She wondered if this were only by contrast with the faces she had been watching on the screen. It seemed possible even that he had been napping during the last episodes of that incomparable Bergman film! . . . How *could* he? Yet Ginnie had to concede that, after all, this had been an exhausting sort of day for a man—particularly for a young man of Alan Gunter's practical nature . . . and . . . and of his energetic temperament.

Alan, looking down at Ginnie, had not at all dissimilar thoughts about her. She looked tired. To both of them, after the darkened auditorium, the light in the lobby seemed very bright, not the dim, lavender light there, not a ghastly light which was bound to give a weary, ghostly aspect to any countenance one looked into. He saw a strange look come into Ginnie's green eyes. No doubt she was tired. It had, after all, been a wearing kind of day for a girl with Ginnie's intellectual turn of mind. That morning, her picture had appeared on the front page of the old-fashioned society section of their paper, and beneath it the heavy, black caption: MISS PATTERSON BETROTHED TO MR. GUNTER. Alan sighed audibly. Alas, he mused to himself, that picture had been his mother's doing and Ginnie had not been at all prepared for such a prominent display. And then they had had to go to church with his parents, and—most inappropriately, it seemed to him (he appreciated Ginnie's not referring to the fact)—to the country club for an endless, fol-de-rol Sunday dinner afterward. During the afternoon they had to call on three of his aunts whom Ginnie had never met before. And finally they had to join Ginnie's own family, here in the north end, for an intimate Sunday night supper at home—*with* candles in old wine bottles, and *with* Mrs. Patterson's pâté that she had learned to make when she and the professor were in France (on his Guggenheim, twenty-five years ago) and *with* Ginnie's tiresomely precocious little sister as usual dominating the conversation, this time trying to insist that Alan and Ginnie accompany her and her father to a chamber music concert at the university instead of to. . . . Again Alan at this recollection sighed aloud. Small wonder his poor dear fiancée was tired after such a day. Probably he should not even reproach her for having carelessly seized the arm of that stupid-looking bearded fellow. Though how *could* she have done it? What *had* she been thinking of to do such a careless thing?

Squeezing her hand until the stone on her new ring gave his own palm pleasurable pain, he resolved that he would try not even to mention her absurd mistake.

They pressed on through the lobby of the art theater, where the audience waiting for the second show milled about, sipping coffee from paper cups which they held by ridiculous little paper handles. The handles on the paper cups somehow got on Alan's nerves. And these second-show people were very much in the way. Alan reflected that while he approved entirely of the art theater's striving for a salon effect in the lobby, since it humanized a mere movie theater, one had nevertheless to admit that the scheme was not very efficiently carried out. With the first-show people trying to leave the theater, here were the second-show people still sipping their coffee, dawdling over the low, wide tables and thumbing through the magazines strewn thereon, or standing about trying to admire the more or less abstract paintings (every month a different local artist's work) which adorned the sandalwood walls. Alan quickly assured himself that he respected the kind of people who came to the art theater and that he understood why so many of the men wore beards and so many of the women wore no makeup—or wore too much makeup. But somehow he was not in the mood for them at this moment. Perhaps it was because of the Bergman film. He hadn't understood it perfectly, of course—not the way Ginnie would have with . . . with her training in *aesthetic* appreciation—but he did *like* it and approve of it. (He had had an English professor at Williams who liked movies really better than novels, and he was beginning to see what that fellow meant.) At any rate, after the genuine, deep spiritual concerns of that Bergman film, surely everything about this theater and these people seemed merely arty and trite. He longed to get outside. Only then could he discover exactly what he thought of the film.

Finally he and Ginnie had arrived at the blue-tented, plate-glass outer doors of the theater lobby. Other members of the serrying first-show crowd held back momentarily to slip on their coats before going out into the winter night. Alan couldn't wait. Giving the door a shove with his open hand, he sent Ginnie through first, her Chesterfield coat still only draped about her shoulders, his own camel's-hair thrown over his arm. At the very moment when the delicious night air struck his face and the moment when he had just stepped into the cheerful glare of the bright lights under the theater marquee, he heard his own and Ginnie's names being spoken.

To his left, and emerging through another door from the lobby he saw the person who was addressing them. It was none other than one Sass Merriwether—yes, that was who she was—the petite, pretty, vibrant (these were his mother's words), and irrepressible Merriwether girl. She was one of the current harvest of belles out in the east end of town where the country club and the private schools were and where Alan still made his home with his family. It was always unexpected and perhaps disconcerting to see someone from "out there" "up here" at the north end art theater. And it was not unusual when two people from "out there" met "up here" for them to greet each other in just the astonished and elated tone that Sass was using now—as though they were meeting on the moon!

"How *are* you two!" she said. "But what a question for me to ask! Congratulations, you two!" And then, possibly more to Alan than to Ginnie: "What a movie! Wasn't it creepy!"

"Indeed it was," said Alan, hardly aware of what he was saying as he fairly beamed down at the beauteous Sass.

The bright marquee light did no disservice to Sass Merriwether and Alan did not fail to be aware of that fact. Her peaches-and-cream complexion, her intensely blue eyes, her white-gold hair all were created for such light, as also, incidentally, were the muted greens and reds in the plaid coat she wore—a coat cut in the best lines of that season, low-belted, collarless, and with three-quarter-length sleeves revealing just an inch of her peaches-and-cream wrists above marshmallow gloves. Of course if either Alan Gunter or Ginnie Patterson with their own brand of good looks had glanced at each other, during this interval under the marquee, each would have in fact discovered that the other suffered no more than Sass from being caught in such light. But it was on Sass they both found their eyes fixed. Alan was not in the least infatuated by the little Merriwether girl. She was several years younger than he. He was not well acquainted with her even; he was simply well acquainted with her sort, with the world he had grown up in. . . . Yet at this particular moment she seemed to him one with the very freshness and wholesomeness of the night air and the frankness of the bright lights, and she came as a blessed relief after the atmosphere of the art theater lobby.

The girl's own escort, a tall, bland-looking young man with roses in his cheeks, was smiling vaguely and politely over Sass's shoulder at Alan and Ginnie but since the two couples would be separated almost immediately, no introduction was really called for. Just before they parted, Sass bent in front of Alan and said to Ginnie, "It was such a *lovely* picture, Joanie—I mean, Ginnie."

"Indeed it was," Alan heard Ginnie say and he saw Sass blink her eyes nervously.

"Who did it?" Sass asked as if quickly to overcome her embarrassment.

"Why, Bergman, of course."

Sass burst into rather loud laughter and so did her escort. And so, unfortunately, did Alan. But immediately Sass reached out and squeezed Ginnie's hand. "I meant *your* picture in the paper this morning," she said in an apologetic tone.

"Oh," said Ginnie, "oh." Then, suddenly tugging at Alan's arm she led him off in the direction of the parking lot. Sass and her escort moved off in the opposite direction and soon disappeared in the bundled-up crowd.

As Alan Gunter and Ginnie Patterson hurried off to the parking lot beside the theater, Alan noticed that Ginnie had slipped into her Chesterfield without any assistance from him. She had done it while they stood speaking with Sass. It was a regrettable oversight on Alan's part, and he knew it. But, even so, how *rude* Ginnie had been to that girl! She must have really *known* Sass meant the picture in the paper! But he reminded himself that it had been a difficult day for Ginnie and he refrained from criticizing her.

At the car, while he was fumbling with the lock on the door, he heard Ginnie bring out in a queer kind of drawl, "So you thought it was a 'creepy' movie?" It was as though while he bent over to unlock the door she had struck him over the back of his head with a wrench. He felt himself fairly staggering from the blow.

Under his breath, still working with the key, he muttered, "My God, my God." Then, finally swinging the door open, he drew himself up very straight. "That's just Sass's lingo," he said, curling his lip. "I *liked* the movie, and so did Sass for that matter."

"As if it mattered, for that matter," said Ginnie.

As their eyes met, she blinked her eyelids. Her lower lip trembled, and then was brought under control. At last she hurled herself into the car, feeling stunned, feeling as though she had been slapped across the face. She yanked the door closed so quickly that the outside handle slipped out of Alan's grasp. He stood a moment looking through the car window at the girl he was going to marry, then he ran around the back end of the car to the door at the driver's seat. Ginnie made no effort to open the driver's door from inside, and so he had to open this door with his key, but there was no fumbling this time. He was intent upon what he was doing. He could barely wait to climb in there beside her and tell her what he thought of her behavior. And Ginnie could barely wait, too, to tell him what she thought of his.

With their first blasts at each other, both sensed that this was going to be their first really fearsome fight; and it was. It was awful.

They were married two months later, but as long as a year after they were happily wed, each of them would sometimes think of that quarrel in the car while they were driving toward the Pattersons' house that night. What they said to each other in that quarter hour was of no real significance. How could it be since neither of them had the vaguest conception of why he or she felt so utterly outraged or why he or she felt the necessity to set the other straight on certain points once and for all? Everything they said on the way to Ginnie's house was surely irrelevant to any real quarrel they had between them, and so need not be reported here. But for a time each was insisting periodically to himself or herself that something had gone out of their life. Each had the feeling that he or she had seen something or someone for the last time, that something was over. Each had the transitory feeling of wishing to hold on to something that was lost forever.

Cousin Aubrey

IN THE TENNESSEE COUNTRY of my forebears it was not
uncommon for a man of good character suddenly to disappear.
He might be a young man or a middle-aged man or even
sometimes a very old man. Few questions were ever asked.
Only rarely was it even speculated that perhaps he had an
"ugly situation at home." It was always assumed, moreover,
that such a man had gone away of his own volition and that
he had good and sufficient reason for resettling himself elsewhere. Such disappearances were especially common in our
earliest history, before Tennessee achieved statehood even, but
they continued all through the nineteenth century and even
into the twentieth. We were brought up on stories of such
disappearances. I very early came to think of them as a significant part of our history: the men who had disappeared without
leaving behind any explanation of their going.

When in recent years I found myself strangely preoccupied
with the possible present whereabouts of one of my mother's
aged cousins, one Aubrey Tucker Bradbury, I could not but
be mindful of those old stories I had heard about other men
who had vanished. By this time I was already a middle-aged
man with grown-up children of my own, and my mother
herself had been dead for some while. This middle-aged preoccupation of mine would soon develop into what amounted to

an obsession. What seemed particularly impressive to me was that this Cousin Aubrey had managed to vanish three times from our midst before his disappearance was complete and permanent, so to speak. Anyhow, I came to find myself wishing above all things, almost, to know what had finally happened to my old cousin and where he might be living out his days. It did not occur to me either that he had had some great good fortune in life or that he had come to an ignominious or perhaps violent end. But somehow I could not rest until I knew what had become of the man. I realized that even as a child I had a good many times wondered what had happened to him. I suppose I had reason enough to wonder, since on every occasion of our meeting before his final departure he had taken particular pains to show a special dislike for the small boy—and later, the adolescent—who was brought forward to meet him, a dislike which seemed totally unwarranted since our meetings were so few and so brief. But all that aside, my sudden and unaccountable preoccupation with finding Cousin Aubrey Bradbury was like some old passion of my youth that had been suppressed and was now in late middle age manifesting itself in a more virulent form.

All the while that I was making the first few tentative inquiries and investigations concerning this missing cousin and even later when we had found him—as a result of my own and my younger son's efforts—I continued to think of those other vanished men who had captured my imagination when I was a boy. I felt that they might offer an explanation of Aubrey's disappearance. I knew how little similarity there could have been between those men and himself—as little as there could also have been between himself and any one of our great achievers, such as my maternal grandfather, for instance, who scaled the great heights of Tennessee politics to end his days in a no less exalted role than that of United States senator and an entrenched power in the capital at Washington. But nonetheless, the names and stories of those other men's disappearances would keep returning to my inflamed and strangely excited mind. My constant reference to them in conversation during this time very nearly drove my wife, Melissa, as well as my son Braxton to distraction. They spoke of this habit I had fallen into as my "mania." But they listened sympathetically, too—they and the rest of the family—as again and again I catalogued the names of vanished Tennesseans. Apparently I spoke of them always in tones of such particular veneration that Braxton especially found it wonderfully amusing. He compared it to the listing of Homeric heroes! At any rate, by all means the most famous name in my said catalogue was that of our old warrior-hero, Governor Sam Houston. Everyone, especially Braxton and his mother, knew the story: On the morning following the night of Governor Sam Houston's marriage to a Nashville belle, he abandoned his bride and abandoned as well his newly won gubernatorial chair. It is well known that Houston went then for a time to live among the Indians. And afterward, of course, he went on to found the independent Republic of Texas. But, for us, the point is that he never returned to Tennessee. . . . Only somewhat less famous in the annals of the state was a man who had been one of our two Confederate senators and who, after the war, without seeing his family or his constituents again, went off to live in Brazil. From there he sent back photographs of himself posed in opulent surroundings and attired in romantic Portuguese costume. But when some relative, later on, made a point of looking him up, he was found in pathetic rags living in dreadful squalor and quite alone in the slums of Rio de Janeiro.

Not all of our vanished men, however, were public men. They were, some of them, simple, landless men who seemed unable to put down roots anywhere. Sometimes they took their wives right along with them when they went away, as well as whatever children they had and perhaps an old grandmother or some other dependent or relative or, in the earliest time, perhaps a little clutch of black slaves and even an indentured servant or two. But even these rootless men, when they departed, frequently left under the cover of night, as if the act of moving in itself were a disgrace. I am told that in the first quarter of the last century it was indeed quite common in Tennessee to see a crudely lettered sign nailed to a tree trunk in the front yard of an abandoned farmhouse, reading simply GONE TO TEXAS. And that was only a manner of speaking, of course. It was merely a statement that another disenchanted man had put forever behind him the long, green hinterland that is Tennessee, and that he never intended returning to her salubrious clime.

CERTAINLY AMONG my earliest memories is my experience aboard the special funeral train bearing the body of my late grandfather, who was in the United States Senate and who died in Washington in 1916. I was the only grandchild taken along on this journey since the others were of school age and would have been too long absent from classes. Aboard that funeral train the Senator's widow occupied the drawing room in the first of the two Pullman cars. I remember such details not merely because I was present but because I would afterward hear accounts of that train ride repeated endlessly by other members of the family, for whom without exception it was the most important journey of their entire lives. I particularly remember that in the drawing room of the second Pullman car were the late Senator's three daughters by an earlier marriage, one of them being my mother—young matrons they must be called in the language of that day, though despite each being married and the mother of one or more children they were scarcely more than girls, really. And in lower berths nearest to their private compartments would sleep their young husbands, each taking his turn during the long journey to Tennessee at sitting with the dead Senator's corpse up in the baggage car. Among these, also taking his turn at sitting with the corpse, was of course my father. A certain nephew of the Senator, the aforementioned Aubrey Tucker Bradbury, would from time to time offer to relieve one or another of three sons-in-law at his watch. But the sons-in-law regarded their vigil by the Senator's coffin as their exclusive privilege. And the fact was that the very presence on the train of this odd-looking and eccentric kinsman of the Senator's—this Aubrey Tucker Bradbury—was resented by all members of the immediate family. The three sons-in-law agreed among themselves that even the wide black armband on the sleeve of Aubrey's dark suit was a presumption and an affront. More than anyone else, perhaps, they bore in mind a certain irregularity in Aubrey's very kinship to the family—that is, that he had been born out of wedlock, being the child of the Senator's deceased elder brother and a "mountain woman" of obscure background. In the eyes of the family there was something infinitely lugubrious, if not sinister, in the young man's very bearing. The eldest of the three sisters was moved to remark (while I, her little nephew, was sitting on her lap in the drawing room) that only by the black mourning band on his sleeve could their cousin Aubrey be distinguished from the long-faced undertakers who had abounded on the scene at the railway platform as they were setting out.

That special train would leave the Union Station in Washington at 2:40 in the afternoon on September 18. The year of course was 1916. Although the funeral procession from the Willard Hotel to the station had been led by a horse-drawn hearse bedecked with a mountain of floral wreaths, the rest of the official procession consisted of four elegant black limousines and eleven other black motor cars. In the uncovered driver's seat of each of the high-set limousines rode not only a chauffeur uniformed in black but a black-uniformed footman as well. I remember my father's commenting that these funeral vehicles and their funeral attendants were supplied not by the federal government, as one might have supposed, but by the Washington undertaker who would be in charge of all procedure and all protocol until that moment when the Senator's coffin would be lifted into the baggage car.

It must be mentioned that alongside the highly polished limousines rode a number of government-provided plain-clothesmen—outriders on horseback, as it were. And it cannot go without mention that these men were present because inside the limousines, among other notables, rode two very great personages indeed. Though the American manners of the day forbade that the bereaved family openly acknowledge the presence of any such person at this solemn occasion, I think it all right, so long afterward and in this latter day, so to speak, for me to make known the rank of those great personages. They were none other than a former president of the United States and the incumbent himself! Their presence is, however, scarcely a significant part of my story. The important point is that the mounted presidential guards with automatic pistols showing on their belts underneath their jackets seemed impressive to me, at the age of four, and actually frightening to my mother and her two sisters. It gave those young-lady daughters of the dead Senator the uneasy and altogether absurd feeling that the funeral procession might be attacked as it moved along Pennsylvania Avenue.

One of these three sisters who had this irrational response to the armed guards was of course my mother. This youngest daughter of the Senator was of an apprehensive and nervous temperament. Already, at earlier events of the funeral, she had kept glancing almost suspiciously in the direction of her eccentric cousin, Aubrey Tucker Bradbury, as if to see if he were experiencing an anxiety similar to her own. (I do think I observed this for myself at the time and was not merely told of it by my mother long afterward.) It was always at Aubrey she glanced during the funeral service and not at her handsome and youthful husband. The sight of Aubrey Bradbury was somehow reassuring to her during the early period of the funeral, as his presence had often been to her as a child and particularly just after the death of her own mother. Aubrey had actually been her confidant in those earlier times, as he had been also for her sisters during certain times of insecurity in *their* girlhood, and there had even been a period when this cousin had lived in the house with them and served briefly as their papa's private secretary. And at one time or another this same Aubrey had made declarations of undying love to each of the three sisters. (All three of the sisters would in later life give me hints of these outbursts of Aubrey's.) Anyhow, my mother knew of Aubrey's sensitive, serious nature, and though she had since her marriage—and probably through the influence of her husband—come to think of Aubrey as a ridiculous, unmanly sort of creature, she wondered if he were not today imagining, like herself, that outrageous and terrifying things were going to happen to the funeral party. As a matter of fact, I think that without being conscious of it my mother sensed that this occasion marked the end of an era in the life they had all known.

The two other sisters, my two aunts, who were destined to help bring me up after my father's early death, were persons of a far less apprehensive nature than my mother, and so they were able to speak more openly of the absurd anxiety they felt that day. Even as they rode along the avenue between the Willard Hotel and the Union Station and observed total strangers standing at the curb, with hats removed in the old-fashioned way in the presence of death, my Aunt Bertie and Aunt Felicia spoke to each other openly of their anxiety. But my mother, whose name was Gertrude, was of a more introspective and questioning temperament and was unable to speak out about her fear. Her hesitation was due, in part at least, to the peculiar nature of her anxieties. The fantasy she entertained was not merely that those men on horseback would suddenly turn on the procession and perhaps upset the coffin and the precious corpse inside. (*That* was the "crazy feeling" openly confessed to by my aunts and which, as a matter of fact, they would long afterward laughingly tell me about.) But Trudie, as my mother was always called by her older sisters, imagined those armed men as actually forcing open the coffin and revealing to her that her worst fantasy-fear was come true: that it was not Senator Nathan Tucker's body locked in the casket but that of someone known to her but whom she could not quite recognize, someone whose identity somehow eluded her or, rather, whose identity she could not quite bring herself to acknowledge.

My mother knew in reason, of course, that her father's body

was present, but during the short funeral service in the hotel ballroom it had occurred to her several times that her father was not really dead at all and locked away in the elaborate, brass-trimmed coffin. She would learn in later years that during the very moments when the three sons-in-law, along with her cousin Aubrey Bradbury and two other young kinsmen, were bearing the coffin down a center aisle that was arranged between hotel ballroom chairs—she would learn, that is to say, that other mourners beside herself had had that same fantasy.

Perhaps it seemed to nearly everyone present that day that whatever else might be inside that coffin it could not be the body of Senator Nathan Tucker of Tennessee. The Senator had always seemed to nearly everybody the liveliest and most alive of men. To all present, moreover, the tragedy of the Senator's death seemed almost beyond belief, if only because of the unlikeliness of the circumstance. They could not accept that this noble, gifted, vigorous, healthy man of sixty, who had been more of a gentleman–folk hero than a mere politician, had been brought down by something as ignoble and trivial-sounding as a gallstone operation.

Of far greater and more lasting significance, though, was the shock to the mourners that this ambitious and talented man would be destroyed at the very peak of his illustrious career in public life. (He had served three terms as governor and was at the beginning of his second term in the Senate.) No doubt the most difficult fact to be faced—or perhaps *not* to be faced—was that this distinguished son of an old country family, a family that had been distinguishing itself to an ever greater degree during every generation for more than a hundred years, should now be stricken at the very peak of his family's supreme elevation. Perhaps all the kin and connections assembled at the funeral were in fact saying to themselves, "We have invested so much confidence and hope in this man as chief of our tribe! In him who helped lead us back into the Union and resolved so many other conflicts within us! If he be dead now, to whom shall we turn to bolster our collective ego, and *where* shall we turn?" These Tennessee people were, in 1916, a people who still

identified themselves most often in terms of family ties. To
them the Senator's achievement represented generations of
hanging together in all things. Perhaps everyone present at the
funeral service understood this. Perhaps the notables present as
well as the fashionable Washington friends of the three daughters were more observing of the antediluvian family feelings
than were members of the family themselves. There was something altogether archaic about this family, something that made
it seem to step out of an earlier, simpler, nobler age.

Even while riding in the procession to the Union Station
and even when the coffin was being hoisted clumsily into the
baggage car of the waiting train, Gertrude Tucker Longford,
my mother, continued now and again to entertain her ugly
fantasy. Her papa's body *could not* lie inside that coffin! It was
not her gentle, witty, silver-maned, silver-tongued, her almost
beautiful papa who was dead, but some other senator, somebody else's head of family and chief of tribe, or just some other,
ordinary man of lower degree and less beloved than her papa.
Probably this seemed so to a lesser extent for her two sisters
also. Because once the three of them were closeted in their
drawing room, there in the second Pullman car of the funeral
train, with me sitting on the lap of first one of them then
another, each young woman positioned herself in the remotest-
seeming corner of the green-upholstered seats, fondling or
vaguely trying to entertain me from time to time but totally
disregarding her sisters and staring disconsolately into space as
if the end of the world had come and she were entirely alone
with her grief.

As Trudie Longford, my mother, quietly closed the drawing
room door that afternoon, the last face she saw out in the aisle
of the Pullman car was that of her cousin Aubrey Bradbury.
I was standing close by Mother's side, and Aubrey must have
observed the two of us there. I don't recall what my own
impression was. But Trudie observed, as she would tell me
many times afterward, that Aubrey wore a wounded expression on his heavy but weak-chinned face, and as she closed the
door he lowered his eyelids submissively as if acknowledging

Trudie's right to shut the door in his face. My own impression was, and remained so ever afterward, that his seemingly lowering his eyes actually represented his glancing down at me with a mixture of ire and resentment. My mother, at any rate, would be confronted by her cousin a good many other times before that journey was over, but she retained her impression always that that was the last time they ever looked directly into each other's eyes, that there was never again the exchange of communicative glances there once had been. After the Senator's lying-in-state in Nashville and after the subsequent burial at the cemetery in Knoxville, Trudie would never in effect look upon Aubrey's countenance again. When he did return rather mysteriously to attend my two aunts' funerals, not too many years later, he was unrecognizable to most people, and Mother had no substantive exchanges with him. His reappearances on those occasions seemed afterward more like apparitions, in most respects. And nobody learned anything of the whereabouts of his present residence or of his present mode of life—not that anybody knew how he learned about the funerals he attended, either. For more than forty years his real whereabouts would remain unknown to any member of the Tucker clan or to anyone in the entire connection. It was, as my mother and her sisters said, as though that day in the Knoxville cemetery the earth of East Tennessee had simply opened up and swallowed Aubrey Bradbury whole. From that moment he was no more among them, no more among us. From that time he became another of those men of good character who disappeared without leaving any explanation of their going.

MY POINTS OF reference regarding Cousin Aubrey's severance from the world he knew best would not be complete without mention of some other examples that come to mind. My father had a cousin in West Tennessee who set fire to his house and went off with a woman from a neighboring farm. His house was long since heavily insured, perhaps by design, and so he supposed he was not behaving dishonorably or even inconsiderately with his family. He had no concern about the welfare of his wife and children. At a later time word would come that this man wished to return home. But his wife's brothers went to him, wherever he had revealed himself to be, and forbade his coming back or even manifesting his present whereabouts to his wife and children. Most of us never knew where it was he had resettled or whether or not he and the woman from the neighboring farm had stayed together.

And then there was a banker in Nashville whom I would hear about during my childhood who left his office in the middle of one afternoon, without so much as taking his derby hat or his gold-headed cane with his monogram on the crown. They say he went out through the revolving door, like one of the ordinary clerks, with a pencil stuck behind his ear and just as though he were only stepping across the street for a few moments. His whereabouts were not known to us for more than twenty-five years. He did not abscond with any bank funds when he left, and his affairs were in perfect order. His greatest problem was said to be with demon rum. One sad part of the story was that when at last he was found he had altogether rid his life of that difficulty and was regarded as a model citizen in his new location. Sad, though, was not the word for what happened after he was discovered. When he was at last hunted down by a Nashville newspaper reporter ("Just for the story in it," so it was said), the two oldest children of the new family he had started locked themselves in their rooms and put bullets through their heads. It turned out that the banker and his former secretary, whom he had run off with, had opened a small hardware store somewhere in the Northeast and were operating a moderately successful business there. . . . I can assure you there were other instances, all the details of which I once knew as well as I know these. As for my wife and my son Braxton, they have always shown more interest in these stories with unhappy endings than in those that end merely in tantalizing mystery, which are more to my liking. Brax used to predict perversely that to find my cousin Aubrey Bradbury might do him irreparable harm. From the outset I felt that it was likely that the old man's rediscovery by a long-lost cousin, scarcely more than half his own age, might just as easily turn out to be a great boon for the old fellow—and would somehow certainly turn out so for me. Yet in my nightly dreams about him throughout the entire period of my search it would sometimes turn out one way and sometimes another. I cannot even now say for sure what our eventual reunion meant to either Aubrey or to me.

IF WHEN I WAS growing up I asked one of my fragile and ever-ailing aunts or my fragile but long-enduring mother whatever became of Aubrey, she was apt to stare off into space, genuinely bewildered—so it seemed to me—and murmur something like: "We don't know whatever happened to poor Aubrey. I am afraid none of us has kept track of him. Finally he just seemed to have vanished into thin air." They did not want to think about what may have become of him. They only wanted to talk of the trying times they had had with him on the funeral train. If at some other time and in quite another mood I asked if Aubrey had been like my manly father or like my equally manly uncles as a young man, I would likely be answered with a hoot of laughter. They thought my question utterly ridiculous. If all three of these ladies were present when I asked this question, there would come a chorus of "Oh, heavens, no! Not a bit! Not in the least! Not at all like any one of *them!* They were real men, your father and your uncles!" If at still another time I persisted, trying to arrive at some notion of the man, and suggested that perhaps after all he had been rather like those other men who disappeared, I was apt to be given a very straight look. Then there came an emphatic answer: "No *indeed!* Aubrey Tucker Bradbury was most certainly not like one of them! For Aubrey there was no ugly situation at home that *he* had to run away from!"

The phrase "ugly situation at home" was often used in connection with the hero Sam Houston and with our relative in West Tennessee who burned his own house, as well as with a good many others. Once during very recent years I happened to use that very phrase in discussing Cousin Aubrey with my son Brax, and when I quoted my mother to him on this subject I was at first shocked by Brax's burst of laughter. The fact was, Braxton was quite a young man at the time I speak of, and it only recently had been revealed to him that Aubrey Bradbury was actually an "outside cousin" of the Tucker family. I think this had not consciously been concealed from him, but it was rather that Aubrey's irregular kinship was seldom referred to by anyone. I don't recall at what age I stumbled upon the information that Aubrey was the illegitimate son of one of my maternal great-uncles and that Bradbury was actually his mother's surname. Upon my use of the all-too-familiar phrase, Brax, laughing out at me and slapping his thigh in the coarse manner he sometimes exhibits, exclaimed to me, "And you, Daddy—you and your mother and your aunts—you didn't call that 'an ugly situation at home'? Poor Cousin Aubrey! I hope you will never find him again!"

What I then felt I must explain to this son of mine was that in my mother's day—if not quite in my own—an illegitimate child like Aubrey was not put out for adoption and was not left to be brought up in disgrace by his unwed mother. Rather, he was drawn into the extended family, which was a reality in those quaint and distant days in Tennessee, and he was given the family's special protection both at home and abroad in the world. I said this was so, at any rate—or that I had been told so by my forebears—in the really best, the "most long-settled and best-regulated families" in our little up-country corner of the world. As soon as I had insisted upon this to Brax, however, I found myself recalling how my mother and aunts had come at last to regard Aubrey with the condescension and even contempt that their husbands had taught them to feel for him, and that the husbands, in their particular, masculine pride of that period, had always felt. My father and my uncles were all three of them sons of Confederate veterans and were themselves so thoroughly versed in Civil War history that aboard the funeral train they delighted in pointing out the sites of great battles and even small skirmishes. More than once I heard them laughing at Aubrey's ignorance of military history. At Culpeper, my father (whose name, incidentally, was Braxton Bragg Longford) went through the Pullman cars announcing to all that nearby was the spot where "the Gallant Pelham fell," and it had to be explained to Aubrey who that hero had been. Aboard the train there were many whispered conversations about the eccentric cousin's behavior. One night he was discovered in the area between the two Pullman cars, with his face in the crook of his arm, weeping aloud—ostensibly out of grief for his dead benefactor, the Senator. My two uncles discovered him there and led him into the men's smoking room where they administered large doses of whiskey out of their own flasks. And it was at some time on that long journey that I heard Uncle Hobart repeating what was allegedly my grandfather's own account of how he had gone to the simple mountain cabin where Aubrey was being reared until he was about school age and had "rescued" him from the rough people there, had placed him in Mr. Webb's school in Bell Buckle, where he was rather harshly disciplined and received a severely supervised classical education. But I think these incidents and stories did not impress me so strongly as did Cousin Aubrey's own contumelious glances at myself. Very early, though, I began to understand the resentment inspired in him by the mere sight of a boy who enjoyed every protection such a life as mine provided and the affection and even adoration of those three particular women who presided over my every activity. And by the time I was an adolescent I believe I could already conceive that an experience so totally different from mine could have a hardening and corrupting effect upon a being as sensitive to the affection and consideration of others as I believed myself to be.

I MUST TELL YOU now that when Aubrey Tucker Bradbury resurfaced in my life at last—nearly forty years after his first disappearance—he would resurface little by little, so to speak, inch by inch. That is, I began first of all merely to hear rumors of the existence of a man with a name much like his own, though not exactly like. The surname and the middle name had been reversed. And on the second occasion of my hearing of him it was indicated that the two names had been hyphenated—a most unusual practice for someone hailing from Tennessee. The old Cousin Aubrey in all representations of him had been so modest-sounding and unpretentious that I tended to dismiss the possibility of the two being one and the same. But once I had heard of the existence of this other man it registered indelibly on my mind. After the first report of him I was ever conscious of the remote possibility that this obviously different sort of man might still somehow be Aubrey.

Though it was always some place other than Tennessee that I heard his name spoken, it was inevitably added that his origins were there. It was this that made me first suspect that my mother and my two aunts might have been wrong in their assumption that Aubrey had merely disappeared into the East Tennessee countryside and had there resumed the role of a Tennessee bumpkin. It so happened that the first mention of his name reached my ears not in this country even but when I was traveling in Europe. Since I was not over there on a pleasure trip and was not paying my own expenses, I was put up at a rather better hotel than I normally would have been booked into. (My expenses were being paid by the very generous university where I taught art history in those days and partly by the Italian government, for whom I was helping to direct restoration of art works after the disastrous flood in Florence.) There in the dining room of the great hotel by the Arno I heard someone at the next table pronounce the name of Aubrey Bradbury-Tucker. The people at the table were alternately speaking English, German, and Italian. I listened carefully but was unable to grasp precisely the subject of the conversation. But I heard once again the articulation of that name. The party left the dining room without my ever making out their identity, though I assumed, correctly I think, that they too were involved somehow in the restoration at the Uffizi.

The next time I heard the man's name spoken was on a shuttle flight between New York City and Washington. A garrulous old lady sitting beside me on that short flight insisted on knowing where I was "from." When I told her I was from Charlottesville, she said knowingly that my accent didn't sound like "old Charlottesville" and that I must teach at the university there. (She of course "knew people" there and had often been a visitor.) I confirmed that all she said was so and confessed that I was originally from Tennessee. "Ah, Tennessee," she exclaimed. "Nashville I'll bet it is!" Then she proceeded to tell me about a wonderfully attractive man from Nashville—"so he claimed." She had made his acquaintance aboard a South American cruise ship and he had flirted with her "most scandalously." His name was Mr. Bradbury-Tucker —"hyphenated no less!" she said. And then she laughed her merry laugh again. Suddenly I could see just how attractive she herself had once been, and I could understand how delightful it would have been then to have found oneself on the South American cruise with her. She said that Mr. Bradbury-Tucker had had the most beautiful Vandyke beard she had ever seen on any man. And she said that when she told him so, he replied, with a twinkle in his bewitching brown eyes, that he only wore the beard in order to conceal "a very weak chin." Then she went on to say that Mr. Bradbury-Tucker had deceived her wickedly and that *she* had clearly meant nothing to *him*. Only on the last day of the cruise did she discover that Mr. Bradbury-Tucker was traveling in the company of another woman, a rich woman older than herself who during the voyage had kept mostly to their stateroom. I tried to reassure her—facetiously I suppose—that all Tennesseans were not such rascals, and I told her that my mother's maiden name had been Tucker and she had had a cousin named Bradbury. At this, the lady blushed to the roots of her snow-white hair. She made no further effort at conversation and managed not to hear further questions that

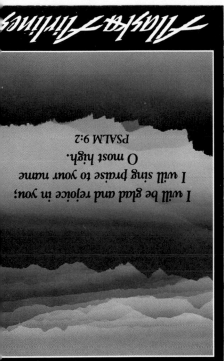

felt she was berating herself for
much to a stranger. When she got
way with the crowd without my
ne. But it was then that the fantasy
he country bumpkin, the outside
into the countryside of East Ten-
d with his erstwhile protector, the
at a new Aubrey had been released
ke on a new persona and perhaps
e upon the world.

ille some two years after that ride
really constructive piece of evi-
Tucker and our Cousin Aubrey
and the same. It was at a men's
fashioned academic circles—given
visiting lecturer, a man who was
appointment at the university.
tions committee, I felt reasonably
ccept such an appointment as we
was too celebrated, too "interna-
tional" an expert in his field, to be willing to settle down in
Charlottesville, Virginia. But he was our guest lecturer of the
day and we wished to please him. We happened on the subject
of the old days of railways and what a delight traveling had
been then. It turned out that our lecturer was a veritable collec-
tor of stories about trains. And of course, wishing to please
him, we all brought forward our stories on the subject. Perhaps
I, more than the others, insisted on being heard and was soon
running through my own repertoire. Yet I think everyone
present would have acknowledged that our guest more or less
urged me on.

When at length I proceeded to tell our lecturer about
Grandfather's funeral train, I was careful to speak only of the
comic aspects of the journey. In fact, I told him only about how
my two uncles ended by getting very drunk and so altogether
out of control that they had finally, first one and then a while
later the other, to be turned over to the constabulary in the first

two county seats where the train stopped after passing over the Tennessee state border.

Indeed I had hardly sketched in my account of those two incidents when our guest lecturer burst out at me, exclaiming "What a strange coincidence this is!" He bent forward and placed his well-manicured hand on my arm. But he was not even looking at me as he spoke. "This is a true story that I have heard before!" he said, bending toward me as he spoke. "How very strange! I do love such stories and most of all how I love to have them turn up in such dissimilar circumstances. I first heard of that train journey from a man by the name of Colonel A. N. Bradbury-Tucker and who himself was present on that funeral train and who was, moreover, a relative of this dead Senator whom you referred to up in the baggage car." (Obviously our guest lecturer had not bothered to catch my own name and my connection to the Senator, though I had already spent a day and a half in his company, squiring him about the university, introducing him to senior professors, deans, and one vice-president. Clearly he did not recall that I had identified the dead Senator as my grandfather.) Presently he continued: "He was a very odd sort of person, this Colonel Bradbury-Tucker, who told me his version of the same story. He was a very urbane and distinguished-seeming person. He was more like someone you might meet in Europe. One could not have guessed that his clothes even were American. He had a handsome beard, very beautifully trimmed. Altogether he was wonderfully well groomed in the old-fashioned way. He and I met in the house of a very wealthy old lady in Bristol, Rhode Island. I never knew exactly what *that* relationship was—his and the Rhode Island lady's—but I gathered from little things he let drop that he saw himself as a great lady's man. Anyway, he loved to talk about women—ever so confidingly. Perhaps he had a lot of money. He wished one, at any rate, to think so. Or perhaps he was the sort of man who lives off women. But the thing that interested me most about that funeral train he had been aboard was the presence there of the dead Senator's three young married daughters. I remember his holding up his forefinger and thumb like this and saying, 'They were absolutely delicious.' He was like some very cultivated gourmet describing a variety of his favorite dishes! He made great distinctions and differentiations with regard to the young ladies' three kinds of beauty. He referred to them as innocent young matrons all properly married and perfectly protected, of course, but knowing nothing of the world. 'Genuine provincials!' he said. 'And absolutely delicious!' "

Suddenly I felt deeply offended and wished to hear no more from our lecturer and no more of Colonel Bradbury-Tucker's view of my mother and my aunts. It was undoubtedly my Cousin Aubrey that the lecturer had known, but the picture that this latter-day Colonel Bradbury had painted was so far from what I had received from my mother and my aunts that I felt a kind of electric shock pass through me. When presently our talk was interrupted, I moved away from our guest lecturer and soon took my leave from the smoker. I was afraid that some faculty colleague present might mention to him that my mother's maiden name had been Tucker and that like the colonel, I too originally hailed from Tennessee. . . . I hardly need add that the lecturer did not receive the nomination of the selection committee, and that though I continued to read his distinguished scholarly works I never saw him in person again.

From that day forward I was sure of course that the man I had kept hearing about was my mother's cousin. For a certain period after that I was less sure than formerly that I still wished to come face to face with Cousin Aubrey. Yet curiosity about his incredible transformation caused my interest in his whereabouts and his ultimate fate to persist. If the long-ago journey on the Senator's funeral train changed all our lives in some degree and if the significance of those changes was what I longed to understand, then a meeting with Colonel Bradbury-Tucker—surely the most altered of us all—might facilitate my understanding. Only to look upon the man's countenance might solve mysteries about myself.

Very soon Aubrey's resurfacing in my life was destined to come one inch closer. In Charlottesville, Virginia, there are many people, especially among the university faculty, who subscribe to the *Washington Post* as their morning newspaper. But since my wife is a native of a small town in Southside Virginia, we have always read the *Richmond Times-Dispatch* for our morning paper and purchased the *New York Times* at the newsstand on the corner. And that is how I happened to miss—or very nearly miss—seeing the newspaper picture of Colonel Bradbury-Tucker. I first beheld his visage not in a paper that was delivered to my doorstep, and not in one for sale at a newsstand, but in a fragment of newsprint wrapped around a vegetable that my wife brought from the curb market. It was from an issue of the *Washington Post* that was at least three weeks old. Even as the newspaper crossed my vision on its way to the trash can I received an impression of the erect figure and the slightly out-of-focus face that was in the background of the photograph reproduced thereon. I quickly fished it out and spread it on the enamel-topped kitchen table. It purported to be a picture of one of those Washington hostesses whose entertainments one generally avoids unless one is seeking office or has some other self-interested purpose requiring one's presence there. The caption under the picture gave the famously rich hostess's name, of course, describing her as one of Washington's most celebrated socialites. She was apparently so rich and so celebrated that it seemed worthwhile to mention even her slightly out-of-focus escort in the background, one Colonel A. N. Bradbury-Tucker. At last I had a blurred but indubitable image of the man Aubrey Tucker Bradbury had become. Though his beard was white, it seemed to me an absolute facsimile of the streaked gray beard my grandfather had worn in pictures taken not long before his death. And even though the image of his face was blurred, the dark eyes looked out piercingly toward the camera, just as the Senator's had always done in his campaign pictures, those which Mother kept locked away in her leather-bound scrapbook and produced periodically for my admiration and edification. And I had the eerie feeling that indeed it had been the old Cousin Aubrey whose death had come that September day in 1916 and that it was his body that had been substituted for the dead Senator's in the elaborately brass-trimmed coffin that was handed so clumsily onto the special funeral train.

The Real Ghost

HE WAS A MAN who kept nearly always to his own style; and
not even in the present unlikely circumstances would it have
been Hal's style to make a headlong retreat down the stairs. He
prided himself above all things on "keeping his cool." Before
beginning his descent he had halted abruptly at the next to top
step of the stairway, and he brought his hand up to his parted
lips, feeling with his fingers the very dry coolness of those lips.

How long he remained poised so on the top step he couldn't
afterward have said. But he did know afterward, when he stood
at the foot of the stairs again, just what he had confronted
upstairs, though he did not know for how long a time he saw
what he saw. What he had clearly seen was a face illumined in
a bedroom looking glass and again in an uncurtained glass of
a hall window, the outside louvered blinds of which were
closed against the reflecting pane. In both instances it was the
living and distinctly roseate face of someone other than himself
that he saw. And yet he recognized there a being so like himself, too! That was the primary observation that he had had
time to make. On the other hand the face in both reflections
seemed to wear an expression that was wan and strangely eager
to find some focus for its at once vacuous and possessive eye.
It was not really of course a face that a man of his style and
temperament could believe in. He instinctively doubted every

appearance of self-possession or possibility of emotion that it presented to his view. Yet he knew that for a time the image that repeated itself in each pane of glass caused his teeth literally to chatter in his head. But he was not sure for how long a duration the chattering continued. It might almost have been in each instance for only a matter of seconds.

Anyway, when he turned and headed back down the stairs, the turn backward had been abrupt and his descent was swift if not precipitant (precipitance would certainly not have been his style!). It was at something less than a run that he came down. Yet at the bottom of the long, curved flight, while passing his left hand over the well-remembered newel post there, Hal Crawley saw that hand of his tremble—oh, ever so lightly, indeed almost imperceptibly.

The sight of the trembling hand and the thought of the teeth chattering upstairs now almost made Hal laugh aloud. But not quite. That too was not his style. Trembling and teeth-chattering were so exactly what one was supposed to manifest on seeing a ghost! And who believed in ghosts nowadays? Especially in broad daylight, especially in a house where one had grown up, and more especially in the house which, though full of furniture, had stood empty of people since the day of its late owner, who was of course Hal Crawley's own late father. The house and the furniture in it seemed positively unfamiliar to Hal. But houses and furniture were not the sorts of things he ever paid much attention to. And strangely enough that was what his father's banker, and the trust officer, and the crass real estate broker, too, had had the gall downtown to laugh at him about—as though it were something missing in his nature. And *this* from men who were supposed to be men of business.

He had not quite run down the stairs; he didn't quite laugh while crossing the familiar front hallway to the living room, and seeing the mist of his own breath before him, he told himself it was much too serious a circumstance for laughing. At his age and with his tendencies—at near fifty and with his lifelong tendency to "rigors"—he was apt to take his death of cold hanging about this long-unheated house. *That's* what was serious! Whatever the apparition he had experienced at the top of the stairs had been, it was most likely, so he told himself now, the *result* of the chill which had come into his bones—*not* the cause of that chill.

He went striding across the hall and into the living room. He did so with a sudden hope that he might actually find a fire already laid in the fireplace there. Or, more accurately, he went with the sudden knowledge that he would find such a fire laid. For if the house was truly furnished just as his father left it—as the Trust Department at the bank insisted it be, in order to make it more attractive to a prospective buyer—then there would most certainly be a log fire, complete with paper and lightwood, laid on the brass andirons.

The fireplace was seldom used when Hal was growing up in the house—only at Thanksgiving, at Christmas, at New Year's. But his father had forever insisted that the servants keep a fire laid, in case of an emergency, a fire laid and a box of matches on the mantel shelf. The contingency which the old man had explicitly anticipated was a power failure. But of course there were other kinds of contingencies. Although a power failure had occurred only once during all the years past—when a winter ice storm deprived the whole city of electricity for a few hours—still old Mr. Crawley had remained eternally vigilant; so long as he had lived he was fond of reminding his son of the one occasion when the fire did become a necessity, sometimes exaggerating the duration of that emergency by many hours. And always, under the metal match box on the mantel shelf he had kept written instructions of how to open the damper and at what place to drop the match.

Hal found that there was indeed, as he had predicted, a fire laid in the living room! There was even the inevitable box of wooden kitchen matches on the mantel shelf. As he hurriedly took down the box and withdrew a match it seemed a wonder to him that the Trust Department, with all the rules and regulations imposed upon him since his father's death, had not had all matches removed from the house. The trust officers had been so damnably thoroughgoing in their other safety precautions! It was all like something left over from his childhood. Because of them the furnace could not be kept in operation. They had had the electricity and gas and water cut off last March 15, the very day following his father's funeral. But the regular cardboard match box he found on the mantel was contained in the ornamented copper casing that Hal's mother had felt, in her day, made kitchen matches acceptable in the living room. He felt before him one last trial of obedience to household customs that had once ruled his life. Perhaps the bank people had not recognized the object on the mantel shelf as a match box or had considered the copper casing a sufficient safety precaution.

But the matches *were* there in their old accustomed place. And as he stooped down, match in hand, Hal saw that the fire was laid precisely in its old, accustomed place in the very style his father had perfected. It had clearly been laid under the direction of his father—not last year, because in that year of his father's final illness there had certainly been no fire lit during the winter holidays; and probably not during the entire winter before, because that was the year when Hal's mother lay wasting away in the big bedroom above the living room. Mr. Crawley had been too dispirited to think of fires then, too concerned over the physical suffering of his wife and possibly too absorbed in memories of anguish that his own awful bursts of bad temper and his own overbearing nature had caused his wife in her lifetime. It seemed to Hal that his father and mother had been forever apologizing for things they had said to each other or each continually reassuring the other about imagined slights that neither of them had intended. What a trying household it had been to grow up in! Perhaps that was why he never himself ever thought of marrying. Perhaps it was why he went into the army for three years and came back to live not at home but in an apartment-hotel downtown. (*Everything* furnished!) And now every old piece of furniture and every old feeling of any kind devolved upon him to be disposed of! And, oh, he would dispose of it all forthwith. Momentarily he felt sure that the fire had been laid there in the living room a number of years back, during the last year of his father's life, when the old man had seemed to spend most of his hours mulling over things he and "Mother" had said or not said to each other.

Now striking the match on the hearth and lighting the crumpled newspaper, which would no doubt have given him the very date on which the fire was laid if he had really cared to know, Hal Crawley watched the flames blaze up from the paper, watched those flames ignite the knotty lightwood with small explosions and then blaze over the dry bark of the neatly stacked logs. At first there was no smoke, only clear golden flames. Then, squatting on the hearth, with the fire screen set to one side, Hal seemed to be hurled back suddenly by the very heat itself. No, it was more than the heat that made him go back so suddenly on his haunches! And now in the eccentric configuration of the flames he saw again the ghostly face that had appeared to him in the looking glass and in the window pane upstairs.

He had pushed himself backward halfway across the room before his sight returned. He saw that the smoke was now pouring out the upper corners of the fireplace opening and rising along the paneled overmantel toward the ceiling. In his stupefaction he could only think of how "excellently" his father had always maintained that that chimney drew. When he had built the house his father had not left a matter so important as chimney construction to the architect, much less to the contractor. He had supervised the chimney's construction himself. If there was one thing he did know, Mr. Crawley had said, it was how a chimney must be built if it was to draw properly. (What a thing to know!) Above all, it had to be *shouldered* correctly! He was a man who had grown up in the country, in the days when the draft in a fireplace was a vital matter. It had been in an old end-chimneyed house on the Tennessee-Kentucky state line, forty miles above the city of Nashville where he subsequently established himself in business and brought up his own family. Suddenly now Hal could visualize the wide, open chimney flues in his grandfather's old house and recalled his father's complaint that they had had no dampers in them. Then all at once Hal sprang forward into the billowing smoke before him, pushing his own face into the face he saw there. He had forgotten after all to open the damper! Even at the risk of encountering that same face again he rushed headlong—so to speak—into the smoke, seized the iron ring just below the lintel, and opened the damper which his father had designed and installed there. The smoke poured upward and the flames brightened and shot upward following the smoke, and immediately much of that smoke which had been hovering over the hearth whooshed inside the iron facing and up the chimney. And suddenly Hal felt completely detached from the whole room he was in. And the whole house seemed not at all his style!

Now Hal moved about the living room, hoisting up windows and fanning the air with the morning newspaper, which until then had been folded under his arm. Though he felt an essential shiver run through his body, he was warmed somewhat by the activity itself and by the fire which now blazed handsomely inside and beyond the hearth. His thoughts were temporarily diverted from the apparition at the top of the stairs as well as that in the first burst of smoke. All at once he felt firm in a new resolve to sell the house. The faces in the windows and in the smoke disappeared forever from view. The banker and the trust officer and the dread real estate broker—all expected to join him here this morning and whose arrival was already overdue—haunted him momentarily as spirits and then vanished into reality. Hal could already imagine himself being blamed for filling the house with smoke and thus perhaps making decoration of the living room necessary before the house could be sold. But he scoffed at the idea as he stood before the flames and was his own master.

In the Waiting Room

ANYONE COULD TELL at a glance the two men were brothers. They entered the hospital waiting room speaking to each other in whispers, each holding his hand up to his mouth in precisely the same way. The family resemblance was unmistakable—in their features, in their gestures, even in the way middle age was beginning to tug at their under-chins. Yet their dress was so different—one's was so roughly rural looking, and the other's so very elegantly urban—their haircuts were so different, and even the trim of their fingernails, that they seemed in a sense hardly creatures of the same species. It was nine-thirty of a Saturday morning, and these two brothers were entering the seventh-floor waiting room of the Methodist Hospital. Outside the row of windows on the west side of the room was spread the city of Memphis. In the relatively near distance out there— some eight or nine blocks away—could be seen the brick and concrete towers of the Baptist Hospital and Campbell's Clinic and the U.T. Medical Complex. Two miles or so beyond that were the half-dozen near-skyscrapers of downtown Memphis, stretched out along the Mississippi River. And beyond the river, as everyone in the waiting room that morning so well knew, lay Arkansas.

In the row of chairs by the windows sat a red-haired man and two women. The man, in plaid jacket and gray trousers, was seated between the women. On his left was his sister, also with red hair, not so coppery as the man's and showing more signs of gray. The diminutive brown-haired woman on his right was his wife. All three figures were twisted halfway round in their chairs and were gazing silently out the windows. Against the north wall of the room sat a solitary young man. He was dark haired, dark eyed, dark suited—he even wore dark, pointed-toe shoes. But his socks were white, and he wore a white shirt, open at the collar. When the two whispering brothers entered the room, the threesome at the window turned around. The diminutive brown-haired woman straightened herself in her chair and asked formally, "How do you find Mrs. Schofield this morning? Did she rest well?"

"She's resting nicely," said the brother in khaki trousers—the brother, that is, in a homeknit-looking cardigan sweater and high, waterproof shoes.

The other brother smiled politely and shrugged. He clearly meant, by so doing, to qualify or even contradict his brother's favorable report on the patient in question. This patient, Mrs. Schofield, was the two brothers' aged mother, who at eighty-seven lay in a coma in a private room down the corridor. The old lady's heart had begun weakening two days before, and in the time since her two sons were called to her bedside her condition had continued to worsen almost hourly. Except that he knew his brother so well, it would have been difficult for the brother in the navy blue suit (and neatly knotted houndstooth tie) to understand how anyone could describe their mother as "resting nicely." Only his brother's country timidity, he reasoned, and his country way of wishing to answer all questions as briefly as possible could account for the falsehood he uttered in reply. And when they had seated themselves on a vinyl couch against the south wall of the waiting room, the blue-suited brother, after carefully adjusting his tie and straightening his ribbed socks, returned the little, brown-haired woman's courtesy, asking, "And how is your father-in-law this morning?"

BEFORE THE WOMAN could answer, both her red-haired husband and her red-haired sister-in-law spoke for her, spoke almost in one voice and in identical words: "He is still a very sick man." Then the two of them smiled at the rather comical coincidences of their expressions, as also did the two brothers. Apparently the coincidence struck the solitary young man, across the room, as being somewhat more than merely comical. He gave a sudden, loud guffaw.

Everyone's attention was at once turned on him. But in the split second required for them to direct their eyes toward him, all sign of mirth vanished from his sallow face. He gazed at them solemnly for a moment with his dark eyes. Then casting his eyes downward and lifting one rather delicately formed hand, he pretended to brush imaginary crumbs from his shirt-front. Since he was the only decidedly young person in the room, the others were able to view his indiscretion with some degree of tolerance. Perhaps they felt especially indulgent toward him since, on the preceding two days, he had always appeared there in the company of an old woman, an old country woman whom he had permitted to describe herself to the group—without any protest on his part—as his "grandma" and whom he had suffered to pat him on the knee or hand each time she did so.

The other occupants rested their eyes on the young man for a moment, and then they looked at each other. Regardless of this interruption, the brown-haired little woman who had first spoken now seemed determined to give her own account of her father-in-law's condition this morning. She sat on the edge of her chair and gave two little clicks to the latch of her handbag. "Dad Jones is still a very sick man," she said in an almost challenging tone to her red-haired husband and sister-in-law. And in a politer tone to the two brothers on her right she added, "But he is doing as well as could be expected after surgery—and at his age. We are quite hopeful that he may

improve as the day goes on." Her husband and her sister-in-
law looked at her in open dismay. Her optimistic tone seemed
almost to make them laugh. And presently they both seemed
to be trying to get the attention of the brother in the houndstooth tie, to try to convey to him with a look the true state of
their father's health: that he most probably would not last the
day. Yet they only looked; they said nothing.

ALL OF THESE people had made each other's acquaintance
during the previous two days. All—even the young man seated
against the north wall, as well as his grandma who was this
morning in the sick-room with her husband—all were aware
of a number of important factors in their lives which they had
in common. Each of them, for instance, had originated either
on a farm or in a small town in Arkansas; the family of each
had been generally dispersed and were for the most part living
in Memphis, if not still farther afield; and the old persons to
whose bedsides all had now come were alike not only in being
regarded as "terminal cases" but in having been brought to the
Methodist Hospital after long sojourns in Memphis nursing
homes. This body of information about the experience they
shared had not been revealed or comprehended by them in any
one dramatic moment or in any series of such moments, and
no open acknowledgment of it had been made at all. But during the previous days the information had been gradually and
quietly assimilated. A general knowledge had been repressed,
most probably, because—until this morning—there had always
been present some non-Arkansan, some hospital visitor whose
patient was not critically ill, some visitor whose patient was not
his eldest and nearest of kin, someone, that is, who could not
have understood all they had in common.

Just when the two brothers and the threesome at the window had completed their exchanges—both spoken and silent—
and the brothers had seated themselves across the room from
the solitary young man, there appeared in the doorway an old
country woman. Although she was wearing a different dress

this morning and had combed her long, gray hair more carefully than yesterday, even having inserted additional combs
where her hair was thickest above the temples, she was recognized by all as the young man's grandma. She was a remarkably
tall old woman with narrow shoulders and wide hips, and she
wore an ankle-length dress made of a bright cotton print—
orange splashes mixed with greens and blues. One could not
fail to notice the dress before noticing the face of the woman,
its colors were so bright and cheerful and the cut of the material so generous. She glided into view there in the wide doorway like a boat with a calico sail. Instantly upon seeing her, the
dark young man turned his face away to the window. It was
as though he were embarrassed by the sight. But the old
woman, whose eyes were as bright a blue as any of the several
blues in her dress, seemed momentarily unaware of her grandson, or at least no more aware of him than of the others present.
"Well, I declare," she said, still hesitating in the doorway and
looking about the room. "Well, I declare. It's nobody but *us*
this morning."

Her declaration was made in a rather high-pitched drawl,
and her voice revealed more astonishment than joy over the
company she found. Her blue eyes, in their deep sockets,
darted glances about the room as though she were made uncomfortable by her discovery, or even were frightened by it.
Remaining just inside the doorway, it was almost as if she had
stumbled into the wrong waiting room and might yet turn
back. While she stood there, her glance did not once settle
upon the figure of her grandson. Finally she repeated in a more
composed and cheerful tone: "Nobody but *us* this morning."

As if in response to this somehow, the brother in the sweater
and khaki trousers came quickly to his feet. "Now, don't go
getting up for me," the old woman protested. "There are
plenty of chairs and to spare." But the red-haired man by the
window stood up also. And after him the brother in the
houndstooth tie—he smiling, and somewhat shame-faced.
Surely their getting up this way in a public room, for a woman
whose very name they barely knew, was something none of

them would have done if there had been anyone besides themselves present.

And now the wife of the red-haired man was about to inquire about the old woman's husband. She had parted her lips to speak when the old woman herself interrupted. "I do declare," she said, looking at the men who were still on their feet, "I never saw so many gentlemen in one room."

At this, her grandson came also to his feet. As he did so he continued to gaze toward the window without having once looked at the old woman in the doorway. It was as if he could not bear to look at her, or perhaps did not dare to. Yet it was his rising that the old woman seemed to find altogether overwhelming. The moment he was on his feet, she rushed to his side and threw her great frame down in a chair beside him. "Now!" she said. "Now you all sit down. Standing up that way you make me feel a thousand and one years old." She sounded positively silly, almost flirtatious. "I may have one foot in the grave," she went on, "but I still don't want everybody putting themselves out for me."

When the men had sat down again, this old country woman bent forward in her chair and fixed her gaze on the view outside the window, the view from which her grandson had still not taken his eyes. "I do declare it's a beautiful day out there, despite everything," she said. "And hasn't this Memphis grown into a fine city. It don't seem like the same place it used to be. Not the town I came to fifteen years ago when my own mamma was sick and I had brought her over here to Methodist. Nothing looks the same. It's a lot prettier place now, though. Tall skyscrapers over yonder, so flat and white, like fence posts coming up so straight out of the green trees. Like so many tombstones, they are—like whitewashed tombstones in some nice, well-kept cemetery."

The old woman's burst of loquacity seemed to be amazing to everybody present. Even her grandson stole a glance at her. Yesterday and the day before—at moments when self-introductions were being made—she had rather grudgingly explained to the other visitors who she was, who her grandson was, and who their patient was, but for the most part she had remained grim faced and silent—no less so than her grandson, himself. And now they all suddenly recognized in her a different type, recognized the garrulous old country woman whom you could not afford to encourage lest she bend your ear all day.

Except for the stolen glance from her grandson, there was no response whatsoever to her lyrical outburst about Memphis. After a moment or two of silence, during which she and the young man beside her continued to gaze out the window, she spoke again. "We had a right bad time with Mr. Glover last night," she said, her eyes still on the skyline. "He took a notion he *would* leave the hospital!"

The brother in the cardigan sweater exclaimed, "You don't say!"

The tiny, brown-haired woman sat forward in her chair, and her eyes widened noticeably.

The others looked at her with obvious interest. Who "Mr. Glover" was there could be no doubt. Even if they had not known the woman's own name was Glover, her listeners could have told from her old-fashioned, wifely tone that it was her husband she referred to. "I was nodding in my chair beside his bed," she went on, "when all of a sudden the poor patient in the *other* bed commenced shouting, 'He's out of his head. You better watch him!' Or maybe he said, 'He's out of his bed.' That's what woke me. And *there* was Mr. Glover leaning against the bed, so weak he couldn't hardly stand, peeling off his nightshirt. I hauled myself up out of my chair and asked him, 'And where do you think you're going, Mr. Glover— naked as a bluejay?' . . . 'I want my clothes,' he said, like some bad little old boy." The old woman rolled her eyes around the room almost kittenishly. She put her hand to her mouth and seemed to laugh into it.

The young man turned and faced the old woman. "And how come you didn't send after me," he asked, "if he was making trouble?"

"Oh, you've done your share of sitting with him," she answered solemnly, and then she addressed the room: "He sat with his granddaddy many an hour of the night when he was a little fellow coming along."

"Only to keep you from having to, I did," the young man growled, turning back toward the window.

"Many's the night he'd rub his granddaddy's legs and his back and hear his complaints about how he hurt. You see, he stayed home with us till he was near twenty, and then, of course, he went off to New York City where he'd always said he was going to go when he got to be grown." She had told all of this to the room only yesterday, but it had been something dragged out of her then. "You see, we raised the boy ourselves," she continued with enthusiasm. "His daddy left his mamma and cleared out before the little fellow was a year old, and his mamma—she was mine and Mr. Glover's only child— died on us, passed away not two years after her husband left. The boy stayed with us till he was near twenty, and after he left, it wasn't long till Mr. Glover became more than I could handle. He was in such pain we didn't reckon he'd last long, so we put him over here in Mrs. Hooker's Nursing Home, all against his will, poor fellow."

The young man crossed his legs and recrossed them again. "You mean *I* did," he growled. And then he addressed the room: "The old guy was killing her, what with her having to wait on him hand and foot around the clock. He would have done her in, in no time. Besides which, he saw his end was coming on and, clear as anything, he wanted to take her with him was what he wanted. It was *me* that put him in the nursing home."

"Why, yes, indeed," agreed the old woman. "This here boy has sent back the money for it every month that comes. And to begin with he came back to Memphis from New York City and rented a car and came over and carried Mr. Glover over here to Mrs. Hooker's Nursing Home."

The young man crossed his legs again, his white socks flashing. "Against his will," he said with emphasis. "He hasn't ever forgave me for it, either. Against *her* will, too. It's a nice, clean place, though, where we put him, and they know how to look after him. He's been there four years, and *she's* still alive because of it."

"Which Home is that you've had him in?" asked the red-haired man. "Did you say 'Hook's'?"

"No, Hook's—" …

…suited brother, who, like …ung man's words with … private Homes here in …ssman and spoke with … is way in the Memphis … subject he had made a … he felt his information … some use of. "I believe … colored—and that the … st above average."

…," said the red-haired … onsidered himself also …expert. We've learned a good deal about them through trial and error," he said, smiling meaningfully at his sister. "And we've come to the conclusion that they're all about the same."

"Yes," said his sister. "Give a little here, take a little there, they're all about the same. We should know." She, too, felt that here was a subject she could speak on with some authority and therefore with some pleasure. "We've had Father in five places, all told. Each one was a little more expensive than the one before, and, as for Dad, he's liked each one we've put him in a little bit less than the one before. But they're all about the same."

"Relatively speaking, yes," said the blue-suited brother. He gave a depreciative laugh. "Anyway, however good they are, the old folks don't seem to like them. It's like sending a child to his first day of school. He doesn't like it and doesn't know it's for his own good."

The old woman shifted in her chair and cleared her throat. Then she ventured, "Well, some places, they tell me, are pretty bad."

"Ah, listen to her," said the young man, his eyes still on the window.

"Oh, yes, some of them *are* bad," said the little wife by the window. "They treat the patients—the residents, that is—like animals, as Dad Jones used to say of one place, like animals in a zoo. And I heard of another place where they regularly get the patients' medicine mixed up."

Her husband came in quickly: "That's only hearsay. And, furthermore, Dad was ever one of the worst to complain. *We* knew that as children. Even Mamma used to say so. You've just known him as an old man." He looked at his sister out of the corner of his eye, and they smiled at each other rather sadly, shaking their heads. His wife was overly indulgent, they seemed to say.

But his wife, diminutive and bright-eyed, cocked her head to one side, and as she spoke, it was hard to tell if she was addressing her husband and sister-in-law or the whole room. "I don't care," she began, "but if we had kept him at home out at Marianna, he would have been happier, he wouldn't have been so bored. Why, his mind—his memory—began to slip as soon as he left our house."

Her husband looked at her sympathetically and said, "My father stayed with *us,* and she was working herself to the bone for *my* father. She was ruining her health. People ought not to do that, not even for their *own* kin."

"We could have—" his wife began again.

But the old woman interrupted. "I don't mean to say that Mrs. Hooker's Home is one of these bad ones." She was clearly afraid she had offended her grandson and wished to placate him. "Not at all. They're nice folks there, and we were lucky to have gotten Mr. Glover in, and mighty lucky, I say, to have the money to keep him there. It's only because the boy here worked so hard in New York City and sent the money back. But, still, I do hear some of the places are pretty bad."

"They're all fairly well regulated nowadays," said the blue-suited brother reassuringly. "The quality of the meals may differ, and the beds, I suppose. I made a thorough investigation of them before we decided on one for Mother."

The other brother, in his cardigan and waterproof shoes and khaki trousers, had sat with his eyes lowered during most of this talk. Even now he kept his eyes lowered to his hands, and he spoke in a gentle and rather cultivated voice that contrasted with his rough clothing. "There's only this," he said. "There's only this: there are things that cannot be foreseen about these arrangements we make." He lifted his eyes and let his gaze move from face to face around the room. All his timidity seemed gone suddenly. "We had an uncle, our mother's brother—an old bachelor like me, he was—who farmed Mother's home-place near Jonesboro after our grandfather over there died. When he, our uncle, got too old to farm and to look after himself he went into a—a church-run rest home over near Pine Bluff. What they have to do in those church-run places, you know, is sign over all their property and savings to the church home, which agrees to care for them for the rest of their lives and even give them pocket money. Well, they put him in a nice private room and all that. It was fine for the first six months or so. But he came down with a chest cold. They transferred him to an infirmary, put him in an open ward. When he improved, he found he had to be put on a waiting list in order to get his private room back. He was a timid, country fellow and hated being in the ward with all the talkative, retired preachers who were there. He got worse again, and he died before he could ever get his private room back."

There was a general head-shaking around the room and a chorus of "oh"s. But the blue-suited brother, who was clearly distressed by being reminded of this family story, said, "They treated the old fellow badly, no doubt about that. But there are nearly always two sides to such a story. Uncle Ned never made a good trade in his life. Yet he was very independent; he didn't consult any of the family about his agreement with that place. And Lord knows it wasn't much he had to sign over to the church. They didn't make any fortune off him, that's certain."

"Your Uncle Ned's story," said the red-haired man spirit-edly, as though he were in an argument and had thought of a good point, "is just the opposite of the way the story usually goes. Your uncle went into the home of his own volition and then regretted it. My father, for instance, didn't want to go, but it became a way of life with him. Much as he has complained and moved from one place to another, he has almost never talked about coming back to us or to my sister here. He's made friends in each place and he keeps up with which ones are still around and which have passed on."

"Well, as for our mother in there," said the blue-suited brother, gesturing toward a door down the corridor, "she has made some awfully good friends and had some awfully gay times since she settled at Mount Holly, which is where she had been for three years until now. When my wife and I went by to see her on her last birthday, they were having a big birthday party for her. Why, those old ladies and old gentlemen at Mount Holly had loaded her with presents, and they were all having the time of their lives. And it isn't just the social life Mother has liked at Mount Holly. There are charity patients—even there at Mount Holly. Mother likes giving them money and clothes. And there are even colored patients, and Mother has found it interesting working out relationships with them. In fact, it is a regular microcosm of life there—not at all a feeling of isolation. I don't believe Mother has had an unhappy day since she settled at Mount Holly."

"You mean, don't you," said the brother in khaki, "since *we* settled her there."

"Yes, we had a time making her decide to go," agreed his brother in blue. "They couldn't keep her on the farm. Someone would have to be forever preparing special meals for her and driving her in town to the doctor. And here in Memphis—well, my teenage children would have driven her out of her head. And my wife and I go out—"

"That night," his brother interrupted, "when we went to her on the porch and told her we had made the arrangements at Mount Holly, she took her cane and got up and walked without help down into the yard. She wouldn't let us help her or go with her. She went by herself. And we had a hard time finding her, later. But when we did, she laughed at us and asked if we thought she was going to do harm to herself. She kept up her teasing ways with us and her good sense of humor through it all. I still think sometimes she might have got along all right there at the farm with me."

His brother threw back his head and laughed. "Without another woman on the farm? Why, you'd have had to get married, Harry, so you'd have a wife to look after her." Now his laughter was hearty. "You know you wouldn't have liked that, Harry," he said.

The little, brown-haired wife said quite earnestly, "Yes, a woman on the place might really have made it so you could."

The bachelor brother smiled and shrugged. And the married brother said, "Anyway, she gave us quite a scare that night and, believe you me, she enjoyed it. She's always been a great tease."

"But that's nothing," said the red-haired man. "That's nothing at all to what Dad put us through. You wouldn't have thought a man with his diabetic neuritis, a serious heart ailment, and nearly blind and deaf could put us through what he did. At home, he kept firing the nurses we got him, as if to prove he didn't need looking after. And he swore that the nurses beat him whenever all the rest of us were out of the house. If the nurses beat him in his own house, he meant for us to understand, what would they do to him at a nursing home? And then finally he proposed marriage to a neighbor woman who came in to see him, promising to leave her all his property but forgetting she already had one invalid husband to take care of."

There was a general tittering in the room. Then the red-haired sister-in-law asked, "But what is one to do with old people?" It was quite as though this woman and the others present didn't understand that the old woman sitting against the north wall was really an old person who might soon be facing the fate of those they were discussing. But even the old woman, herself, didn't seem to realize it. With the others, she nodded sympathetically to the rhetorical question. "What is one to do?" the red-haired woman repeated. "We all wish they didn't have to end their days in those places. But I live in an apartment two blocks from here, with my husband and our two children. My husband and I both work downtown, and we're not young anymore. Yes, you know, the trouble is this: the old people's young people are not really young people any longer. And in every case there are the problems of the home and children. Life has to go on even where there are old people and sick people. The problems become just too much. It's not like the old days on an Arkansas farm where there was plenty of time and plenty of room, and plenty of hands, too, for taking care of the old folks."

"Let me tell you," the dark young man joined in abruptly, turning his eyes from the window to the room. "Yes, just let me tell you. The day when I came back home in the car I had rented in Memphis, I found my grandma here looking like a skeleton. She was worked to the bone and about fit for burying, herself. I ran up the stairs to my granddaddy's room and told him to get out of that bed, told him I knew a doctor in Memphis could cure him and get rid of all that pain in his legs and back, and told him I had the money to pay for it, which part was true. I don't think I'd ever told him a lie before in my life. And no matter how many lickings he had give me, I hadn't ever hated him before, either, because in his way he was good to me when I was coming along without any dad of my own— as good to me in his way as *she* was. I hadn't ever hated him until I saw what skin and bones he had wore her down to. But I knew I had to hate him, that day, and lie to him till I got him over here to Mrs. Hooker's Home, where I had already paid a hundred dollars down for him. He and I left Grandma crying in the hall there at home and I lied to him all the way over to Memphis and even after he was in his room at Mrs. Hooker's. Oh, he found out in a few days that the doctor who came to see him was nothing special and that we weren't going to let him go home again. But it was too late then. He hasn't ever forgave me, either. He hasn't ever forgave me. Every time my grandmother would go to see him there at Mrs. Hooker's, he would spend half the visit railing against me. But I had to do it, and I'm not a bit sorry. You can't let them take the living with them!"

"No," said the blue-suited brother.

"No, you can't," agreed the red-haired man. And his sister nodded her head in agreement.

"But it's hard," said the little wife.

"I've found it hard," said the brother in the sweater, "to think of her over here in Memphis when she might have been at home where she wanted to be."

The old woman shifted her weight in her chair. Then she cleared her throat and spoke openly to the whole company: "The worst part of it, though, you haven't come near touching on. And like as not, you haven't known it yet. When Mr. Glover climbed out of bed last night, and I asked, 'Where do you think you're going, naked as a bluejay?' he answered me, 'Get me my clothes, woman. I'm leaving out of here. It's going home, I am.' 'All right,' I say to him, 'but not tonight. It's some fifty miles to Mark Tree. We'll have to wait till sun-up.' I could see he was half out of his head and only meant to humor him. But he said, 'It ain't your home I want to go to, woman. I want to go back to Mrs. Hooker's Home. That's where the only friends I have are. That's where they know how to give me some ease.' "

Suddenly the old woman, looking out across the room to the doorway, began to shed silent tears. The young man looked up as if he had never before in his life seen her cry and so didn't know what to do. And it was just then that he and the others saw the nurse who had appeared in the doorway. Silently, the plump little nurse crossed the tile floor and stood before the old woman. "He's gone," the nurse said in a voice full of gentleness.

"What do y' mean?" asked the young man, coming to his feet.

"All right, ma'am," said the old woman to the nurse. Then she said, "Sit down, son." The nurse glanced at the young man, then turned and left the room without looking at anyone else.

"Does she mean—he's dead?" asked the young man, sitting down beside the old woman.

"No, son, he died somewhile earlier," she answered gently. "The nurse means they've taken his remains out and to the undertaker's."

"How come you didn't say so? How come you sat here talking?"

Now it was only the old woman who stared out the window. She raised her two hands to her head, lifted the combs that were just above her temples and replaced them more firmly in her thick hair. "You wouldn't have liked being in there," she explained. "Now, you know you wouldn't," she said, as if remonstrating with a child. "Not seeing him the way he was at the last. And I didn't want you to." As she rose from her chair, her eyes seemed dry again. And as she turned from the window to leave the room, all the men stirred in their chairs. She motioned to them to remain seated. But her grandson came up beside her and placed his arm about her waist and walked beside her through the doorway. The other occupants of the room glanced at each other briefly, and then everyone watched the grandmother and grandson pass down the corridor toward the elevator, the old woman seeming to lean more of her weight on the young man with every step. Just as the doors slid closed, those in the waiting room saw the young man withdraw his arm from his grandmother's waist, turn away from her in a sudden, spasmodic motion, and quickly throw both his hands up to his face. Then they saw the old woman, herself, turn her back to the young man and hide her own face in her hands.

The people left in the waiting room looked at each other in silence. When the elevator doors were closed, not a word was spoken among them, not between brother and sister, husband and wife, or brother and brother. Perhaps until the moment just before the elevator doors closed they had imagined that the death of the old man would draw his old wife and his grandson closer together, would draw them into closer understanding of each other, that for all their differences they would be of comfort to each other now. As they sat gazing down the corridor toward the closed elevator doors, they could only have been reflecting on how near the end was for their own old ones. And for them was there any other prospect than that view down the corridor and the image of the pair on the elevator, turning their backs to each other, burying their faces in their hands, each giving way to his own sobs and shedding his own tears for what he had not been able to do and all he had had to do?

Nerves

IT WAS PURE CHANCE that he and I had happened to sit down on the same bench in Centennial Park. I can't remember which of us was there first. Each had his own newspaper, and I am sure we'd have kept behind our papers if each of us had not had a small son playing some fifty or sixty feet away. The two little boys were not playing together, and they were hardly aware of each other, I suppose, but both were hopping about rather carelessly on the wide cement steps that go up to the Parthenon—that is to say, the stucco replica of that edifice, which serves as one of Nashville's museums. Each of us had had to call out two or three times to his charge before there was any direct exchange between us. "Watch it there!" was my phrase, or sometimes merely "Look out!" His admonitions were more succinct than mine, but somehow they sounded softer and more old-fashioned, too. For him it was simply "Oh-oh!" or "Mind!"

My first impression was that he was an older man than I. But that is a mistake I'm always making. From the long spiel he gave me presently, and which I am going to set down, I now judge that he must have been born in Nashville at about the same time I was—during the First World War, or not long before. From what he was to say, I gather, too, that he had always lived near the park and was still living somewhere in that neighborhood. It was a Saturday morning, and probably his wife was shopping in one of the supermarkets that have gone up over on West End Avenue. As for me, I was only back home on a visit. I had taken my son to the park while my wife went to call on an old-maid aunt who had never liked men or small children.

It happened finally, as it was almost bound to do, that we both called out at the very same moment.

"Watch out there!"

"Mind!"

The result was that we opened our conversation by making apologies for our nervousness about the two boys. Modern parents, we agreed, were much too protective for their children's own good. Children ought to be left to learn *something* from the school of hard knocks, we said. And after saying that, we managed to restrain ourselves and called out to the boys no more. Nobody was ever so nervous about *us,* we said. But we agreed also that it was not our fathers or even our mothers who had taken us to Centennial Park. It was always some colored nurse. From this we got on the subject of how the park had changed, noting especially the disappearance of the Japanese garden. Only one small pagoda and one of the pretty arched footbridges remained, though here and there were heaps of rocks with broken mortar sticking to them to remind us how it had all been in our day. It seemed too bad. Did he happen to know, I asked, if the garden had been done away with during the war—because of Pearl Harbor, perhaps?

He didn't know. He couldn't remember when it had gone. Then, as if still thinking about this question, he turned his head and gazed back toward the heavy rush of traffic that was coursing along West End Avenue. It was, so far as I could make out, that chance turn of his head that brought on the totally unexpected and, I think, quite remarkable speech he then delivered. It was the sight of the traffic that seemed actually to set him off, but I believe he never could have arrived where he finally did without the silent prompting and encouragement that I gave him—without what was really my participation in everything he brought forth. I became so absorbed in what he was saying and in my own speculations about what he would say next that there may even have been moments when my lips moved to form the words as he spoke them.

"I remember very well, don't you," he began, in the most leisurely and casual tone imaginable, "when the streetcars ran along Broad Street and all the way out West End? There was nowhere you couldn't go on a streetcar when you and I were growing up. And streetcars had their points; they were lovely things in their way." He paused here, and, with his eyes fixed momentarily on the toe of one of his shoes, he smiled rather foolishly and even apologetically. Then presently he looked up and let his eyes meet mine directly. After that, he continued. And he did not interrupt himself again. "My own father remembered the days of mule cars," he went on, "though, of course, my father was still a small boy when the trolleys went up. But my grandfather, he remembered the mule cars very well indeed, and used to ride them to town every day. The old man—my grandfather—used to say, 'I never thought I would see the town change so much in my lifetime.' But I say the same nowadays. And I say, like him, no change can be altogether for the good. I say streetcars were really beautiful things in their way.

"There was a life lived on streetcars that isn't lived anymore. One time, my mother made me get up and give my seat to a Negro woman we didn't even know. Not that my mother had any modern ideas, and not that it was any more than I ought to have done. But it was something that could happen then and that couldn't happen now, or wouldn't be the same thing if it did. The woman was tired, my mother said. She had likely been on her feet all day in somebody's kitchen and was no doubt going home to cook another dinner for her own family, whereas Mother and I were only going out to see a picture show. Another time, when I was somewhat older and able to ride around town alone, a skinny old mountain woman touched me on the shoulder and *made* me get up and give her my place. After she sat down, she tried to sell me some berries she had in a basket. When I refused, shaking my head and carefully turning my eyes away from her, she laughed out at me and said, 'Anyways I'm proud to have your seat.' I was such a city boy that I didn't know what she meant by 'proud' until later, when I asked at home.

"I grew up riding streetcars to school and back. One time, I played hooky from school and took the car that went to the Glendale Zoo, though I never got that far. Something awful happened. At first, I thought the car had jumped the rails. But it was worse than that. A small boy had wandered out onto the tracks. I heard someone say, 'It's a child!' And I couldn't stop myself. I whirled about and I saw the mess back there. Or maybe I imagined I saw it. Because I'd hardly turned when a big hand was slapped over my eyes. It was broad and calloused, and it was distinctly and agreeably cool to the touch. From the feel of it, I knew at once whose hand it was! It belonged to the workman in overalls who had sat across the aisle from me. And presently he pulled me around so roughly that I cried out 'Hey!' When I got free of his hand and gaped up at him, I thought I could tell from the look in his eyes that he knew I was playing hooky that day. But of course it wasn't that. 'What you want to look at it for?' he said. 'And what are you waiting for, boy? You git off this thing, and you head out for home, and don't you look back once!' I did just what he told me. He was a man and I was a boy, and I thought I had to.

"Things happened on streetcars that couldn't happen now. Why, the governor of the state himself used to ride downtown to the capitol every day—right in the car with everybody else. Once (it was a long time ago), the governor and the governor-elect sat side by side going to town one morning. It may have been in the days of mule cars, but no matter. The young governor-elect, in his pride, sat up very straight, showing everybody how much taller he was than the old governor, who was on the dumpy side. But just before they got to town, the young governor-elect turned toward the window beside him and spat tobacco juice. He had thought the window was open, and it turned out not to be. Everybody was watching. They say the old governor laughed until he cried.

"My grandfather who remembered the mule cars so well said that the mule cars weren't really very different from the electrics. Only not quite so noisy. He *liked* the noise, though. It gave him a sense of privacy, he said. With all that noise, he could talk out loud to himself without feeling such a fool. I remember his doing it, too. After he got to be very, very old and couldn't even hear a peal of thunder, he claimed he could still hear the rumbling of the streetcars from up in his room at night. And it comforted him to know they were still running out there on the West End. I suppose it was somehow comforting to know that there were people out there awake with him when the rest of us in the house were asleep.

"And certain strange things happened on streetcars, which you may have heard about and which you may or may not believe in. Banshees and ordinary ghosts and headless men were known to appear on the late-night runs. Mr. Ben Allen, the famous Nashville spiritualist, after he'd been dead for thirty years, got on one night at the reservoir and rode the Eighth Avenue car to Douglas Corners. Before he alighted, he went up and down the aisle shaking hands with all the other passengers, some of whom had known him as children and remembered what a friendly soul he was, alive. The Bell Witch also used to appear from time to time. She was the most fun of all. She always was, of course. A hundred and fifty years ago, she turned Andy Jackson into a jackass and rode him around the world seven times in one night. You've heard that story, I'm sure. He wrote down an account of it, and said it happened when he was passing a night at the original Bell home-place, out north of town. But then, *she'd* play her pranks on anyone— Bells, Donelsons, Dickensons, or anybody. Black, white, or in between, she didn't care. And why should she? The Bell Witch was really everybody's witch, not just the Bells'. She'd been around Nashville ever since there was anyone here to scare. Why, she wasn't even afraid of the grumpy old conductors who ran the streetcars and who ruled on board them like old sea captains—every last one of them a sort of second Captain Bligh. One night at the end of the line, on the last run of the night, Cap'm Jimmy Clark opened the doors of his car to let off an old woman who had got aboard right here at Centennial Park. But when he looked in his mirror and even when he turned around, he saw there was no old woman for him to let off. He went back and searched the car. He searched beneath the seats and everywhere. He couldn't find a soul, but he guessed easily enough who it had been and he knew, all right, that she was still there. Cap'm Jimmy got off his car, closed the doors, and walked back to town through the dark. He left the old streetcar sitting there all night with its lights still on. Way down the track, when he was walking the ties back to town, he heard her laughing at him. Her witch's laugh followed him all the way in to where the streetlamps began. Cap'm Jimmy vowed, afterward, that he didn't run one step of the way. He wasn't going to give any witch that satisfaction.

"But now, of course, the whole of Nashville's transit system has gone over to buses. And I ask you, who in the world's afraid of buses or bus drivers? Those big, smelly buses sneak along through traffic with no bells to clang, no rights of their own, no dignity of any kind. The passengers all sit looking out the windows as if none of them knew anybody else was on board, never speaking a word to each other. They're all of them only counting the months till they can make their down payments and ride home from work in their own private automobiles.

"Even when something happens on a bus, it's not something you'd be sorry to miss. Or not something *I'd* be sorry to miss, like the Bell Witch or Mr. Ben Allen. But let me tell you! When I came home late one night last month, I did see something happen, or almost happen—something that made me wish there was some friendly stranger there to put a hand over my eyes. There were just the driver and the four of us on board. When the bus stopped, we weren't at a real stop. We just stopped where we were. I was sitting up toward the front, and I was glad enough to look up from the kind of bad news you get out of a paper nowadays. The driver, still peering into his narrow little mirror, stood up and said, 'What's going on back there?'

"That seemed to be all he knew how to say. And he said it over and over again—'What's going on back there?' Said it as if he didn't see plain enough what *was* going on, and kept looking into his mirror as if he was afraid to turn around.

"I don't know how long it had been going on. When I turned my head to see, the colored girl was hunched up in the corner of that long seat at the very rear. The two white boys were on their feet, standing over her in a threatening way. It was almost as if they were posed there for a picture. No, they were more like an unposed picture I might have seen in that damned newspaper I had just put down. And I just don't *remember* it like that; it seemed like that at the time—like a wire photo from some scene of trouble on the other side of the world, not like something that was really happening there on the bus. One of the boys had his fists clenched, with his right fist drawn back—like this. He was in shirt-sleeves. The other was wearing an old army field jacket, and he had one hand raised to slap with. From where I was sitting, I could see only the head and hunched-up shoulders of the girl. I remember very clearly the picture that it made. It didn't become at all real until finally I had got up out of my seat and seen the knife blade gleaming in that girl's black hand.

"It was how she wielded the knife, I suppose, that really brought me to. She was moving it back and forth in front of her in a slow, sort of clocklike rhythm. It was the only movement in the whole bus—in the whole world, it seemed to me at the time. I remember thinking to myself during the first split second after I saw the knife that she didn't seem to have a very firm grip on it. The underside of her wrist was turned up, and the handle seemed to lie rather loosely in her half-open palm. She had her legs drawn up on the seat, and I could see her elbow pivoting on one knee as she kept the blade going back and forth. And after a second, I noticed that her eyes were moving right along with the blade, making the same line from the one boy's fist to the other one's open hand.

"I don't know what had gone before this, and don't suppose a word had passed amongst them. But suddenly, for no reason I could understand, the black girl let out a scream to wake the dead. The white boys rushed her, and then they pulled back quicker than they'd gone in. And at once each boy took his same old pose again. Everything about them was the same as before, except there was blood on the cheek of the boy with the clenched fists.

"The girl was standing now. She held the blade steady, not moving it anymore, just steady and straight out before her. 'Don't nobody come no closer,' she said. It seemed to have taken that scream to give her her voice, but, like the driver, she didn't have but one thing to say. 'Don't nobody come no closer to me,' she said.

"I had forgotten about the driver until I heard him say again, 'All right now, I want to know what's going on back there.' His voice sounded all trembly.

" 'Don't nobody come no closer.'

" '*What* is going *on?*' the bus driver said. He was nearly shouting. Finally, I saw him step out of his little cage and face the business. 'You boys better tell me what's going on,' he said.

" 'Don't come no closer, none of you,' the colored girl said.

" 'What's going *on?*' the bus driver said.

" 'Just don't nobody who don't want to get cut up come no closer. That's all I got to say.'

" 'What's it all about, gal?' said the driver, just as though he didn't know.

" 'Don't you come no closer neither, Mr. Conductor,' she said.

"It was clear that the two white boys weren't going to say anything, and the girl and the driver had already said all they knew how to say. For a long time—it seemed like hours to me—all five of us stood there on the lighted bus like so many dummies in a department-store window. That was the worst part of it, really. I won't ride a bus again as long as I live without thinking how it was while we were all standing there like that. Finally, the bus driver looked at me. 'You've got to go somewhere and phone the police,' he said. I knew I would have to, and I wish I had made a dash for it right then without waiting to hear what he would say next. '*You'll* have to go,' he said, 'because I can't leave the bus. They might get rough and tear things up while I was gone. It could cost me my job.'

"And I realized then it wasn't the colored girl or the white boys he was afraid of. It was losing his job. It was his miserable job and the bus system's property he had on his mind at a time like that.

" 'Just don't come no closer to me,' the girl said.

" 'Well, I want to know what's going on,' that driver said again.

"That's how I left them. I got off the bus as quick as I could, and I went and found a telephone in a little café that was still open, and called the police. The desk sergeant who answered the phone made me give him my name and address. Then I struck out for home on foot. It was a dark, gusty sort of night, and I had the uneasy feeling I would find something wrong at home. I suppose it was having to give my name and address to the police that started me imagining things about my own family. Actually, everything was fine at home, but all the way I kept thinking of my house with my wife there alone with the boy and how easy it would be for something to happen. Then, just before I got to our corner, I heard a police car's siren. And it had a queer effect on me. Suddenly I could imagine exactly how the siren would sound to my wife inside the house. It would be a very familiar sound, I realized, and somehow comforting—familiar and comforting to us in the same way probably that the clanging and rumbling of the streetcars used to seem familiar and comforting to my grandfather. It was an awful thought. I hate the idea of it. Yet I don't know what we'd do without the police and their sirens nowadays. You have to hand it to the police.

I imagine they must have got out there to that bus before anything serious happened. They must have managed the situation all right, because I looked for something about it in the paper the next day—I looked for several days—but I never could find a word about it."

The Decline and Fall of the Episcopal Church
(in the Year of Our Lord 1952)

TOM ELKINS WAS SITTING on Mr. Thurston Roundtree's front porch, uninvited. Moreover, he was about to say a kind of thing he didn't often say. He said, "Mr. Roundtree, sir, it's your decision." Such directness wasn't customary in the talk between the two men. An inevitable silence followed. During the silence old Mr. Roundtree didn't look at Tom Elkins. The old man was sitting alone at one end of the porch swing. Every now and then he would give himself a push with the toe of his soft-sole house slipper. And all the while he kept his eyes fixed on some point far down in the lawn beyond the area where the largest clump of white lilac bushes grew.

After a minute or so had passed, still not looking at Tom Elkins, the old man said, "So far as any decision from me is concerned, I made it years ago. It didn't matter, though. I didn't care, of course. But all the same the church wasn't doing any harm, Tom."

"It was a hazard, Mr. Roundtree," said Tom, returning to his usual tone of inexhaustible patience with people. He was a lawyer who was not very effective in the courtroom but who had a reputation for being very persuasive in private consultation, very effective in negotiated settlements. As a member of the town council he had, during the past two years and more, spent a good many hours on Mr. Roundtree's front porch, uninvited.

"Yes, Tom, the church was a hazard," Mr. Roundtree consented, still continuing to gaze off into the shady lawn which stretched away in grassy undulations toward the narrow macadam street. Mr. Roundtree's old house was set at least fifty yards back from the street, and besides the clumps of lilacs and yellow jasmine and Christmas honeysuckle there were a half-dozen or so old forest trees that broke the monotony of the lawn's gentle roll. "The church was a hazard, Tom," said Mr. Roundtree, "a hazard to those who went snooping around inside when they had no call to be there." Until this point the old man had continued to gaze off into the lawn. Then, seeming to realize how harsh and unfeeling he sounded in the light of the boy who had been badly hurt falling from the gallery of the abandoned church and the hobo who was found dead behind the altar rail two years before, Mr. Roundtree did look directly at Tom. But he looked with raised eyebrows that seemed to say, Now, see what an ugly thing you have driven me to saying? Now, see the position you have forced me into? The old gentleman was known for his kindliness and tolerance and for his philosophical acceptance of most of the changes he had seen in the world. He was generally regarded as being different from the rest of the old-timers in town. Yet he was a man of firm character—nobody ever doubted that—and in all matters pertaining to the old church building he had taken a firm, an almost obstinate stand. He had taken a firmly and obstinately indifferent stand, that is to say, in a case where some expression of bias might have made things a bit easier. Even Tom Elkins, the very soul of personal consideration and long-suffering patience with other men, was driven to the wall in this case. It was not often in his career that Tom had said anything so severe and so final-sounding as "Well, Mr. Roundtree, sir, it's your decision"—either to a client of his own or even to the "other party" in a case.

The church in question had been an Episcopal church—an "Episcopalian" church most people called it. Its congregation, never large out there in that little West Tennessee town, had so diminished during the first years of the present century that services were finally discontinued. At last the old building fell into such a bad state of repair that—after a number of unfortunate incidents—the town council condemned the property and had the structure torn down. This action took place more than thirty years ago—back in the middle twenties—and it was only a few weeks after the actual demolition that Tom Elkins came to sit on Mr. Roundtree's front porch, that afternoon, for their final consultation.

Mr. Thurston Roundtree was not only the sole surviving vestryman of the vanished St. John's; after the death of his spinster sister, three or four years previously, he had become the only member of the otherwise dispersed congregation still living in the town of Blackwell. In later years, other Episcopalians have moved into Blackwell, and a new, very tiny church has been built on the outskirts of town. But the new Episcopalians are different from the old sort that used to be there. One feels that they are all converts from other denominations. One feels this even about the Episcopal rector himself, nowadays. And the services in the new church are so high that they seem almost Roman. At any rate, as sole survivor of the old Episcopalians, Mr. Roundtree was the man the town council had consulted during every step of the condemnation and demolition proceedings. He had not made difficulties for them in any legal way. He had not written to the diocesan headquarters in Memphis, where some claim to the property might have been made. And he had not tried to get in touch with former parishioners of the church who were scattered about the country. He had made no formal protest whatsoever. But every time Tom Elkins was sent to see him he would only say, "If I were you, Tom, I'd just let the old church stand. It doesn't matter to me, though. I don't care, of course. But it's doing no harm." If only he had said it mattered. If only he had said he cared. Then some kind of settlement might have been arranged, and everybody's conscience would have been put to rest.

Even after the town council had employed Sam Flemming

and his wrecking crew, even after the work of destruction was underway, Mr. Roundtree said nothing. And yet while the building was coming down he disturbed many people by going each day to stand quietly for several hours under a rangy black walnut tree across the street from the church. Although his presence didn't seem to disturb Sam Flemming or Sam's rough crew of men, the sight of him there worried all conscientious souls like Tom Elkins when they drove past. Somehow it must have made them feel guilty. Sam Flemming, a great hulking fellow with a fine, manly stomach and a shock of black hair as coarse as a horse's mane, would sometimes lean against the clapboard wall of the church, eating his lunch or enjoying a plug of tobacco, and frankly return old Mr. Roundtree's silent stare. They eyed each other across the asphalt street and spoke not a word. Each was as open in his staring as if he thought the other did not see him there. It seemed no embarrassment to either of them that there was no conversation, and it was certainly not a question of their not being acquainted. They knew each other as all men in such a little country town know each other, or as they used to know each other in those days.

Yet the way the two men looked at each other perturbed other people who passed by. And Tom Elkins bore the brunt of the general perturbation. Tom was not a married man, but for more than twenty years he had been informally engaged to a fine girl named Emma Broadhead. Literally speaking, Emma was no longer a girl, of course, but in a town like Blackwell a single woman will often be spoken of as a girl so long as she continues to receive attentions from any man. It was mostly through Emma that Tom was kept informed of how upset the town was by the two men's silent confrontations. Emma said that what she and others feared was that Sam Flemming and Mr. Roundtree *would* speak and that there would be an ugly incident in which Mr. Roundtree was bound to get hurt. As a responsible citizen and councilman Tom must *not* permit that to happen.

Emma had a very strong sense of social responsibility, and Tom Elkins respected her for it. She had not developed this sense until fairly recent years. It was connected, curiously, to her continuing in the single state. Perhaps it grew out of the gratitude she felt toward friends and neighbors who had cherished and comforted her when they might have ostracized her. For although she had never married Tom Elkins—it was her dying father's wish, a wish which he did not fail to mention in his will, that she remain single and at home as long as her invalid mother lived; and finally it seemed the mother would live forever—although she had never married Tom, she and he had made no secret of their true relationship. Many an early dawn saw one of them leaving the house of the other. And hardly a month passed without both of them being simultaneously out of town for a long weekend. The effect upon Emma was to inspire liberal feelings in her in nearly all matters. And since Tom was a lawyer with vague, if frustrated, political ambitions, she quite naturally came to express her sense of social responsibility in vaguely political terms. She was concerned for the common good and she did not forget the rights of the individual. (It was she, for instance, who had urged the tearing down of the church to protect hoboes and children who wandered in there.) Tom's ineffectiveness in the courtroom and in the rôle of a public speaker was, of course, what served to frustrate his political ambitions. But with Emma's encouragement he had come to see himself as the town's public peacemaker and great conciliator. Emma kept this ideal polished bright for him, and it was her scrupulosity that would not let Tom blind himself to dangers that might lie ahead in the demolition of the Episcopal church. "You must do what you know in your heart is right," Emma said to him. "And what you know in your heart is right is that such matters must not be allowed to drift."

Tom felt quite certain that there would be no real altercation between Mr. Roundtree and Mr. Flemming. The two men, being of very different sorts, were merely curious about each other. But although no altercation ever occurred, there were indeed two occasions when Tom went away as upset as if he had witnessed the ugly incident which Emma and some of her friends feared. Once he had come on the scene when stacks of rotten rafters were being carried out and thrown on a truck. Observing the rotted rafters, Tom had crossed the street to Mr. Roundtree and said cheerfully, "You can't deny that the old place was pretty dilapidated, can you, sir?" And Mr. Roundtree's reply had sent Tom away deeply concerned about the old man's state of mind and perhaps even the state of his soul.

"It wasn't dilapidated," Mr. Roundtree had said, smiling a rather puzzling smile. "It may have been a shambles, but it wasn't dilapidated. It was originally roofed with cedar shingles, its timbers were white oak and heart of pine, and the bricks in the foundation were hard bricks made on my own grandfather's farm, a mile west of town. It was a good building. But still there was no rock in it. The church wasn't built of rock, Tom, and so we couldn't properly say it was dilapidated, could we?"

The old man's smile at that moment bothered Tom more than what he had said. But when he reported the incident to Emma, she paid more attention to Mr. Roundtree's words. Was he merely being pedantic, she asked, or did that business about the rock mean that Mr. Thurston Roundtree had lost his faith? "I think it may have something to do with Miss Jenny," she said, remembering how close the old man had been to his dead sister. Perhaps he was a disillusioned man. Perhaps a secret loss of faith explained his unwillingness either to fight or to condone the condemnation of the church building.

Another time when Tom stopped to chat with Mr. Roundtree under the black walnut tree, something even more upsetting occurred. Tom and Mr. Roundtree had chatted for some five or ten minutes when Tom realized that Sam Flemming had left the work he had been doing with his crew and had come to lean against the wall of the church. The clapboard siding had been mostly stripped away by then, but the old lathing with the thick plaster bulging through in places was still there, and Sam leaned heavily against one of the uprights. Tom resented the man's common stare and he felt somehow that it would be an act of rudeness to Mr. Roundtree for him

to acknowledge Sam's presence. While Tom and Mr. Roundtree continued talking, a number of cars passed along the street.
Inside the cars were other good citizens of Blackwell, and Tom
could see them rubbernecking as they rode by. Presently matters grew worse. Tom realized that Sam Flemming had now
come forward and was standing at the curb on the opposite
side of the street. At last Tom turned and gave the man what
was intended as an angry look. Meanwhile, more cars were
passing along the asphalt street between them. Tom felt that
the whole town was participating in the moment. He even
sensed that certain cars had passed more than once. Then,
before he could turn his attention back to Mr. Roundtree,
Tom understood that he was about to be addressed by Sam
Flemming.

"Tom, tell him," Sam's voice boomed forth, as another car-
load of rubbernecks passed slowly between them, "tell him if
there's a thing or two inside he'd like to have, he can have
it—and free. The whole frame of the building will be a-coming
down tomorrow or the next day; so let him speak. If there's
something he craves, Tom, he can have it." Since all material
coming out of the building would belong to him, Sam spoke
with genuine authority. He kept his eyes on Tom as he spoke,
and when Tom glanced back at Mr. Roundtree he found the
old man's eyes also on him—not on Sam. Moreover, the old
man pretended that he had not heard what Sam had said.
His lifted eyebrows demanded that Tom repeat Sam's offer.
Yet when Tom did repeat it, Mr. Roundtree only burst into
laughter.

"Why, what in the world would I want with any of it?" he
drawled in the most casual, good-natured tone. "What is any
of it to me?" And without saying more, he lifted his hat to
Tom, gave him the most genial smile, and so took his leave.

Tom Elkins gazed after the old man for a moment as he
ambled away up the street. Then he turned back to Sam. Sam
seemed still to be waiting for an answer from him. Tom simply
shook his head. When he did so, he saw Sam Flemming's face
go crimson. Then presently the man turned away and began

shouting orders to his crew of workmen. Tom Elkins went and got into his car and drove off to lunch, continuing to shake his head now and again all along the way. He had lunch with Emma at the Blue Bird Tea Room on the public square, and they agreed that all Tom could do was watch and wait.

Only a few days after that, the church was leveled. Neither Tom Elkins nor anyone else observed whether it was on the very day that the demolition job was finished, or perhaps a few days later, that a marble birdbath appeared in Sam Flemming's side yard. Sam lived in an unpainted ramshackle cottage on the main street of Blackwell. Since the widening of that street, back in the twenties, the old cottage with its narrow, bannistered porch was left perched right on the sidewalk with no front yard. When the Depression had come, Sam had bought the place for a song and had moved his family over from the Mill Hill. Two of the town's finest old houses were on either side of him, and they were set back from the street in groves of maples and elms and ancient white oaks. But on Sam's place there were no trees left, and the little bit of a side yard had long since been denuded of grass by the play of Sam's half-dozen children.

Awareness of the birdbath's presence in Sam's side yard dawned slowly on everyone. (Perhaps people usually avoided looking at the run-down place.) And the realization that the new birdbath could be nothing other than the baptismal font from the erstwhile Episcopal church came more slowly still. Or perhaps realization did not come so slowly as it appeared to. At any rate, a good many days passed before anyone spoke to anyone else of what the birdbath really was. Finally Emma Broadhead said to Tom, "There is no use in our not admitting to each other what Sam Flemming's birdbath really is." Simultaneously other honest souls seemed to have spoken their minds to those nearest them. And when at last the word *was* spoken, it seemed for a time that no one could speak any other word. Tom was made to understand that a sacrilege had been committed that must somehow be righted! The town council was blamed by everybody, and the members of the council were informed that the font must be removed from Sam's yard.

Sam Flemming, however, not resting after the completion of the church demolition, knew his rights. He had contracted to tear down the church for a very small sum and on the condition that all the building materials and all he found inside would belong to him. He had found the font locked in a closet that opened off the sacristy, where the last rector had no doubt placed it for safekeeping against vandals. Sam recognized it at once as a thing of value. His first thought had been of old Mr. Thurston Roundtree. Old Roundtree was a queer duck, and was a man who held himself too high for Sam's liking. He was one of those old-time Episcopalians. You couldn't go to him directly about something like this. But then, with the aid of Tom Elkins, Sam had got his chance to hint to the old man that there was something valuable inside. He was sure the old codger knew what he meant, and yet the man was too proud to meet him halfway. Sam was vexed. He meditated long on how he should dispose of his treasure. Then absent-mindedly one night he mentioned it to his wife. It seemed an awful mistake at the time. She was down at the church next morning, calling the thing a birdbath and talking on about how she *would* have it. She wasn't a woman who complained much of her lot and of things she didn't have in life. She worked hard, spent sparingly, and nearly always let Sam have his way about things. But now and then she would forget herself—forget her children even, Sam told her, and forget *him* even—and take a fancy to some pretty piece of foolishness like bantam chickens or inside plumbing, or this birdbath! He didn't mind. He liked it in her except when she carried it too far. Besides, he knew that his work would be finished there at the church within a few days. He might not have a chance to approach old Round-tree again. What else could he do with it, for the moment, but take it home with him?

After the font had been set up in the Flemmings' side yard for only a few days, the wife and the two youngest girls had worked the earth all around it into a circular bed for flowers. How strange that the town was so slow to observe it there. It was not only the Flemmings' first birdbath; it was also the first flower bed the Flemming family had ever had.

Naturally, Tom Elkins was the person to go to Sam Flemming and suggest that the birdbath was bound to give offense to Mr. Thurston Roundtree, the only surviving Episcopalian. Others had already appealed to Sam on the grounds that it was an offense against religion in general. But Tom knew that Sam was a godless man, and though it was in their behalf that he went to see Sam, Tom knew that the sensitive feelings of the Baptists and Presbyterians and Methodists in Blackwell would not be something to move the man. It was clear to Tom, however, that Sam had some special feeling about Mr. Roundtree and about that old church building. He went to Sam's house and stood on the sidewalk talking to Sam, who sat on the porch with his sock feet on the bannister rail. Tom talked first about how strange it was that Mr. Roundtree had come and watched the church being torn down. Then he said that when Mr. Roundtree had laughed at the idea of wishing to have anything out of the church he must have been only covering up his real feelings. Tom could see that Sam was listening carefully to all he said, but he made no direct reference to the birdbath until he was turning to leave. Even then he said only that it was "bound" to offend the old man, because he could not truthfully say that Mr. Roundtree had voiced complaint. Without taking formal leave, Tom had walked off across the street and was already behind the wheel of his car when he heard Sam call his name. "Tom!" came Sam's resonant voice across the asphalt. He was still seated on the porch and was looking out at Tom between his two black-socked feet on the bannister rail. "Tom, tell him," he called, "tell him he can still have it if he wants it. If he wants it, Tom, and if he sends me word direct, he can have it."

Tom looked back at Sam but made no reply. Behind Sam, in the shadowy doorway to the house, Tom could see Mrs. Flemming. She was a woman of slight build and with dark hair pulled tight back on her head. She stood in the doorway, clearly watching and listening, with one hand raised and resting on the doorjamb.

The result of Sam's offer was, of course, that final consultation between Tom Elkins and Mr. Thurston Roundtree. Tom went the very next afternoon to sit on the old gentleman's front porch. After a respectable preamble, in which the history of the condemnation and demolition of the church was traced once again, Tom at last got round to asking permission to say that he, Mr. Roundtree, would like to own the baptismal font. He asked it in the name of all their fellow Christians, who were greatly offended by the use being made of the font. He told Mr. Roundtree that he was there only in an effort to serve the community, that he was giving time to this business that he ought to be devoting to his own law practice.

But Mr. Roundtree declined to send the word that Sam Flemming required. He would only shrug his narrow, rather humped, old shoulders, smile to himself, and say that it simply didn't matter about the font. In the end, it was really as much the church as the font that the two men were talking about, because from the outset Mr. Roundtree was clearly determined to show the same unconcern for the one as for the other. And after their exchange over whether or not the old church had been a hazard, Tom knew that they were now exactly where they had started two years before. He was inclined now to consider the incident closed. But he wondered if Emma would consider it so. . . . Surely there was no more he should or could undertake.

But somehow he found himself still unwilling to stir from the big wicker chair on Mr. Roundtree's porch. He was not comfortable in the chair. Little broken sticks of wicker stuck in his back however much he shifted about. And the sight of the toe of Mr. Roundtree's house slipper pushing at the porch floor every so often was now irritating to him. He had found it painful to have to say anything as direct as, "Well, Mr. Roundtree, sir, it's your decision." One didn't say that sort of thing to an old gentleman in Blackwell, Tennessee. And yet

now he *wished* to say something that would sound even more
insolent. He felt a need to understand Mr. Roundtree's stub-
born indifference to the whole affair. He longed to look the old
man in the eye and speak the one word "Why?" Yet this was
Mr. Roundtree, this was an old gentleman of one of those
old-time Blackwell families—one of the old-time Episcopalians.

Tom himself was a Methodist. He mother had been a Methodist and his father a Cumberland Presbyterian. He was one
of the regular, easy hybrids that the town was made up of.
Emma represented a similar mélange. But the Episcopalians,
the little band that once existed in Blackwell, had been different. At this time—the time of the church's demolition—Tom
was a man in his early forties, and so he was able to remember
back to the turn of the century when there were still enough
parishioners to justify services being held at St. John's. What
a different breed they had been from their Methodist and Presbyterian contemporaries. They danced and they played cards,
of course, and they drank whiskey, and they did just about
whatever they wanted on Sunday. They indulged in what
their Baptist neighbors called "that barbarous ritual, infant
baptism." They starved themselves during Lent, and they attended services on Christmas Day, even when it didn't fall on
a Sunday. There were no graven images in the old church, and
there was no altar stone, of course, but the Episcopalians had
talked about the church as though it were the temple in Jerusa-
lem itself. That was what their neighbors resented. Yes, they
always spoke of it as *"the* Church," as though there were no
other church in town. They lavished a loving care on the
church building that no other church received. It was not
merely that they were the richest congregation; they were, in
all respects, the most attentive. Everyone else felt that there
was something idolatrous in the congregation's affection for
and pride in the old building. The grass on the little lot was
always neatly cut. If one of the boxwoods that lined the brick
walk to the entrance died, it was immediately replaced. The
English ivy on the brick foundation and about the front steps

was meticulously trimmed. And a great fuss was made about obtaining the right, deep shade of green paint for the window blinds. About the interior there was quite as much fuss made—by the ladies. Somebody was forever doing new needlepoint covers for the kneeling stools or sewing new velvet covers for the altar rail. And there was the somewhat mysterious and embarrassing business about the care of the altar cloths and the polishing of the silver chalice and the candelabra. The care of the church kept the whole congregation busy. And then almost overnight, it seemed—in one short decade—the Episcopalians, all but Mr. Roundtree, either died out or moved away from Blackwell.

Sitting that last afternoon on Mr. Roundtree's front porch, Tom Elkins felt, momentarily, a revival in himself of all the old resentments the town had once had against the Episcopalians—primarily, it seemed now, against their pride in their old church. It was Mr. Roundtree's obstinate indifference to its ultimate decay and destruction that stirred the old feelings. His indifference seemed but the same old pride in a different garment! Suddenly he heard Mr. Roundtree address him. "Tom," the old man began, and then paused. Tom had his eyes focused on the worn toe of the old man's house slipper. He looked up, embarrassed to be caught staring at the threadbare toe of the slipper. But he found he wasn't, after all, caught. Mr. Roundtree was once again gazing off in the general direction of that largest clump of lilac bushes. "Tom," he said, "you see that Corinthian capital on the ground down at the foot of my yard, beyond where those lilacs are? It came off the old courthouse."

Tom couldn't, from his position, actually see the capital but he knew where it was and he knew where it had come from without being told. He knew that Mr. Roundtree had had it put there when the old courthouse was replaced by a modern structure a few years earlier. Without making any effort to see it now, he replied, "Yes, sir, I do."

"I had it placed there," said Mr. Roundtree, still not looking at Tom, "because I have a romantic fondness for ruins. I don't attach any importance to this feeling of mine. But I indulge myself in it so long as it does nobody any harm. And I suppose that's how I felt about the old church, Tom. My feelings had nothing at all to do with religion, of course. Perhaps the building had, after all, become a hazard. I don't know. I simply enjoyed seeing it there. Nothing more or less."

"But, Mr. Roundtree," Tom began, hardly knowing what he was going to say, yet sitting up very straight in his chair as though he were going to make a lengthy objection to the old man's confession. It flashed through his mind that Mr. Round-tree was not telling the truth. Or perhaps the old man was merely trying to end all these months of talk on an amiable note. That was the more likely explanation. But Tom could not let it go at that. The questions in his mind were too pressing. And the opportunity presented was too good to be missed. He fairly stammered out, "But, sir, that church was your house of worship. Wasn't it a sacred place to you? Wasn't everything in it sacred? We—on the council—have been afraid that you would feel—"

But he was interrupted by the intense gaze which Mr. Roundtree settled on him. Simultaneously giving himself a little push in the swing, the old man turned his eyes from the distant Corinthian capital and the lilac bushes to Tom Elkins there on the porch. He looked at him with an amazed and amused expression. "Why, no, Tom," he said, "not at all. No, not at all." And then he actually laughed in just the ironic way he had laughed at Sam Flemming's offer that day. "I suppose it isn't generally known," he then went on, wearing a somewhat more serious expression, as if only now grasping Tom's failure to comprehend. "I suppose it isn't generally known, but at the insistence of my late sister Jenny the Bishop came out here some fifteen years ago and held a little deconsecration ceremony. One couldn't regard the old building as a sacred place after that. It would have been sacrilegious, in the most literal sense of the word. Old St. John's hasn't been a holy place for nearly fifteen years."

Tom sank into his chair, again insensible of the piercing pieces of broken wicker at his back. He could hardly believe what he had just heard. Was the old man trying to make a fool of him? Was this something he had invented to cover up the real truth of the matter? Somehow it didn't ring true. Something was still missing. And yet, after all, that was what Episcopalians *were* like! For them it was as simple as that: the holiness was removed with the wave of that bishop's hand. It was as primitive as that. It was a matter of pure magic. And why hadn't the old man mentioned it before now? Suddenly it seemed plain to Tom that Mr. Roundtree had not wanted anybody to know how little he cared about the church building. He had been laughing at Tom's efforts at conciliation all along, or simply being contrary. Tom yearned to wash his hands of the whole business. He would go to Emma and tell her finally that nothing more could be done, that his conscience as a public servant was clear.

Yet when Tom Elkins rose to leave, Mr. Thurston Roundtree seized his hand warmly and told him to come again soon. He didn't have many visitors, said Mr. Roundtree, and would always welcome a chance to chat with someone as intelligent and as generous with his time as Tom was. The old man even walked halfway down the path toward the street with his visitor. It was as though he were parting from a dear friend. Mr. Thurston Roundtree was experiencing, momentarily, that cordial feeling toward Tom that one inevitably feels toward someone to whom he has confided an old, long-locked-up secret. For, yes, Tom was the first person in Blackwell he had ever told about Jenny's deconsecration ceremony. It was something he was sure other people would not understand, might even interpret as a reflection upon the town. He had himself been strongly opposed to having the ceremony. But Jenny had insisted she was acting, as much as anything else, for *his* own good. In their long years together—an unmarried sister and brother living in the same house—they had got on famously, without any quarrels or squabbles. Yet in the very realm in which they seemed most solidly united there was the one great division between them—that is to say, in their religion. It was simply that Jenny questioned her brother's inner piety and spiritual depth. As they grew older she accused him more and more often of caring only for the ritual, the music, and the general attractiveness of the little church itself. When the church was finally no longer in use, and she and he were forced to travel twenty miles into the next county to attend services, she disapproved of his continuing to see after the upkeep of St. John's. Several times when the bishop was in the next county for confirmations, she threatened to have him over to deconsecrate the building. Each time, Mr. Roundtree would give up having the grass cut for a while and neglect to have broken windowpanes replaced. But then one year he made the mistake of having the window blinds taken down and repainted. That was when she struck the blow. The bishop came, and the building was no longer a church. His sister lived only a few years after that, but she had lived to see his idolatrous spirit broken. He had not imagined how the deconsecration would affect him. But somehow *she* must have known. For from that day forward old St. John's was to him but another of the town's outdated, picturesque buildings. When Jenny lay on her deathbed he had to confess to her that she had been right, that he had cared too much for the mere trappings of religion. He knelt beside her bed, and together they prayed God for forgiveness of His faithful but errant servant, Thurston.

TOM WENT DIRECTLY from Mr. Roundtree's to Emma Broadhead's house. "Enough," he said to Emma, "is enough."

But Emma, whose figure was just beginning to acquire a middle-aged heaviness, settled herself in a large chintz-covered armchair, gazed up at Tom with her still girlishly soulful eyes, and said, "I know my Tom better than that."

"But there's no more to be done," Tom tried to insist. "Mr. Roundtree doesn't care a fig for that font."

"It is not Mr. Roundtree's feelings, is it," said Emma quietly, "and not yours or mine, that you are concerned about, Tom. The offense is against the good people of this town. That is what one mustn't forget if one is to serve the community."

"But what more am I to do, my dear?"

"You will have to see Sam Flemming again."

"And what can I say to him?"

"It is not for us women to tell you men what to say to each other. *That* is not our function. *That's* the other side of the coin. You will know what to say."

Tom didn't wait even till the next day to go see Sam. He went that very afternoon. And he didn't talk to Sam from the sidewalk this time. He went up to the narrow porch, without being invited to do so, and sat down beside Sam. He was ready, if necessary, to take off his shoes and put his feet on the bannister rail beside Sam's. He didn't know what the terms were going to be. It had not really occurred to him yet. But he knew he was going to meet them somehow.

Tom sat there on Sam's porch in silence for several minutes. Finally, in an offhand tone, he asked, "What church do you belong to, Sam?"

Sam looked at Tom and grinned. He ran his long, rough fingers through his black hair. Then he leaned forward a little and spat a stream of tobacco juice between his two big toes and out into the gutter beyond the sidewalk. "I call myself a lapsed Free Will Baptist," he said and laughed.

Another silence ensued. Then Tom said, "Is that so?" After a moment he said it again: "Is that so?" He was recalling that Sam and his family had once upon a time attended some church over on the Mill Hill. But they had apparently given up religion altogether since their move. People had supposed that they might begin attending one of the churches in the new neighborhood, but it was never urged on them. "What made you lapse?" Tom asked.

"It wasn't much of a church," Sam said. He spat between his toes again, hitting almost precisely the same mark in the gutter as before. "They were all so bone-ignorant, even the preachers. It was just a lot of talk and shouting and going on, nothing you could put your finger on or spit at." He grinned at Tom again and said, "It was all a lot of loose talk, and I guess I never *was* a good listener with ignorant folks."

"Didn't you ever think of trying another church?" Tom asked. Was it possible that Sam Flemming's conversion to one of the regular denominations might yet be the solution to their problem?

"Not me," said Sam. All at once he took his feet off the rail, slapping them resoundingly on the wooden floor of the porch. And he turned such a suspicious look on Tom that Tom felt sure the man had read his thoughts.

In reply—in denial—Tom Elkins merely shrugged and began examining his fingernails. When an interrogation took a wrong turn, he was the first to sense it. He knew that silence was often the best policy at such a moment. He waited now for something else to occur to him, and it wasn't long in doing so.

"I don't know how you vote, Sam," Tom began cautiously.

Sam looked at him out of the corner of his eye. "I don't vote," he said abruptly. Then after a moment he explained. "My old daddy was a Republican, like his own daddy before him. I don't know how they ever come to be so. But I know, sure God, it never done them no good hereabouts." Sam bent forward over the bannister rail and spat out his chew of tobacco. "Generally speaking, Tom," he then went on, "I don't know much. But I know enough to keep out of politics and to keep to myself what little I know about politics."

"All I was going to say," Tom said, trying to sound reassuring, "is that I guess you do believe that what the majority of people in a place want is what that place ought to have."

"In most matters, I'd say as much," said Sam with a certain caginess in his tone. Presently he touched first one and then the other of the two breast pockets on his denim shirt, feeling for his tobacco. There was none there. He slapped each of his trousers pockets and found none there, either. Since his gestures were self-explanatory, he got up and went inside the house to get a new packet of tobacco without making any explanation to Tom Elkins. In the doorway, as he was returning, he stopped to break off a plug from the new packet he had opened. Easing it into his mouth and masticating slowly and thoughtfully, he gazed out through the screen door at his visitor, who still sat by the porch bannisters, facing the street. The back of Tom Elkins's head, the hair thin on the flat plane of his double crown, struck Sam as just a little bit pathetic. He wondered if the thinning hair didn't come from wearing a hat too much; he smiled slyly at the notion. And the white shirt collar showing above Tom's suit jacket made Sam lift his own chin and twist his neck about. There the poor fellow sat, waiting to ask more questions. There was *nothing* such a fellow wouldn't ask you. Off to his left, Sam could see the marble birdbath in the side yard.

Sam knew, of course, it was the business of the birdbath Tom had come about. It was a bad business, too, and wasn't going to end well for anybody. How could it? From the moment he had got that closet door open, at the church, and had first laid eyes on it he knew it had some kind of worth—some kind he couldn't put his finger on, couldn't spit at. The wife hadn't had to tell him that. He knew *that* before the wife had ever come down to look at it and name it a birdbath. Both before and after she saw it he had tried his damnedest to get Old Roundtree to claim the thing. He hadn't for a moment kidded himself about *giving* it away. Whatever the thing was worth to Old Roundtree, Old Roundtree would have paid in full—of his own accord. That's the sort of gentleman the old man was, but somehow the old man was fouled up about whatever was connected with that church. Just how and why was beyond knowing. But it was plain now that he wasn't ever going to take the birdbath off Sam's hands. That's what made the mess. . . . And it was always bad luck to bring home something you couldn't afford to own. A birdbath with flowers all around it! In Sam Flemming's yard! He couldn't stop the wife from setting it up out there for the time being. Moreover, it was all right—for the time being. He knew the woman *had* to like it. A woman had to be the one to ask some foolishness in life. *He* liked it, too. But a man doesn't kid himself about how much foolishness he can afford. Well, she wasn't going to make it easy for him this time, he knew that. Not this time nor next, either. She didn't change. But when it was done it would be done. And she would still be his wife. He would still, also, be the man.

PRESENTLY SAM'S two black sock-feet, with a perfectly round hole showing the white flesh of each heel, returned to the bannister rail. Tom watched the feet go back to their place. He said nothing. It was Sam who spoke first. "It wasn't just me," Sam said, "who thought the Free Will Baptists hadn't much of a church. My old daddy didn't think so, either. He used to be what they called the section for old St. John's. I was a little fellow then and he used to take me up there with him sometimes when he was cutting the grass or cleaning outside. He'd point out how pretty and dignified the place was and how they even had it printed in a little book what they was going to do every Sunday of the year. Daddy told me how one time he said to one of the ladies—Mr. Roundtree's sister, it was—that he thought he'd leave the Baptists and join the Episcopalians. But she said to him, 'No, Jack, you have your church and we have ours. It's better to keep it that way.' " Sam, while he spoke, had been looking directly at Tom, but when he quoted the Episcopal lady he dropped his eyes momentarily, and a smile came to his lips, a somewhat mechanical smile that parted his lips and showed a row of uneven, tobacco-stained teeth. "That's why I was kind of glad," he said presently, raising his eyes again and looking quite solemn, "to keep something out of the old church like my woman's birdbath yonder—sort of in memory of my old man. Of course, the wife and the kids set great store by it too. They would hate to part with it. I don't know what they might do. They think it's about the prettiest thing they ever saw."

Under Sam's seemingly honest gaze and listening to his expression of sentiment about his dead father and his delight in the pleasure which the font gave to his wife and children, Tom wondered now if he could ever broach the subject he had come to discuss with him. He had promised himself that he *would* come to terms with Sam that very day; yet the kind of terms that had come into his mind just now seemed suddenly so crass, and so vile even, that he felt quite ashamed of himself. All at once he felt so humble in the presence of this honest, hard-working, tenderhearted Sam Flemming that he could not resist the impulse to confess his own wicked intentions. "Sam," he said, "I have to tell you that I was just now about to offer you money for that—that birdbath out there."

He was watching Sam's face closely as he spoke the words. In the straight lines on either side of the serious mouth he read strength of character. In the wide, brown eyes he read gentleness and charity. Here was a face Tom had known most of his life, and he felt now that he had never seen it before. Wasn't the coarseness he had attributed to it really a rugged loftiness? Wasn't Sam Flemming, after all, the very salt of the earth, a man whose kind of virtue was incorruptible? Yet at the very moment when Tom was really making such acknowledgment of Sam's virtue he observed a smile beginning to form on the man's lips. Moreover, he recognized it as the same smile that had played momentarily when Sam quoted the Episcopal lady speaking to his father. There was something unreal about it. It was the smile a man smiles in his sleep. And though Sam's eyes were open, it was somehow as though the lids had closed over them again. "Well, Tom," he began, his voice growing thicker and taking on more perceptibly the accent of that particular West Tennessee county in which Blackwell is situated, "I'll tell you, Tom, money speaks louder than most anything I know of." His smile broadened until all of his tobacco-browned teeth were showing. "What kind of money was you of a mind to offer?" he asked.

Tom rose from his chair and turned his face away from the man. So it was all a lie—all that about Sam's old daddy and his wife and kiddies. Even the bits about his daddy's being the sexton and about Mr. Roundtree's sister. But why would he take the pains to make up such stuff? What went on inside such a man? He tried to look at him again but found himself looking over his head and out toward the baptismal font in the side yard. His eyes refused to be directed toward those heavy features and that sly smile. Pursing his lips, he pretended to be reckoning the value of the font. "I'll give you fifteen bucks," he said at last.

"Make it twenty," said Sam. And he spat once again between his toes and out into the gutter.

Meanwhile, Tom had drawn two ten-dollar bills from his wallet. Instead of handing them to Sam, he placed the bills neatly, one on top of the other, on the bannister rail just next to Sam's right foot.

"I'm much obliged to you," said Sam, lifting his heel and putting it down on the two bills.

"I'll send someone to fetch the font after dinner tomorrow," Tom Elkins said and went down the porch steps to the sidewalk.

THE EXACT HOUR when Tom Elkins would send for the baptismal font became generally known in Blackwell by midmorning of the next day. Word had got round through some mysterious grapevine of information which neither Tom nor Sam would willingly have acknowledged feeding. Mr. Thurston Roundtree, for instance, as well as those rubbernecks who had witnessed the scenes at the church, knew that at half past one o'clock two members of Sam Flemming's own demolition crew, temporarily in the hire of Tom Elkins, would appear at Sam's place for the purpose of removing the birdbath from his yard. The general knowledge was so accurate that Tom himself, who had planned to direct the operation, was later than the spectators in arriving on the spot.

Tom, as a matter of fact, was so late in arriving that when he drew up to the curb, on the opposite side of the street, he saw his two workmen already standing in Sam's side yard. Their rusty old pickup truck was parked nearby, and it was clear that they would require hardly three minutes to do their work. It would not really be necessary, Tom reflected, to get out of his car, even. Yet when he presently observed that Sam

Flemming was seated on his porch, staring out into the street between his two feet, and that just opposite Sam on the far side of the street stood Mr. Roundtree with his old eyes shaded by the broad brim of his felt hat, and that between them was moving a fairly steady stream of slow, rubbernecking traffic, Tom then feared it might seem cowardly of him to remain concealed in his car. He stepped out into the street and went and leaned against his front fender. He nodded first to Mr. Roundtree and next to Sam Flemming. Each man returned his nod and somehow did so as though the other were not present. Cars moved along the street at a snail's pace. At last, Tom gestured to his two workmen that they should proceed.

From his porch, Sam Flemming suddenly called out, "Tom, you tell him he can have it still, and I'll give you your money back."

Tom, almost despite himself, turned his eyes to Mr. Round-tree. Mr. Roundtree's eyes were not visible under the hat brim, but Tom could feel that he was waiting to have the message relayed. It was like something from a dream, or something remembered from another existence. "Sam says you can still have the font, Mr. Roundtree," Tom said without spirit, without conviction, even.

The old man threw back his head and laughed. And with his face still tilted and exposed to view he said, "Tell him I think it looks pretty up there, Tom. Why not leave it there?"

At that precise moment, a woman, followed by two barefoot little girls, came running unheralded from Sam Flemming's house. They came out a side door onto a little wooden stoop there. And before the screen door had well slammed behind them, they were scurrying down the steps to the yard, and all three of them were crying out at the top of their voices. The woman's voice was more shrill even than the children's and she was shouting the sort of angry words a woman shouts when animals have got into her garden: "Shoo! No! Stoopid! Git!" She was Sam Flemming's wife, of course, and her cries along with her daughters' were directed at the workmen tampering with their birdbath. It happened also that at that moment in time two bluejays and a catbird were just swooping down to the birdbath to refresh themselves. Whether the birds' fury was directed also at the workmen or merely at each other, they gave forth fierce, almost human cries, and with a great fluttering of wings they stirred the air about the two men's bare heads.

"Don't you dare! Don't you dare!" Mrs. Flemming was shouting as she came up to the two men. Stepping into the flower bed, she threw herself forward on the rim of the font, shouting again, "Don't you dare! Don't you dare lay a hand on it!" But the men had already laid hands on the bowl of the font and were trying to lift it off the pedestal. With a quick glance over her shoulder at her husband on the porch, Mrs. Flemming called out, "Sam! Sam!" Sam didn't so much as turn his head to look at her.

One of the workmen said to her in a sympathetic voice, "He's sold it on you, Mrs. Flemming."

"No! Hit ain't for sale," Mrs. Flemming screeched. "He mought give it away, but hit ain't for sale." And with that she took her hands off the font and threw herself upon the man who had spoken to her, pulling at his fingers with one hand and at the collar of his khaki shirt with the other. Like her husband, the woman was of a sallow complexion, and her hair was perhaps thicker and blacker than his. But her face was thin and hollow-eyed, and her figure lean almost to boniness. Seeing her, ordinarily, one would not have supposed that she possessed any of her husband's vigor, nor that she was capable of the frenzy she had thrown herself into. She was shouting now at the older of her two dark-haired daughters, both of whom were moving threateningly against the other workman. "Sarah," she cried out, "grab his leg!" And then to the younger girl, who was no more than seven or eight years old, "Emmaline, sink your little teeth into his arm, honey!" Both girls obeyed her instructions with energy and with obvious relish. But the workman whom they attacked was a big man like Sam and he shook them off like flies, hardly seeming to notice their bites and blows. And Mrs. Flemming's attack upon the other man was equally ineffective. He and his colleague were now lifting the stone basin and emptying the water on the ground.

For Tom, the spilling of the clear water onto the ground acted as a totally unexpected release. Suddenly his spirits soared. It was as if he had seen a miracle performed. And he could not understand why he felt such joy. He had failed utterly, hadn't he, to moderate among the various parties. And he still could not understand the nature of the conflict itself. Moreover, he was disenchanted with the characters of both Mr. Roundtree and Sam Flemming. He turned his eyes slowly toward Sam, who had even now not removed his two feet from the porch railing. Then he looked at Mr. Roundtree, whose face was in the shadow of his wide-brimmed hat but who obviously had his eyes fixed on the sprawling figure of Sam. Had the old man perhaps known all along what Sam was trying to offer him from the church and had he counted on finally witnessing such a scene as this one? And why? Why? And now Tom looked at Sam again. What low manner of man was this that he could not be moved by that spectacle in the yard? He cursed the man under his breath. But even so he was not able to dispel his own state of near rapture.

Despite the unremitting attacks from the woman and the two little girls, the workmen carried first the basin and then the pedestal out to the street and hoisted them into the truck bed. And meanwhile Sam Flemming continued to sit on his porch, occasionally spitting a stream of amber juice between his two feet, giving no notice to the ruckus his wife and daughters were creating. At last some of the other bystanders began to appeal at first to Tom and then to old Roundtree, imploring them to intervene. Mr. Roundtree responded only by taking off his hat to some of the ladies who were beseeching him. Tom merely shook his head sadly. Only once did the two men's eyes meet. And Mr. Roundtree's eyes said, "Take back your money, Tom." And Tom's eyes said, "Accept the Episcopal baptismal font." But each was as deaf to the other's appeal as to that of the bystanders.

Both men stood seemingly in a kind of transport until after the birdbath, slipping and sliding about the floor of the truck and making a noise like thunder, had been hauled away down the street and out of sight. In fact, they continued to stand there just so until Mrs. Flemming and her two little daughters, straightening their dresses and pushing back their disarrayed hair, had reentered the Flemming cottage by the same side door they had emerged from. Then without any exchange with Sam Flemming or between themselves, the two men turned and went their separate ways.

The workmen had their instructions to dispose of the baptismal font however they might wish to, so long as it was never seen again in Blackwell. When, years later, the new St. John's was built, some effort was made to locate the old font for tradition's sake. But the workmen had done their work well. The font seemed to have vanished from the face of the earth, as even the two workmen themselves had. During the intervening years they had drifted away from Blackwell to some other community, and no trace of them or of the font they had carted off in their truck that day was to be found. Tom Elkins was by then married to Emma Broadhead (her mother having not, after all, lived forever) but neither he nor Emma could give any clue as to the font's whereabouts. Mr. Roundtree had by that time, of course, joined his sister Jenny in the town cemetery. Sam Flemming was not dead, but he had had a disabling stroke and in his immobile and speechless condition was being cared for by the wife and daughters whose birdbath he had sold. The fate of the font remained unknown, and the parishioners of the new St. John's have had to establish their new church without any relic from the past.

The End of Play

THERE WAS SOMETHING about the Political Convention game that my father disapproved of from the start, or at least something about it that got on his nerves. One night at dinner, at a time when the rules of the game might be said to have been still in the formative stage—though, as a matter of fact, they remained in the formative stage to the very end—I was speaking to my brother about how the roll call of the states would work. My father suddenly railed out at me. I was too old to be making up such a childish game, he said, and particularly to be basing it on something I was too young to understand and knew nothing about. Mother intervened. She said that apparently I knew a great deal about it—far more than *she* did, she said. Then she explained to Father how faithfully I had listened to the real conventions on the radio earlier in the summer. "Hasn't the boy anything better to do?" Father said quietly, hardly looking at Mother, trying to sound calm and reasonable. "Has he nothing better to do than to sit around listening to the radio all summer?"

And then my mother said, "It seems an innocent enough pastime to me. What would you have him do?" But as soon as she had spoken, she smiled. She knew well enough that what he would have me do was to go trekking off to Tennessee with him every two weeks or so and knew that it was because he was irritated with me for refusing to go that he let my talk get on his nerves.

This was during that hottest and driest of summers, the summer when the Hoover-Roosevelt campaign was being launched upon the nation. And my father was trying to make a fateful decision: Should he stay on and struggle with the ever worsening business conditions in St. Louis or should he take his family back to live in Thornton, the small Tennessee town he had come from? The temptation to go back to the comfort of his home town was very great. Down there in Cameron County, Tennessee, he owned twelve hundred acres of productive land, and in the county seat of Thornton he retained his partnership in what had been his father's and grandfather's law firm. He could hole up in that little Southern town till the Depression was over and then make a new start in the great world of finance that so fascinated him. Even at the time, he had no doubt that he would have his second chance. He was only forty-four.

I suppose I had no notion of the seriousness of the decision my father was making that summer. At least, looking back on it, I can't imagine that I did. I entered into my play with a joy, or an intensity, that I had never known before. I was already a boy of eleven, but I was the youngest of my parents' four children and still enjoyed the prerogative of the baby in the family: my life was still all play. Among our servants I was known as the playingest child they had ever seen. I had played dolls with my two sisters till I was nearly nine years old. After that, I played war in much the same spirit I had played dolls, with more emphasis on the tragic fates of my individual soldiers than on armaments and battles—this, to the constant annoyance of my brother. From war play I graduated to play based upon the books I read, on the history in *Puck of Pook's Hill* and on the romance in Page's *In Ole Virginia*. It seemed to be my right, as the baby in a family like ours, to go on indefinitely adapting everything to my play.

And so during that summer of 1932 I was playing Political Convention. From the little balcony above the side entrance to our house in Washington Terrace, I waved my arms in silent gestures as I made my silent campaign speeches. That was how it began. And neither the neighbors' smiles nor the protests from my brother and sisters had any effect upon me. As I further developed the idea, even choosing a name and a platform for my party, I came to speak openly to everyone about the Convention I was planning. Somehow the fun in it appealed to the imagination of several of my friends. At last I won not only the approval but even the participation of my rather grown-up brother and sisters.

I don't know how many sessions of the Convention were actually held. We had no set place or hour for meeting. There would simply come an hour when time hung heavy on our hands. Word would go round the house, and then round the neighborhood, that we were going to convene. And wherever it was coolest at that hour, there we would gather—in the front living room, or on the side porch, or out under the trees in the yard. And there was one notable session held round the dining room table with my friend Tommy Ganter, as chairman, pounding for order, which he never obtained, and without which I was to suffer one of the severest defeats of my life. Much of the rhetoric used in that Convention I can still remember—especially my own, especially that which I lifted from books we had in the house, books that contained speeches made by certain of my Tennessee forebears. The one brilliant stroke of the imagination I take credit for, however, is the invention of a delegate from Tennessee, a sort of Senator Claghorn created ten years or so before the radio reproduced him. All his speeches opened with the words "When I was a boy roaming the green fields of Tennessee. . . ." During the first sessions, his preamble would invariably bring laughter from the other delegates. But as the hot summer wore on and my filibustering delegate would not let the Convention conclude its business in a democratic manner, his opening line would elicit boos and jeers which, toward the end, became genuinely fierce. I know now that I just could not bear the thought of the Convention's adjournment. It had become very

real to me, more real than anything else about that particular
summer vacation when all of us except Father had to stick so
at home there in St. Louis.

My father, in trying to make his decision about his projected
move from St. Louis to Tennessee, went down to Thornton
a half-dozen times that summer. Again and again he asked me
to go along with him. Invariably, without any hesitation, I
declined. In fact, the moment I saw that an invitation was
forthcoming, I would begin shaking my head. Yet it was I who
rode with him to the Union Station to see him off nearly every
time he went. And it was often I who was there with the
colored driver to meet him when he returned. The rest of the
family would say goodbye to him when he left the house and
they would welcome him at the front door when he returned.
After packing his suitcase my mother would go out to the car
with him to say goodbye, and she would be standing just inside
the screen door to welcome him when he came home again.
But it was never once suggested that she or the older children
make the journey with him or even go down to the station to
see him off. The trip was a tedious piece of business that he had
to attend to, and there was no reason at all for the rest of the
family to share the inconvenience and discomfort of the long,
hot trip.

But as for me, I *wanted* to go to the station with him.
Further, the reason I wanted to go to the station was that I
really yearned to take the train ride too. If only I could have
found it in me to say that I wanted also to pay a visit to
Thornton and to the kin down there! For that was my father's
stipulation: I must say that I longed to see my relatives and
longed to visit that old country town. There was something in
his nature, or something in his old-fashioned country upbringing perhaps, that made "using" people abhorrent to him above
all else. I suppose it was this that made his decision about
whether or not to go back and live in Thornton so difficult for
him.

At any rate, he was very firm about not letting me go along
just for the ride. "You ought to want to know your relatives,"

he said to me. "You ought to want to be acquainted with the town and the country we all came from." And he would assure me that the trip would be no extravagance. "We still have our railroad passes," he would say, sometimes when we were already on the way to the station. "And since we would put you up at Aunt Lillian's or at Cousin Jenny's, it wouldn't cost any more for both of us to go than it will for me by myself." But I would already have begun shaking my head vigorously. I couldn't go. I *couldn't.*

Our railroad passes were not on the direct route from St. Louis to Thornton, but even I could recall how in better days the whole family had once traveled to Thornton over what *was* the direct route—and riding in a Pullman car, too. I could recall most clearly our making jokes about how we *ought* to be using our passes. That was how things used to be. That was when my grandparents were alive and when people could joke about spending money they ought not to. But nowadays I could visualize my father riding half the night on a coach that he boarded in the St. Louis Union Station, I could see him sitting for an hour or two in the little country depot where he made his connection, and I could imagine him riding the three or four hours after that on a coach that brought him into Thornton in the early dawn. These were the hardships that the rest of the family were glad to be spared. Yet these very hardships were what I would have relished: sitting up on the day coach all night and waiting at the little junction for the light of the train on the other line to appear out of the dark. I knew even that I could have endured the real hardship of visiting among the Thornton relatives for a few days. But could I lie about liking it? It was the prospect of lying to my father about why I wanted to go that set me to shaking my head—or so I told myself—of lying to him in advance and of pretending, under his eyes, to enjoy the visit once we arrived.

I sincerely *thought* it was that that made me refuse to go with him. But one night in St. Louis, after I had ridden to the station with my father, I dreamed that I had gotten on the train and made the trip with him, and that after we had been in Thornton for some time I discovered that *he* had lied to me. For, instead of my being allowed to return home to St. Louis when he did, as I had been promised, it seemed that I had to remain in Thornton among the relatives until he came on his next trip. Moreover, I discovered that Thornton was not the town I remembered visiting when my grandparents were still alive. The place had the appearance of just such a small town, but it was a hopelessly large small town. Instead of there being three or four streets like the one my Aunt Lillian lived on, there seemed to be hundreds of streets like hers—all shaded with the same oak and tulip poplars and lined with the same white clapboard houses. In that dream I wandered through the countless streets, searching for the house of one of my grandfathers, but I wasn't able to find it. And I wasn't able to find my aunt's house. Rather, I thought every house I came to was my aunt's. I would ring the doorbell and a woman looking very much like Aunt Lillian, as I remembered her, would open the door and say she thought my aunt lived in the next house. At last I met a boy, walking in the opposite direction, who had a pair of ice skates thrown over his shoulder. I recognized him as someone named Junior Lockout (actually I knew no such person) and I remembered I had had an appointment to go skating with him at the Wintergarden in St. Louis, that day. "Why aren't you where you are supposed to be?" he said, and then hurried on out of sight. When I awoke from the dream I sat up in bed and turned on my light to make sure I was in my room in St. Louis.

My sisters and my brother took a very special view of me, I think. In my father's eyes I was simply the youngest child, the baby. And to my mother I was merely the child who had been the least trouble to her—because we were much more prosperous when I came along—and the child who, as "a little thing," had most doted on her. But my brother's and my sisters' view of me was that I, unlike them, was altogether a child of the family's affluent St. Louis years. *They* could actually remember living in Tennessee. My sisters had even attended the primary grades in the Thornton grade school. They could recall the academic difficulties experienced on transferring from a country school to Mary Institute and could recall how astonished they were to find that each little St. Louisan could already tell you which eastern college she or he planned to enter. But I shared no such experience, shared no memory of having had to make my own way. I was one of the elect—a born St. Louisan. And instead of its making my sisters and my brother resent me, it produced a protective spirit in them. They imagined that this difference in me would make it more difficult for me to face the catastrophe our father was threatening us all with—the removal to a country town. They did not *want* me to face it; they wanted me to go on with my playing and not face the thought of it even. I suspect there was much talk among them about how hard it would be on me, because sometimes when I would enter a room that summer, they would quickly break off the conversation. And then at other times I would wander into a room and hear one or another of them talking about how adversely the move to the country town would affect his or her future. On those latter occasions they seemed not to notice my presence, or perhaps they supposed I could not understand the complicated family problems they were discussing and supposed that I would not bother to listen.

That summer was a dull time for my sisters and my brother—for young people of high school age, that is, who were used to choosing between various kinds of summer vacations and entertainments. To such young people all of the Depression summers were dull. It was not so bad for children my age and younger. It didn't matter to me that the family no longer belonged to a country club or to the Racquet Club. I could go swimming at the public pool and enjoy it just as much as I had enjoyed the club pool. And instead of putting on the country club greens, my contemporaries and I took up miniature golf. (On the neighborhood miniature golf course we found new charm in the game by watching the ladies' necklines when they bent over to putt.) We were very much at home in our city world, whether in its private or its public aspect. Moreover, I was still young enough—still babyish enough perhaps—to have made up that childish game of Political Convention, just to pass the time.

I found it hard to understand why Father had so set his heart upon *my* company on those trips to Tennessee. Finally one night, Mother undertook to explain it to me, and she did so without my asking her to. We had been to the Municipal Opera together, at the open air theater in Forest Park, and were walking home through the park together, just she and I. She may have felt somewhat uneasy about walking through the park at night. The way was well lit, but there was a breeze in the treetops that rustled the broad leaves of the sycamores. Now and then a mass of leaves would come between the streetlight and the sidewalk to cast moving shadows all around us. I felt no uneasiness, myself, because I knew Forest Park as I knew my own back yard. With my friends, I had played many a game of "The Three Musketeers" and "Beau Geste" in the very area where we were walking that night. When we had walked for some distance in the park, Mother became momentarily confused about our direction, about whether we were heading toward Kings Highway or toward Lindell Boulevard, which latter was our proper direction. When I laughed at her and showed her how near we were to Lindell Boulevard, she took my arm, as though I were a man, and told me to lead the way. A few minutes later, after we had left the park and were walking along Union Avenue and past the gates to Portland Place and Westmoreland Place, where so many of the very rich, old St. Louis families lived, she quite abruptly began trying to explain my father's behavior to me.

She said he worried about the prospect of uprooting me and taking me away from life in St. Louis, which was the only life I had ever known. She said that life on a Tennessee farm or in a small town would be very different and would require some adjustment on my part. And then she hesitated, as if expecting me to reassure her. But I didn't know how to reassure her; I didn't know what I could say. When she didn't continue to explain and defend my father, we walked along in

silence. She made no further effort to explain Father's attitude
and she expressed no concern of her own about how I might
adjust. But she continued to hold on to my arm the rest of the
way home, and by the time we reached Washington Terrace
she and I were chatting easily about the operetta we had seen
and about whether we liked Guy Robertson's voice better than
that of Leonard Cely.

Even in those days I think I felt a kind of gratitude toward
my mother for her seeming reticence toward me and for her
not having allowed me, as the baby boy in the family, to
dispossess the other children and my father in her affections.
A little earlier in life I had so wanted to do just that! It may
be that her rejection, however gentle, caused me to seek satisfaction in my fantasies and play-pretends for a number of
years. But even at the age of eleven, I think I already sensed
how great a danger there had been for me in doting so on her
and already understood that she had protected me from some
unnameable pitfall.

The Political Convention game had been suggested, to some
extent, by a game I had made up the summer before. The other
game, which I had played with a friend named Dick Kilpatrick, was known as Big League Baseball. It consisted merely
of the two of us playing pop-up ball in the back yard, with
whoever was at bat playing the part not only of a major league
team and the umpire but of the radio announcer as well. That
is, between swings, the batter carried on a running commen-
tary of the game. After a hit and while running to base, he
would be exclaiming, "He's coming in, folks! The crowd has
gone wild! And the score, oh, the score!" The Convention
game was suggested through the fact that this summer we had
had to listen to the broadcast of the two national conventions
during the very hours when we might have listened to the
baseball games. At any rate, Dick Kilpatrick soon seemed quite
as enthusiastic about playing Convention as he had been about
Big League Baseball. And two other friends of mine, two
brothers named Henry and Tommy Ganter, were easily
drawn into it. I have never been able to decide what signifi-

cance, if any, should be attached to the fact that the parents of both Dick and the Ganter brothers were of the same kind of Southern, country origin that my parents were. But almost certainly both their families were going through a crisis that summer not too dissimilar to ours. I know that eventually Mr. Ganter managed to weather the Depression years in St. Louis. Mr. Kilpatrick was not so lucky; his business failed the following winter and he died soon after. Perhaps for all three boys that unending game I had invented offered the kind of escape they needed just then. And perhaps for my brother and sisters it did somewhat the same, bored as they were with sitting about the house most of the time or, in the case of my brother, out looking for a summer job that wasn't to be found. My memory is that in some of our sessions they all completely lost themselves in the play-pretend, and were carried away with it almost to the same degree that I was. For a time at least I am sure they were. As delegates they made eloquent speeches, which were usually terminated by a demonstration for a favorite son; and when one's turn came to act as chairman he gleefully accepted the chance to pound away with my grandfather's rosewood gavel, calling for order and threatening to have the sergeant-at-arms remove some delegate from the Convention floor. Very early, and by unanimous vote, they adopted the name for the party which I had chosen for it: the Minority Rights Party. And in a spirited meeting held out under a giant sycamore tree in the side yard, we adopted a platform whose only two planks—so far as I can remember—provided for the enfranchisement of all minors and the disenfranchisement of all adults.

My mother warned us several times that the Convention was getting on Father's nerves and that we had better plan a final session and bring the thing to a conclusion. I never had any intention of heeding her warning, and I believe it was resented even by the others. We met irregularly, of course, just whenever the mood struck us and whenever we could all be assembled. As I have said, the rules remained in a formative stage till the end. The only records ever kept were a record of whose turn it was to serve as chairman (the chair rotated, with a new man in it at every meeting) and a record of where the roll call of the states left off at the last session. We first went through the roll of the states asking for nominations, the six of us who were not in the chair taking turns at answering. We ended with seven nominees, after a number of sessions, each of us pretending to be the head of a delegation and actually nominating himself or herself, then seconding the nomination, and casting all votes for himself each time it came his turn to answer for a state. It is a little fuzzy in my mind about how the rules worked beyond that, and it was fuzzy in all our minds at the time. There was a great deal of squabbling and calling out for recognition from the chair. But somehow I obtained a permanent claim to the delegation from Tennessee, and in nearly all moments of confusion I could manage to gain the floor and open up with "When I was a boy roaming the green fields of Tennessee. . . ."

I came to all meetings not in costume but with the makings of costume, so to speak, at a moment's notice. As soon as I gained the floor I would snatch out my pocket comb and roughly part my hair down the middle. On my nose I would fix a pair of pince-nez which my mother had long since discarded in favor of her horn-rims. And then I would whip out the black shoestring that constituted my tie. "When I was a boy roaming the green fields of Tennessee," I began on one occasion, "I had a dear, dear friend. And though I did not then dream that I would one day place his name in nomination at this Convention, as I have done recently, there *were* traits of leadership in him that I could not fail to recognize in him. . . ."

The name I had placed in nomination was of course my own. It was to praise this great Tennessee statesman, myself, who had begun life as an honest country boy, that I delivered all my speeches. My speeches did not always begin so relevantly. I astonished the assembly once with this opening: "Americans, awake! We are here free born in our native land! But liberty is not license, and preparation for defense is not war! We need every citizen to develop and build up our national resources!" It was, of course, something I had gotten out of one of the books in our library. I knew it had no bearing on my subject, but it did have the right ring to it. And since I was carrying on a sort of intermittent filibuster I had to make use of whatever came to hand.

My father was no Southern chauvinist. I had seldom heard him speak of the Civil War, and never of the War Between the States. He thought of himself as a modern American businessman. Yet I know that he did not like to hear people make fun of things Southern. What I don't know is whether or not *that* was my intention in acting out the rôle of my delegate from Tennessee. Perhaps I was doing a sort of probing. Perhaps I was making a statement about how little I knew of things Southern, and saying that all I could make out was a not very attractive stereotype. I do not even know that I intentionally arranged that the Convention should so often be in session at that time of day when he came home from his office. But there were certainly a number of times when it *was* in session at that time, even after my mother's warning. And since I didn't always know when he arrived, I can only speculate on what rhetorical flourishes he heard from my lips, from the lips of the boy who wouldn't say he wanted to visit his Thornton kin. I think of passages, sentences, phrases that I uttered before the Convention that summer, words I had copied down or memorized from my father's own books, and I can imagine what he might have heard me declaiming—declaiming to the amusement of the Ganter boys, Dick Kilpatrick, and my brother and sisters. "Speak not to me of the new South! There is no new South! There is only the old South resurrected with the print of the nails in her hands!" Or another time: "They accuse me of being a Tennessee mountaineer! Well, I plead guilty to the soft impeachment!" and: "We are not ashamed of Fort Donelson or Shiloh! We are not ashamed of Stone River or Missionary Ridge! No more than we are ashamed of the heroes of King's Mountain!" Or possibly: "It doesn't matter whether you come from East, Middle, or West Tennessee! All of the three Grand Divisions are grand divisions!"

And then suddenly, one afternoon in late August, the Convention took a turn and became merely a contest between two personalities. Dick Kilpatrick had overnight created a delegate from Missouri, a delegate colorful enough to rival my own. He arrived at the meeting wearing a derby hat and a checkered vest, and with a rubber cigar in his mouth. Dick was just my own age and he was my oldest friend. I suppose I had always dominated him somewhat, had made him play many a game that was not to his taste. He was rather short and too pudgy for a boy his age, whereas I was on the skinny and angular side. His face was round, and until that afternoon I think I had always felt there was something effeminate about his expression. But one couldn't feel so, seeing him under that riding derby of his mother's and with that cigar between his protruding lips. And when he removed the derby to reveal the bald-headed effect achieved by a silk-stocking cap, we didn't have to be told how tough a nut he was going to play the rôle of. No St. Louis or Kansas City political boss ever looked more brutal or more self-assured.

He informed us in short order that he was going to offer a dark-horse candidate. The man he was going to place in nomination—himself, of course—was a man's man, a red-blooded American who would know how to run things down there in Washington. "The man I give you," he shouted, "is a *winner!* And that's what we all want!" I don't know whether I really knew from that moment that my cause was lost and that Dick Kilpatrick was going to capture the nomination. How *could* it be lost? It was *my* game, wasn't it?

Yet I ought to have known. The other delegates had already wearied of the game. My sisters particularly had only gone on with it at my insistence. My own behavior when I had the floor had become increasingly frenetic, so much so that the other delegates were now probably half bored, half disturbed by it. Dick Kilpatrick gave them their release from my spell. My brother, as the delegate from Michigan—where he had formerly gone to summer camp—was the first to go over. Making his only speech of any length during the entire Convention, he said he was proud to cast his vote for the gentleman from Missouri. Somehow at that moment I thought of my father, remembering that he was on one of his trips to Tennessee and would not be coming in tonight. I did not know whether I was glad or sorry.

My two sisters divided their votes. Tommy Ganter wavered. He was the youngest of the delegates and really seemed quite confused and uncertain as to where his loyalty should go. But by and large he continued to cast his votes for me whenever it came his turn to answer in the roll call. Everyone but Dick and me had by now given up his own candidacy. Henry Ganter was in the chair, calling the roll, and so he could not vote that session. Henry was by nature a quiet, reflective boy, and the brightest student in our class at the Country Day School. He was highly amused by the contest that had developed and during the first part of the meeting he laughed so much that it frequently interfered with his roll call. But later I noticed him smiling quietly to himself, as if at his own thoughts, and I was not entirely surprised when he beat upon the wicker table and abruptly called for a motion for adjournment. He said that he and Tommy had to hurry home for an early dinner. The adjournment was agreed to only after Henry consented to my demand that we meet the following night.

Meet the following night we did—in the dining room, after dinner. The chairmanship, I realized only as we were seating ourselves around the table, had automatically passed from Henry to Tommy Ganter! And so Tommy could not vote, and except for my sister, I had lost my only semblance of support. I knew too well how eager both my sisters were to bring the Convention to an end. There was clearly no hope. The session did not go on very long that last night. Yet at least there *was* a dramatic climax. And without it I don't know how we would ever have brought that awful, hot summer of uncertainty, that hiatus we had all been enduring, to a satisfactory end. I came well prepared to challenge Dick's claim for attention. To my costume I had added an old broad-brimmed straw hat of my father's, the band stuffed with tissue paper. And in my father's absence I even got Mother's permission to wear one of his linen vests under my own linen jacket. I had no difficulty getting the floor since Tommy Ganter was in the chair. But almost as soon as I began speaking, Dick Kilpatrick, once again in *his* costume, began a demonstration for his candidate, marching around the table, playing "America the Beautiful" on his kazoo. Henry Ganter joined in the demonstration at once. And despite Tommy Ganter's pounding for order on the mahogany table, all the others, including my one faithful sister, soon joined in. Along with our kazoo playing, our marching, our table pounding, and our speechmaking we were all of us laughing at our own spectacle, laughing with satisfaction and at the same time with a certain hysteria, I think. Above the din, I continued to plead the cause of my candidate, though this time I took a different line. "The man I give you," I shouted, "never had a pair of shoes till he was twenty-one. And his children down there in Tennessee go barefoot to school even nowadays. They git turnip greens and hominy grits for breakfast, corn bread and black-eyed peas for dinner, and sourbelly for supper. They go to the Baptist Sunday School and wash each other's feet on Sunday and drop a copper-cent in the plate when it's passed."

It was several moments before the demonstrators seemed to hear what I was saying. But all at once they left off cheering Dick Kilpatrick and began jeering me. My sister, the one who had supported me longest, even hissed, "Hush up!" And I could tell from her facial expression in what bad taste she considered my remarks.

I was seated at one end of the oval dining table, and Tommy Ganter at the other. Presently I saw Henry Ganter step over to Tommy and heard him say, "I move we nominate Dick Kilpatrick for president by acclamation." My sister who had told me to hush up seconded the motion. Then Henry stepped behind Tommy's chair, and placing both hands on his little brother's shoulders, as though usurping his power, said, "All those in favor will signify by saying 'aye.' "

Hearing the chorus of "aye"s, I rose from the table. My pince-nez were clouded with tears. Removing them from my nose and slipping them into my pocket, I turned away from the table; and there in the dining room doorway a few feet behind my chair stood my father.

He was wearing a seersucker suit and a bright blue bow tie. In one hand he held his hard-crowned straw hat, in the other he still held his suitcase. He had just returned from the last of his summer trips to Tennessee. Without a word, and to the consternation of all, I ran and threw myself into his arms. I think it was the last time I threw myself into my father's arms in that babyish way, but it created a warmth between us that never afterward cooled. He dropped both his suitcase and his hat to the floor, and placing one hand on the back of my head he said, "One thing is sure, son. Tennessee is not as bad as you make it out."

"How's Aunt Lillian?" I asked softly.

He laughed outright at me. "She's fine and she wants us to come see her."

"I want to go," I said.

"We're *going* to go back to Tennessee," he said. "The whole family—to live. Not to Thornton, but to Tennessee."

I saw my mother, just behind my father, smiling gravely at me. Then she turned her eyes to the other children, and wearing the same smile she said, "Let us consider that the Convention is adjourned."

WE DID MOVE BACK to Tennessee that fall. Instead of going to live in Thornton, however, we went to live in Memphis, where my father had certain business interests. But Memphis was near enough to Cameron County for us to spend many weekends and holidays either on the farm or in Thornton itself with Aunt Lillian or Cousin Jenny. I became genuinely found of visiting among the relatives after I got used to their ways.

In fact, while I was in my teens, I spent several summers up there when the rest of the family preferred going to our cottage in the Cumberland Mountains or going off for a few weeks on the Gulf Coast. I became interested in the family history, and even in local and regional history. I developed an ear for the differences between Memphis speech and Cameron County speech. And yet in a sense I remained self-conscious about it all to a degree that my brother and my sisters did not. Within a few weeks after we arrived in Memphis, my brother was speaking with what was almost a Mississippi accent. Both my sisters married Southern men and have raised families of Southern children. To my brother and sisters, as to my parents, the period in St. Louis represents a relatively brief interlude in their lives. They are vague about a lot of things there that are very clear in my mind and they will ask me to refresh their memories about people and addresses and even events that took place in that period. For me, of course, almost the reverse is true since I lived there during those years of life when one is taking his measure of the world.

Sometimes during the war when I was overseas, I would have to visualize very concretely just how long a distance a mile is, and I would inevitably think of the distance between our house in Washington Terrace and the ice skating rink on DeBolivar Avenue. Or if I had to reckon what fifteen miles was like I would think of the distance between our house and the Florrisant Valley Club. And even to this day I am apt to describe someone to my brother by saying that he has a freckled face and a dimple in his chin, rather like Tommy Ganter, or by saying that someone is the roly-poly type, not unlike Dick Kilpatrick himself.

An Overwhelming Question

"I DON'T UNDERSTAND YOU, Rudy. We've known each other all our lives, and if we can't—"

"We have not known each other all our lives, Isabel," he said flatly.

They were a comical pair at such moments. Her speech would suddenly become littered with diphthongs and elisions. His became hard and flat. A foreigner listening in at these moments might have supposed them to have grown up in two different regions of the country. But as a matter of fact, she had merely assumed the more specially feminine and he the more specially masculine form of genteel, city speech as it is spoken in the great heartland. And it signified no more than that they had reached an impasse in some kind of argument. Of far greater significance was their reference to how long they had, or had not, known each other. . . . Sometimes it was she who said they *had* known each other all their young lives, and sometimes it was he. Neither of them ever meant to say it, but in the heat of argument the untruth would sometimes slip out. Not very often, but sometimes. Otherwise, it was acknowledged between them that they had met only a few months before they got engaged. That was what was real and true. Other Isabels and other Rudys whom they had known at fourteen, at sixteen, at eighteen (and even earlier than fourteen) had no connection with the grown-up and matured Isabel Havens and Rudy Banks.

Last winter, the grown-up Isabel and Rudy had fallen romantically and passionately in love at a Hunt and Polo Club dance. They said yes to each other a few nights later (to each other and to what was a lot more than just each other) and very shortly now they were going to be married—in three days' time, in fact. Their bond was in their present and in their future. Any memories they had in common—old awarenesses and unawarenesses of each other, growing up as they had in the same town—were like memories that each might have shared with some other boy or girl, or, still more likely, with a succession of others. Looking back from twenty and a little beyond, all that part of life seemed utter nonsense and not to be thought of as in any way real.

"I just don't understand your attitude," Isabel said, trying to begin the present argument all over again. But again words failed her. For a full minute they stood there not saying anything. Rudy pretended to go on looking at the pieces of Danish glassware that had come in recently. (Isabel's mother liked grouping the presents in kinds, and as their treasure had accumulated during the past eight weeks, Mrs. Havens had managed to make this room look more and more like a well-ordered coupon store—one for royalty, or even celestial beings.) "Lately," Isabel finally managed to continue, "lately, Rudy, you have treated me like a leper. A mixture of a leper and a lunatic. Or a pet that might bite you if you didn't watch out. I am just fed up with it."

Gently he took her hand, and she at once lifted his hand to her lips and kissed it fervently. "Right now," she said, "even your hand is as cold as ice."

"It's cold in *here,*" Rudy Banks said, shivering.

She dropped his hand, and moved over to the wall and turned up the thermostat. The room was in the basement of the house and had its own gas-fired space heater. It had been the laundry once, but a dozen years back Mr. Havens had converted it into a rumpus room for Isabel and her playmates. More recently, Mr. and Mrs. Havens themselves had used it for a card room on hot summer nights. And now all the furniture except the Ping-Pong table had been stored away and replaced with sawhorses with planks laid across them. The improvised tables and the Ping-Pong table and the built-in shelves held most of the wedding treasure.

From the thermostat, Isabel looked back over her shoulder at Rudy. He was fingering the Danish glass again, but his eyes were just trained on her. When the gas jet in the heater flickered on, she saw him smile and shake his head. She said, "You'll be surprised how fast it will warm up."

"You *are* a wastrel," he said. "We'll be back upstairs before the blower comes on." He knew all about such heaters.

"I don't think we will." She turned to the door that led to the basement corridor, and closed it.

"Isabel," he said, "honest to God!"

"I'm serious this time, Rudy," she said.

"You aren't serious. You may think you are, but you aren't." He tossed his head back and laughed, as though that would show her she wasn't serious. "Look where we are," he said. "Just consider what the possibilities are. It gives me goose bumps to think about it. All this glass! And the cement floors!" The room was lit by a single bright globe in the center of the low ceiling. The crystal, the china, the silverware winked at them from every surface and from the open shelves. From the far end of the room, two brand-new television sets gawked. And in a nearer corner crouched an outdoor cooker, brandishing its copper and stainless-steel accouterments.

"If I'm not serious now," Isabel said, "you'll never see me serious."

"Don't talk baloney," he said.

"It's not just talk."

"Baloney," he said, still smiling. He was not going to be drawn into more talk. If he had managed this long, he could somehow make it the rest of the way. She was really incredible, but he was confident that in another moment or so he could make her see what a ridiculous time and place she had chosen for *this* onslaught.

She moved toward him along the aisle between the tables. "Now see here, Rudy. We've been engaged for three months. We've—"

He raised three fingers and shook them at her. "And we'll be married in just three days from now," he said.

She drew nearer. He retreated around the corner of the heavily laden Ping-Pong table. She laughed, but he didn't feel any safety in it for him. She wasn't conceding anything. She was merely humoring him in his playfulness. He went round to the other side of the table. As he turned the corner there, his jacket brushed against a sherbet glass, which fell against one of its companions and gave off an elegant tinkle.

"You'll break something," she said sharply. "You know what a clumsy ox you are." It was a sudden change in tactics on her part, but he recognized it. She was really very clever. She would make him angry, and then there would have to be a reconciliation. Then anything could happen, anywhere.

He leaned across the glassware between them and gave her a glittering smile. "You know how much I love you," he said. "Why are you so silly and persistent? You know I am not going to let you have your way."

But she had lowered her eyes to the table. She didn't seem to hear him, though of course she did hear him. She was thinking that probably she *wouldn't* have her way. She could feel the blood rising in her cheeks. And she was blaming herself for not realizing weeks earlier that he was consciously opposing her. What a dupe she had been! How she had let the time go by! Oh, the evenings they had idled away! The opportunities they had passed up! The kisses she had wasted! . . .

THE SPACE HEATER's fan came on—the blower. He heard its soft whir and then almost instantly he felt the new warmth on his ankles. It seemed to him that probably she *would* have her way. For there she stood, opposite him, a picture of maidenly surrender—surrender to his refusal, which made her doubly irresistible—her eyes cast down so modestly, all her features in a gentle repose he had never imagined they had resort to, and her face and neck and even her bare shoulders pink with blushes. The warmth about his ankles rose to his knees. Or was he only imagining it? No, it kept on rising. He thought of what it must be like to drown—half with horror, half with pleasure he thought of it. And now he imagined that the whir of the heater's motor was coming directly from Isabel herself. He knew she was going to look up at him in another moment, and he supposed there might be tears. Then he *would* drown. If she wept—he had never seen her weep, not this Isabel—then it *would* be settled.

Afterward, he realized that she must have heard the footsteps before he did, and that that, somehow or other, was why she never looked up. It was the first of the arrivals amongst the dinner guests, and they were on the basement stairs. Isabel's mother would be sending them down; everybody who came to see the house had to see the presents. Rudy sprinted on tiptoe down the aisle between the tables, threw open the door to the corridor, pushed down the thermostat, sprinted back along the other aisle to Isabel. Taking her in his arms, he kissed her passionately. He observed, with relief, that there were no tears on her cheeks. . . . That's how they were when they were discovered by the utterly delighted first arrivals.

It was a fine party that night. After dinner they all went dancing. Rudy and Isabel were rather quiet throughout the evening. They held hands a lot, and kissed frequently. But they were noticeably abstemious. Some of the young men in the party had a great deal too much to drink, and one of the girls did. She was Isabel's cousin, who had come from out of town for the wedding and was staying at the Havenses' house. When they returned home at half past two, Isabel was forced to take charge of her cousin and see her up to bed. Rudy and Isabel said only a quick good-night at the doorstep.

HE TELEPHONED at eleven the next morning—from his office. Isabel was not at home. Her cousin was still asleep, but Isabel had risen an hour earlier and had gone out by herself for a drive in her car. Rudy talked to the maid first, but Isabel's mother got on the upstairs extension and dismissed the maid. Mrs. Havens said she felt she must take this opportunity to tell Rudy that she detected a "mounting nervousness" in Isabel, and she hoped he understood it was only to be expected in a bride as "the great day" approached. He did, he did—he assured her—he did indeed. And *she* wasn't worried, was she, by Isabel's going out for a drive? He hoped not. He didn't think she ought to be. . . . Heavens no, she wasn't. But with so much going on she was merely afraid she mightn't find another chance to speak to him privately, et cetera.

A few minutes later, Rudy stood watching them bring his car down on the elevator in the parking garage. He drove eastward a few blocks and then turned south. He had no particular destination in mind—no particular purpose. But the car seemed to know what it was doing. Was he in flight or in pursuit? he wondered. Or by keeping in motion was he trying to stand still? After last night, she might be capable of coming to his office—just barely. On the other hand, if he were in pursuit the town had grown too large during the past five years for him to think of looking for her. And it was not as though they had a trysting place. That wasn't in Isabel's line; Isabel was a born homebody! Suddenly he began to laugh rather hysterically at his own unexpected *bon mot*—a homebody—and he only managed to check himself when he saw two men in another car eyeing him curiously.

Half an hour later, he came on her car—her long yellow convertible—parked on the edge of the golf course and near the seventh green, in Riverside Park. . . . God, he breathed. What was she thinking? Those moonlight picnics! . . . "Get your big toe out of the egg sandwiches." . . . Snipe-hunting and all that. . . . Jesus, sweet sixteen! . . . Did she—could she—think those times in Riverside Park meant anything to him or to the other boys who went along? Had the other girls thought so too—that those playful, necking-party picnics were *something?* It seemed an eternity since he had ever thought about that summer, the summer when he had come home from college and decided to try dating some of the younger girls. Had she actually been amongst them? Yes, he could see her sitting very near the edge of the bluff above the river and holding on to a beer bottle and trying to yodel. And possibly he was the only one near enough to her to observe that the bottle, which she finally hurled down toward the river, was still almost full of beer.

He parked his car alongside hers and got out. There seemed to be no one playing the course. He set off in the direction of the seventh green, walking south and parallel with the bluff. The only sign of life was a man riding a big power mower several hundred yards ahead. The grass he walked through had already been cut, and blackbirds and pigeons mingled indiscriminately in the area. Each time he approached them, the blackbirds rose up and moved farther off. The pigeons waited till he was in their midst. His only feeling was one of boredom. Such stupid, ugly birds they were. What had they to do with him? What had revisiting Riverside Park to do with him and Isabel? . . . He went on, despite himself, knowing that she would not be glad to see him. . . . Though it was May, the sky was like pale wood ashes, with only a white disc of a sun showing through the overcast. Along the crest of the bluff, a growth of young scrub oak and sweet gum saplings hid all view of the great muddy river that was below. As he walked, he kept watching for the opening—the break in the growth. He knew it must still be there, and at last he saw it. He stepped through and out onto the little point of eroded, red-clay earth.

SHE WAS SITTING very near the edge with her plaid coat spread out beneath her, and she had on tan Bermuda shorts and a white cardigan. She looked up at him, not so much in surprise as in disappointment. Moreover, her glance accused him. Now it was he, wasn't it, who—by finding her here—said they had known each other all their lives. But no, his raised eyebrows replied, it was she who said so by being found here. He sat beside her on the plaid coat. Two hundred feet below them, down the clay bluff, the ugly red-brown river labored energetically and senselessly. It spread before them, half a mile wide. The flat landscape to the west of it was still victim to the last of the spring floods. There were islands over there with shapes like continents, familiar-looking but unnameable continents. It was a scene they both felt they had always known and never known.

They were a solemn pair, sitting there; they had met this morning in a region where they were dead to each other, where they must not and could not be otherwise. . . . One summer he had thrown pebbles at her window! No, it was a lie! But he had.

"Are you up there?"

"I'm up here."

"Coming down?"

"Have to get dressed."

"I'll be on the steps."

She was thirteen and it was almost midnight. But he was only a neighborhood boy, and their families were such friends it didn't matter. And he was so much *older* than she was. Why, she was a child. It was like having a little sister or even a little brother to talk to. He did not like her or dislike her. She was merely an excuse to keep from going on home. When he came pebble-throwing at her window he had always been somewhere else before. Probably he had spent the evening talking with boys his own age and older about whether or not one ought to go East to college, about when and whether-or-not the next war would come, about careers that would take them to Africa and South America—conversations that ended with somebody's saying, "I'll do anything so long as it takes me away from this hellhole." And then on the way home, he stopped to throw pebbles at the little Havens girl's window.

She and he would sit on her porch steps and chatter for half an hour or so. With her head of tight, black curls and with her lean, freckled face, and with no figure at all yet, she looked as much like a boy as a girl. It amused him to talk to her. It touched him, somehow. To think that two years ago he had been that young! Poor child, she had not begun to live. But he! Africa . . . war . . . college . . . I'll do anything so long as it takes me away from this hellhole!

What he did not know was that at thirteen she was already a Roman Catholic nun. She was sent by her family to the Methodist Sunday school every Sunday morning, but that did not alter the larger fact. And at fifteen, the summer of the necking-party picnics, she was soon to be the successor to Maria Tallchief. It was one of those secrets that had to be kept from those about you. *They* said it sounded so childish in a girl who was already having dates. She had at least to try to seem like the other girls. She even made fun of her dancing lessons. But she knew her worth, and she pitied people like Rudy Banks. Such boys were attractive to her, naturally. She even envied them. They asked so little of life and were able to live for the present moment only. (She knew about the really wild girls that boys like Rudy went out with sometimes.) But how would life be bearable without some high purpose like her own? . . . That was at fifteen. At seventeen, her purpose was more practical, she thought, and again more selfless. Her destiny, she knew now, was to become a social worker. Her heart went out to unwed mothers and prostitutes. She read serious articles in magazines. Boys like Rudy Banks were amusing still, but she knew it was a type which the society of the future must eliminate. Such men brought about the downfall of the very girls she was going to devote her life to helping. After an evening of dancing in the arms of some Rudy Banks or other, after sometimes allowing herself to be kissed by an especially ardent admirer, she felt she could hardly wait to be released from these demands which her life made upon her. It all seemed very degrading and to no purpose.

What she did not know, of course, was that when she was

seventeen and Rudy was nineteen he was making a fateful decision: Should he become a nuclear physicist or a professor of political science? . . . That year passed, and by the time he was in law school, two years later, Isabel was engrossed in her serious Junior League work. That year they were thrown together on several occasions and talked openly, not specifically to each other, but in groups which included the other, about their absorbing interests—law and charity work. They typed each other. He heard that she was still a puritan. She knew about his affairs. But it was to be still another year before they really met. By then they were properly prepared for the meeting. Rudy Banks had finished school and Isabel Havens had finished her Junior League apprenticeship. The time was at hand, the time for each of them to meet the right someone, to fall desperately in love, to get married. They were a sleeping beauty and a sleeping prince waking, conveniently, at the same time and in the same place. It would have seemed a profanation of the miracle to say that in their long sleep they had dreamed anything sweeter or nobler than the love which they were created for and which was going to light them through the rest of their waking life. Whoever said so was a liar.

During the half hour that they sat together looking at the wide river and its false islands, they spoke little. There were no kisses, and he didn't even take her hand till they rose to leave. The things that they did say were only simple things that touched on the dreariness of the scene. It seemed wrong, they said, that a brown river could not be thought as beautiful as a blue river. But the simple truth was, it couldn't. They wondered how it might be to have grown up beside a blue river with water so clear you could see right down into its depths, a clear river in a well-defined channel cut between white limestone bluffs and with possibly a little green island in the center, very real, and possibly, even, on that island the ruins of a small castle for the eye to focus on.

THAT NIGHT'S PARTY was out at the Hunt and Polo Club. The hostess was Rudy's Aunt Polly—his somewhat youthful, not unworldly Aunt Polly Norris. The guests were a mixed lot. There were Isabel's attendants, of course, including her cousin from out of town, who bored everybody with her remorse and total abstinence tonight. But the party was made up mostly from a rather frolicsome, wildish set that Rudy felt particularly at home in and from a somewhat less youthful but even more frolicsome set his aunt belonged to. Isabel's parents, as well as Rudy's own, decided, wisely, to spend the evening at home. They said there had been so much festivity already, and there was so much to be done tomorrow and the day after, et cetera, et cetera.

It was a fine party, like all the others. There was dancing on the glassed-in terrace after dinner, which was served at ten— after drinks which were served at seven-thirty. The little combo that Aunt Polly had hired finished playing at two a.m., as agreed upon, and departed. Before three, most of the young men, mindful of office desks that awaited them just six hours hence, dragged their young ladies away from the scene. And by that hour most husbands and wives from Aunt Polly's set had taken their leave—together or separately. Aunt Polly herself had already slipped away.

Isabel and Rudy wandered into the little corner of the lounge that the combo had occupied. It was just beside the door to the terrace, and it was banked with giant potted plants. They sat down together on the piano bench. They were holding hands, and without looking at Rudy, Isabel lifted his hand to her lips and kissed it—kissed the back of the hand, then the fingers.

"Hey now!" he said.

"Yes, hey now," she said, smiling to herself, still not looking at him.

"This morning in the park—" he began.

"In what park?" she coaxed, smiling. "Have you been meeting people in the park?"

"Oh," he said. "No, not I. Have you?"

"I slept all morning," she said.

"I was at the office."

"Well, then."

"Let's walk some," he said.

"Yes, let us do so." He realized that she was faking tipsiness, and an inspiration came to him.

The bar was at the other end of the big lounge. They set off in that general direction. They moved through a cigarette smog, in near darkness. Off at the drear edges of the room a few sad, last table lamps were still lit. In the mammoth field-stone fireplace, some last embers sputtered and sent up a feeble show of sparks. But in the central gloom, Rudy and Isabel had to pick their way amongst tables and chairs without always knowing whether the chairs, or even the tables, were occupied by one or more persons. As they drew near the bar, they passed one final little company sitting upright around a table. Someone in the group said, "Look at 'em. They're walking on air."

Someone else said, "They think they're in love."

"What do you mean *think?*" said the first voice.

"I mean *think.*"

"What are the odds?" said a new voice. "Has he or hasn't he?"

"It's always even money."

"Not in this case. For if he hasn't, she's the only woman under forty at this party he hasn't."

"Are you speaking from experience?"

"I'm not under forty."

"Well, she's pure as the snow."

"It's always even money."

Hand in hand, they had moved on to the bar. They smiled at each other. He even bent forward and kissed her on the lips. Then, almost under his breath, he said to the barkeep, "Two whiskey and water—heavy."

The table behind them was silent. Presently the barkeep set two bronze-colored drinks on the counter. A long, low, breathless whistle came from the table. Not-in-this-case said, "Look, he's going to slug her. That's the most loathsome sight I've ever seen."

And walking-on-air said, "With the wedding only the day after tomorrow—*really* only tomorrow now!"

Isabel looked at the drink before her on the counter, and then looked at Rudy. He gave her his glittering smile. How artless he was. Oh, how she loved him for his artlessness. She knew all about him. She loved his thinking that he could use the same smile and the same drink for all his purposes. She knew who it was that had slugged her cousin from out of town last night. She knew how he and her cousin had spent that twenty minutes when he escorted her to make the long-distance telephone call to her own fiancé back home. She believed still that all that was all right for him. She believed still that she had made a mistake in her self-denial; her heart, or her mind, was still set upon remedying her mistake, upon breaking the solemn resolution which some other Isabel, in one of her other lives, had made for her. That was still her fierce, firm purpose, her overwhelming necessity even. And now something strengthened her resolve. As Rudy's smile faded, she saw a look in his eyes that was unbearable to her. . . . She *would not* serve his purpose. She would not allow him to keep the resolution made by another Rudy Banks. She would not, on their wedding night, be there merely as his idealized something or other.

She took his arm, without ever touching the glass set before her—and without his having touched his—and led him away into the gloom.

"Did you see her face?" said a voice at the table.

"Beautiful!" said another.

"Oh God, now I've seen life's other face," said a man's voice. It would have been difficult to distinguish which amongst the other husky voices were male and which female. "I've seen it," the man's said. And then, after a moment, the same voice was giving utterance to a chain of muffled, broken sobs.

"Get hold of yourself, Doug," said a voice that was distinctly a woman's. "You're not that far out."

Two chairs scraped on the stone floor, and the barkeep was relieved of his neglected drinks.

ISABEL STEERED RUDY in the direction of the nearest door to the glassed-in terrace. When finally they stood in the doorway, Rudy drew back. There was more light on the terrace than in the lounge, but it had been deserted by the guests. He pulled her away from the doorway, and they walked in the light along the edge of the lounge till they reached another door leading to the terrace. Isabel stepped out onto the terrace alone. Rudy leaned against the doorjamb and watched her wandering about out there. She had never seemed more maidenly, never more womanly, never more desirable, never more precisely the very girl that she must be. He did not know why it mattered so much to him, but at any rate he knew that it did. He no longer regarded himself as a serious person, he had long since come to think of himself as a kind of clown and to think of his life's most serious activities as clownish acrobatics which he was peculiarly well qualified to perform; but there remained this one last absurd point of semi-seriousness. For it, he was willing to risk Isabel's most indignant and righteous rage. He was, in fact, determined to risk it now, in the light of her will to use him in the way she so clearly intended, her will to have her cake and eat it too, her willingness to make him the battle-ground of her conflicting purposes.

On the terrace, Isabel peered out through the glass walls and then gazed upward through the glass overhead. "It has cleared," she said breathlessly. "Stars are out."

Rudy burst into laughter.

Isabel seized the latch on one of the panels in the glass wall and threw open the door to the outside. She gave one little shriek of laughter. It seemed half in response to Rudy's laughter and half in response to her first breath of the night air—half anguish, half delight. Without looking back at Rudy, she ran out-of-doors.

"You can't go out there," he shouted after her, quickly crossing the terrace to the open door. "It's all a mess!"

THE MESS OUTSIDE was a very real one. The Hunt and Polo had moved its location during the previous fall—very late in the previous fall. And there had followed such a severe winter and such a wet spring that almost no work had been done on the grounds. Members and their guests still came and went, between the asphalt parking area and the front entrance to the clubhouse, over a series of rough planks laid across the mud.

From the doorway to the glassed-in terrace there were not even any planks. When Rudy reached the doorway he saw Isabel bounding off through the mire with her white evening dress pulled up about her knees. He gave one regretful glance at his patent leather slippers and then set out after her. With his first steps he felt the mud oozing over the sides of his slippers, and it passed through his mind that he, Rudy Banks, might end his days a wife-beater! He might not even wait till she *was* his wife! Why hadn't he thought of that solution before? A beating might just do the trick.

He gained on her rapidly, much more rapidly than he had expected or intended. She was heading toward the woods that began a hundred feet or so distant from the clubhouse. As she approached the woods she was obviously slowing her pace. Suddenly Rudy stopped in his deep tracks. For the first time, she looked back at him. And she, too, stopped. But presently, still holding up her skirt, she began to trot along the edge of the woods where the ground was not so soft. Rudy remained where he was, lifting first one foot and then the other to shake off the mud, the way a small dog will do. When Isabel had traveled about thirty feet, she turned in toward the clubhouse again. She was circling back! Before Rudy knew it, she had outflanked him and cut him off from any easy retreat to the terrace doorway.

He glanced to the right and then to the left. Isabel was

moving toward him now. In an open space, several hundred feet to his left, was an assemblage of dark objects that he recognized—clumps and stacks and bunches of leftover building materials as well as certain other bulky objects. His choice was between this junkyard and the woods, and instinct told him that he must at all cost avoid the woods. He bolted for the junkyard.

The Hunt and Polo's new site was ten miles farther from town than its old location, and in conjunction with the move (a very profitable move, the old site's having been sold at a fine figure for use as a new suburban development)—in conjunction with the move the members made one extremely sage decision: they entirely eliminated the role of horses, hounds, and polo ponies from the club's program of activities, and so were relieved from making any provisions for barns, paddocks, kennels, or polo field on the new site. This was a very realistic step and would save them many thousands of dollars in years to come. And to placate a few stodgy members who disapproved, it was resolved that a good many accessories and appurtenances from the old installation should be brought along to decorate the new site and thus preserve some of the old atmosphere. If spring would only come, these ornaments would be duly set up in places appointed for them by the landscape architect. But, meanwhile, they rested with the remnants of lumber and cement blocks in the club's private junkyard. And it was in their precincts, on this starry April night, that Rudy Banks took final refuge from Isabel Havens.

Once he had entered the area, Isabel had difficulty catching sight of him again. The lumber piles and the stacks of cement blocks were like so many small buildings with dark little alleys of mud between. And much of what was brought from the old club consisted literally of quaint outbuildings and dependencies—a dovecote, a saddle and harness shack, a two-room playhouse for young children, as well as stacks of doghouses, barrels, feed-troughs and drinking-troughs, even heaps of gates and rails from the old fences—and nearly all of these heaps and stacks covered over with sheets of canvas. Along the muddy passages between, Isabel pursued him doggedly. Or suddenly she did an about-face, sure she would run squarely into him around the corner she had just turned. But he was never there. Soon she ceased to imagine even that she had caught glimpses of him. She could hear the smacking and sucking of his quick footwork in the mud, and now and again she would hear him laughing to himself. She heard him mutter, "God, what's this?" Half a minute later, she heard him say something like that again. And each time, she would presently come on the thing she supposed he had seen or perhaps even stumbled over—first an iron hitching post, next an old mounting block. The noises he made sounded always just around the corner ahead or behind, or just over the nearest bulk of canvas. She never once called out to him, or she did not *think* she did. And she would never know how long she went on stalking him after it was no use. She never lost her confidence that she would find him at last.

He was never certain how close behind him she might be. He could not hear a sound she made, but he knew always that she was back there or maybe just ahead around the next corner. At last, he knew his only safety would be in hiding from her somewhere. He had led her through the whole complex of junk and rubbish, and now was back at the largest pile of lumber. He began to climb. Beyond the lumber he could see the gable of the children's playhouse. The climbing was very easy. He went up and up, ever so silently. Then at the very top, his right foot caught between two planks. Pulling the foot free, he twisted his ankle painfully. He bent over to massage the ankle, hopping unsteadily on the other foot. He lost his balance, and in an effort to regain it, whirled about and fell backward. As he fell, the back of his neck came down heavily against the pointed gable-end of the playhouse.

The poor fellow died instantly. His body folded up as though he were a life-sized Raggedy Andy, his two feet flying upward to either side of his head. He slipped, bottom first, down into the narrow crevice between the lumber and the playhouse. It would be many hours before they found him there, and meanwhile the stars shone on his uncovered head and on the muddy soles of his dress slippers. He was wedged in between the rough edges of the unfinished lumber and the smooth clapboard of the playhouse. His neck was broken, the life gone out of his body, but he was safe from Isabel at last, poor fellow.

THREE
ONE-ACT PLAYS

Familiar Haunts

Meg, a woman of thirty-five, wears an elegant, floor-length negligee. She stands before a monumental pink marble mantelpiece which has carved nude figures on either side of the relatively small fireplace opening as well as on either side of the expanse of mirror in the overmantel. Between two enormous brass andirons is a tiny glow of flames. On one side of the fireplace opening is an embossed, brass-plated woodbox. On the other side is an elaborate brass fire set—shovel, poker, tongs, et cetera, all highly polished. The rest of the room, except for the chair in which Meg's brother Nicky is seated, is furnished more like a lady's boudoir than the proportions of the room indicate. There is no bed, but among other tables and chairs is a small writing desk and an accompanying fragile chair.

Nicky, two or three years younger than Meg and still very youthful looking, wears a topcoat and is holding his hat in his lap. He is sitting very erect in a straight, high-backed armchair—a reproduction of Stuart oak. The chair is placed against the wall beside a large entrance, closed off by double doors.

. . .

NICKY   I used always to be known hereabouts as my father's son. Now I'm known as the brother of the rich Mrs. Bitch.

MEG *(taken off guard but replying sharply, quickly)*　I may not be as rich a bitch as you think I am.

NICKY *(placating)*　Why, you're not a bitch at all. That's only an expression. But they do say you're right rich. At the moment they say you are the richest single woman in St. Louis.

MEG *(pleased)*　They say.

NICKY　You are single at the moment, Meg?

MEG　Now and forever more. I've gone into retirement.

NICKY　But a woman doesn't marry and divorce four times in a dozen years without clearing something. Every time I write you either you've got a new hubby or you've shed one. I must always think of myself as the brother-in-law of a different tycoon.

MEG　If you came home more often you would see the real truth.

NICKY　Dearest Meg, you have never said that before.

MEG　I don't know, of course, how often you may have come home. You don't usually honor me with a call. To what do I owe—

NICKY　One time you will be Mrs. Harris, and the next Mrs. Amesbury, and the next Mrs. So-and-so. What is your name now, Meg? *(Meg laughs.)* And each hubby richer than the one before, they say.

MEG　They say. *(her tone hardening)*

NICKY　I have to believe them. I see how you live. You keep the old homeplace up wonderfully. And, dearest Meg, you would not have been allowed to marry that pigeon-toed little brewer if Father had not known his worth. But Father saw your talent. Father set you on the right path.

MEG *(indignant at the reference)*　How dare you. *How* dare you, you spineless ne'er-do-well.

NICKY　Lord, what have I said now?

MEG　How dare you speak that way of Father.

NICKY　Oh. Oh, Father.

MEG　He would die a thousand deaths to hear you. You and

I were everything to him. And whatever he did for me, he left *you* every cent he had, remember that.

NICKY And now it's all gone.

MEG Can that be true? In less than ten years you've run through it all?

NICKY It's gone, at any rate.

MEG Oh, oh, Nicky, how could you? . . . You mustn't sit there like a beggar, hat in hand. Come closer to the fire, we'll have a drink.

NICKY But I *am* a beggar! I need—

MEG Nicky! I won't have you asking me for more money. I will entertain you. You may even come here and live in the house again, if you like. We can be children again. But I won't give you more money.

NICKY Why not, Meg? What's so important about money?

MEG *(laughing)* Ah, Nicky, Nicky. The same old Nicky. I will never give you more money. No woman should ever begin giving money to a man—not even to her brother. It has to work the other way round. Don't you remember that Father would always try to keep me from giving you money even when you were a boy? Father used to say that I spoiled you worse than any mother could have done when you were a little thing. In most respects I suspect I did. If Mother had lived, she could not have had more concern for your welfare than I did. And Father gave his life to the two of us. He was an attractive, vital man, but because of us he never thought of marrying again.

NICKY No, Meg, not of marrying! But marriage isn't the only solution to such a man's needs. He took the other solution, my solution.

MEG *(quite angry)* Now, I won't have you talking that way in this house! Not sitting there in the chair that Father always directed you to!

NICKY *(rising)* Then I'd better go. But I should tell you it was *he* who suggested I see you tonight.

MEG *(staring at him in silence for a moment, then:)* I don't believe you have any intention of going until you get the money you came for. *(Nicky smiles and sits down again.)* And though I love you dearly, Nicky, I have no intention of giving you more money.

(She offers him the highball she has been mixing for him, but he holds up his hand and shakes his head, refusing it. She shrugs and sips her own drink.)

NICKY I came tonight because Father suggested I come. Father says—

MEG *(ignoring his last speech)* Father used to say that if one understood the correct female role and the correct male role in our corner of the world then one needn't understand anything else.

NICKY You and Father talked openly about *sex!* With me he never acknowledged that such a thing existed—not in his *lifetime.*

MEG *(stomping her foot)* Nicky, stop it!

NICKY Father never spoke directly to me about anything but work. It was always work he had in mind for me, not sex. When he was alive, I mean. It's a different matter now, of course.

MEG *(after a silence)* Nicky, it was your own good that Father had in mind for you. I consider it very unmanly of you to be so critical of him when he is not here to defend himself.

NICKY Ha.

MEG I also consider that you are being unfair to me, to come begging money from me and making all these innuendos about Father! I don't know what half your remarks have meant. I don't want to know. But I know you, Nicky. You could be up to anything, *anything.* You're not going to frighten me, though, with your insinuations. Let me tell you this, if Father didn't speak directly about many things, he did speak directly to me about you. Oh, we had it out many a time about you and your unwillingness to work and your expensive tastes.

NICKY As for all that, he spoke directly enough with me about it. But he doesn't get away with such talk anymore.

MEG   Nicky, that is absolutely enough. You are not going to scare me with those little parentheses of yours. When I was a girl, I really thought sometimes you *were* going mad. But I used to call your hand on such games even then. So don't try to pull any tricks out of that old bag.

NICKY   I was never more sane in my life than now.

MEG *(moving farther away from him)* And you were never more unfair to me. There is something I have never told you before, Nicky. It was I who persuaded Father to leave you the entire estate, except for the house. "Nicky has expensive tastes," I said, "and as for me, I can look after myself." We talked about it many times, Father and I. It was very hard to make him understand. He said, "Meg, you're worse than any mother would be." Why, he and I used to sit right here before the fire and talk about such matters, hour after hour. Even then, Nicky, I felt as though you were my own child and I was setting matters right between you and your father. I would be monogramming a shirt for him or knitting a sweater. Oh, Nicky, how he *loved* to have everything he wore especially made for him and when I was working on something for him he would say what a good wife I would make somebody. "That," I would say, "is why I don't need money of my own. All I want is the house, Father," I would say, "because whatever or whoever my husband may be, I intend to spend the rest of my life right here where we have been so happy together."

NICKY *(He has come up behind the couch where she is now sitting.)* It was always clear to me you didn't *want* his money. You *would not* have it! But why? Why, Meg? It was tainted money for you, somehow.

MEG   That's not true! It's not true! How can you be such an ingrate! *(rising from the couch)*

NICKY   But it is true. It was tainted for you but not for me. That's how you thought of it. *I* was not too good to receive it. And you knew I would "run through it." You wanted me to run through it, Meg. What was wrong with his money?

Was it ill gotten? Was there something low and crooked about the way Father made his pile?

MEG *(She slaps him.)* You common, ungrateful brat! Get out of this house! There is nothing you will not accuse your own father of!

NICKY But *he* doesn't care, Meg. *He* doesn't care what I accuse him of, Meg. And he doesn't know why you wouldn't have his money, Meg. I have asked him . . . just last night.

MEG *(She slaps him again.)* I will not listen to such rot. I will not listen to such nonsense . . . about . . . the dead.

NICKY He told me to come here to see you. Dead or not, he wants to know why you did not want his money. It disturbs him. It disturbs his peace.

MEG I tell you not to talk that kind of rot to me. Either you are hoping to make me think you are mad or you hope to drive *me* mad. But I warn you, Nicky—

NICKY He thinks maybe you suspect him of having accepted money from his lady-friends.

MEG *(She is silent for a moment.)* He never had any lady-friends. Not after he was married to Mother. Not after Mother died. His interest was all in . . . in us, in his family.

NICKY *(laughing)* Oh, Meg.

MEG Don't "oh Meg" me. Get out of my house. Go on, get out, I tell you.

NICKY *(fearless)* He had as many lady-friends when we were growing up as I've had lady-friends in my lifetime, as *you've* had husbands in ten years. And why shouldn't he? It was after Mother died, of course.

(Meg goes and rests her arm on the mantel shelf, putting her forehead on her arm, and looks desolately into the fire.)

NICKY There was Mrs. Susie Morris, the rich and voluptuous widow of old Judge Joe Morris. Father used to go to see her just after noon on Sunday.

MEG You're lying, Nicky. Father played golf on Sunday afternoons.

NICKY I would sometimes be in the vacant lot next to Billy

Fletcher's house. There would be a whole gang of us, playing baseball or touch, and it never occurred to him that I was among those boys and watching him come and go. He would arrive after Mrs. Morris's servants left at noon and he would stay for three or four hours. He would always arrive on foot; he must have parked the car several blocks away. And although other people would sometimes come calling on those Sunday afternoons, Mrs. Morris and Father would never answer the door.

MEG Your disordered mind! Your perverse nature! You *evil, evil* creature!

NICKY There were others, too, Meg. You know there were others. You could name them as well as I. You have just never been willing to name them to yourself. Everybody in town knew about him and that "notorious old libertine" Mrs. Templeton. *(laughing)* They took trips together all over the country. While you and I were away at school, he and Mrs. T. were off to Florida and California—even Honolulu. I know people who *saw* them there. . . . His lady-friends were all rich women. He was right clever about it. They didn't need his money, and they were so well fixed here in St. Louis they could behave pretty much as they pleased. *(Meg goes and sits down on the couch.)* Oh, don't tell me, Meg, you never had any thoughts about Mrs. Linda Perkins, and Mrs. Rousse, and Mrs. Battenberg.

MEG He used to be put with them at dinner parties, that's all.

NICKY Why, you know more about life out here in St. Louis than that, Meg. How can you pretend to such innocence. You, the much-married Mrs. Whatchamaycallher. Just remember how most of those old lady-friends of his ended their days—hopeless alcoholics or married to some horse trainer or even to her chauffeur in one case, or jumping out a window or taking too many sleeping pills. I'm not exaggerating. And I'm not blaming *him* for how they ended. I'm only pointing out the kind of company he kept.

MEG I don't believe a word you're saying. I don't believe you believe it, either. But I see now what it is you're saying to me. Those *women* you describe—you see me, Nicky, as one of their sort. In your eyes I'm one of that contemptible lot, another rich Mrs. Bitch. Well, let me give you some small insight into what it is like to live as I have done. I have never once been in love. I have yearned for love. I have dreamed of it. But that is all. Yet I have found the men I married interesting men. Even "the pigeon-toed little brewer" interested me. They were not idiots—any of them. Maybe their money interested me first of all, but in each instance I sincerely believed I would come to love the man I was marrying. I was sure I would; and then month after month went by, and it was the same story. It wasn't in me. I was lacking the ability to love them.

NICKY   And don't you really know why you haven't the ability to love them? Don't you really know who is responsible for that?

MEG *(despondent)*   You go back to him, you blame him for everything. Yet when he was alive he dedicated his life to us.

NICKY *(angry)*   *Why* couldn't you ever see him as he is? A greater hypocrite never lived than our father. All those years when he was having one fine affair after another—in those very years—he was declining to acknowledge the existence of sex so far as I, his son, was concerned; and later on when he was still in hot pursuit of every woman within his reach, he was advising me, with the straightest face, to "beware of womankind," not to "involve myself," that "a young man should go to his marriage bed pure as any virgin." When I had finished college he used to say I wouldn't work, but when I was in my teens he wouldn't allow me to take a little job after school—he said I should study or get "my exercise"—and he would not give me money to spend on girls. You and he agreed I had expensive tastes because I learned to like clothes and cars. I *had* to like *something*, by God! And then when I did get a girl and she and I got drunk (on money you gave me, Meg dear) and were picked up asleep in my car at the roadside—because we had nowhere else to go—

what did he do? He came to the police station and beat me!
(clenching his fists, enraged by the memory)

MEG   No, Nicky, he didn't! You know you're lying!

NICKY *(pressing his fists against his temples)*   Yes, he beat me
while the cop held me.

(Meg weeps.)

NICKY *(suddenly laughing)*   No, don't cry, Meg. There's no
need crying about it now. I've got back at him. You should
see how I treat him nowadays.

MEG *(looking up at him from the couch)*   What *are* you saying,
Nick—my poor Nick?

(Silence)

NICKY   I'm saying that he comes back to me. All through the
years he has. I assumed he came back to you, too.

MEG   Oh, God. Please, my dear, don't say these things.

NICKY *(incredulous)*   You've *never* seen him? Why, it's here
in St. Louis that I see him nearly always. In fact, I never
come without seeing him. He'll turn up in a taxi or in a hotel
room. Once he turned up at the airport when I came in on
a late flight.

MEG   No, Nick. How crude of you. You're trying to torture
me. *(passionately)* I loved him. I loved him. *(weeping)* Don't
you know that if he were to appear anywhere at all it would
certainly be *here*? *(She hides her face on the back of the couch
as she sobs.)*

NICKY   Of course it would! Of course! See him there! There,
Meg!

*(Ghost appears. He is an overweight, disheveled, middle-aged
man.)*

NICKY *(to Ghost)*   I didn't really think you would follow me
here and let her see you for what you are. *(laughing)* Put
your shirttail in, you old bastard. Do you want your own
daughter to guess what you have been up to? And fasten
your tie. I guess your collar won't button. *(to Meg)* He got
to be such a slob, you know—in those last years. But he was
always essentially that. *(walking around Ghost and addressing*

him) Suck your gut in! Do you want me to give you a kick in the pants? *(The Ghost throws back his head and laughs silently. Then suddenly he pulls himself up and strikes out at Nicky, missing him.)* You couldn't hit a fly! *(to Meg)* Well, now what do you say?

MEG You know very well what I say. I don't see a thing. Or hear a thing.

NICKY *(to Ghost)* What the hell are you up to? Make yourself known. Speak up. Tell her how much you regret all your sorry ways. That's the tune you are always singing to me. Tell her how you appear to me for the very purpose of letting me abuse you and lighten your burden. *(The Ghost opens and closes its mouth as Nicky intones:)* I am thy father's ghost, doomed for a certain period of the night—*(suddenly laughing)* Well, that's the only Shakespeare you know. *(to Meg)* He's only trying to impress you. He could always make himself impressive to the ladies.

MEG *(seizing Nicky's arm)* Nicky, darling—really, there is no one there!

NICKY You were always blind as a bat, Meg. But I can make him talk. I can make him say things you'll remember. *(to Ghost)* Tell us about your love-life, and tell us how you took money from those widow-ladies. Oh, he had *something* the ladies liked. He might look like an old slob to you and me, but he had *something* we couldn't see at home.

MEG *(springing to her feet)* Nick, how much do you want? I'll fetch my checkbook. It's over here. How much? Say the amount and then go. *(She is already making out the check.)*

NICKY You really don't see him, do you?

MEG How much, Nick?

NICKY *(throws hand in air, gesturing to ghost)* Take off! *(Ghost leaves.)*

MEG How much, Nick? I want you to go.

NICKY Twenty thousand.

MEG And you won't come back? *(writing check)*

NICKY Not unless you send for me. Not unless *he* should turn up here, and you should need me.

MEG   Here, Nick. Go quickly. *(She stuffs check in his jacket pocket.)*

NICKY   Goodbye, Meg. *(He extends a hand, but she turns away.)*

MEG   Please go, Nick. I am very tired.

(Exit Nick. Meg lowers the lights. She goes to the fireplace and leans on mantel, as before, her face hidden. The Second Ghost appears in the room. He is slender, straight, correct in his dress, moves with dignity. As he moves silently across the room, she lifts her head, as if hearing his footsteps, but doesn't look around.)

GHOST   Meg, darling.

(She turns quickly from the fireplace but in the opposite direction from the Second Ghost. She takes a sip from her drink, replaces glass on the table, puts away her checkbook.)

GHOST   Meg, darling. *(She stands very still, her back to him.)* Turn and face me, Meg. *(She puts her hands to her ears.)* Meg. *(Lowering her hands, she braces herself against a table, turns slowly toward him. He is now standing directly beside the couch, with his hand on the couch back.)*

MEG *(in a hoarse whisper)*   God in heaven!

GHOST   Meg, do you see me? Do you hear me?

MEG   Yes. Yes, I do. I see you. I hear you. I must be out of my mind.

GHOST   No, you are not out of your mind. But it took Nick— poor Nicky—to make you let yourself see me. But it doesn't matter how or who. *(He begins moving around the couch toward her.)*

MEG   Stay where you are. I am not afraid of you. This is some kind of trick. *(backing away)* I will throw myself out that window if you come any nearer—whoever you are.

GHOST   But you know who I am, Meg. And it is not as though you didn't recognize me. You do. I am just as I always was, am I not, Meg?

MEG   If you come one step closer I'll throw myself out that window.

GHOST *(laughing)*   Meg, you and I know that window has a burglar guard. It would be very difficult.

MEG I'll wake the neighbors. I'll call for help. I'll scream. At least they would come in and tell me I am mad.

GHOST But why the histrionics, Meg? You have nothing to fear from me, have you, Meg? *(He is drawing very near to her.)*

MEG *(looking up into his face, yielding completely)* But why have you never come before?

GHOST I have been here always, Meg darling. *(He takes her in his arms. She puts her arms about his neck. They kiss. They remain in a lovers' embrace as there comes the sound of Nicky's slamming closed the great double front doors of the house.)*

Curtain

A Redheaded Man

The library, in a fine old city house in St. Louis, has been converted into an invalid's room. Nathan, very pale, very old and ailing, though still fiercely masculine, reclines in his chair, his eyes now open, now closed. His daughter is with him. Her clothes are elegant but hopelessly out of fashion and ill-fitting. She wears a hat which hides her face much of the time.

. . .

SHE   What more can I do for you, Father? Jack will be here any minute now.

NATHAN   Why, you've done everything, I think.

SHE   I've done nothing, of course, but be here with you.

NATHAN *(irritated)*   It's your presence that *is* everything.

SHE   You're very sweet to say that.

NATHAN *(stirring in his chair)*   Sweet, hell! Why, if your mother herself should come back, *her* presence could not be more comfort to me.

SHE *(gently)*   What a way to speak to me, Father. *(soothing)* But it doesn't matter, dearest. My only wish is to make you more comfortable. I am here to answer your needs. I am here because you want me here. If it had been Mother you wished for most, it is she who would no doubt be here.

NATHAN   Of course, of course. *(roughly, shaking his head)*

That was only a manner of speaking. Of course it is you I wanted here. Damn it, I don't deny it! I don't deny it!

SHE   Don't upset yourself, Father honey. *(She pats his hand.)* *(A pause)*

NATHAN   All through the years I've told myself that if I trusted you it was to me and my house you would come— when your *time* came.

SHE   But how did you ever imagine that I would come at all? You didn't always believe in such possibilities. *(all the while ministering to him)*

NATHAN   I believed always in you . . . despite anything, despite your abandoning me for that sorry, redheaded, low-born bastard—abandoning me and—

SHE *(calming him)*   Father, don't. *(shaking her head and smiling)* What a silly you are.

NATHAN   And never even bring your child to see me.

SHE *(ministering to him)*   But didn't it ever occur to you that "when my time came" I might be drawn elsewhere?

NATHAN   To your child? To the son of—

SHE   Now, now. *(laughing at him)*

NATHAN   To the son of such a union!

SHE *(hesitating)*   Well, yes, why not to my son, to Jack? He has been a wonderful son to me, an adoring son. You two are very much like each other, really. High-strung and *so* demanding of other people, and *awfully* lovable. My Jack's a fine young man. He will be here in a few minutes now. You two will meet for the first time, and I shall witness the meeting—myself unseen. It will be a moment of great satisfaction for me.

NATHAN   It will be as unlikely a meeting as ever was. You should put down a cloth of gold.

SHE   This house will be the cloth of gold for that meeting. At last to see the two of you together under one roof! Under *this* roof! What a satisfaction it will be for me.

NATHAN   I wish you could be with us in more than spirit. *(She lifts her face and laughs gently.)* I wish you could be *present* then—visible to both of us.

SHE No! I can't be, Father. *(Her voice trembles slightly. The tone is somewhat nervous but affectionate still.)* You know I can't be.

NATHAN *(laughing)* Of course not. It would scare the wits out of the young fellow, coming to this old house and finding the spirit of his dead mother chatting quietly with his nearly dead old grandfather. *(laughing bitterly, hatefully)* Oh, God damn! *(slapping chair arm)* God damn! What a picture!

SHE *(affectionately)* Father, you *are* awful. Now, aren't you?

NATHAN Awful? If you think I'm so awful, why are you here? And most daughters in the world wouldn't do what you did.

SHE Do you want me to go now?

NATHAN No! *(desperately)* No, of course I don't. Don't leave me yet.

SHE *(gently still)* Why, I'm not threatening to leave you, Father. Not till Jack comes. *(A pause)* But why did you imagine it was not to Jack I'd be drawn if I were to be drawn to anyone on this side?

NATHAN *(leaning forward in chair)* Because your son did not want you and did not believe, as I did, in your coming back. He is young. His thoughts are no doubt on other things . . . already. My thoughts have never been on anything or anyone but you. From the night you left my house with that redheaded sybarite, that seducer, that low-born—

SHE *(quietly, gently)* Remember, we don't talk of him, Father.

NATHAN No, I agree with you about that, by Christ. His name is not mentioned in this house.

SHE Nor my name.

NATHAN Nor your name.

SHE But, again, how did you ever imagine I would be drawn back here?

NATHAN *(with assurance)* Because this was the house in which you were loved most.

SHE *(She goes and kisses him on the top of his head.)* I'm not sure about that. . . . I'd like to think so. Or would I?

NATHAN You think—

SHE How could one ever be sure? *(all gentleness)*

NATHAN You think *Jack* loved you more?

(She is silent for several moments and still as a statue.)

SHE Jack is a wonderful son. *You* are a wonderful father. But—

(Nathan opens his mouth to speak but remains silent for a moment. Then, looking directly at her, he speaks.)

NATHAN You have not been coming to see me so faithfully during the last month or so, yet you have *never* seemed so close or so clear as tonight.

(She now stands behind his chair, with her hands on his chair back.)

SHE It is because, dearest Father, my feelings are so intense about this meeting between my two loved ones. It is more important to me now than ever. *(in a whisper)* He is almost here! Now! Now! *(She runs toward the doorway at center, rear.)*

NATHAN *(irritated)* The maid will let him in.

SHE *(serene)* Ah, but I must see him as he enters this house the first time. *(Now she is standing in the broad doorway. To herself:)* It is he! My dearest Jack! *(then, glancing back at Nathan)* And my dearest Father! Ah, my two innocents!

(She passes through the doorway and backs away to the right. Jack's voice is heard. He appears in the doorway from right, a handsome young man with dark hair. As he enters he is speaking over his shoulder.)

JACK In here?

NATHAN Yes, in here. . . . Well, well . . . *(with formality)* I am very glad you have come.

JACK *(advancing)* How do you do, sir. It's fine to be here.

(They look at each other. Then they shake hands.)

NATHAN Won't you sit down?

JACK Yes. . . . Where would you prefer I sit?

NATHAN *(impatiently)* It doesn't matter, it doesn't matter. . . . Over there.

JACK Here?

NATHAN   Yes, yes, it don't matter. Sit down. You mustn't be so diffident with me.
(A silence)
JACK   I thought you might hear me better on one side or the other.
NATHAN   I am not so infirm as I may appear to be.
JACK *(edgy)*   I didn't mean that. But I believe Mother once said your hearing was always better in one ear than in the other.
NATHAN *(laughing acidly)*   Well, well. Is that the most interesting kind of comment she had to make on me? Or perhaps the only kind of comment you chose to recall.
JACK   It wasn't my intention to offend you, sir.
(A silence)
NATHAN   Well, I suppose you came in on the throughway.
JACK   What do you mean, sir?
NATHAN   Why, I mean what route did you take to get here?
JACK   Oh, I came—
NATHAN   It doesn't really matter!
JACK   No, of course it doesn't matter how I came. What matters, I would suppose, is that I got here—at last. You have never been to—our little apartment.
(A pause)
NATHAN   I don't go about much anymore.
JACK   Of course. I understand that.
NATHAN   And I don't know why I should ask what route you took to get here. They've put in all those new streets. I wouldn't know my way—
JACK   Yet I can see you do really want to know. . . . Well, I came along Pershing Avenue to Union and turned—
NATHAN *(impatiently)*   But that's right out here, right over yonder. I mean the route from where you live. You do live out in the county, don't you?
JACK   Ah, you don't know where I live! *(laughing)* I see. That's what you're trying to find out. *(laughing again)* Well, it's not exactly in the county. I live in Parkview.
NATHAN   Oh, so . . . I've never thought Parkview was very

attractive, but then I've never been in that section of town much. I remember when it was all corn fields. And then it was all just another subdivision with new development houses and apartments. Lots of duplexes, aren't there?

JACK I grew up in one.

NATHAN Ah, yes.

JACK I grew up in Parkview. I rather like it. In fact, it's my favorite part of St. Louis. I think I'll never leave it.

NATHAN Well, bully for you.

(A silence)

JACK I suppose you prefer Clayton to Parkview.

NATHAN Well, I prefer Clayton to Ladue. The further you get out of there, the poorer the construction is, the more impermanent and unreal it seems. It just doesn't seem like St. Louis to me.

JACK But it is cleaner out there; it is more open.

NATHAN Who minds a little dirt, who minds close neighbors, if it means living among permanent people?

JACK *(barely suppressing a smile)* Permanent people? . . . Well, I acknowledge this was once a very fine neighborhood.

NATHAN It still is.

JACK It has changed, though, hasn't it, since the days when—

NATHAN It hasn't changed. This is a part of town no one ever leaves.

JACK No one?

NATHAN Not anyone who belongs here.

JACK People don't leave Parkview, either. Not anybody who belongs there. And I like it the way it is. I wouldn't want to see it changed—not for anything. You like the old West End because it is *yours*. I like Parkview because it is *mine*.

NATHAN I can't imagine equating them.

JACK No, I suppose not. Certainly *I* couldn't. . . . You know Mother used to tell me about how fine this section was when she was living here—when she was a child, that is. It was the fashionable West End then. But most of it has got to look awfully seedy and run-down. Waterman Avenue is a slum, and so is Washington Avenue.

NATHAN   Well, around here is not a slum. And I don't relish your reflections on this section of town in general.

JACK   No sir, I suppose you don't, sir. And I don't relish your reflections on Parkview, sir.

NATHAN   Oh, "sir, sir, sir"! What kind of talk is that from a man this day and age? Is there something you're after from me? *(laughing—unpleasantly)*

JACK *(rising and speaking very loud)*   I didn't mean to offend you! But I didn't come here to be offended, either!

NATHAN   Sit down. And keep your voice down, too.

JACK   I won't have you speaking so to me. If this is what having a grandfather is like, it's just as well to have done without one till now.

NATHAN *(slowly)*   So you do actually regard me as your grandfather, eh?

JACK   Yes, I think of you as that.

NATHAN   Even though your mother and that father of yours would never let us meet so long as your mother lived?

JACK   Yes, even so. But I am not going to take such talk from you. I am only a *disinherited* grandson, not an *illegitimate* grandson.

NATHAN   See here! I won't take such dirty language as that from you, either. Not in my house!

JACK   Ha! Dirty language! I've been told that *you* can swear like a trooper. And have often done so in *your* time.

NATHAN *(beating on chair arm)*   Why in God's name did you come here? Was it to persuade me to change my will?

JACK   That is a laugh. I've heard how you spend money on yourself. My impression is that you have just barely enough left to last your lifetime.

NATHAN   Then *why are you here? (very loud) Why* did you come?

JACK   Well, that's a better question than how I *got* here, anyway. . . . *(quietly, leaning forward)* But don't you know why? . . . *(They gaze at each other in silence.)* Because of her. *(with strong emotion)* Because I saw her suffer from him through all the years—as *you* had predicted she would.

NATHAN   From that father of yours, that—that redheaded devil!

JACK   From that redheaded devil, that father of mine. . . . *(again with great emotion)* I loved her, as you did, and I saw the suffering he caused her through all the years and could do nothing about it.
(Nathan suddenly buries his face in his hands. Jack rises and stands gazing at Nathan. A silence.)

NATHAN   Well, she is free now.

JACK   Free?

NATHAN   Free of *him.*

JACK   Perhaps now. But for how long?

NATHAN   For eternity, for eternity. Don't you see?

JACK   No . . . not for so long. . . . And not so free today as yesterday. And not so free yesterday as the day before. Each day her freedom—

NATHAN   Will you try to make yourself clearer? You're not making any kind of sense.

JACK   I thought perhaps you understood matters better than that. I thought perhaps you understood how things stand.

NATHAN   *(assertively)*   She is free now, free of him.

JACK   Something has happened. I thought possibly you knew. She is threatened. . . . *(with emotion)* I have to tell you, my grandfather: I see my mother almost daily.

NATHAN   How can that be so?

JACK   *(quietly)*   You don't believe in ghosts, do you?
(They are both silent.)

NATHAN   It is not a matter of belief. She is here with *me,* too—for much of the time.

JACK   I suspected so. She is with you most of the time, because you need her more. That's what she's like. But she comes to me—briefly.

NATHAN   Her devotion is something truly wonderful. I misunderstood her while she was alive.

JACK   *(walking about)*   She could not help herself then.

NATHAN   Yes, she did what she did to me because she could

not help herself. He was always such an ugly, wizened, unattractive fellow—even when he was young. I think she believed no one else had ever been kind to him.

JACK *(still walking about)* While she was alive she could not help herself. He dominated her completely. But recently have you not noticed a difference in her, just recently—just since *he* died?

NATHAN She has not told me he is dead.

JACK He died six weeks ago. Have you not noticed a change in her just since then? Hasn't she seemed more withdrawn? Have there not been lapses—times when she was not with you so much as before?

NATHAN What in hell's name, young man! What are you getting at?

JACK But isn't it so?

NATHAN Hell, yes, it's so! Damn right it's so!

JACK Then you know why I have come here.

NATHAN Like hell I do!

JACK Yes, you do. My life is empty, but I am tortured by thoughts of what she is suffering. It is far worse than when she died. Then there was the consolation that she was free, at last. *(Nathan hides his face in his hands again.)* You don't want to face it. But you know who it is that's taking possession of her.

NATHAN *(removing his hands, whispering)* What's to be done? Oh, Jesus!

JACK What was ever to be done? You haven't witnessed all that I have. Let me tell you—

NATHAN No, I forbid you! I won't let you tell me. What I saw was bad enough—even before they were married.

JACK I used to hear them quarreling in the night. The sound of her weeping is the earliest of my memories. And when I was sick in the night he wouldn't let her come to me. He was always saying that she spoiled me. *(laughing)* The truth is, he was always insanely jealous of me—of *me*, a child who needed its mother's attention.

NATHAN   And why do you think he would never permit her
to come back here to visit? He couldn't endure the thought
of her attentions to me.

JACK   I thought it was *you* who would not allow her to come.

NATHAN   I would not allow her to come with *him*. Can you
blame me for that?

JACK   Honestly, I cannot.

NATHAN   Oh, Jack, I had seen too much before they were
married. I warned her. Oh, I warned her. He wouldn't wait
until they were married to go to bed with her, you understand. She was a schoolgirl still, and he was nearly thirty,
and he delighted in fornicating with such a girl, a girl who
had never really had a beau before. And it gave *him* special
pleasure that it was here in this house where she had been
brought up, with her parents practically in the next room.
Afterward, he would be gone for weeks, and she wouldn't
know where he was or whether she would ever set eyes on
him again. Her mother and I knew what it was all about, and
she didn't pretend that it was otherwise. He had corrupted
her, you see, and I had to make her understand that any man
who would do that was capable of far greater bestiality and
cruelty. She wouldn't believe it.

JACK   Yes, but that was nothing to what came later. I have
seen him slap her across the face with the back of his hand.
(Nathan weeps.) It was when he was drunk, of course. He
would stay drunk for weeks on end, and sometimes he
would be gone for months. Once when I was barely in my
teens and Mother was working at a gift shop out on Skinker
Boulevard, she heard that he was in jail in some little place
like Joplin or Sikeston—a hundred miles or more from here.
He was there for forging a check, I think. She and I got on
a bus and went out there to bring him back. It cost Mother
nearly all her savings. We barely had the money for bus fare
home. But before we started home she took him to a barber
shop in the basement of a hotel, where he got a shave and
took a bath. And then on the bus, going back, she let him
sleep with his wiry red hair in her lap. I sat in another seat,

across the aisle, and looked at him with what I realized then for the first time was my hatred for him. I think the realization came to me because I understood for the first time that he was killing her. . . . Ten years later when she died, I had not spoken to my father in five years.

(Jack has now turned his back to Nathan and stands looking out a window.)

NATHAN   Jack . . . she has never told me how you felt about your father. I didn't know till now.

JACK   Of course not. She wouldn't tell you. I used to try to persuade her to leave him. I said she and I could go up East to another part of the country and change our names, but she said he could find her anywhere in the world. I would say, *"Any*where, Mother?" Then she would smile and say, *"Any*where—anywhere in this world, son." And I thought I could tell then that she was thinking about how it would be to be dead. It seems to me I always knew she would not live to be old. One could sense how she looked forward to the freedom death would mean for her, or that she thought it would mean. But now he's dead, too, and her peace is all over for her.

NATHAN   My dear girl, my dear child. . . . *(his eyes closed)* You and I did love her, didn't we. We have that consolation. Even if she is beyond any help from us now she knows that she has our love.

JACK   But the emptiness of our lives now if he comes to possess her altogether! If the time comes when she is taken from us altogether! I think of her suffering.

NATHAN   *(holding up his hand)*   Don't! You lacerate me! The pain's too damned much to bear! You must go now and let me rest. But come again, Jack. You must come again very soon. Neither of us can live alone with the thought of her agony. But I must rest now.

(He closes his eyes and sleeps. Jack backs out of the room and is heard in the distance leaving the house, closing an outside door. Presently She reappears from the right, dressed as formerly but without her hat and with her clothes seeming to fit her figure as

when new. She comes to where Nathan is sleeping and gazes down at him affectionately. After a few moments her husband, a redheaded young man with a suitcase in one hand and his hat in the other, appears from the left. She looks up at him and throws him a kiss.)

HE   Let's be off.

SHE   Sh-sh-sh. *(And from this point on all lines are spoken sotto voce.)*

HE *(coming closer)*   The old rascal's asleep.

SHE   Yes, he's tired from Jack. We mustn't wake him.

HE   The arrogant old cuss. . . . He and Jack will make a fine pair.

SHE   Poor darlings. If only they could understand what it is to love someone.

HE   It isn't easy. But *we* know a thing or two, don't we?

SHE   I have known since the first moment—the first time I saw you looking at me and felt you touch my hand. I have been yours since that moment.

(He takes her in his arms and kisses her neck.)

SHE   My love, you're hurting me.

HE   Of course I am.

SHE   But not here!

HE *(laughing)*   No, not here.

(Together they run from the room, to the left, both of them laughing. Nathan stirs in his sleep, muttering.)

NATHAN   Jack! Jack! There must be some way! We must follow her. We must follow her!

Curtain

Missing Person

There are suggestions of affluence in the decor of the Patter-
sons' living room—Chinese lamp bases, vases, handsomely
framed prints on the walls, a French clock on the mantel shelf
at the left end of the room. Here and there is a choice family
antique. But the chairs and the couch near the fireplace have
clearly been chosen for comfort. Altogether, the emphasis is
upon comfort and conventional good taste. It is a modest house
with the front door opening directly into the right end of the
living room, but the room itself is spacious. Above the clock
on the mantel hangs a pastel portrait of a child. It is Emma
and Harry Patterson's son Tom. A charcoal drawing of the
boy as an adolescent hangs to the right of the doorway in the
rear wall, a doorway leading to the boxed stair that twists
upward to the bedrooms above.

It is nearly four o'clock in the morning. Emma sits alone
on a small bench, occasionally poking the wood fire. After
several moments of silence, she speaks in a monotone to herself.

. . .

EMMA He always liked to have a fire. Especially when all
three of us were up late at night. He said a fire made it seem
like there were more of us. *(laughing dully)* He used to wish
so for brothers and sisters. . . . *(A silence. She pokes the fire.)*

He may be poking up a fire somewhere at this moment, not for effect but for warmth. . . . *(The delicate chime of the clock strikes four.)* It's four here. What time *is* it over there? *(Several moments pass in silence. Emma yawns. She rests her forehead on the heels of her hands momentarily. "Oh, God," she mutters, without feeling. "If only I could pray." After another silence, Emma yawns again. At the sound of an automobile outside, she comes slowly to her feet. A car door is heard to slam, but Emma doesn't turn around until there comes the sound of Harry's footstep outside the door at the opposite end of the room. When he opens the door, she only stands looking at him.*

Harry speaks without really looking at Emma. He drops his small suitcase beside the door, removes his hat, and begins clumsily getting out of his coat.)

EMMA Nothing?

HARRY I know nothing I didn't know before I left here.

EMMA *(laughing scornfully)* Washington!

HARRY "Missing in action, presumed to be dead." Like some kind of chorus they keep repeating.

EMMA *(tearful)* Yes, why can't it be "Missing in action, presumed to be alive"?

HARRY And "in enemy hands"?

Emma gives way to tears. Harry runs the length of the room to her, with uncertain step and dragging his overcoat. His movements and gestures, but never his speech, suggest how much he has had to drink.

EMMA *(weeping, bordering on hysterics)* Why? Why? Why not "presumed to be alive"?

HARRY *(taking hold of her)* We do know the circumstances, Emma. We do know the circumstances. The platoon was ambushed there in the foothills. It is an honest presumption.

EMMA *(still tearful)* Hearsay! Hearsay!

HARRY It's all we have. It's all *they* have. *(His coat falls to the floor.)*

EMMA And you've been drinking! *(Pulling away from him, she picks up his coat and folds it over the chair arm.)* Drinking and driving on that highway at this hour.

HARRY   There wasn't much traffic.

EMMA   You're trembling all over. You're staggering drunk.

HARRY   *(moving farther away from her)*   And why are you waiting up? You promised you'd sleep.

EMMA   Sleep? When this was our last hope?

HARRY   You ought to have gone to bed. I'll bet you haven't even tried to sleep. Have you taken one of your pills? *(She shakes her head.)* But you can't start this sort of thing, Emma. I told you I wouldn't be coming back till tomorrow.

EMMA   And I knew you *would* be coming back tonight. If the news had been good, you would have telephoned. And with it bad, do you think I would imagine you settling down in a hotel room with a good book or even a good bottle? I knew you would drive straight through, the whole five hundred miles, and drink all the way, too.

HARRY   Yes, and I knew you knew.

(Suddenly she throws herself into his arms. He holds her a moment. Then she draws away, in command of herself.)

HARRY   And now I am going to have one more drink. There would be no use in my going to bed. It will be morning soon. And after a while I'm going to the office and try to start life. *(He has opened a small cabinet and is making himself a drink.)*

EMMA   You are giving up hope, Harry?

HARRY   *(He stares at her a moment before he speaks.)*   Not until he is brought in this house, dead.

EMMA   Don't say that. Don't say it that way.

HARRY   *(after a silence)*   I sent him.

EMMA   *(with a moan that comes just short of being a scream)* We mustn't begin saying such things. . . . He's alive somewhere, Harry. I would feel it if he were not.

HARRY   He came to me and stood right where you're standing now. He said, "Dad, I'm against this war. What would you think of my registering as a conscientious objector?" At first I think I only just smiled at him. What a way to answer a young person. What a way to answer the most serious question your child ever asked you.

EMMA Don't tell it again, Harry. It doesn't help to go over and over it.

HARRY And finally I said to him, "I suppose you *could*, Tom, if that's how you feel about matters." Then I asked, "How would you feel about the others in the category you would be putting yourself in?" Then I smiled again—idiotically—and said, "Have you ever had the impulse to let your hair grow—maybe down on your shoulders—and wear one of those necklaces?"

EMMA Harry—

HARRY *(lifting his hand)* No, don't interrupt. The awful thing was—

EMMA Stop it, Harry. It doesn't matter.

HARRY The awful thing was, he gave me a look—or, rather, he looked right through me for a moment as though he were considering right at that moment what it would be like to dress so, or as though he actually had been considering the possibility for some time.

EMMA You imagined that, Harry. Tom has never once considered doing that sort of thing. He's too sensible for that. He has too much sense of humor for it. Why, I used to try to get him to let his sideburns be a little longer. I thought it would be sort of cute. I—

HARRY Let me finish, Emma.

EMMA No, I don't want you to finish.

HARRY I said, "I would rather see you in an infantryman's uniform than dressed like that." I said, "Do you know what I would do if I were your age, Tom? Well, I'll tell you. I wouldn't be going to my father with talk about pacifism. And I wouldn't be waiting around for my draft number to be called. I would go out and enlist in the Marines and get my ass over to where the fighting is so that I wouldn't feel ashamed the rest of my life every time the subject of the war came up. . . ." *(raising his voice)* Emma, I didn't mean it, I didn't mean it! It wasn't what I had intended to say to him! It wasn't what I really thought or felt!

EMMA Hush, Harry. Don't you know that you're torturing me? I said worse things to him, myself.

HARRY *(He sits down in a straight chair and speaks softly.)* And when I had finished, he just said, "Well, you're not me, you're not my age." And then, as if we had been discussing something that wasn't very important to either of us, he bent over and began tightening his shoelaces, and then went over to the mirror there and tightened his necktie, and began whistling softly to himself. *(laughs quietly)* He was always whistling. He had a whistle for every occasion.

(Harry has not observed that Emma has turned her back to him and, no longer listening, is standing rigid before the fire.)

EMMA Harry, I haven't ever told you what *I* said to him.

HARRY *(after a silence)* It doesn't matter, Emma. As you say, it doesn't help to go over it.

EMMA I have never told you that I knew he was going to enlist before he wrote us.

HARRY I suspected you knew in advance, and suspected that you blamed me for it.

EMMA No, you're wrong. He never repeated to me what you had said. Not even on the day he let me know he was going to enlist. It was during his spring holidays. Our conversation, too, took place in this room. *(smiling fondly)* He came in whistling, of course. I was over there, poking at my needlepoint. I didn't notice at first what he was whistling. When I did notice, I looked up. He was standing there at attention. When I looked up at him, he quit whistling. It had been the Marine Corps song, of course. "What do you mean?" I asked him. "I mean I'm going to leave college and join the Marines." Naturally I didn't think he was serious. I went back to my needlepoint. "I really am going to, Mother," he said. "You are not, either," I said. "Or over my dead body you are." . . . After a minute he asked me why not. I said that he should finish his education, that he should plan on graduate school, even. "Bull," he said. . . . That was when I first realized he was serious, when he said, "Bull," and I put away my needlework. . . . "I hope you won't tell Dad," he said. "Not yet. But I've already made up my mind. I'm going back to school after the holidays, but as soon as I get there I'm going to see the man at the enlistment office. It takes time, you know." I told him that I certainly would tell you and that we were not going to let him do it. He said to wait a while before telling you and he agreed to think about it some more. We had another conversation about it the night before he went back to school. That was when I said the awful things to him. I said he didn't appreciate all we had done for him, that if he loved us the way a son should he wouldn't think for a moment about stopping his education and going into the Marines. I said *(her voice breaking)* I said it was a coward's way out.

(Emma and Harry look at each other in silence for several moments, neither of them moving a muscle.)

HARRY   He got it from us both ways.

EMMA   But that's not the worst of what I said.

HARRY   That's enough, though, Emma.

EMMA   But it's not all. . . . I felt he was not listening to me. He was standing by that window, looking out, whistling under his breath. It was almost as if he were already on his way. I suppose I felt I *had* to make an impression on him. "Stop that infernal whistling, Tom," I said, "and listen to me." He faced around, and if my life drags out for a thousand years, I won't forget his eyes while I said what I said to him. "Tom," I said, "war isn't what men make it out to be. It never has been. The worst of it has never got into history books. The killing is not the worst of it. It's what the killing does to the killers. You would ask me how I know. Well, I heard it from my mother and from my grandmother. It's something that women have always known and feared to speak of above a whisper—even among themselves." Tom laughed at me. "You laugh," I said, "but you listen! It's not killing the enemy I'm speaking of. It's the other killing that does things to men and that never gets into history books. Soldiers of an army kill each other, Tom. They always have.

They shoot each other in the back, over nothing almost."
(Harry comes to Emma and tries to stop her.)

HARRY   Now, you hush this, Emma.

EMMA   He tried to stop me, too. Just at this point. But I won't
be stopped. "Once they have killed," I told him, "it doesn't
matter whom they kill. When they don't want to obey their
officers, they shoot them. When their subordinates won't
obey, they shoot them. And there's worse to come," I fairly
shouted at him. But then he did stop me. Yes, Harry, he put
his hand over my mouth very gently and firmly and held me
till he could see I had gone limp and till he could see the tears
on my cheeks. When he let me go, I blurted out, "It will
make an animal of you! I had rather see you in your grave!"
(Harry takes her in his arms.) I didn't mean it, either, Harry,
I didn't. But Tom looked down at me and said, "Who are
you to decide I should be alive or dead?"

HARRY   *(taking his drink from the table)*   Have a few sips of
this—

EMMA   I don't want it, Harry. That's all right for you, but I
don't want tranquilizers or sleeping pills.

HARRY   *(forcing her to take a few swallows)*   Have a few sips
and then go up and make yourself lie down for a while. I'm
going to sit here or maybe lie down on the couch. We had
better not talk anymore. It will be morning soon.

EMMA   *(brushing back her hair, staring about the room as though
she hardly knows where she is)*   All right, Harry. I'll go up for
a while.

*(Harry goes with her to the doorway, kisses her on the forehead
and on the cheek. She goes up the stairs. He sets his empty glass
on a table. He goes and pokes the fire, puts on another log. Then
he drifts halfway across the room and drops down into a straight
chair beside the liquor cabinet. He sits there in silence for several
moments. Footsteps are heard outside. Harry rises mechanically
and gazes toward the front door, at the right end of the room.
The knob on the door turns. A tall, stooped young man with
shoulder-length hair and wearing striped bell-bottom trousers
and a pea coat opens the door slowly and enters. Under his*

*unbuttoned coat a heavy necklace is visible, hung about his
turtleneck shirt. As Harry watches, the young man carefully,
even stealthily, closes the door after him.*

HARRY *(coming forward)* Hold it, my friend! What do you
think you're doing?

TOM Don't you know me?

*(Tom laughs nervously. Then he quietly whistles a few bars of
"Over There." Harry rushes toward him. But Tom raises his two
hands in a rather delicate gesture, to stop him.)*

HARRY Tom! Oh, Tom, my boy!

TOM Yes, "Tom." Long hair, necklace, and all.

HARRY But—but what does it mean? Tom, you can't
know—Tom, my boy, what a miracle.

TOM You're glad to see me? Even like this?

HARRY It's all I've dreamed of: if I could just see you like this!
I can ask for no more except to have you forgive me the
things I said. Let me call your mother.

TOM No. No, don't call her.

HARRY But what does it mean, your coming in like this—
unannounced and at this hour of the night.

TOM It's almost morning.

HARRY Yes, but the time doesn't matter. What I mean is—
Let me call your mother now.

TOM The time does matter. And you mustn't call Mother. I
had to come at this time.

HARRY Tom, son, how wrong I was.

TOM You'd really take me back like this? *(incredulous)* With
no complaints?

HARRY Of course we will. All we want is to have you back,
alive and safe. Let me have your coat. Come over by the fire.

TOM No. I won't take off my coat, Dad. I am alive, yes, but
not safe.

HARRY What is it, son? Come over by the fire. We'll talk
some, and then we'll call your mother.

*(They walk together the length of the room, Tom looking all
about him with much affection in his glance. Harry's eyes are on
Tom.)*

HARRY   I've just got back from Washington this very night, making one last insistent check. Tom, do you know the report we've had?

TOM   Yes, sir, I read it in the paper on the West Coast. That's why I'm here, you see. I came in on a bus a week ago. I've been watching the house to see if *you* were being watched by them. *(He sits down near the fire.)*

HARRY   Watched by whom?

TOM   Like the Army, like the State Department, like the F.B.I. By God knows who. I saw you come in a while ago. Not another car had gone by in two hours. I knew this was my chance.

HARRY   But how did you—how did you ever get back into the country? What happened to you? You weren't ambushed in the foothills, the way they said?

TOM   I never left this country. And they well knew it in Washington. Unless there has been some mix-up about names, this is all a trick to try to bring me out of cover.

HARRY   Tom, believe me, you must—

TOM   No, I won't turn myself in. . . . Are you going to turn me in?

HARRY   Of course I'm not, Tom! You know we'll do everything we can do to help you; but you can't stay in hiding the rest of your life.

TOM   Oh, yes I can. But I sort of wanted you and Mother to know for certain that I am alive. I watched you through the window. I saw Mother go upstairs. I knew when I headed back here that I mustn't let her see me. She would never let me leave. *(He rises.)* But I have to go. Only say to her when she comes down that I am alive. *(begins moving toward door)*

HARRY   But is there nothing I can do?

TOM *(after a moment's hesitation)*   I need money, Dad. I need a *lot* of money.

HARRY   Well, you know I'm not a rich man, Tom, but—

TOM *(smiling)*   What I live on takes a lot of money, Dad.

HARRY *(pretending not to understand)*   Hiding yourself, that is? You can't hold a job?

TOM *(still smiling)*   I can't hold a job.

HARRY   I could write you a check for some amount.

TOM   A check wouldn't do.

HARRY   But you know I never keep any cash, Tom.

TOM   Yes, I remember.

HARRY *(feeling for his wallet, though not producing it)*   And I spent the last dollar I had in Washington. I drove home—

TOM *(looking about the room as if appraising everything)*   Could you let me have something I might sell?

HARRY   Well, then your mother would have to know.

TOM   I must run, Dad. *(He is nearly at the door. Harry has followed him and stands only a few feet from him.)*

HARRY   Tom, son. You know that you were our pride and joy.

TOM   I know.

(Tom turns and runs out, closing the door silently behind him. Harry gazes at the closed door. At last he begins backing away and across the room. Midway, he turns and goes back to the straight chair where he had been sitting before. He sits there for several moments, staring straight before him. Finally he gets up, finds his glass, makes himself another drink. He drinks it down in three swallows. Makes himself another. With the drink in his hand he goes to the couch, near the fireplace, and sits down. He finishes the second drink and lies down on the couch, setting the glass on the floor beside him. He sleeps.

Presently Emma is heard on the stairway and makes her entrance. She goes to Harry and looks down at him tenderly. She covers him to his waist with a plaid rug. Then she takes up his glass and places it on the cabinet. She moves to the window at right and rear, stands there looking out. It has grown somewhat lighter outside. A whistle is heard from out of doors, at right. Emma draws back, one hand brought to her mouth. "Harry," she whispers. She turns back to the window for a few moments, then toward the door. Hurried footsteps are heard. The door bursts open. Tom, with close-cropped hair, holding himself very erect, and wearing the same pea jacket but with a sports jacket

underneath, with tie and gray flannel trousers, enters. Emma
takes a step toward him. Tom holds up one hand, belligerently.)

TOM Stay there, Mother. Don't come any closer. *(Emma takes*
another step.) Don't make me tell you again, Mother. Stay
where you are.

EMMA *(frightened)* Harry!

TOM And don't call Dad.

EMMA Tom, my child, where have you come from? Let me
come to you, Tom.

TOM No, that's what I won't do.

EMMA Tom, Tom—

TOM *(seeing his father)* Sh-sh. Is he asleep?

EMMA He's dead to the world, poor fellow. He's been drinking all night. Tom, we thought—

TOM I know, I know. *(toughly)* But here I am alive and
kicking.

EMMA *(suddenly skeptical, moving farther away from him)*
You look like Tom, but is it really you?

TOM *(laughing at her)* It's me all right. I thought you recognized me out in the street. I saw you at the window.

EMMA It was the whistle made me think you were Tom.
How can it be you? But of course it is. Oh let me come to
you, Tom.

TOM *(laughing at her)* You keep backing off and saying, "Let
me come to you." *(She takes a step toward him.)* Stay there
where you are! You might be sorry if you don't do as I say.

EMMA But, Tommy, you're home, my love. I don't know
how you got here. I don't care. But this is the moment we've
lived for. *(She weeps.)* I've never doubted, my dear child. I
felt you were alive, and I have only wanted you to come back
and let me beg you to forgive me. I know you had to go. You
did what you had to do.

TOM *(laughing)* You're right, there. I did what I had to do if
I was ever going to get stateside again.

EMMA *(Speaking to him as to a madman, with fake calm, she eases*
herself down into a chair.) Tom, my baby, sit down. Take

off your coat. You're home, my baby. Everything is all right now.

TOM You needn't be afraid of me. I wouldn't have come all this way to see you if I were going to harm you. But keep your voice down. I don't want to wake Dad.

EMMA Tom, would you mind telling me what happened? Your father has just got back tonight from Washington, making one last desperate effort to get information about you.

TOM They don't have any information about me. They won't ever have any if you don't give it to them.

EMMA How can I give them any? I don't know what's happened and don't want to know.

TOM I'm afraid you're going to have to know.

EMMA All I need to know is that you're really here.

TOM You mean, I could come home with no questions asked?

EMMA Absolutely, Tom. We are your parents. Nothing you could do could make us stop loving you. And nothing you could do could make me wish for anything but to have you safely back home.

TOM Well, unfortunately, I'm afraid you're going to have to know my whole story. But first let me make this clear: I had to come here and see you once more and tell you I was alive.

EMMA That's all that matters.

TOM I'm afraid it isn't.

EMMA What is it, son? Are you absent without leave?

TOM *(laughing)* Absent without leave, indeed? . . . Can't you look at me and tell I'm a killer now? Can you honestly look at me and say, "My son is a killer but I want him home, alive"?

EMMA My son is a killer and I want him home, alive.

TOM *(going to her and leaning over her, threateningly)* Say it again.

EMMA My son is a killer and I want him home, alive.

TOM Now say this: "My son killed more of the enemy than he could count, more than was necessary. My son killed prisoners of war, rather than bring them in. And I want him home, alive."

EMMA   My son killed more of the enemy than he could count, more than was necessary. My son killed prisoners of war, rather than bring them in. And I want him home, alive.

TOM   Say this: "My son left his best buddy to die in a ditch, and I want him home, alive."

EMMA   My son left his best buddy to die in a ditch, and I want him home, alive.

TOM   Say this: "My son killed his officer who had twice saved his life, and I want him home, alive."

EMMA   *(weeping)*   My son killed his officer who had twice saved his life, and I want him home, alive.

TOM   Say this: "My son murdered ignorant, innocent women and children, and I want him home, alive."

EMMA   *(weeping)*   Stop! Stop!

TOM   Say it.

EMMA   *(weeping)*   My son murdered ignorant, innocent women and children, and I want him home, alive.

TOM   *(turning and walking toward the front door)*   I came home to hear you tell those lies. I deserted to escape court-martial and execution, and I crossed the mountains into another country, and I made my way halfway round the world just to hear those lies. It was all that kept me going.

EMMA   They are not lies. *(She has buried her face in her hands.)* They are not lies.

TOM   But why don't you look at me? Somehow you can't look at me now.

EMMA   Wait a moment. Only wait a moment. . . . *(removing her hands from her face and rising)* Poor Tom. My poor Tommy. . . . Let me come to you now. You must stay with us here. We'll help you work things out.

TOM   No, there are some things that can't be worked out. I only wanted to see you this once more in the house. Beyond that, there is only one other piece of business—a favor, the greatest favor I could ask.

EMMA   Ask it, ask it. Anything in the world, Tom.

TOM   Come away with me. You and Dad simply put on your coats and come away with me. I made a fortune in the Marines. I need not tell you how. I can get us all three out of this country by noon today. You will never want for anything.

EMMA   Tom, let me wake Harry.

TOM   No, you must decide before you wake him. If you have decided, then he will agree to go along. If you have not, he will make the decision. And I know what that would be. And he would never let me leave. He would make me stay here and "work things out."

EMMA   Tom, I've never lived anywhere else. You know how lost I would be.

TOM   You would have *me*.

EMMA   But we would not have you here. We would be lost anywhere else.

TOM   Yes, I know you would. . . . *(after a silence)* Well, there's a plane waiting. I have to hurry. *(peering over at his father)* Tell him, tell Dad—

EMMA   Yes, what shall I tell him, Tom?

TOM   Only tell him that I am alive. *(He goes out quickly.)*
    (Emma returns to the window and looks out. After several moments she begins to sob. Harry sits up on the couch. He hears her sobbing and looks about for her. Finally he locates her at the window. It is growing light outside.)

HARRY   Emma, dear.
    (He rises from the couch and crosses slowly toward her. She manages to stifle her sobs. She turns and faces him. He comes closer, reaches out and takes one of her hands.)

HARRY   He is dead, Emma.

EMMA   Yes, he is dead. We mustn't deny it again.

Curtain

A NOTE ABOUT THE AUTHOR

Peter Taylor was born in Tennessee in 1917. He is the author of seven books of stories, including *The Collected Stories of Peter Taylor, A Long Fourth, In the Miro District and Other Stories*, and *The Old Forest and Other Stories* (which won the PEN/Faulkner Award for Fiction in 1985); two novels, including *A Summons to Memphis* (which won the Pulitzer Prize for fiction in 1987); and three books of plays. Mr. Taylor has taught at Harvard University, the University of North Carolina, and Kenyon College, from which he graduated in 1940. Since 1967, he has been Commonwealth Professor of English at the University of Virginia. He lives with his wife, the poet Eleanor Ross Taylor, in Charlottesville, Virginia, and Sewanee, Tennessee.

A NOTE ON THE TYPE

This book was set in Janson, a redrawing of type cast from matrices long thought to have been made by the Dutchman Anton Janson, who was a practicing typefounder in Leipzig during the years 1668–87. However, it has been conclusively demonstrated that these types are actually the work of Nicholas Kis (1650–1702), a Hungarian, who most probably learned his trade from the master Dutch typefounder Dirk Voskens. The type is an excellent example of the influential and sturdy Dutch types that prevailed in England up to the time William Caslon developed his own incomparable designs from them.

Composed by ComCom,
a division of Haddon Craftsmen,
Allentown, Pennsylvania

Printed and bound by
Arcata Graphics/Martinsburg,
Martinsburg, West Virginia

Typography and binding design by
Dorothy Schmiderer Baker